D1164364

My Saving Grace

Danelle Harmon

All rights reserved.

No part of this publication may be sold, copied, distributed, reproduced or transmitted in any form or by any means, mechanical or digital, including photocopying and recording or by any information storage and retrieval system without the prior written permission of both the publisher, Oliver Heber Books and the author, Danelle Harmon, except in the case of brief quotations embodied in critical articles and reviews.

PUBLISHER'S NOTE: This is a work of fiction. Names, characters, places, and incidents either are the product of the author's imagination or are used fictitiously. Any resemblance to actual persons, living or dead, business establishments, events, or locales is entirely coincidental.

COPYRIGHT 2020 © Danelle Harmon

Edited by Christine Zikas

Published by Oliver-Heber Books & Gnarly Wool Publishing

0 9 8 7 6 5 4 3 2 1

PRAISE FOR DANELLE HARMON

"One of my all-time favorite authors!"

— JULIA QUINN, #1 NEW YORK
TIMES BESTSELLING AUTHOR OF
THE BRIDGERTONS

"Provocative and passionate!"

— LISA KLEYPAS, NEW YORK TIMES
BESTSELLING AUTHOR

"Danelle Harmon's style is as bold and
sexy as her unforgettable characters!"

— LORETTA CHASE, NEW YORK
TIMES BESTSELLING AUTHOR

To you, EI-LBT, my beloved partner in beating aerophobia. Flying high again ... but in a far different sky. Thank you for all that you gave me, all that you taught me, and all that you helped me to overcome. I will never, ever forget you, my beautiful friend.

St. Brendan
2014–2020

The ancient Celtic cross that hung from their mother's neck was a source of awe and mystery for all of Deirdre O'Devir Lord's children.

Gathering in a circle for story time was a bedtime ritual, and it had been so for as long as any of them could remember. Tales of her homeland in faraway Connemara. Tales of green pastures and brooding gray skies, windswept mountains, rocky cliffs and barren wastelands of limestone. Tales of the sea, of life in a small cottage, of a land far, far away from the stately English manor house the children knew as home. And most fascinating, tales of Irish heroes, heroines and saints vividly brought to life with each retelling. Finn McCool. Cu Chulainn. St. Patrick. St. Brendan the Navigator. Brigid and Aoife and Queen Maeve of Connacht. All well and good, but she always saved the best for last.

Grace O'Malley.

Or rather, as their mother called her, *Gráinne Ní Mháille*.

They'd push their way closer, tightening the circle and staring up at her with wide eyes as she began to reach for the chain around her neck that held the cross. *Shhhushing* each other for quiet. Upturned faces rapt with attention. Squirming. Waiting. And then, she would begin the story of Ireland's fierce and famous lady pirate who had lived during the time of Queen Elizabeth so long, long ago and to whom the ancient relic had belonged. The story never changed, though over the years, the children's ages did. Colin, fair-haired and handsome, the image of their English father. The four girls, born one after another and each, like Colin, a pale blonde.

And finally, Del. Sensitive and serious, he was the youngest of Admiral Christian and Deirdre Lord's brood and the only one to inherit the wild black curls of their mother.

He sat now, quietly waiting his turn to hold the heavy cross of beaten gold and raw emeralds as it began to make the round of their circle. Colin, the oldest, preparing to go off to sea under the watchful eye of their uncle Elliott, quickly passing it to the sister beside him with a shrug, as though such childish things were now quite beneath him. Niamh, Kathleen, Brigid and Tara, each fingering it with wonder and reverence before passing it to the child on her right. Del waited his turn. He knew what to expect. But today...

Today was different.

Beside him, Tara stared down at the relic while their mother told the familiar tale of their ancestress, the formidable *Gráinne*, sea-queen of Ireland's wild western coast.

"Her blood runs through your veins," she murmured, speaking in her native Irish—a language she had taught each of the children. "And every so often—" her voice softened, grew so low that the children had to lean forward to hear her— "*Gráinne* returns for the sake of one of her descendants. Someone that she herself chooses, someone she takes a fancy to, someone that needs her protection. Her wisdom. Her guidance."

Tara passed the heavy cross to Del. He had held the relic many times before, had felt its metal against his palm, the heavy chain falling over his fingers. What stories could it tell? What things had it seen? Did it still bear a trace of the salt spray it must have gleaned as it had hung from around the neck of *Gráinne* herself?

Wonder. That had been all he'd ever felt.

This time was different.

He closed his hands around the ancient metal, and something moved in his blood. At just five years old he couldn't identify it, but it was there all the same and he felt it in a way that was raw and physical. A quickening. Something ignited. Awakened. He couldn't put words to it but it made him uneasy, aware, and he was quick to pass the cross to the last person in the circle, his mother.

She took it from him, smiled, and fastened it around her own neck, tucking it back beneath the bodice of her gown so that it rested near her heart. Storytelling was over. It was time to go to sleep. She listened as each child recited their prayers, helped them into their beds, kissed foreheads and tucked blankets around little shoulders and finally blew out candles, taking her stories and her warmth and the cross, which was suddenly no longer mysterious but frightening to little Del, with her.

He lay there in the darkness of this room he shared with Colin, whose soft breathing he could hear from the curtained bed nearby. Colin, who seemed a million miles away. Colin, whose dreams would surely be of ships and the sea and girls, most particularly the Honourable Miss Jane Drury of the neighboring Rathmore House. Colin, who had fallen asleep quickly, not a care in the world.

But Del was afraid to go to sleep.

Afraid to close his eyes, and be all alone with himself.

He had felt shaken and somehow different since holding the cross tonight, but as the stars wheeled in the heavens above, passing in and out behind the clouds scudding across the Hampshire sky, and rain fell gently against the heavy, lead-paned windows from a very English night, his young eyelids grew heavy. It was probably raining in Ireland, he thought. The Ireland of Grace O'-Malley, a place he had never seen but which, thanks to his mother's stories, lived vividly in his imagination. Rain and mists, seabirds and rock, church ruins and lonely wind and restless, wandering spirits...

The wind hit him, and pelting rain, and he realized he was on a boat. Not a massive, stately square rigger such as the one his father was off commanding, but a primitive, many-oared vessel like those he'd seen in ancient paintings. The boat was empty save for one person.

A woman.

She stood there near a long tiller, feet braced against the motion of the sea and arms folded across her bosom, her head thrown back and her very stance commanding and bold.

She was about his mother's age and her hair was wild and dark and long, dull with sea mist and spray, lashing her cheeks and mouth. Her eyes were fierce beneath slashing black brows, her nose strong and her lips full and smiling. She wore strange clothes, partly masculine, partly feminine, but he recognized the good serviceable sea-boots and the dagger in a heavy belt at her waist, the easy way her body absorbed the wild roll of the ship as though she were born to it.

"Delmore," she said, and greeted him warmly in Irish.

He spoke Irish, of course. Spoke it as well as he did English. He understood.

He reached up to clutch the shrouds, steadying himself against the vessel's pitch, sea-spray as cold as ice soaking his clothes as the galley's bow dipped, rose, and flung it aft in a hissing shower of foam that spattered the woman's long skirts and the mannish coat she wore over it, belted at her waist.

"Do you not speak, young man?" she asked, humor in her bold eyes. Her voice was strong. Father would call it a quarterdeck voice. Again, she spoke in Irish.

"I don't know what to say, nor whom I'm addressing."

"You know who I am, Delmore."

He was suddenly afraid to speak. His fist tightened on the tarry rope and he shook with cold.

"Gráinne Ni Mhaille," she said. "Your English father —" at this, her smile changed ever so subtly, and he caught the disdain there— "would call me Granuaile."

"Grace O'Malley?"

She inclined her head, her smile broadening, and he wondered why there was nobody on this strange boat except for the two of them, and how it could sail with just her to crew it.

"Then that makes you my grandmother."

"Aye, several times great," she replied.

"Am I dead?"

She laughed, no ladylike twitter but a full, gusty sound that cut through the roar of the thrashing sea. "Not dead, young man, but dreaming. It's the only way I could reach you. Now listen closely, because you will not see me again for a long, long while."

"I'm listening," Del replied, wide-eyed, holding on for dear life as the galley's pitch and yaw grew more noticeable, his small arms straining with the effort.

"You, like so many in our family before you, will grow up to be a great and famous mariner. This, despite the wretched English blood you carry from your sire's side!" The wind strengthened, snapping the pennant above, pushing the galley over on her lee rail until Del's arms began to ache. The wind tore at the woman's hair, flung wild, wet strands of it across her fierce eyes. "You will grow up and you will find your true love. There will be many who'll have your heart, and many who will break it, but don't despair, little lad. I'll send someone who will be your soulmate. Someone that God made just for you. A mariner, like yourself. A woman worthy of the man that you'll be."

Del just stood there. Girls, marriage, a wife... they were the farthest things from his mind.

The howl of the wind strengthened, and water was streaming through the scuppers now, washing down the decks, soaking his feet, pouring out into the sea. His body was tiring from the effort it took to cling to the shroud as the vessel leaped and dove beneath him. The apparition was fading, losing substance, losing form, and Del felt a great pulling and wondered if the sea was sucking him down into its depths or if the galley was driving herself into the rising waves, into the sea itself, with each building swell.

"Gráinne!" he yelled, desperate, unwilling to be left alone on what he now knew was a sinking ship. "Don't leave me!"

She was already moving away, the waves washing over her boots, her cloud of dark hair tangling in the wind, whipping across her face and shoulders in a wild, snarling cloud.

I will never leave you.

"Gráinne!"

She was fading into the sea mists, the ship going with her.

"How will I know her?" he cried desperately. "How?"

She turned back then, and through the screaming wind he heard her strong, resolute voice.

"She will bear my name."

The wild pitching gentled and ceased. His ancestress shimmered in the salty mist and flying foam and was gone. Del jerked awake, his heart pounding so hard that he felt the throbbing in his throat. The dream was vivid. Real enough that he felt he could reach out and touch it. He lay there in the bed, quite dry save for the sweat beneath his back, staring up into the darkness and his pulse hammering in his ears. *Bang, bang, bang.* He shuddered and blinked, finally hearing the sound of Colin's measured breathing in the other bed as his heartbeat began to quiet.

A dream.

He could not know then that it would fade, as dreams almost always do, and as he grew to adulthood it would be all but lost in the pick-and-choose array of memories that the adult mind remembers when looking back at its childhood years. He could not know then that he would suppress his imaginative and sensitive side to become the mariner the strange woman had said he would be, not because she'd foretold it but because it was in his blood, like it was for all the Lord men and, truth be told, all of the O'Devir men of his mother's side as well. He could not know that the dream would become less vivid, its colors and emotion fading as the years passed and that eventually he'd dismiss it entirely, when he even bothered to think about it as all, as silly childhood fantasy.

But for now, he lay there in the darkness, trembling in fear and awe.

It was a long time before he slept.

❧ I ❧

BARBADOS, APRIL, 1814

The letter came by fast-sailing packet to the commander of the Leeward Islands squadron of the Royal Navy's West Indies Station, a celebrated Vice Admiral named Sir Graham Falconer who happened to be married to an ex-pirate queen named Maeve. The letter's bearer, a hapless lieutenant wilting in the day's heat, stood by with tense expectation. That hapless lieutenant happened to be under the command of one Delmore Lord, flag captain of said admiral and commander of His Majesty's Ship *Orion*, and the flag captain himself stood quietly at attention, hands clasped behind his back, as Sir Graham broke the wax seal and began to read.

Orion, a massive floating fortress of a hundred guns, was currently sleeping in the sun out in Carlisle Bay, happily at anchor, and Del had the feeling her repose would soon be interrupted given the thunderclouds darkening his admiral's face.

"Damnation! Is there no end to my being summoned back to England under the most ridiculous of circumstances?"

Del held himself rigidly straight. "Ridiculous, sir?"

"Aye, bloody ridiculous! A wedding. This place is crawling with privateers and the French are ever a concern, and I'm being summoned home for a damned wedding!"

Del exchanged a look with the trembling messenger and cut his eyes toward the door in a crisp motion. *I will handle this. You are dismissed.*

The young man bolted.

"I suppose," said Del carefully, "that would depend on whose wedding you are being asked to attend."

"My sister Ariannah's! Damn it to hell, it's not like she hasn't been married before, what, two times now?"

"I believe it to be three, sir."

"Three! And what is this, number four? The safety of the Leeward Islands is to be compromised because I have to go home to attend a damned wedding? What madness is this?"

"I should say, sir, that that would depend on who she is marrying, and who's demanding your attendance."

"She's marrying a relation of the king, a relation who enjoys favor with the royal family, and when the Prince Regent says his admiral must go home to attend the nuptials, that admiral cannot refuse. Damn it. Damn it all to hell!"

Movement at the doorway; for a moment, Del thought that the terrified junior officer was coming back, but no, it was only Kieran Merrick, one of the said American privateers who complicated family matters on the other side of Sir Graham's pedigree— that is, the side into which he'd married.

"Something amiss, Gray?" asked the American, pouring himself a glass of lemonade from the sweating glass pitcher that dominated the table on which the admiral had thrown the letter. "I heard you from the veranda."

"I have to return to England. *Again.*" He slanted a look of pained exasperation at his brother-in-law. "And what am I to do with you whilst I'm gone? Leave you here to run rampant over British shipping?"

Kieran shrugged, his warm amber eyes twinkling. "You could."

Sir Graham just made a noise that sounded like a cross between a snarl, a growl and a curse and slammed out of the room.

Del relaxed, finally, and poured himself a glass of the lemonade. "And you shouldn't," he muttered, toasting his American cousin with his glass as he pulled out a chair and sat down, taking care to keep the fine gold lace of his uniform sleeve out of the condensation that was forming a puddle beneath the pitcher. "Sir Graham has enough on his mind these days... knowing you're not causing trouble back here would do much to alleviate at least one of those concerns."

Kieran pulled out the chair across from him and sat, tilting his head back to enjoy the breeze coming through the open windows. "I suppose it probably *is* time for me to end my visit here," he reflected, using his thumb to draw circles in the condensation of his glass. "Unlike my brother Connor, I don't take pleasure in raiding British ships right out from under Sir Graham's nose. I need better hunting grounds than these."

"Spoken like a gentleman and not the pirate you are."

"Privateer."

Del just shook his head, knowing the argument was pointless.

"Besides," Kieran said levelly, "I'm always a gentleman."

"You should go home to Newburyport, Kieran. Take care of your own family matters. You can't hide from things forever."

His cousin's eyes darkened with pain and he looked away. "Aye, I should."

The recent tragedy loomed in both their minds, unspoken. In the other room, the admiral wasn't happy. Both men, sipping their lemonade, could hear Sir

Graham ranting to someone about the letter, probably his wife.

"And what will you do, Del?"

"I go where Sir Graham goes, of course. He's my admiral. *Orion* carries his flag. Unless he chooses to return on that fast-sailing packet, he's going to want *Orion* which means, of course, that he'll need her captain."

"Which means you."

"*Delmore!*"

"Which means me," Del said hopelessly, as the admiral's roar preceded the man himself.

Sir Graham strode back into the room, his oldest son Ned running happily in his wake. "Uncle Kieran! Captain Lord! We're going to England!"

Sir Graham went straight to the table, bypassing the lemonade and seizing the bottle of Bajan rum instead. "No sense delaying the damned inevitable," he snapped, pouring a hefty measure of it into a glass. "Go ready *Orion* for a transatlantic crossing. We're going home to England."

2

RUSCOMBE HALL, SURREY, ENGLAND, FIVE
WEEKS LATER

I 'm going to grow up and marry him.

It had been her fourteenth summer and Sir Peter
Danvers, whom Mama had married two years after con-
sumption had claimed the earl who had been Lady
Grace Fairchild's father, had organized a foxhunt. Her
stepfather had been popular in the circles in which he'd
traveled, most of which had been naval, for he'd been
knighted for bravery at sea and his friends were many.
They had come from far and wide to the hunt, and that
had been the first time Grace had set eyes on the
golden Adonis who had been Midshipman Sheldon
Ponsonby.

He'd been attached to Sir Peter's ship, so it was
quite natural that he was there at the hunt. Grace's fascination was piqued at first sight of him in his handsome blue uniform, stoked when he'd come over to hold
the reins for her as she'd prepared to mount her horse,
firmly anchored in her impressionable young heart
when he'd turned a blinding smile on her, cupped his
hands for her to step into, and lightly boosted her up
into the saddle.

Right then and there, she'd fallen in love.

Off they'd all gone on the hunt, and off he'd gone
with Sir Peter when her new stepfather had returned to

sea, and off to sea he'd stayed after Sir Peter's leg had been carried off by a French cannonball and her stepfather succumbed to his injuries a week later. Once again, her mother had been a widow, once again, there were black mourning clothes and no Seasons for her two lovely daughters. Several years and several Seasons had come and gone since then as well as a third husband who had run off with a baronet's daughter, leaving the dark-haired beauty who'd been born Ariannah Falconer no choice but the shame and scandal of divorce. And all during that time, Grace had held out for Sheldon Ponsonby, following his career as he made lieutenant, and then post-captain, his achievements noted in the newspapers they took from London.

She vowed that she'd be luckier in love than her beautiful mother had been.

Captain Sheldon Ponsonby would never die and leave her a widow. He would never forsake her for another, younger woman. He would be the perfect match and Mama, having just pledged her vows to Husband Number Four, was inclined to agree.

Wasn't that, after all, the reason he'd been invited to *this* wedding, since he was home on an exceedingly rare leave from the sea?

Invited, with the hopes of making a match?

Now, with the ceremony an hour behind them, Grace sat on a blanket spread on the cropped grass of Ruscombe Hall— her new home, she figured, since it was owned by her newest stepfather— watching the breeze ruffle the lake that provided a focal point for the estate.

A focal point for the benefit of anyone but herself.

Her focal point happened to be the couple strolling hand-in-hand at the water's edge, the young woman's blonde tresses carefully arranged beneath her bonnet to frame her heart-shaped face, the man on whose arm she clung, tall and handsome in his naval uniform. He bent down to hear something she said, smiling as though she was the center of his existence, and Grace's heart burned with jealousy.

That man was Royal Navy Captain Sheldon Ponsonby.

And despite her and Mama's hopes, he had altogether failed to notice her.

"Really, Grace. You should not be so transparent about your feelings. It's unbecoming."

Grace tightened her mouth and forced a smile.

"That's a grimace and it's even worse."

"Well, look at them, Hannah! He's about ready to lay a rose at her feet!" Grace all but cried in her frustration. "Why doesn't he look at *me* like that?"

"Jealousy does not become you either, my dear sister."

"Oh, I would give anything to be her, right now!"

"She's his cousin. I doubt his interest in her is anything more than familial."

Grace tore her gaze away from the couple. Anything so that she wouldn't have to look at the two of them. She shut her eyes and fantasized about him doting on her the way he was the Honourable Miss Cecily de Montforte. Fantasized kisses in darkened gardens and sidelong glances and what her name would sound like on his lips. Fantasized about his warship, and a special tour of it with her hand tucked into his arm. Lud, she'd fantasized about him even *noticing* her. She was twenty-one years old now, no longer the awkward girl he'd solicitously helped into the saddle that long ago day. She had dreamed about him. Waited for him all this time, even while in mourning for Sir Peter, even while hiding out from the gossips after the horrid scandal with Lord Anthony, the one-time husband whose name both she and Mama had promised never again to speak. Why didn't he even seem to know she existed?

"He's smitten with her," she continued wistfully, as

her gaze slid back to the beautiful couple walking some distance away. "It's so unfair."

"Well, she *is* quite beautiful."

Grace tightened her lips and said nothing.

"And from a very powerful family," Hannah went on.

"Well, so are we."

"Indeed, and Uncle Graham has certainly given us fame and prominence with his heroism at sea, but we are not a ducal family like the de Montfortes, Grace. It makes a difference when it comes to the marriage mart and you know it as well as I do."

"You just said they are cousins."

"Distant cousins, I believe."

"And it's not as if I can make my feelings just... *go away*."

"No, but you're wasting your energy, and possibly even your best years, waiting for him. And for what?" Hannah plucked at a blade of grass. "Plenty of other fish in the sea."

"You don't understand." Grace gnawed at her bottom lip. "I can't think of anyone but him. I don't want anyone but him. I've waited for him all this time and he doesn't even notice me!"

"Well then, maybe you need to *do* something to make him notice you."

"Do something?"

"Well, yes, why not? He's a mariner. A decorated naval officer. You need to develop an interest in the sea and ships so that you can converse with him on such matters, and hold an intelligent discourse."

"And you think Cecily de Montforte knows anything about ships?"

Both women knew that the young blonde upon whom the gallant Captain Ponsonby was lavishing attention didn't need to know anything about ships. She was one of those rare creatures whose beauty was such that it would stun the most hardened male and make the shining sun wonder if it had light enough to surpass her.

"You're staring, Grace."

Grace jerked her gaze away for a second time. More people were arriving from the chapel, now. Ladies in elegant silks, men in well-cut frock coats, a family with children, all headed down to the lake, taking seats upon the sloping grass to enjoy this fine summer day and the food sitting in covered dishes on long tables whose bright linen cloths fluttered in the breeze. Someone was setting up a game of bowls. A terrier, barking, ran between people finding spots on the grass, eliciting a shriek from a young woman whose chicken drumstick it stole from her plate.

Despite herself, Grace laughed.

"So what are you going to do?"

"You said I need to develop an interest in the sea and ships so that I can hold a conversation with Captain Ponsonby. I know little about either, but it's never too late to learn, is it?"

Hannah frowned.

Especially when she noticed where her sister's gaze was now directed.

"Don't even think about it, Grace. You know nothing about boats."

But Grace was already on her feet. "Nonsense. I've read stories about boats, I daresay I know how to work one. Besides, it's in the blood. Our Uncle Gray is a famous admiral. It'll come naturally to me. You stay here. I'm going to go and make sure Captain Ponsonby notices my existence."

Prophetic words.

He would soon notice her, alright.

Except, not quite in the manner that Grace intended.

3

T here were worse places to spend a summer afternoon than in comparatively-cool England, enjoying the pleasantries of good food, genteel company, a lazy day and a sun that knew how to be kind, when it felt inclined to appear at all, instead of brutal.

Which was more than could be said for Barbados.

Sir Graham might've been grumbling like a thunderstorm for the entire crossing, but Del, whose Irish blood inherited from his mother tended to make him sensitive to the heat, was quite happy to be away from the scorching sun of the tropics. Nice to be here where not a soul knew him, where no one except his coxswain Jimmy Thorne— whom he'd brought with him as a manservant— deferred to him as the second most senior man in the fleet, nice not to have to solve problems or disputes and nice, quite nice, really, to just be out of uniform and dressed in civilian clothes without a care in the world.

He felt quite invisible in this crowd, really.

Not a bad thing. Especially for a man who didn't really know how to abandon the stiff requirements of protocol, of expected dress and behavior and comportment, and to just be... anonymous.

Sir Graham, though, was more relaxed than he'd

been in some time and for that, Del was grateful. Happy admirals were good things. They made one's life a hell of a lot easier, even when the nearest ship to be found was many miles away and one was, for all intents and purposes, off duty.

He told Thorne to go enjoy himself and wandered to the refreshment tables that had been set up on the lawn. There, he took a plate, selected some chicken, rolls and fruit salad, and headed for the grassy slope overlooking the lake, quite alone, content to just absorb the sun and warmth and clean wind and to do pretty much nothing.

The wedding had been earlier, the royal guests come and gone, the festivities now more casual following their departure. Sir Graham's eldest sister, with fawning husband number four in tow, made the rounds of the guests, her dark hair swept up in an elegant coil atop her head, her blue eyes alight. She was ravishing, and the love-struck man at her side who puffed out his chest and made it clear that she was his by every language his body possessed, could barely take his eyes off her. Sir Graham, at least, had put his irritation at being summoned for what he'd decried as complete foolishness destined to end in yet another death or disaster, behind him, and now sat in a chair beside his lovely wife. Lady Falconer, laughing at something he said, grabbed one of her runaway children headed straight for the lake, and giving their yawning infant a kiss, handed her up to her nanny.

"Time for your nap, sweets," she murmured, watching fondly as the woman carried the baby off to the house.

Del caught her eye and smiled. Lady Falconer, he thought loyally, outshone her sister-in-law in beauty and vivaciousness.

And she didn't even have to try.

A servant made the rounds with a tray, and Del selected a glass of punch. He sipped at it as he walked, idly wondering how he would fill his time here in England. He didn't know anyone here save for the Falconers and Alannah, one of Sir Graham's many sisters. She had made the crossing from Barbados with them in her own return to England, and would be departing soon for her townhouse in London. What to do? Perhaps a visit to nearby Hampshire to see his parents. Certainly, a trip up to Norfolk to visit his brother Colin and his wife, and meet the little nephews he'd heard so much about but, given how long he'd been attached to the West Indies squadron, never even laid eyes on.

In the meantime, he had this rather dull party to get through.

Leaving Sir Graham to his family, Del strode toward the small lake and lowered himself to the grass, avoiding a cluster of sheep droppings lurking on the ground nearby. It was a breezy day, with gusts that threatened to snatch the fine beaver hat from his head and send it flying out over the water. He eyed the lake, little more than a pond, really, its surface ruffled by breeze and sparkling in the sun. A small dingy and a sprit-rigged skiff were pulled up on the shore and as he gazed idly at the two boats, he saw a young woman walking toward the skiff with confident authority.

She was pretty, with a slender, pleasing figure and dark hair showing from beneath her bonnet, and soon enough her back was to him as she bent down and pushed the skiff out into the water. Del watched with a mild detachment, allowing his thoughts to go no further. His luck with women was abysmal, and he doubted very much that it would be any better on this side of the Atlantic than it had been back in Barbados.

He sensed a presence beside him and looked up.

"Ahoy, Ned," he said to the boy. Smiling, he patted the ground beside him. "Are you enjoying yourself?"

"Not at all, Captain Lord."

Del raised a brow. "Too many aunties?"

"Six of them. Alannah, Ariannah, Annalisa, Anastasia, Arabella, Anaconda—"

Your grandmother named one of them for a snake?

"Damnation, I don't remember her name, I hardly know any of them except for Alannah."

"Do not swear, young man."

"Why not? Mama does. Papa does. Everyone does, and if I want to grow up to be an admiral some day then I should probably get started on the swearing, spitting and shouting bit while I'm in my formative years."

"You don't see your father spitting."

"No, but he does swear and shout, and I doubt he's enjoying himself as much as he's pretending. I know my mother would rather be anywhere else. I wish we could've stayed in Barbados. There's nothing to do here. We've not been in England for three days and I'm already bored out of my mind."

Del smiled, his attention wandering back to the young woman and the boat.

"Aren't *you* bored, Captain Lord?"

Del bit into a chicken drumstick and chewed thoughtfully. "Give me time. For now, it's nice to just sit here and enjoy a few moments without giving orders, tending to a ship, keeping your father happy or solving a problem."

"I wish Uncle Connor were here. I miss him."

Del, who had found Kieran's older brother Connor yet more proof that he was terminally unlucky when it came to competing for the opposite sex, only smiled a bit wistfully. *Deadly Dull-more*, Connor had called him. And he was, really. Dull. Quite dull. Still, he'd have preferred something a little more flattering... perhaps Dutiful Del. Was he really so dull? How Connor had tried to get him to "live a little," as his American cousin had liked to say. But thinking of Connor Merrick made him remember the beautiful Welshwoman, Rhiannon. Rhiannon, who had fallen head-over-heels with the impetuous, insanely reckless Connor and for whom he, Del, might not have even existed.

Yes, he was quite invisible when it came to the fair sex— and he was resigned to it.

He wiped his fingers on a napkin and chased the chicken with another sip of punch. Set the glass on the ground beside him, leaned back on his elbows, tilted his head back and let the gentle English sun warm his face. He closed his eyes, enjoying the idleness, the utter freedom of having absolutely nothing to do, nowhere to go, nothing to plan for, but to just exist. His limbs felt suddenly heavy, his eyelids weighted. He yawned.

"Captain Lord?"

"Aye, Ned?"

"That's one of my cousins over there in that skiff. D'you think she knows what she's doing?"

Del cracked open an eye. The young woman sat alone in the boat, clutching a paddle as she rowed her way farther out into the lake. She was not only a clumsy rower, but failed to switch the paddle from one side of the boat to the other and the little craft, helpless against the one-sided pulling, was tracking in a circle.

"No," he said. "I do not."

He took another sip of his punch.

"I don't think so, either."

"It's about to get worse, Captain Lord. She's attempting to figure out the mainsheet and sail."

Del put down his glass and sat up, arms draped loosely over his knees. He felt himself tensing.

The craft's one sail was affixed to its single mast, so there was nothing to raise. The boat had obeyed the weather helm and swung itself into irons, the sail fluttering helplessly from the mast. Del would have liked it to stay that way for the sake of the young woman's safety but as he watched, she took up the single sheet, dropped the paddle, and began to shorten sail. To her credit, she reached up to seize the boom and hold it to starboard as she attempted to get the boat out of irons. It immediately responded, nose coming around and beginning to gather way. The girl frantically let out the mainsheet as the craft heeled sharply and a moment later, it was moving swiftly across the lake, her fingers clenched around the tiller.

For a moment all looked well. Del, watching keenly, saw the young woman tip her head back to check the trim of the sail. Sunlight on rosy cheeks, a determined set to a pretty mouth, exhilaration mixed with fear and a certain triumph in her eyes as she glanced over her shoulder to where Captain Ponsonby and a stunning blonde sat together on the grass, watching her.

And then Del tensed.

He heard the distant sigh from far off over the meadows and trees and knew what was coming before it actually did.

The chestnut trees that bordered the lawn suddenly bent and clawed at the blue, blue sky as the next gust of wind came and the young woman, not paying attention, not realizing that she'd let the wind move across the stern, was unprepared for the accidental jibe when it came.

And come, it did.

Hard.

Del was already on his feet as the boom slammed over with killing force, already running toward the lake when it connected with the girl's ear, already throwing himself headlong into the water as she was clouted overboard in a tumble of pale skirts and flailing legs.

Ned's prophetic words rang in his ears.

It's about to get worse.

About to get a *lot* worse.

❧ 4 ❧

"**H**urry, Captain Lord!"

The boy's shouts were lost behind him as Del kicked rapidly toward where the boat, already back in irons, the boom swinging back and forth, lay helplessly on the surface. Behind him he heard people yelling encouragement, a woman screaming, felt the water streaming past him with each pull of his arms and powerful kick of his feet.

The young woman had already slipped beneath the surface.

Panic assailed him, and he dived.

Instantly the clamor from the lawn was drowned out, to be replaced by the suffocating muffle of the water around him. No clear, pure crystalline saltiness like he'd left behind in Barbados, but warm murk, fouled with goose shit and weeds, the sun striking bars down through shifting silt, his hands suddenly tangling in plants, muck—

Hair.

Through the murkiness he could just see her, sinking into the bottom sludge. He grabbed her arm and kicked hard to the surface, pulling her. His head broke the surface and he yanked her up with him, turning her so that her face was toward the fresh wind that had brought her to such grief. She was lifeless in his grasp, her eyes closed, her bonnet lost. He swam hard toward shore, kicking on his side, one hand pulling, the other wrapped around the girl to keep her afloat, and a moment later his booted feet found the squishing, sucking mud of the bottom where a horde of people had come running to meet him.

He lifted the girl, dripping and lifeless in his arms, and sloshed onto the little beach. She weighed nothing, her head lolling against his chest and her wet hair swinging over his elbow. People converged on him and crowded close, hands shading eyes, a woman crying, another swooning. Sir Graham burst through the crowd with Lady Falconer, young Ned leading the way.

"Dear God," the admiral said, reaching for the girl. Del handed her over, watching as Sir Graham bent and placed her on the grass, turning her on her side until she coughed and around them, people began to cheer.

Sir Graham's gaze cut to the helpless skiff drifting out in the middle of the pond. No words were needed.

Bring the damned thing in, would you, Captain?

Aye, sir.

Pulling off his ruined top boots and dumping the water from them, Del waded back into the lake, swam out to the hapless vessel, hauled himself aboard and quite expertly, sailed it back to the shore.

He hauled it onto the beach and moved to the perimeter of the small crowd surrounding the young lady. The new bride was there, sobbing and wringing her hands, and her portly new husband was trying his best to comfort her. Del remained carefully impassive. He stood there dripping, able to see only a small part of the young lady through moving, shifting people and now, Lady Falconer ministering to her. Nobody acknowledged him, nor made room for him. He was just another bystander.

Already forgotten.

Invisible.

Ned was small enough to squeeze his way through the press and return with a report.

"Is she all right?" Del asked, lamenting the loss of his hat which floated out in the middle of the pond. He plucked at his shirt sleeve, drenched and clinging to his skin beneath. He stank of mud. Oh, did he stink.

"She's alive." And then, soberly, "But she wouldn't be if not for you, Captain Lord. You're a hero."

Del shrugged. Saving one girl from her own foolhardiness was child's play, really.

"And to think she's my cousin. How embarrassing. She obviously didn't inherit the seafaring skills that come naturally to *our* side of the family, that's for sure..."

Del moved slightly, his commanding height allowing him to see over the tops of bonnets, feathers, turbans and top-hats. He had a clear view of her now, of dainty cream slippers and small feet resting on the bright green grass. They were attached to equally dainty ankles, and her skirts lay drenched and molded to shapely legs, the sight of which caused a sudden bump in Del's normally reined-in composure. He looked away, not wanting to compromise her modesty, feeling a surge of angry disgust toward those men who did not do the same. Thankfully, someone brought a blanket and placed it over her legs and torso, and Del allowed his gaze to return to her face. A lovely, beautifully-drawn, heavily-lashed face with clear skin and a pert little nose. He stood there, feeling stricken from all sides, as the girl's eyes fluttered open.

"Thank God!" someone exclaimed.

"She'd be dead if not for that man who saved her!"

"Who was he?"

"Some sailor, I'm told."

"Are you alright, Lady Grace?"

The girl's hand went to her ear, where blood and

water trickled from her scalp. Confusion darkened her eyes. As she came back to herself, Del saw her eyes register dawning realization of what had happened and then, as they caught sight of Captain Ponsonby standing and looking down at her with everyone else, Captain Ponsonby dressed in his naval uniform which she immediately connected with "sailor" and "rescue," she reddened with mortification.

"I... I am quite fine, thank you," she murmured. She stared up at Ponsonby. "Thank you, Captain, for saving me. I owe you my life."

Del never heard his naval peer refute the statement of gratitude. He never heard young Ned proudly proclaiming that it hadn't been Captain Ponsonby who'd dived into the mucky lake to fish her out, never heard the girl asking who had, indeed, rescued her from certain drowning.

He had already turned on his heel and headed back to the house.

A bath. Soap. Towels. Clean clothes.

Really, that was all he wanted.

27

❧ 5 ❧

No person reached the age of twenty-one years without at least one deeply embarrassing incident to mark their life, and Grace had had more than her share of them. There was the time she'd sent her father's favorite hunter toward a fence and when the horse balked, the fence had been taken all alone by an unseated Grace, who landed on the other side with a sprained wrist and her skirts nearly around her ears and in front of the whole house party, too.

There was the time she'd been asked to dance with the fashionably handsome William Roundstone during her first Season and after a breathtaking turn around the dance floor with him while everyone watched and twittered behind their fans, she'd been silently drawn aside by Lady Sarah Marlowe only to be told that she'd started her menses and the back of her gown was—

No, that was too mortifying to even think about.

But this incident, though...

Nothing. Nothing, could be this... this *awful*.

Her head spinning, she realized she was propped against Lady Falconer's ribs and bosom. Her aunt had one arm wrapped protectively around her while expressing her vexation with the other.

"Get back, all of you," the ex-pirate queen snapped,

flicking her hand at the crowd in an impatient shooing motion. "Give the poor girl some air!"

"Oh, my daughter! *My daughter*! My head, oh! My heart! Grace! My *baby*!"

Mama, pressing down against her, cradling her face in both hands, smothering her with perfumed kisses, making her head spin, crushing her.

"Mama, please," Grace managed, pushing helplessly at her. "I can't breathe."

"Oh, my dear Grace! My darling girl!"

"Stop that infernal wailing, Ariannah!" Uncle Gray's voice rumbled somewhere above, annoyed. "Take my sister back to the house, Angus, and get her calmed down, would you?"

Mama was pulled up and off her, and as awareness flooded fully in, Grace looked up at the faces all staring down at her and wanted to die. Concerned faces, relieved faces, disapproving faces.

And *his* face.

Captain Ponsonby's.

She heard the low murmurs about her rescue... the man who saved her... some sailor...

A sailor.

Oh, *no*...

Oh, *yes*.

Someone's voice, drifting down from above. "Are you all right, Lady Grace?"

"I... I am quite fine, thank you," she said, gingerly touching the side of her aching head and feeling a goose-egg already rising there. She looked shyly up at the man who had risked all to save her. "Thank you, Captain, for jumping in after me. I owe you my life."

"Why thank you, but the credit doesn't go to me, though had I been closer I should think I'd have done the same. No, it was another, my lady."

Young Ned was yelling something.

"Another?" she asked, confused.

"Delmore Lord," said Captain Ponsonby, raising his head and scanning the gathered crowd. "But I daresay he's taken himself off. Pity, that, or you could thank him yourself."

What?

Captain Ponsonby hadn't rescued her?

Grace looked into that handsome face, hoping against hope for a sliver of concern for her injured person or relief at her recovery. Nothing there to read though, and already he was offering his elbow to the blonde and leaning down to murmur some words to her.

"Shall we?"

The woman nodded, and the couple moved away.

As Grace sat up, the small crowd began to disperse, murmuring words of gratitude that she had not drowned, some appearing dismayed that the excitement was over. Sheldon Ponsonby didn't glance back. No more words from the good captain, then. No words, no long looks of simmering heat or grave concern. He had eyes only for the beauty on his arm though to be fair, her china blue eyes were soft with compassion as she looked back over her shoulder at Grace and raised a brow.

Are you all right? those kind blue eyes asked silently, as though their owner perceived Grace's embarrassment and sought to spare her any more.

Grace nodded and shut her eyes. She seemed like a nice person, did Cecily de Montforte. It was hard to dislike a nice person. Harder, still, when they were concerned about you.

Even so, it would've been nice if Captain Ponsonby had been the one showing the concern.

She got shakily to her feet with the help of Lady Falconer. The movement stirred the air, filling it with the scent of muck and pond water, both of which clung to her wet clothes and dripped from her unbound hair.

She must look like a bedraggled creature indeed. A drowned rat.

She certainly smelled like one.

Not to mention what her mishap had cost Lady Falconer's exquisite gold gown.

"I'm so sorry... I ruined your beautiful clothes," Grace said, looking with dismay at the mud and water stains where she had rested. "I was so foolish... I thought I knew what I was doing... I'm so sorry, Aunt Maeve."

"Nonsense, I've been dying to change into something less fancy all morning. You did me a favor." She looked up at her husband. "Gray, where did Del go?"

Her uncle shaded his eyes and surveyed the lawn. "He was here a moment ago."

"And where are the twins? Ned! Weren't you watching them?"

"I—"

With a below-her-breath curse, Lady Falconer went racing toward the lake, where her two toddlers were climbing into the same boat that had brought Grace to such trouble.

"Come, I'll help you into the house," Uncle Gray was saying. "You should rest."

Hannah was suddenly there, covering her shoulders with a blanket to preserve her modesty, her lips tight with disapproval.

Grace clung to the admiral's arm and flanked by her sister, allowed them to lead her toward the house, shimmering in the heat haze atop a carpet of green.

"Mortifying," she muttered, grateful for her uncle's support and wishing with all her heart that his was Captain Ponsonby's arm instead as they moved slowly up the stairs into the house. "Absolutely mortifying."

"You were lucky, young lady."

She murmured her assent, wondering who *had* rescued her. And where he had gone.

They went into the foyer and stopped in the great hall. It took a moment for Grace's eyes to adjust to the shadows after the bright sunlight outside and she stood there, blinking. The cavernous room was not empty. In the gloom, a tall figure stood silently looking out the window toward the distant pond, hands clasped behind his back. The shadows obscured his face, but he was lean, with broad shoulders under a transparently wet shirt that clung to his arms and the muscles in his back and showed transparent patches where his tanned skin showed beneath. He stood in his stockings, a discarded coat and waistcoat in a crumpled heap near one foot and leaching out a puddle of water. In that moment he turned and looked at them, and as her vision adjusted to the gloom, Grace got an impression of black hair curling in tight, dripping ringlets around a proud face; of a bold nose and high cheekbones, of steady gray eyes that were carefully guarded, alert, their emotions veiled and sharply contained. Immediately, her uncle left Grace in the care of her sister and crossed the room to the man.

Hannah, taking advantage of the moment, seized her arm and thrust her face into Grace's, yanking her attention away from him.

"What were you *thinking*, you ninny?!" she hissed.

Grace closed her eyes. "Yes, I'm fine, thank you."

"I can't believe you took a boat out into that lake all by yourself when you hardly knew what you were doing. You could have been killed!"

"I knew what I was doing. The wind came up."

"The wind was already up!"

"It moved, then. Who would have thought?"

"You weren't paying attention. And you weren't paying attention because you were too busy trying to impress Captain Ponsonby!"

Grace colored again, especially as the tall stranger by the window was quietly watching her as Sir Graham spoke with him, and it was at that moment that her addled brain put two and two together and she realized who the man actually was.

Drenched clothes. Dripping hair. The wet garments and the puddle at his feet, spreading out in a circle on the marbled floor.

No, it hadn't been the dry, unruffled, utterly gorgeous Captain Ponsonby who had dived into a murky pond to rescue her.

It had been this man.

Just who was he?

❧ 6 ❧

D el had returned to the house, thinking to quietly slip away to put himself to rights, and after hailing a footman and telling him to find Jimmy Thorne, wherever he'd gone, waited in the foyer. A blushing maid with a case of the giggles had run past and a moment later there was his coxswain, tucking his shirt into his breeches and trying to look as though he hadn't just been tumbling the lass in some hidden alcove. Thorne's reputation held on land as it did at sea, Del thought hopelessly, and sent the man off to prepare him a bath.

He waited, wondering what to do with himself as the bath was readied. He unbuttoned his coat, peeled it off, dropped it to the floor. The waistcoat followed, as did his cravat, wet and itchy and all but choking him. Best to shed what he could here, since otherwise he'd be tracking muck and stagnant water all up the fine carpeted stairs— as well as any rugs he'd have to tread once up there. At least the marble floor could be easily cleaned, which was more than could be said for any expensive rugs, and he wasn't one to cause extra work to another, just because he could.

He went to the window and looked out, waiting. He recognized Lady Falconer in the distance, helping the girls into the boat as Ned took up the paddle. Alannah, talking with the new bride, who seemed quite recovered. Ladies in pastels, men in fitted coats and tails and beaver hats such as the one whose acquaintance he'd known so briefly. Sir Graham was nowhere to be seen.

Neither was the girl.

He clasped his hands behind his back and rocked back on his heels, wishing Thorne would make haste. Although the room was empty, he was already in a shocking state of undress and if someone came in—

Someone came in.

"Del!"

It was his missing admiral. Two young women were with him, including the one he'd rescued. And she was staring. She, who had brought about the loss of his hat, the ruination of his clothes, and the need for the bath that, now that he was in the presence of genteel company, he knew he needed more than ever.

He summoned his usual rigidity to cover his embarrassment at being caught in such a state of undress, and in front of young ladies, as well. They were coming toward him. She was still staring. What the devil was he supposed to say to her?

"Del, I've been wondering where you'd gone. So's everyone else. What are you doing in here?"

"Waiting for a bath to be drawn, sir."

"Of course. Most fastidious man I know. Anyhow, I've been looking for you. Thought you might like a proper introduction to my nieces here, one of whom owes you her life. Grace, Hannah, may I present to you my... my friend, Delmore Lord. Del, these two are my sister Ariannah's daughters, Lady Grace and Lady Hannah Fairchild."

Del, feeling very self-conscious in his wet, stinking, transparent shirt and bedraggled hair, let alone the scent of *eau de pond* that clung to him, obligingly took each of their hands and bowed over them, wondering why Sir Graham didn't introduce him as his flag captain.

But of course.

He'd wanted to keep a low profile while here in England. To relax and wind down and not have to think about his duties or command. He didn't want his high station to be known or people to make too much of him, and he'd made that perfectly clear to the Falconers as well as Alannah before they'd even left the flagship. He didn't want to be asked the questions that civilians would ask of him, if he had known Nelson (no), if he had served at Trafalgar (no), if he had ever seen battle (yes), if he'd ever seen someone get their head taken off by a cannonball (it was called round shot, not a cannonball, and no, he had not and did not care to ever see it, no).

But now, he just felt awkward.

As though his identity were just out of reach, and the person who stood here in wet, stinking civilian clothes wasn't really a person at all, but an illusion. An imposter. To correct his admiral in order to reclaim an identity he'd willingly relinquished, even if just for a short time, would appear ridiculous, perhaps even petty. And what would Sir Graham think?

"Pleased to make your acquaintance, Mr. Lord."

Mr. Lord.

He would have laughed if the situation hadn't become so irretrievable to begin with. And now he looked down at her, this lovely young woman he'd fished from the pond. She had the same dark blue eyes as Sir Graham did, the same jet black hair, and she was looking up at him with a smile that did funny things to his insides.

She was the fairest creature he'd ever met.

No.

I will not, I most definitely not, even entertain the idea of getting my heart broken again.

I will not.

"Thank you for saving my life," she said, laying a hand on his damp sleeve. Her voice was soft and lively, her smile sweet and genuine, but her eyes held none of the adoration they'd had for Ponsonby. A realist by nature, Del certainly hadn't expected any. He was responsible for some six hundred lives on HMS *Orion* every day the ship was under his command. What he'd done for the girl was something any gentleman would have done, let alone an officer of king and crown.

Ponsonby hadn't done it, though.

Maybe Ponsonby just wasn't as quick to react as you were.

Maybe Ponsonby hadn't seen her as soon as you had.

Maybe Ponsonby cared more about preserving the state of his fine uniform than he did the life of the young lady.

It didn't matter. He would get the pleasantries over and done with and hopefully at any moment Thorne would be calling down to tell him his bath was ready and he'd have an excuse to escape this... this bizarre awkwardness.

"It was nothing that any quick-thinking man wouldn't have done," Del said dutifully. "I happened to be nearby, and so I acted. I hope you are quite recovered, Lady Grace."

She smiled then, and her eyes, heavily lashed, darkly fringed, took on a sudden sparkle. "My body is quite recovered, but my pride has been sorely wounded. Everyone was watching, including— oh, that doesn't matter, does it? Everyone was watching and now I've given the world something to talk about. But then, I always do. Really, I bring embarrassment to everyone who knows me, myself included." She laughed. "Aren't you glad you don't know me? I'd embarrass you too, to be sure. Still, I hadn't planned to be the talk of the afternoon. Oh, the mortification!"

"An accidental jibe can happen to any sailor," Del offered lamely.

"Is that what it's called?"

Del stared at her, thinking that if she didn't know what an accidental jibe was, she had no business being in a boat. So this was a sampling of the civilian population whose protection fell upon the hapless Royal Navy?

God help them all.

"Yes, a jibe occurs when the stern passes through the wind. In turn, it causes the sail to be caught by the resultant change in wind direction and the boom to come swinging 'round. When unintentional, the motion is usually quite violent, and can be dangerous."

"As I discovered." She slid two fingers behind her ear, wincing. "I suppose that if I'm going to sail, I should take proper lessons."

"I daresay that would be advisable."

"Well, I *was* doing quite well until the wind gusted," she challenged. "Don't you think?"

Again, Del was struck speechless; between her incompetent attempts to row the boat let alone sail it, he'd not seen such a cock-up on the water since an Eton classmate had made a paper sailboat that had promptly sunk the moment it got waterlogged.

"Your efforts were quite—" he cast about for the correct word —"notable."

She fixed her gaze on him then, studying him for a long moment with her head slightly tilted and a sparkle in her eyes and her teeth worrying her bottom lip in a way that made Del think of what that lip must taste like, how plush and sweet it might be beneath his own.

"Notable," she repeated, head still cocked to one side, and he saw the laughter in her eyes and knew that she knew very well what he thought of her seamanship.

"Well, yes."

"The next time you see me in a boat, sir, I'll give you reason to think it *memorable* as opposed to just *notable*."

"Do us all a favor and stay out of boats, Grace," said Sir Graham. "Leave the sailing to the navy."

"Yes, I agree with Uncle Gray," her sister added. "We've seen notable. We don't need memorable."

"Nonsense. You are a pessimist, Hannah, if you think 'memorable' carries connotations that are negative. In fact, I declare that my performance will be... unforgettable."

"That promises to be even worse."

Del stood there, unsure what to think of such a strange and silly conversation and decided that the clout to the girl's head must have knocked something asunder within it. And in that moment, seemingly on impulse, she took a step forward, stood on her tiptoes, and anchoring herself with a hand against his shoulder, kissed him lightly on the cheek.

Del stood there, blinking.

"Thank you, sir. I shall forever be grateful to you for your kindness. And—" she grinned, her eyes sparkling with self-deprecation—"your seamanship that I so obviously lack."

Del, resisting the urge to touch his kissed cheek, tried to muster words from his suddenly dry throat and failed. He was saved by a most opportune source. A loud *ahem* from the top of the stairs revealed Thorne's presence, and the coxswain was grinning as he noted the exchange between his captain, the two women, and the admiral.

"Your bath is ready, sir."

Thank God.

Del, his cheek still tingling where her lips had touched it, said the right things, bowed the right depth, and grabbing at the lifeline that had been offered him, all but ran for the stairs.

G race, still chewing her bottom lip and thinking about the subtle rasp of Delmore Lord's cheek beneath it, thinking about the strange electric jolt that had rattled her senses at that contact, watched her unlikely savior move quickly up the stairs.

Hmm.

"Shall I help you up to your room?" the admiral asked kindly.

His words shook her out of her momentary confusion. Confusion that she'd felt the blood hum through her veins when she'd put her lips to Mr. Lord's cheek. Confusion as she'd touched his wet shirt and the rock that was his shoulder beneath, and how that had made her senses swim with a sudden longing she didn't understand. Confusion at feeling these odd things that she had thought, really, she might only experience with a similar imagined encounter with Captain Ponsonby.

What is the matter with me?

"Grace?"

"Oh thank you, Uncle Gray, but I'm feeling much better," she said briskly, coming back to herself. "I've got the banister and Hannah to help me, so I will be fine. Your friend... he seems rather stiff. I don't think he likes me much."

The admiral shrugged. "I'm sure he likes you quite well, Grace," he reassured her. "But Del is obsessively fastidious and I suspect he just wants to get out of his wet clothes."

"Is he a sailor?"

"He... uh... has a boat, yes."

"I can't believe he jumped into the lake to rescue me. He doesn't even know me!"

"Well, thank God he was close and saw what had happened. You were quite lucky today, young lady."

Her spirits sank a bit. "Pity it wasn't Captain Ponsonby who'd been close. But I don't even exist where he's concerned."

"I am sure that if Captain Ponsonby had been the first one to notice that you were in trouble, he too would have jumped into the lake to save you."

Hannah sniffed. "He was sitting near enough. He could've jumped in to save her but he didn't."

Grace frowned. Surely, Captain Ponsonby had been too occupied with Cecily de Montforte to notice anything, really. Her face mirrored that unhappy thought and the admiral, probably wishing to extricate himself from such awkwardness as he sought to defend both his friend and a subordinate, was quick to make his excuses.

"Well, I'll leave you two to your own devices," he said. "Try and rest, Grace. And I forbid you being out on that pond in a boat of any sort from now on."

She grinned and touched her fist to her brow in what she hoped was a proper naval salute. "Yes, Admiral."

He laughed, catching the mockery in her grin. "Enough of that. I'm off. If you're up to it, Maeve and I look forward to seeing you at dinner."

He bowed and turned, and went back outside to join his family and the guests.

Hannah didn't even wait for the door to close before

she turned on Grace. "I can't believe you actually *kissed* that man!" she hissed. "Whatever must he think of you, Grace? You don't even know him!"

"I do, now." *And what a dreadful impression I've made on him. Not to mention Captain Ponsonby.*

"It's a good thing nobody but us saw you do that. Tongues would be wagging like a tail on a dog!"

"Do stop being so dramatic, Hannah. The man saved my life. An impulsive expression of gratitude shouldn't be criticized so harshly."

"Did you see his face? He was clearly uncomfortable."

"Well, I can't take it back. And I wouldn't want to. But if it makes you feel better, when I see him next, I'll apologize for my impulsiveness."

"Let's hope he'll be at dinner this evening so you *can* apologize, then!"

"Dinner?" Grace shook her head, causing a fresh stab of pain to lance it. "Ugh. The last thing I want is to remind anyone of that humiliating incident by appearing in company tonight." She lifted the heavy wet hank of hair that hung over her shoulder in dismay and gave it an uncertain sniff before dropping it in disgust. "Oh, Hannah. What a disaster. How am I ever going to get Captain Ponsonby to notice me?"

"Oh, he noticed you all right."

Grace began climbing the stairs, steadying herself on the banister and shunning Hannah's help. "You know what I mean."

"Honestly, Grace, after your antics this afternoon I think you forfeited all chance of him noticing you."

"Nonsense. I just need to... to hone my sailing skills. He's a naval captain. He'll be impressed if I can prove that I really *do* know how to sail a boat."

"But you really *don't* know how to sail a boat."

"I can learn."

"That would require finding a good teacher."

"And a body of water that doesn't stink of mud and duck droppings, should the unfortunate happen."

"Really, Grace, you are in no way ready to practice your skills on any body of water bigger than a bathtub."

"And, I'll never learn those skills if they're *not* practiced." She paused on a stair, catching her breath against a wave of dizziness. "I suppose I could ask Uncle Gray to help me, but he seems to have his hands full between his children and his duties."

"You could."

"Or I could ask Captain Ponsonby himself."

"That would be too forward."

"Then who can I find who might teach me?"

Hannah's gaze lifted, past the top of the stairs and to the hall beyond, where Sir Graham's darkly mysterious friend had disappeared. "Well, you could ask the one who saved you. Didn't Uncle Gray say he's got a boat?"

Grace made a noise of dismissal and waved her hand. "Now that *would* be forward, and I don't get the impression he likes me much. I'm not going to make him even more uncomfortable than I already have."

"Well," Hannah said, shrugging. "It was just a thought."

Just a thought.

They continued on and reached the top of the stairs. There, a window stood open and laughter drifted in from the party outside. A chestnut tree cast dancing shadows over the lawn as the breeze moved through its lofty branches and in the distance, Grace could see Ned Falconer helping his two little sisters into the same boat she'd tried to sail, and navigating it with perfect competence out into the lake.

Fresh mortification tore through her.

"I could ask Cousin Ned," she mused. "It would give me the chance to get to know that side of my family better."

"Really, you'd be better off practicing piano than getting back into a boat. Or embroidery. Or French."

"None of which interest me."

"Swordplay?"

Grace laughed. "I'll think about it. Meanwhile," she said, turning from the window, "I'm wet and itchy in these clothes, and I need a bath of my own. This celebration, or party, or whatever Mama is calling it, should last for a few more days. That should be plenty of time for me to think up a way to make a memorable impression upon Captain Ponsonby."

Hannah just shook her head, and the two sisters headed slowly down the hall, each step causing Grace's head to pound a little harder until she realized that she had a proper headache brewing within her skull. She couldn't wait to lie down.

No, she didn't want to attend dinner.

She just wanted to rest.

But Captain Ponsonby would be there and really, she didn't have a choice.

❧ 8 ❧

The bath, served up in a gleaming copper tub with fine milled soap, fluffy towels, and deliciously hot water, was a luxury that was seldom afforded even the flag captain of a famous admiral while at sea, and Del was looking forward to it immensely.

"Thank you, Thorne."

"Aye, sir. Will you have any further need of my services?"

"No. Carry on with whatever you were doing."

Thorne grinned, knuckled his forehead, and swiftly disappeared, leaving Del all alone.

At last.

He peeled off his sodden, clammy shirt and left it balled up in the washbasin so as not to ruin the rug or the furniture. His fine buckskin breeches, stained with mud and what looked suspiciously like the sheep droppings he'd tried so hard to avoid, followed, and finally his stockings. He wrinkled his nose. Yes, the bath was something he was eagerly anticipating, so much so that his skin was almost crawling.

Stark naked, he checked a second time to make sure the door was securely latched behind him and put a tentative foot into the tub. Hot water swallowed up his toes, his ankle, his long, hairy calf. He stepped fully into the steaming water and lowered his weight down, sighing in bliss as the water embraced him, scented with lavender and sending up little curls of steam toward the high plastered ceiling.

He folded his knees to make more room for himself and sliding deeper into the tub, rested his head against the raised lip and regarded that same ceiling.

Lady Grace Fairchild.

He didn't know quite what to make, let alone think, of her. The girl was as foolish as she was pretty because really, what would compel any person of intelligence to go out in a boat they didn't know how to handle and on a windy day, besides?

Of course, that was assuming such person was indeed intelligent.

Del wasn't so sure.

He adjusted his cramped legs and shut his eyes. Again he saw the girl's lively blue gaze, her clear skin, her dark hair falling in haphazard skeins of wet disarray around her shoulders as she'd gazed up at him in amusement just before planting that shocking kiss on his cheek. He hadn't got the impression she was stupid.

Impetuous, yes.

Impulsive, for certain.

But stupid?

No.

Something had compelled her to try such a foolish stunt, and he cursed his mind for continuing to dwell on a question that was, really, none of his business and beneath the normal array of his interests.

And then he remembered her adoring eyes as she'd looked up at Ponsonby, and he had his answer.

Ponsonby. Charismatic, handsome, and confident. The type of man women found irresistible, just as they did Connor. The type of man that Del had never been, would never be, and didn't think he'd want to be.

Why are you still thinking about her?

He sighed and reached for the soap. It was a smooth, fragrant, creamy white square. Soft, and silky. The same color and feel as the girl's skin, really.

He remembered that skin. Remembered the pliancy of her soft flesh, the feel of her heavy wet hair on and over his arm, her warmth beneath the wet gown that had molded itself so... so honestly, to her slender body.

Damnation!

He closed his eyes, willing the thought of her away. Was she also enjoying a bath somewhere, perhaps nearby, perhaps even in the next room? He had no idea where her quarters were. He shouldn't have cared, but he did. He shouldn't have been curious, but he was. Cared that she would make a full recovery. Curious about whether this same soap was wet and slippery as it moved over her soft skin, touching her in places that—

Del swore out loud, realizing, too late that allowing his thoughts to roam as they had, had resulted in his own body responding with an immediate and hard arousal.

Suddenly he wished the bath contained water from the North Sea, instead.

Because he could do with some cold, right about now.

⚓

"I'VE BEEN PONDERING WHAT WE SPOKE OF, EARLIER," Grace said thoughtfully as she sat on her bed following her own bath. She had given her maid, Polly, the afternoon off so she might enjoy the festivities, and now she combed her fingers through her long, freshly washed hair and plaited it into a braid, herself.

"Remind me," said her sister.

"I was thinking of Captain Ponsonby and how to get him to notice me."

Grace tied off the braid with a bit of yellow ribbon. The pond-smell was long gone and she felt fresh and clean in her soft cotton shift. The afternoon sun was setting beyond the mullioned windows. The dizziness had all but subsided, though a dull headache remained. Really, she ought to plead indisposition and keep to her room tonight after the embarrassment of the afternoon. She'd had a dreadful brush with death. Nobody would blame her.

But there was that matter of Captain Ponsonby.

And the more time he got to spend with Cecily de Montforte, the more enamored of her he would be and the more invisible to him that she, Grace, would become.

"Mama was in to visit me earlier, you know. She claims to be concerned about me but she's such a... such a butterfly, it's hard to know what is pretense and what is real. In any case, she says that Captain Ponsonby is only going to be here for another two days, and then he's off to Norfolk to visit his sister Letitia, who is now Lady Weybourne. Therefore, she encouraged me to act fast."

Hannah just slanted her a sideways glance.

"Captain Ponsonby is a seafarer," Grace continued. "He's going to want a wife who knows her way around a boat. I should know my way around a boat better than I do, given that we also come from a seafaring family, but nobody ever spent the time to teach me how to sail."

"Because you're a girl."

"Because I'm a girl."

"But given the fact that I *am* a girl, think how much more of an impact it will make on the Captain and his estimation of me, if I come across as competent. Something that I'll be able to do once I find someone to teach me. Someone who's a sailor himself."

"Ned."

"No, he's a child. He can't possibly know much about sailing. No, I'm going to ask Uncle Gray's friend, Mr. Lord. The one who rescued me today."

"You mean the one you kissed."

"I didn't *kiss* him, I gave him a kiss."

"You kissed him."

"On the cheek."

"Honestly, Grace, no matter what you call it, the man looked *quite* taken aback."

"Well of course he was, he didn't expect it, did he? And I didn't plan it. But what's done is done. Anyhow, there's no harm in asking him. Uncle Gray says he has a boat. So, therefore, that must make him a sailor."

Hannah shut her eyes and shook her head.

Grace pulled her braid over one shoulder and played with its end. "So he has a boat. I wonder if he has a tattoo. All sailors have tattoos, do they not? I wonder if he'll be amenable to teaching me. He is rather mysterious. Something about him isn't quite what it seems, but I can't put my finger on it. He appears to be very well-spoken so I shouldn't think he's a common seaman. Perhaps he works for Uncle Gray... maybe as his clerk? Or do they call secretaries something else in the Navy?"

"I hope you don't plan to ask him if he has a tattoo just to prove he's a sailor."

"Why would I do that?"

"Why do you do anything?"

"Well, that would be rather personal. Of course I'm not going to ask him that, I'm just going to see if he might teach me a bit about boats."

"I still think that's rather forward of you, Grace."

"Nonsense. In fact, I think I shall go down to dinner this evening after all. Not only will Captain Ponsonby likely be there, but so will Mr. Lord. All I have to do is find an opportunity to put my idea to him." She lay back against the propped pillows, smiling once more. "And on that note, I do believe I will rest for a bit. If I'm to be at my best tonight, I need to try and rid myself of this headache."

Del, standing in front of the looking glass with a comb, had been fussing over his appearance— just like a young miss might, he thought sourly, and for what reason, really?— for the past thirty minutes. There wasn't a damned thing to be done with hair so curly it had a life, mind and will of its own. Hair that was drying in haphazard, frizzing, unruly disarray around his face, refusing to be as staunchly under command as everything else about his person, his career, and his life.

For a man as strictly disciplined as he was, such hair was an endless frustration.

He eyed it ruefully. His siblings all had their father's thick blond hair, hair that took a comb with no complaint, hair that shone in the sun and never gave its owner any trouble. But Del's hair was a gift from his mother, and he was the only one who'd inherited it. Irish hair, she laughingly called it. Her own brother, Ruaidri, also had it. Hair that was coarse and wild and curling and quite black, given to corkscrew curls and untamed waves and an explosion of frizz if it met with comb or brush. Hair that one couldn't do a damned thing with and tonight, as Del stood in front of the mirror, frowning, he found himself wishing he'd lived several decades in the past, when at least he could tie the damned curls and kinks and frizz up in a queue and let it go at that.

It was already longer than it should be. But cutting it would cause it to stick up in ways that defied gravity.

"Captain Lord?"

He looked up, reining in his impatience and glad for the distraction. "Good evening, Ned."

"Papa said to tell you they're starting to gather downstairs."

"Already?"

"Well, people want to eat."

"All we've been doing all day is *eating*. And eating some more. I say, Ned, if sailors ate as much as these people did, their combined weight would sink a warship."

"Papa also said you'd try to beg off and ask for a tray in your room, even if you were hungry."

"Your father knows me well."

"He wants you to attend."

"Of course he does. He doesn't want to be alone in the midst of such gluttony and gossip any more than I do. Food. Food! First a wedding, then a wedding banquet, now a wedding dinner. Will there be a wedding nightcap and a wedding midnight snack as well?"

"I hope so. And I also hope they'll be serving more of that lemon cake they brought out earlier. Though I liked the torte with almond icing and cherries on it, as well."

"You'd be wise not to gorge on such confections. You'll be up all night with a bellyache."

Ned grinned. "Advice duly noted, sir."

The boy turned to leave.

"Er, Ned?"

"Aye, sir?"

"That young lady who came to such grief earlier... your cousin." Del turned back to the mirror, checked his freshly-shaven jaw and forced an air of nonchalance. "I trust that she has recovered and is well?"

"Haven't seen her all afternoon but if I do, I'll tell her you were asking about her."

"Oh, no, please do not. I would not wish to give her the impression that I have any... well, any inappropriate interest in her."

"Why would it be inappropriate?"

"Never mind. Forget I said it, actually."

Ned, his eyes gleaming, folded his arms across his chest. "I heard my parents talking, you know."

"You shouldn't eavesdrop."

"I wasn't, intentionally. But I still heard them."

Del went back to the looking glass and lifting his chin, began tying his cravat. "I suppose that's my cue to ask you what they were talking about."

"It is indeed. And they were talking about you. Both of them think you're far too wrapped up in all things Navy and that you've forgotten what it means to be around the fairer sex. They would like to see you find a wife."

Del, tying the folds of his cravat, started such that he nearly choked himself. "I grew up with several sisters. I daresay I know plenty about what it means to be around the fairer sex."

"Well, that was a long time ago. Now that you're old, you've probably forgotten."

"Old? I will turn thirty later this year."

"That *is* old, Captain Lord. Really old. My parents are right. You should find a wife before you start looking grandfatherly. Then it will be too late."

"Spoken from the vantage-point of an eight-year-old."

Ned laughed. "The view up here is quite fine. See you at dinner, sir!"

The boy disappeared, and Del was left alone to ponder his apparent elderliness, to discount the tiny creases at the corners of his eyes to sun and not age, and to resume the fight with his freshly-washed hair.

Really, he should've got it cut. He looked like a damned savage.

He raked a hand through the still-damp curls. Then, buttoning his jacket, he turned from the mirror and headed to the door.

EVENING HAD MADE SHORT WORK OF THE DAY'S HEAT but inside the house, especially with such a crush of people already gathering outside the great dining hall, it was still warm enough to elicit fans, complaints, and excuses for opportunistic ladies to swoon into the arms of handsome men. Grace figured she'd done enough swooning for the day and vowed to bring no further embarrassment upon herself. Nevertheless, she felt warm and cloistered in the press of bodies belonging to those waiting to be announced into the dining room, all of them gaily dressed, showing off jewelry, clothing, the partner who clung to their arm or to whose arm they clung.

That same warmth brought back the dizziness from her earlier clouting, and she wished she had an arm to cling to.

Preferably, Captain Sheldon Ponsonby's.

She followed the announcements into the dining room and found herself sitting, much to both her delight and dismay, amidst a group of blond people.

And, directly across from Captain Ponsonby himself.

For not the first time in her life, she wished she didn't have the Falconer coloring. With her dark tresses and azure eyes, she felt conspicuous and rather lacking. Glancing across the table brought further dismay. Captain Ponsonby, smiling at Cecily de Montforte, obviously liked his women to be fair.

Grace tried to put it out of her mind. People were still arriving and being seated and she forced herself to watch them, instead. She glanced at Hannah, nearby. The three youngest Falconer children had been put to bed under the care of their nanny but Ned was here, trying to emulate the gentleman seated around him in manner, seriousness and look. Colorful fans were appearing all around, directing cool air at damp faces, but the open window at Grace's back admitted a refreshing breeze that relieved her hot nape and shoulders and made her hair, carefully upswept in the back and arranged into ringlets to frame her face, tickle her cheeks when she turned her head.

She sipped from her wine glass, trying to pretend she was oblivious to the handsome blond pair just across from her. The two shared an easy relationship, laughing and smiling as though they'd known each other forever. Grace stared down into her wine, swirling it in the glass, keeping her expression properly cheerful. It was going to be a long evening with this sort of torture, and she willed it to be over. That wouldn't be for some time, unfortunately. People were still coming into the room and being seated.

"How are you feeling, my dear?"

It was her mother, leaning down over her shoulder as she headed to her place at the upper end of the table. She'd entered the room on the arm of Grace's new stepfather, Major Lord Angus McAllister. He was ten years his bride's junior, distinguished in some battle in France against Napoleon, and his adoring gaze lingered on Mama's neck and bosom while his cheeks went as ruddy as autumn apples.

Grace didn't like him much, really, but he'd been kind enough to her.

She wondered if Mama liked him much, either.

She'd certainly seemed rather oblivious to him earlier as she circled the festivities like a butterfly on the wing, laughing, vivacious, beautiful, uncaring that he was staring after her like a love-struck swain.

"Grace?" her mother repeated, growing concerned.

She tore her gaze from her discreet perusal of Captain Ponsonby's hand as it closed around the stem of his wine glass. "I'm well enough, Mama."

Well enough, with having been knocked out of a boat, nearly drowned, and now about to be subjected to two hours of Captain Ponsonby directly in front of me, while he pays court to a beautiful blonde with whom I can never compete.

"I am glad of it. Oh, look, there is your poor Aunt Alannah, she looks so sour these days, one would think she'd want to be back in Barbados!"

"She always looks sour, Mama."

"Grace! Lower your voice, *please!*"

"Well, nobody heard me," Grace muttered sheepishly as her mother, her maternal duties complete and her effervescence in need of feeding, gave her The Look — eyes unnaturally wide open like twin blue beams, staring hard, head slightly tilted, mouth thinned just so — and fluttered off down the table.

Well, at least she'd hoped nobody had heard her, especially Aunt Alannah, who *had* been rather sour since the death of her husband last year. Worry began to assail her, but Alannah, across from her and a few seats down, was shaking out her napkin and nodding a greeting to an older gentleman who was taking a seat beside her. She hadn't heard. *Phew.* More people filing in, and there, the admiral's stiffer-than-starch friend, Mr. Lord, whose cheek had made the blood rush from Grace's head when her lips had impulsively touched upon it.

She was feeling that same bit of dizziness, now. Woozy.

She picked up her fan and directed air toward her face.

The man moved into the room. He didn't look uncomfortable, but there was something about him that made her think he probably longed to be somewhere else. And why not? This was not his family, these were not his people. In fact, why was he even here, aside from the fact that he was Uncle Gray's friend? She watched him as he moved, his stride loose, his shoulders proud and commanding. She rather hoped that he wouldn't be seated next to her; what would she say to him after that kiss? The one she was supposed to apologize for?

You could thank him again for saving your life, you ninny.

She could.

Or, she could launch straight into her plan.

And why not?

Captain Ponsonby was leaving imminently. There was no time to waste.

Mr. Lord moved to his chair, and at that moment his gaze lifted and directly met hers. He gave a barely perceptible nod, and Grace found herself blushing.

Was he thinking about that silly kiss she'd bestowed on him?

Her heart pounded a little faster in her chest, and she took another sip of wine, wishing he hadn't flustered her so.

And wondering why he did.

Mr. Lord was seated beside Aunt Alannah. Only a few years older than Grace herself, she suddenly didn't look so sour, nor did Mr. Lord look so stiff, and Grace wondered what kind of history back on Barbados the two of them must share to enjoy such an easy familiarity. Unreasonably, something stirred inside her; something faintly unpleasant and not altogether welcome, and Grace struggled to identify what it was.

She shook it off. The starter was served, an asparagus soup with some sort of cream base. Grace didn't care for asparagus and left it uneaten following an exploratory spoonful of it that all but made her gag.

She buttered a roll and returned her attention to Captain Ponsonby across the table from her, wondering what the evening would hold.

It was a good thing she could not know.

Disaster was, of course, waiting for Grace.

On this night of nights, it came in the form of a long, dark hair that somehow found its way into Captain Ponsonby's asparagus soup.

Grace had been toying with her roll, waiting for the soup to be taken away, trying to ignore her gnawing envy as she'd observed Cecily's natural grace, her aristocratic elegance as she'd lifted the spoon to her pretty mouth, her china-blue eyes laughing and kind, when it happened.

There was an older gentleman seated beside her, his hair gone to gray, going on about his estate in Shropshire; Grace was dutifully giving him half an ear, trying very hard not to look as sour as she'd observed Aunt Alannah as being earlier when Captain Ponsonby, just lifting his spoon to his mouth, paused and stared at it.

An expression of disgust cinched his handsome brows, his lip curled faintly and it was then that Grace saw it. A bit of asparagus, neatly snared at the end of a nearly-black hair, dangling from his spoon like a swinging fish.

"Oh," the captain said, his lip curling yet further, and in that moment his eyes lifted to hers and he recognized the culprit, the culprit who was the only one in his immediate vicinity with dark hair, who was to windward of him, and who was now, in that brief meeting of gazes, mortified for the second time this day.

He lowered the spoon, the asparagus still dangling from the hair, back into his bowl. Again, a glance up at her, at her dark hair; a pained smile, but the revulsion was there in his eyes, his appetite gone. He pushed the soup away.

His companion had not noticed the reason for his sudden loss of appetite. "Sheldon?"

"The soup is not quite to my liking," he said politely, too much of a gentleman to call attention to the hair, and through flaming face and a crushing sense of humiliation, Grace knew she could not endure another minute here, let alone another two hours. Tears burned behind her lids and she pushed her chair back, getting to her feet.

"I beg your pardon," she managed, her face burning with mortification. "I... I'm not feeling well."

Her mother frowned and began to rise, no doubt unhappy about attention being transferred from herself to another on her special day, but Grace raised a hand to stay her and hurried to the door. She heard chairs scraping behind her, the low murmur of conversation. *Poor thing... she took quite a hit earlier... nobody can blame her for needing to rest!* She put the voices out of her mind, desperate to get out of the room ... desperate to escape the humiliation, desperate to remove herself from Captain Ponsonby's presence, desperate to get upstairs and throw herself down on the bed and have the good cry that was just bursting at the seams to get out.

But they would be looking for her in her room.

Hannah. Her mother. Every single one of her blood-aunts and possibly even Aunt Maeve as well.

And at that moment, Grace did not want to see anyone, talk to anyone or be found by anyone.

At the stairs she turned left instead, and headed outside into the garden.

Her feet could not take her fast enough.

~

IT WAS LADY FALCONER, EYEING THE YOUNG WOMAN as she hurried from the room, who leaned sideways to murmur to her husband's flag captain.

"She looks rather wobbly, Del. You really ought to go see to her welfare."

"Me?"

"Why, yes, you. You've already rescued the poor girl once today, she'll be rather used to it by now."

Del's concern had been aroused when he'd seen her abruptly get to her feet and leave the table. She'd been hit pretty hard during the accidental jibe this afternoon, and though he had no experience with such an injury himself, he'd seen nausea go along with head injuries in others. The sight of food had probably affected her.

"I think, Lady Falconer, that you or her sister or even one of her aunts should be the one to tend to her. She's a young woman without a chaperone. It would be improper if I go see to her—"

"Go see to her," his admiral snapped irritably from nearby. "And that's an order."

One couldn't argue with one's own admiral. Inwardly sighing, Del pushed his chair back, eyed his half-finished soup, and nodding to Alannah, headed for the doors.

Something wasn't right. It was the same feeling he might've had on a perfectly sunny, pleasant day at sea when something in the wind, in the air itself, warned him of an incoming storm. Gut feelings, they were like that. Not always anything obvious, but to be respected, heeded even, all the same.

Del's gut feeling was that Sir Graham and Lady Falconer were up to something.

Reason suggested it might be an ill-conceived attempt at matchmaking, but logic argued against that; there'd been plenty of pretty young women back on or near Barbados, daughters of rich plantation owners, daughters of military colleagues, daughters of local dignitaries. The Falconers had never played matchmaker then, and Del had no reason to think they would do so now. Besides, Sir Graham had been downright furious when Rhiannon, the woman who'd secretly owned Del's heart, had been caught alone on a beach with Connor out in the darkness. Rhiannon had been his ward.

Lady Grace, though, was more than just his ward.

She was his niece.

No, his admiral was just sensitive to the fact that Del was no fan of *ton* gatherings and was giving him an excuse to bail.

But yet, that gut feeling...

He left the noisy, stuffy dining room and shut the door behind him. The great hall was pleasantly cool after the smothering crush in his wake, lighted sconces placed at regular intervals between a gallery of paintings, shining on long-dead faces, throwing shadows across the marble floor and plush rugs.

"Sir?"

It was a footman with a tray of food, heading for the dining room that Del had just vacated. His brows were raised in question.

"A young lady just left here," Del said quietly. "Did you see where she went?"

"Outside, sir."

Outside. Great. In the darkness.

There was that gut feeling again.

He remembered how Connor had been caught out in the darkness with Rhiannon, and the marriage they'd been forced to undergo as a result.

He thought about turning back to the dining room.

He thought about heading upstairs and spending the rest of the night reading a book.

He thought of anything but heading for the door that led out into the darkness and chasing after that beautiful, impetuous, and oh-so-foolish girl.

You can't disobey your admiral.

And if something happens to the young lady out there, and you weren't there to protect her, your head will be the one to roll.

His mouth tight, Del strode for the door.

❧ I I ❧

H e moved lightly down the steps and onto the lawn outside.

The night was cool, the gusty winds that had marked the day having subsided into a harmless collection of faint zephyrs that, were he at sea, he'd be cursing for their inability to move the ship forward at any speed. They were pleasant enough here though, and for a moment he allowed himself to enjoy a soft, lovely night without baking heat.

A night without mosquitoes.

He'd forgotten how much of a luxury that actually was. Above him, stars shot through a dark sky and off in the distance the lights of a village twinkled. He heard a cow lowing somewhere in the night. A fox barking.

A woman's soft weeping.

The gut feeling returned, and it was very clear in its directive.

Turn right around, Del, and go straight back into the house and tell your admiral that his niece is upset and needs tending to. Turn right around and do it quickly, before anyone catches the two of you out here together. So, she's crying. Her head likely hurts. She's not your responsibility and if you go to her, all kinds of bad things may happen to you.

Remember what happened to Connor?

For a moment, Del stood there, torn.

The weeping grew louder, the sound of a wet, mucus-laden nose being sniffed into sinuses punctuating the soft cries.

Turn right around! the gut feeling persisted.

But Del was first and foremost an officer. He had been born the second son of an admiral, been trained by admirals, and now served an admiral, and the idea of disobeying a direct order from one was unthinkable to him no matter how much gut feelings told him to do just that.

He took a deep and bracing breath and damning his obedience to duty, let alone the soft spot in his heart that only wanted to soothe that plaintive anguish, headed toward the sound.

"LADY GRACE?"

The deep voice cut through the darkness in which Grace had retreated, a darkness that covered her shame, soothed her misery, gave her anonymity and escape following the disaster caused by a single, cursed hair.

A hair, of all things.

Oh, how utterly, crushingly, *mortifying*.

Was that to be the end of her dreams with Captain Ponsonby?

Maybe not, because here he was, out here in the darkness and coming to her aid like the gallant rescuer she knew him to be. No doubt, he'd realized his reaction— understandable as it was— had deeply embarrassed her, and had come out to make amends as any proper gentleman would do. No doubt he felt badly about things and wanted to make them right.

She caught her breath, smoothed her carefully curled ringlets back from her face, and passed a knuckle beneath her eye. She considered blowing her nose; sniffling was about as attractive as finding a hair in your soup, but blowing one's nose was a flat-out confession that you'd been crying and right now Grace didn't want Captain Ponsonby to know she'd been doing just that.

"I'm here," she managed, sitting up on the little bench on which she'd sought refuge and wishing her voice didn't sound so nasally, so clogged with tears.

Footsteps approaching, crunching on the gravel. She straightened her spine, sitting primly and thinking, somewhat uneasily, that perhaps Captain Ponsonby might be a bit of a rake if he'd followed her out here in the darkness all by himself. Did anyone know? What were his intentions?

There, a tall form materializing from under the starlight. Powerful shoulders, a trim, lean waist, long legs and an air of quiet authority. He man moved closer, and Grace's heart fell.

"You're not Captain Ponsonby," she said, unable to keep the disappointment from her voice.

"I'm sorry. No, I'm not." He paused a good twenty feet away, unwilling to come closer in respect, she imagined, for her own reputation should anyone find them. "Are you all right, Lady Grace?"

"Yes, Mr. Lord."

"Your uncle sent me to check on you."

"I'm fine. You can go back inside now."

"You don't sound fine."

"Well, I am. And I'd prefer to be left alone, please."

He said nothing for a long moment, and she could sense him thinking. He clasped his hands behind his back and dug at the gravel with his toe before finally speaking. "As a gentleman, I cannot leave you out here alone in the darkness."

"What, are you afraid I might fall into another pond and need rescuing again?"

"On the contrary. To my knowledge there is only

one pond on this property and it is a good distance away. My concerns for your safety have nothing to do with water."

"I'm sure I can see to my own safety, thank you."

"I'm sure you can. But since I was sent to make sure that you're all right, I'll take a seat on this bench opposite your own."

"And do what?"

"Why, stay out here until you decide to go back inside, I imagine."

"I told you, sir, that I wish to be alone."

"And I told you, that I was sent to ensure your well-being."

"By whom?"

"Your uncle."

Her uncle. Well, it was better to have Sir Graham imposing on her life than her new stepfather, she supposed. Because the latter was inevitable.

Still.

He moved closer, and Grace's skin prickled in warning. But he only reached into his pocket, withdrew a crisply folded handkerchief, and gallantly handed it to her before stepping politely away. Then he retreated and took a seat on the bench opposite her. He sat there, a quiet presence in the darkness that, in some odd, confusing way, was rather comforting.

She wiped at her eyes. Irritation crept in, especially when he said nothing, creating awkwardness and a silence she felt obligated to fill. What to say to him? What to do now? Sit here like a bump on a log? Yes, she'd wanted to talk to the man but not quite like this, in these circumstances, and certainly not when she was upset. Worse, she was alone out here in the darkness with him. *Alone.* With him. That was infinitely more dangerous than being out here alone with just herself.

What if they were discovered?

Dear God. That didn't bear thinking about. Nor did the scandal and resultant consequences.

But she wasn't ready to return to the house, to possibly run into Captain Sheldon Ponsonby and the beautiful Cecily de Montforte (who likely *never* shed hairs that ended up in other people's soup), wasn't ready to explain things to her mama and certainly, wasn't ready to face anyone.

So she was stuck here, really. Stuck either talking to him or going back inside. Maybe she could slip up to her room and hide there for the rest of the evening.

Or the rest of the next few days.

But Grace was not one to hide, at least, not for long. She chanced a look at him, sitting there opposite her just across the little stone path, and it hit her, then. Hard. Despite the awkwardness and shocking inappropriateness of being out here in the dark with him, if it weren't for this man she wouldn't even *be* here.

No, Grace. You would be dead.

Dead and drowned.

She suddenly felt lower than the gravel beneath her slippered feet.

"I'm sorry for my crossness," she said quietly, and looked down at his handkerchief, now knotted in her hands. "I've had such an awful day and now, an equally awful night. It's not your fault. I don't mean to take out my feelings on you. Indeed, I should be thanking you for saving my life. For jumping into that lake and ruining your clothes... why, your day was spoiled, too."

He was silent for a moment. "Any decent man would have done the same. I happened to be close enough to predict what was about to happen and take action as needed."

"Well, you may downplay your part in it, but I wouldn't be sitting here breathing if not for you."

"And, uh... forgive me, but crying."

"You noticed?"

"I'm afraid I couldn't help but notice."

"Oh."

She went silent, feeling suddenly very foolish. Of course he'd noticed. It's why he'd given her his handkerchief. She was suddenly glad that he couldn't see her face flaming in the darkness. He probably already thought she was a silly enough ninny, without further confirmation.

"I'm sure your head must hurt," he offered gallantly. "And your pretty gown was ruined."

"You think that's why I'm out here crying?"

He shrugged. "Seems like a good enough reason to me."

"If you think I'd cry over such trivial nonsense, you don't know me very well."

"You are entirely correct in that, Lady Grace. I *don't* know you very well."

Another long silence. In the distance the moon was coming up, tracing a faint track over the distant pond where she'd nearly met her end.

"I was crying," she murmured, looking down at the wadded-up handkerchief in her hands, "because Captain Ponsonby found a hair in his soup."

He paused for a long moment.

"Well, then," he said, finally. "That's an odd reason to cry."

"Not when... when... oh, never mind. I can't explain right now, nor do I wish to. Can you please go back inside, Mr. Lord?"

"That would be disobeying your uncle and I can't do that."

She put her head in her hands and stared down at her feet, her eyes blurring with tears.

"So, he found a hair in his soup," Mr. Lord continued, as though something of such magnitude mattered not one whit. His voice was deep, pleasant and kind.

"He's a mariner. At sea, he'll find weevils in his bread and maggots in his beef. I'm sure he can handle it."

"Do you really not understand?"

"I'm afraid I don't."

"It was a *haaaaair*!" she all but wailed. "One of mine!"

"Maybe it was the cook's."

"It wasn't the cook's, she has gray hair!"

"Lady Grace, I think that—"

"This hair was black," she snapped, tears of humiliation burning in her sinuses once more. "And everyone sitting around me had fair hair save for Mr. whatever-his-name-was. Oh no, Mr. Lord, it was *my* hair. Even if it wasn't, the captain *thought* it was mine and he was plainly revolted— you could see it on his face, and immediately after finding it, he pushed the soup away and went a bit green. He knew it was my hair!"

"And why should that matter?"

"Isn't it obvious?"

"Isn't what obvious?"

"You really are the most impossible person! I don't know if you're just making sport of me or if you really are this obtuse."

"With all due respect, Lady Grace, you are the one talking cryptically, not me."

She leaned forward, tucking her hands between her knees and finding his gaze in the darkness. "I'll spell it out for you then, since you haven't discerned what I'm trying to say while I'm trying not to say it. That is, Mr. Lord... oh, this is embarrassing!... I quite fancy Captain Ponsonby and I don't have a chance of catching his attention except, it would seem, by humiliating myself. He's smitten with Cecily de Montforte and doesn't even know I exist. I need to find a way to get him to notice me. That is why I was out on the lake. He's a captain of a great warship, and I wanted him to know that we had something in common, that I also knew how to sail a boat but the wind, oh! Why did it come up when it did?"

The man across from her went silent, and Grace could not know that he was thinking some thoughts of his own.

Captain of a great warship, my arse. The man commanded a frigate. Frigates were good scouts, they were fast and powerful, but they weren't an admiral's flagship, and they were usually captained by ambitious up-and-comers desperate to prove themselves. He knew, because he'd captained one himself before Sir Graham had given him command of *Orion* and asked him to carry his flag.

This young woman, though... she wouldn't know the difference between a frigate and a hundred-gun ship of the line such as his *Orion*, and despite the stab of annoyance he'd felt when she sang Ponsonby's praises, he was obliged to just let her rattle on for a bit.

"Which is why I was hoping to talk to you," she was saying. "I had planned to approach you when the time was right, but since we're both sitting out here, I'll just say it and be done with it."

"Go on."

"That is, if you're a friend of my uncle, and know something about boats, I'm guessing you're a sailor." She peered at him. "Are you?"

Am I a sailor?

Del's lips twitched. The part of him that was stuffy, that Connor had worked so hard to change, to loosen up, to relax, wanted to draw himself up and retort with proper affront and dignity that he was more than just a sailor, that he was a captain in His Majesty's Royal Navy and commanded a massive warship carrying six hundred men and a famous admiral. He would have liked to have told her that that admiral was one of Nelson's own, his protégée in fact, and he'd have liked to have told her that her precious Captain Ponsonby had a long way to go before he was the "sailor" that Del himself was. But Del was not churlish, nor did he have a wish to cause this poor young lady any more embarrassment than she'd already suffered this day. Besides, he found a certain amusement in letting her believe he was a common tar. As bored as he was here at this wedding where he knew nobody but his admiral and that worthy man's family, amusement was in desperately short supply.

Let her believe that, then.

No harm, there.

"Yes," he replied honestly. "I am a sailor. I work for your uncle."

"Good." She wiped her eyes with one knuckle, raised her chin, and leaned forward. "Because I have a favor to ask of you, and I'm hoping you'll oblige me."

" **A** favor," he repeated, and she heard the slight uncertainty in his voice along with a certain patient humor. "And what might that be, Lady Grace?"

"As I've just told you, I... I fancy Captain Ponsonby, but he doesn't even know I exist. And when my existence becomes known to him, it's always at the expense of unbearable humiliation. I would like to rectify that. I would like to prove to him that I am more than what he's observed to date, that I'd be a worthy counterpart, that I can converse on the subjects that are certainly near and dear to his heart."

In the gloom, she could just see Mr. Lord fold his arms across his chest and let his chin rest on his collarbone. He went very quiet. She wished she could know what he was thinking. Was he silently laughing, using the darkness to hide his amusement? Bemusement? Irritation, even?

She wished she could see his face.

She needed to find her footing.

Rattled, she pressed on. "Obviously, my... um, performance in the lake this afternoon had rather the opposite effect. It proved that my skills are sorely lacking. Since you're a sailor, Mr. Lord, I would be very grateful to you if perhaps you'd be willing to give me a few lessons on how to manage a boat."

"Well, I—"

"I know it's terribly forward of me, but Captain Ponsonby will soon be leaving for Norfolk and I don't have much time to amend the impression I've made on him, not much time to show him that I do indeed have things in common with him. Once they leave for Norfolk, my opportunity will be lost."

"I... see."

"Can you help me?"

Another long silence. "I would be happy to teach you a few things," he said after a long moment, "but you will need a chaperone, of course. I don't want tongues to wag. Or to put you in a position we may both lament."

"So you will you teach me?"

"I can... attempt to," he said, and she heard a faint bit of doubt in his voice.

And this time, yes, most definitely— amusement.

And she noticed something more about that voice. That it was pleasant in timbre, educated and confident. It was smooth and deep, reassuring, measured. The kind of voice a woman could happily listen to, curled up in his protective embrace, her ear against his chest, for hours on end.

Or curled up beside him in bed.

She blushed wildly. Where on God's green earth had *that* thought come from?

Her glance went to the shadowy form on the bench opposite her and she was grateful for the darkness, grateful that he could not see her sudden high color. He sat relaxed some fifteen feet away, but he had such a presence about him that he seemed much closer, and was imbibed with a sort of charisma that wasn't unlike what she sensed in Captain Ponsonby. The captain, though, was resplendent and showy. This man...he was understated. In his own way he was easy to miss unless a person gave him a second thought, and studied him a little bit more than his initial demeanor invited.

A bit of an enigma, really.

"So do we have an agreement?" she asked, leaning forward.

"Yes, but, you should probably know that I too will be leaving for Norfolk, most likely around the same time your quarry is likely to depart."

"My quarry!"

"Is he not?"

"Very well then, but put that way it sounds so... inappropriate."

"No more so than my being out here with you." He rose to his feet. "Will you not come inside now?"

"No, I will not."

"Very well, then. I'll send someone out here to sit with you. In the meantime, we'll have our first lesson tomorrow. Shall I meet you early in the morning? Say, at sunrise? At the pond?"

"The lake?"

"The pond."

"Yes, Mr. Lord. I will be there."

He bowed deeply, straightened up and melted into the darkness, and Grace was alone once more... wondering why she suddenly felt bereft, as though the very air had been sucked from her lungs, as though she'd just come down from a great height and fallen flat on her back, unable to breathe, somehow deflated.

Odd, that.

⚓

"NED, DARLING, WOULD YOU MIND FINISHING YOUR pudding and going to check on your cousin Grace?"

The boy had been trying to pretend interest in the goings-on around the table, adopting the gentlemanly manners he'd been taught, the posture, expressions, and words the adults were using but his mother, discreetly watching him from nearby, must have sensed his restlessness and much to Ned's relief, now offered an escape. There was only so long he could pretend to understand the subtle politics and the not-so-subtle gossip that dominated the dinner conversation, much less show an interest in it. He wished Captain Lord were here. He'd probably be equally bored. At least they could talk ships and naval maneuvers.

But Captain Lord had already been given *his* reprieve when Papa had sent him out of the room on some errand which, his mother admitted in a whisper when he'd asked, was to find his cousin, Lady Grace.

Girls! Did they all require such... caretaking?

Ned decided right then and there that he was never going to be bothered by girls. They were squealing, silly, delicate, ribbon-and-lace festooned creatures anyhow, and required too much effort.

Still, a reprieve was a reprieve and an escape was an escape.

"Yes, Mama," he said dutifully, and cramming a last bite of strawberry tart into his mouth, tried not to leap from his seat. He kept his pace under control. Once out of the dining room, he burst into a run.

His footsteps echoed through the empty hall, and there he paused. Where had his cousin gone?

The big doors that led outside opened, and Captain Lord walked in. He looked preoccupied. Very preoccupied.

"Captain Lord!"

"Why, Ned. What are you doing out here? Is the meal finished already?"

"It is for me. I was so bored I couldn't stand it. Mama sent me out to find cousin Grace. You haven't seen her, have you?"

Captain Lord paused for a moment. "You ought to be in bed, young man. It's late."

"Bed? Why? It's not even nine o'clock. I'm not tired."

"You nearly died a few months back. You should be resting."

"But I didn't die, I don't feel like resting, and you know something you're not telling me."

Captain Lord's firm mouth tightened in the way it always did when he wanted to say something but was holding back, and Ned knew he was lamenting the fact that he, Ned, was not only a young boy but his admiral's son and thus, at an advantage over even his father's powerful flag captain. Captain Lord couldn't really reprimand him, and both of them knew it.

Ned pressed home. "So what aren't you telling me?"

"Your cousin is out in the garden, on a bench, and pining for an absolute rotter. She is also quite alone. If you know what's good for you, young man, you'll go fetch her inside right now before any harm comes to either her person or her reputation."

"Why don't *you* do that?"

"Because you know what happened with your Uncle Connor and Rhiannon. Oh, no. If I'm seen alone with her, harm will indeed come to her reputation, I'd be honor-bound to defend it, but her guns are quite firmly sighted on Captain Ponsonby. I will not get in the way of them."

"You should."

"What?"

"I'd rather have you in the family than Captain Ponsonby any day of the week. I don't like him. Oh, he's probably a good captain and all, but he thinks highly of himself, does he not?"

"That is not for me to say. What is for me to say is that your cousin thinks highly of him, and that is her business, not mine."

Captain Lord turned abruptly on his heel but not before Ned caught the expression on his face. It was the same look of repressed, pinched longing that he'd had when the beautiful Rhiannon had turned her attention on Connor instead of Captain Lord. A look of resigned despair. For not the first time in the last half hour, Ned thanked his lucky stars that he was not prone to the foolishness that men and women exhibited over matters of the heart. He vowed he never would be.

He watched as his father's flag captain headed resolutely back toward the dining room. It was only as he reached the great doors that led inside that Ned saw him pause, thinking for a moment.

He abruptly turned from the door and headed for the stairs instead.

Ned didn't blame him.

That dining room was the most boring place in the world.

He wasn't inclined to go back in there, either.

❧ 13 ❧

D el moved quickly up the stairs.

If he were half the rogue that Ponsonby was, he'd have positioned himself on the bench next to her, taken her hand, turned on the charm and kissed the living daylights out of her.

But Del was not a rogue. And, he lamented, he had no charm to turn on. He was a mariner, and his skills lay in navigation and ship-handling, organization and command, problem-solving, admiral-placating, order-giving, diplomacy, naval tactics, and seamanship.

What the devil did he know about women, save for his sisters and, in the romantic sense, a mistress he'd once set up in Bridgetown, a cunning female who'd turned out to be an expensive and demanding bother? He'd eventually terminated their relationship, and while meeting his needs would have been easy in any of the brothels in that tropical town, Del, as fastidious as his admiral had earlier noted, was not inclined to pick up the pox or any other lover's disease all for the sake of a frolic in the sheets.

No, he had been celibate for a while, and would remain so until such time as he took a wife.

Strangely, the pretty face of his admiral's niece suddenly filled his mind. Stayed there and wouldn't leave.

Allowing it to remain there was folly. He'd learned his lesson following the heartbreak of losing Rhiannon to his cousin Connor, and why would this be any different? The girl was all agog over Ponsonby. A mere *frigate* captain, Del thought rather loftily, and noticing his pettiness, frowned. Not that it mattered. He himself was the captain of a ship-of-the-line and yet the lovely Rhiannon Evans had never even looked at him, so enamored was she of the American privateer.

If he could lose a girl to a veritable pirate, then he had no chance against a frigate captain, no matter how "mere" Del personally found that command in comparison to his own.

She's not for you, anyhow. She's funny and kind-hearted, self-deprecating and pretty, but she's got her cap set for another and it's no sense even trying. Stop thinking about her. Stop fantasizing. Teach her how to sail the damned skiff and let it go at that.

At the top of the stairs, he ran into his admiral's wife just exiting her room. He bowed courteously. "Lady Falconer."

"Hello, Del. Just checking on the little ones. Did you find Lady Grace?"

"I did, and turned her over to the competent care of young Ned."

"Oh." She paused. "Well, then."

Del slanted her a confused look. "I'm sorry?"

"Ariannah despairs of ever finding a husband for the girl. She's got a wild streak in her, to be sure, but it's her propensity for embarrassing mishaps that's been her undoing. Or so her mother says. They invited Ponsonby here in the hopes of making a match, but..."

"But what?"

"I just can't see them together, really."

"Well, the young lady is quite enamored of him. So much so that she's asked me to teach her how to sail in an attempt to impress and win him."

"You should."

"Why?"

"Why not?"

He made a little scoffing noise and shook his head.

"Have you agreed?"

"I felt I had no choice."

Lady Falconer smiled, and her unusual tiger-eyes gleamed. "I can't think of a better instructor. You're patient, Del, and given how you always do everything by-the-book, I cannot, for the life of me, ever imagine her coming to any mishaps under your tutelage. You really ought to tell her what you do for work, you know. Who you are. She seems to like naval captains."

"I have no designs upon the girl," Del said, rather too quickly.

Her smile spread. "Of course you don't."

"Besides," he added hastily, "I'm finding I rather like the anonymity of being Sir Graham's 'sailor friend.' Sometimes it's rather nice to just sit back and watch the world go by, to be an observer instead of a problem-solver or commander."

"Indeed," the former Pirate Queen mused, putting a finger against her mouth to quell the spreading grin.

They stood there for a moment and Del, wondering what was behind that smile, was seized by a sudden desire to escape.

"Lady Falconer," he murmured, and bowed.

"Captain Lord," she said with a formality that was unnecessary given how long he had served as her husband's flag captain— and the fact that she was Connor's and Kieran's sister and thus, after all, his own cousin.

Del resumed his walk down the hall.

"By the way, Del."

He paused and turned, one brow arched.

"While we're here, the admiral would like to visit Norfolk for a few days so he can see your brother,

Colin. We're leaving the day after tomorrow, should you wish to join us."

"And who will be making this journey?"

"Sir Graham and I, and of course, the children. Lady Grace, and possibly her sister Hannah. It's only fair to give Ariannah some private time with her new husband, really. Captain Ponsonby will sail us there to spare us the wretchedness of coach travel."

Norfolk.

Del considered for a moment. He hadn't seen Colin in quite some time. Quite a long time, really. He had planned to visit his brother and maybe his parents in Hampshire as well, before they all returned to the Caribbean, so why not join the Falconers? Besides, it would be far more interesting than staying here where he knew nobody and had little inclination to change that happy fact.

Even if he'd have to clamp down on his unwanted feelings for the girl, stuff them away where they couldn't hurt him, and ignore them as if they didn't exist.

Yes, he'd learned his lesson after Connor and Rhiannon.

"Of course," he said, feeling as though he were sailing toward a lee shore in hurricane force winds. "I would love to go to Norfolk."

⚓

DEL RETURNED TO HIS ROOM, SHED HIS TAILCOAT, shoes and waistcoat, and dressed in just shirt and trousers, stretched out on the bed.

He stared up at the ceiling.

Norfolk.

A trip that would be spent grooming a girl to appeal to a man he was coming to despise. Something he could not understand because really, Ponsonby was a nice enough fellow, if a little too attractive to the fairer sex.

He wondered why that suddenly annoyed him.

Why it seemed like, well, almost a threat.

He was still pondering his curious reaction to a colleague when the distant crowing of a cock penetrated his thoughts and he opened his eyes to faint light beyond the windows and a glow in the sky over the downs. Had he actually fallen asleep in his clothes?

How improper.

To sleep fully clothed aboard ship was one thing; as captain, he had to be ready on a moment's notice to deal with emergencies, weather changes, the sight of a French warship hull up on the horizon. But his idea of slipping into a role of quiet anonymity and living as a landsman for a short time, was falling dreadfully afoul of reality.

Sleeping in his clothing.

Sunup and he hadn't even shaved.

He got up, padded to the corner where a washstand held a ceramic bowl and pitcher, and washed his face. He thought about summoning Thorne, but no... he was not in the mood for the company of his coxswain and certainly, he could shave his own face. He was just searching about for the razor when a shaft of early-morning sunlight came through the window and struck the opposite wall.

Damnation.

He glanced at his pocket watch. The idea of appearing in polite company unshaven, let alone in sleep-rumpled clothes was unimaginable to him, but so was the idea of turning up late. Bad enough to keep a man waiting. Twice, no thrice as bad if it was a lady. Del quickly changed into a fresh shirt, cleaned his teeth, and was just opening the door to dash down the hall when he spied Thorne approaching with a tray that included the coffee with one cube of sugar, otherwise black, that his captain enjoyed every morning.

Del waved him off with a muttered apology and shrugging into his waistcoat, hurried for the stairs.

Behind him, Thorne raised a brow.

The captain was a man of strict routine and rigid protocol. What on earth would compel him to leave his chamber without a shave, let alone his morning coffee?

⚓

GRACE HAD RISEN EARLY. SHE DID NOT WANT TO BE late for her first lesson and was eager to undo or at least repair the damage she had done to her own reputation — let alone Captain Ponsonby's estimation of her— with the debacle she had made of things the day before.

She hurried down to the lake, her maid Polly, sleepy and grumbling about the early hour, tagging in her wake and carrying a blanket. Their footsteps left a darker trail in dewy, silvered grass. Grace had tried to wake Hannah, who had fallen back asleep three times, mumbling something incoherent. Polly, equally somnolent but less likely to argue with her or present some sensible suggestion that would only sour things, had been brought along instead. She would be an adequate chaperone, Grace thought, even if she were likely to fall back asleep the moment she spread the blanket out on the grass.

Sleep, however, was the furthest thing from Grace's mind. She was going to learn to sail today. Properly, that is. And she had a willing and competent instructor.

What could go wrong?

The pond was glassy smooth. In the early morning quiet, a swan, long neck gracefully tucked, looked like a decoy on its surface. Thin sunlight sparkled briefly on the water, throwing diamonds as the gentlest of breezes began to stir.

Mr. Lord was nowhere to be found.

"I'll just sit right here if ye don't mind, Lady Grace?"

"Go ahead, Polly. It seems my instructor isn't here yet, anyhow."

Grace pulled her skirts to one side and sat down on the damp foredeck of the skiff that had brought her to such grief yesterday. Hopefully Mr. Lord hadn't forgotten her or thought better of her request. Maybe he was still asleep.

But movement off in the distance caught her eye and looking up, Grace spotted a tall, lean figure headed her way from the house.

Her heart gave a little leap of excitement, a quick movement that strummed the blood through her veins like a finger plucking the string of a guitar. It was an odd sensation, that, and one she hadn't expected.

Even if Mr. Lord did cut rather a fine figure in the morning sunlight.

He walked with an easy, confident stride, shoulders back and spine as straight as the wall of a house. His crisp white shirt shone in the morning sunlight, and a snug, well-cut waistcoat of plum linen, double-breasted and smart, accented the breadth of his shoulders and the trimness of his waist and hips. As he approached, Grace saw that his steady gray eyes had a hint of purple in them, though whether that was their natural color or a reflection from his vest, she would not have been able to say. He bowed, nodded to a heavy-lidded Polly, and smiled wryly.

"Unless you can conjure some wind, I fear our lesson may not be very productive," he said, looking at the water's still surface.

"It's better now than it was fifteen minutes ago."

"You were here then?"

"I've been here for a while. I didn't want to be late."

"And here I'm the one who is late."

"No, Mr. Lord. You are right on time."

He smiled again, and rubbed at his jaw. It was cloaked with a dark shadow, and she wondered what kind of rogue he must be to have come out without shaving, though she had to admit that it gave him a rather dangerous, darkly handsome look that was not unattractive. He bent to untie the boat from the rock to which it was tethered and despite herself, Grace noticed the breadth of his shoulders and the way the breeze, just awakening, tickled his hair, slightly overlong, wildly curly, thick and unruly.

Why are you noticing Mr. Lord?

He's nothing but your sailing teacher for the morning.

Right. She looked away, studying the swan instead. The regal white bird had now been joined by its mate and several cygnets, and now the little family moved out into the center of the lake, a thin line behind them marking their discreet wake. The cob's head had turned slightly, watching them.

"The first thing one must do," Mr. Lord was saying, "is to study the weather before deciding whether or not it is prudent to take a boat out. Determine the direction of the wind, as well as the strength, and then judge whether you are skilled enough to take on that strength."

"Obviously, yesterday, I was not."

"You were not, but sailing is a skill just like any other, and while I can teach you a rudimentary understanding of it, the best instructor is experience." He straightened up, still holding the rope that had tethered the little craft to the rock, and smiled. "That is, what we'll call 'tiller time'."

"Tiller time."

Their gazes met, and both quickly looked away. Something had been in that quick, electric contact, something that neither would acknowledge, though both understood exactly what it was.

Attraction.

Grace swallowed the sudden dryness in her throat and briskly rubbed her hands together, determined to ignore it. "Well, then, Mr. Lord. Let's get started."

He would not look at her. "Yes. Let's."

$$ \text{❧ I4 ❧} $$

" A nd which direction is the wind coming from?" Del repeated patiently.

The young lady looked at him blankly. She had the Falconer eyes, a deep azure blue, and hers were thickly fringed in black and topped by delicately arched brows. She would be a rather elegant creature, Del thought, if not for her innate talent for getting herself into trouble and her bright, bubbly spirit.

"Well?" he prompted.

She looked over her shoulder, turned, and pointed. "That way."

It was now Del's turn to look at his pupil blankly. "That way?"

"Well, yes. That's where the wind is coming from. That way."

"What I meant, Lady Grace, is this: From which direction of the compass is the wind coming from?"

She looked at him with equal patience. "*That* one."

Del shut his eyes, briefly, and resisted the urge to count to ten in order not to give vent to his rising irritation. "Do you even know which direction *that one*, is?"

"North?"

"It is west."

"Well, how am I to know that?"

"You do know that the sun rises in the east and sets in the west?"

"Well..."

"And given that it is early morning, and the sun is coming up in *that* direction—" it was his turn to point —"which most naturally must be east, doesn't it stand to reason that the opposite direction would be west?"

"What if it's cloudy, and one can't know which direction the sun is rising from?"

"It is not cloudy."

"But it *could* be."

"Lady Grace—"

"I know, I know. Please go on. I'm keen to get on the water. Can we get started?"

"We *are* started. And without a knowledge of direction and wind you will likely end up in the same sorry situation in which you found yourself yesterday."

"I fail to understand—"

"Are we going to have this lesson or not?"

She shot a glance at her maid, sitting on the blanket watching them in the near distance.

"Fine. We have established that the sun is coming up from that direction, which means that the wind is coming from the west."

"Very good. And given that we are standing here on the shoreline, and the wind is coming over our left shoulders—"

"The west."

"Yes, the west, how do you propose to get the boat out into the lake?"

"I thought you were going to do that. That you'd get us out into the middle of the lake since you know what you're doing, and then I'd take over—" she grinned, charmingly— "under your tutelage, of course."

Del stood there, the water lapping gently near his shoes, and he invited, no, *willed* the pastoral quietness of it to soften his rising irritation. He was irritated that he had not risen early enough to complete the morning ablutions necessary for a civilized and respectable appearance. He was irritated with himself for allowing this beautiful creature to talk him into a folly that was destined to benefit yet another rival at the expense of his own heart. And he was irritated that he was irritated because really, it was not gentlemanly to feel, let alone demonstrate, impatience with a gently-bred female.

Especially one who was his admiral's niece.

Really, he should have stayed in bed this morning.

Why the devil hadn't he?

"If you want to impress Captain Ponsonby," he said tersely, "you need to do more than just take over the boat once someone else gets it out into the middle of the lake. You need to do all of it. Push off, trim the sail, and steer it."

She just looked at him.

"And you need to be able to do it alone."

"You're not going to help me?"

"No, I didn't say that. I said that if you wanted to impress a mariner, you must have the skills to be self-sufficient. Just this once, I'll push us out into the water but next time, you'll do it all by yourself."

Her chin came up. "No, no, I want to do it."

"You'll ruin your slippers."

"You just said that if I'm going to do this, I need to learn how to do all of it." She reached down, bent her leg, pulled off the slipper and tossed it into the grass, revealing shapely feet, long toes, trim ankles and high arches.

Del's mouth went dry, and he felt something in his blood kick up and begin to hum.

He quickly looked away and tried to ignore it, but as the girl pulled off her other slipper and stood there in her stockings on the damp grass, he felt that hum beginning to move into a faint burning that sought a place to lodge itself, that thrummed throughout his body, and finally chose the area of his groin.

"Well?" she asked.

I will not look at her feet. I will not. "How do you propose to steer it?"

"With the tiller."

"And where is the tiller?"

She reddened as she noticed the rudder and tiller were both lying in the hull of the little boat, and it occurred to Del that someone, probably young Ned who couldn't bear to see a vessel put away improperly, had likely put them there, and coiled the mainsheet as well.

"Oh," she said, and sloshing through the water, bent to pick up the rudder and drop it into the slot at the stern. Del stood watching, arms crossed loosely over his chest as she attached the tiller to it, thinking that if she at least knew how to do this much, he had something to work with.

"There," she said happily, and looked up.

"Very good."

"Now what?"

"Attach the mainsheet to the little ring at the clew of the sail."

"That rope there?"

"Yes, the line that runs down through the block at the head of the rudder, and which has been left neatly coiled in the hull."

She did as he instructed, the water lapping around her slim, bare ankles. Caressing them. Del looked away, his gaze falling first on the family of swans watching them from nearby, to the maid reposing on the grass. The young woman appeared to be losing her battle to stay awake.

"Now what?"

"Let's get in the boat and go sailing."

He moved the boat out into the water just a little bit so that she wouldn't have to struggle to push it along with his weight through the muddy silt of the shoreline. A stone's throw away, the swan family had moved off but the parents had their long necks curved, their heads twisted, watching them.

Del eyed the mud balefully. The girl had the right idea.

He removed is own shoes, and wished for a moment that he was the common tar she believed him to be. Then he could remove his stockings, too, and wouldn't be clinging to a sense of propriety that served no purpose at best and was about to ruin his stockings, at worst.

There was no help for it. His feet, complete with stockings, sank into the muck with a sucking squish that made Del grimace inside, and the pungent scent of mud filled the air.

He got into the boat and waited.

"Now what do I do?" Lady Grace asked.

"Hold the line and—"

"The line?"

"That rope that tethered it to the rock. Pick it up, hold onto it, walk the boat back into the pond, and get in."

She gingerly picked up the rope with two fingers, her pretty face marred by a grimace of distaste. The sodden hemp was green with slime, damp with mud. She stood there with it, caught his assessing look, and suddenly grinned.

"It's wet."

"Yes."

"And mucky. It smells."

"Yes, it does."

She put her distaste for the moldering object behind her, sloshed into the water, put a leg over the gunwale and got into the boat, sitting on the thwart beside Del.

"Now what?"

Her ankle and a good bit of calf had been exposed

by her entry into the craft and the sight of both had seared itself into Del's mind. He shook his head to clear it and, to get his thoughts off both her and her close proximity to him, picked up the paddle and leveraging it against the bottom, pushed the boat farther out into the little lake, deftly turning it as he did.

The skiff had a single mast to which a sail was permanently affixed; there was no raising of canvas to be done, and the simplicity of the boat's design was something he could appreciate.

"Shouldn't I be doing that?" she asked.

"Yes, but I'll get us clear of obstacles, including that little family of swans, and then you will take over."

"I can paddle a boat."

"If yesterday was a display of your skills, I beg to differ."

"Then all the more reason I should be doing that."

He looked at her. "You're right." He pulled the dripping oar from the water. "Here."

She took the short length of wood and began to paddle. Predictably, the boat began to turn, its stubby nose swinging to starboard, beginning to trace a circle. The girl took up the tiller in hopes of steering it. The boat lost momentum, the rising, still-gentle wind pushing the boom and sail around with helpless abandon.

Del began to rethink his earlier estimation that there was something here with which to work.

"If you move yourself to the bow of the boat," he directed, "and stroke first on the starboard side, and then on the larboard, and repeat that process, you will go in a fairly straight line as long as you exert equal strength on each stroke. You can steer or correct your course by either adding additional strokes to the side from which you wish to turn or, back water with the paddle to get the boat to turn in that direction."

She furrowed her brow and looked at him dubiously.

"Try it," he suggested, and then, as she began to get to her feet, "*don't* stand up."

"Why not?"

"Because I've no mind to go swimming again today."

"What?"

"Meaning, if you lose our balance and tumble overboard, I'll have to fish you out again." As she blushed, he added kindly, "once a week is enough."

"Oh."

She scooted to the bow of the boat, leaned over the prow, and began to stroke clumsily with the paddle. Behind her, Del watched her shoulders working beneath her soft muslin gown, the long dark tendril of hair that had escaped her loose topknot and now curled enticingly against the little knobs of vertebrae at the base of her neck.

His fingers itched to touch it.

Again, he directed his gaze away.

Her maid was definitely asleep and in the distance, the great stone house slumbered in the early-morning mist, a bar of sunshine now finding the peak of its roof.

The boat was moving, the girl's awkward paddling beginning to gain some rhythm, to accomplish some actual purpose. Breaths of wind disturbed the placid surface of the lake, carrying the fresh dewy scent of morning grass and water now that they were well away from the shoreline itself.

Del found himself smiling.

"How am I doing, Mr. Lord?"

Her bright eyes, hopeful and confident, lanced something in his gut and his smile spread. Again, he felt a connection with her. A warming.

He looked away to hide any evidence of it on his face.

"Quite well. Now, take up the mainsheet and the tiller, and let's allow the wind to do the work."

❧ 15 ❧

Curiously, Grace was finding it hard to remember that this lesson was all about learning how to impress Captain Sheldon Ponsonby, and not Mr. Lord, her teacher.

She had managed to get the boat into the middle of the lake, where the cheerful blue water beneath them was lit by errant beams of sunlight that found their way between the branches of a nearby sycamore.

Her gaze followed those amber shafts of light into the depths. She had been down there yesterday, down where those beams of sunlight probed, and she would have died down there if not for this man in the boat with her.

The thought was sobering.

And it awakened something inside her, something she'd been trying to squash, something she'd been willfully trying to ignore... something she intended quite adamantly for someone else.

Desire.

Misplaced, displaced. Unmistakable.

Desire.

She watched him out of the corner of her eye, wondering why she was having such a reaction to him. He was nothing like Captain Ponsonby, who was showy, golden, easily confident in his effect on the ladies. Captain Ponsonby knew just when to turn on a smile or offer a compliment, knew he was blessed with extraordinary good looks, and seemed to take for granted his effect on the fairer sex— a trait which, Grace had to admit, only made him more attractive. Confidence was attractive; that was an undeniable fact. This man in the boat with her, though... by comparison, he was quietly understated— perhaps intentionally, she thought— and she got the impression that he was a person who did his job and went about his business dutifully, without a need for attention or accolades and probably not expecting any, either. Unlike Captain Ponsonby, he didn't command attention in either his behavior or his looks. Not that he wasn't handsome, she thought with a sudden fierceness, because she had to admit that he was quite handsome indeed in a classically masculine sense. It was just that he wasn't... what was the word? Ostentatious. Showy. Or even fashionable.

No, his dark curly hair was too long, and while his face was noble, with a firm jaw and sculpted mouth, his high, lean cheekbones weren't covered in the carefully groomed strips of whisker so many fashionable men— Captain Ponsonby included— sported. His eyes were coolly observant, and fine eyes they were indeed, but they seemed to take life, if not their owner, far too seriously and his taciturn mouth seemed reluctant to smile. She didn't think it must get much practice in laughing, either, because when he did smile the gesture seemed hesitant, guarded, exploratory, much like her first efforts with the oars just moments ago. The word came to her quite suddenly. *Tight.* That was what he was. Tight and stiff and far too serious, and Grace thought that perhaps she ought to do something about that.

Really.

"So now what do I do?" she asked, rolling the long line around her wrist.

His hand shot out, stilling her, and his grave stare held her own. "Don't do that."

She paused, her wrist still caught in his. Her brows raised in surprise, question, and humor.

"Don't do what?"

"Never," he said sternly, minutely lowering the angle of his head to better hold her gaze in his attempt to convey the importance of what he was about to say, "don't *ever*, wrap a line around your wrist."

"Why not?"

"If you were ever to get into trouble like you found yourself in yesterday, you'd be tangled up in the sheet. Lines must have the freedom to run free, to be cast off if need be. If you deny them that, you're looking at a capsize at best and a serious injury at worst."

"Oh."

"Let alone the fact that if the boat did roll and you went with it, you'd be tangled and unable to get free. You would drown."

The gravity of his stare suddenly made her rethink her plan to do something about his seriousness. He'd scared her a bit, really.

"So, what am I supposed to do with it, then?"

He leaned forward and took the rope from her hand. Her skin tingled at his nearness. At his brief touch. She shook off the observation and instead, concentrated on the way he was using a quick, practiced rhythm of his fingers to make perfectly measured loops with it, one after another until the line was neatly coiled and hanging from his grip. He was close to her. So close that she could smell the soapy scent of his freshly-washed hair, the clean linen freshness of his shirt, feel the warmth of his body, so near to her own.

She was suddenly dizzy again, not unlike how she'd felt after her mishap of the day before.

"Here," he said, and handed her back the coiled rope. Or, line. Or whatever the thing was called. "Always keep your rigging in good working order, ensure that it is neatly organized and allowed to run free in an emergency. Don't sit on it, don't allow it to knot, don't wrap it around a body part, and always be mindful of where it is in the boat."

He looked up and caught her gaze once more with steady gray eyes and again, her blood quickened unexpectedly. He was handsome all right, and oh, yes, he had saved her life.

He had saved her life.

Grace swallowed hard, unable to moisten her throat or quell the sudden skip of her pulse.

"Just when I think you are far too serious," she mused, taking the flaked line, "you give me reason to value such a trait." She met his gaze, the sunlight rising through the tree branches and striking a hit across his irises. In them, she saw the faintest hint of purple amongst the gray. It hadn't been his vest, after all.

An unusual color.

An attractive one.

"Have I sufficiently impressed upon you the necessity of allowing a line room to run free?"

"Yes, Mr. Lord."

The corner of his mouth twitched, as though he were about to smile, as though he was on the verge of allowing himself that luxury, but the gesture was fleeting and gone as quickly as it had come.

"Good, then." He shifted a bit in the boat. "Now, you have the mainsheet, and you may lay it down at your feet, holding onto it just here."

"Here?"

He reached out and took her hand. His skin was warm, the hand covering and all but dwarfing her own. "Here."

"All right."

"And then you need to get your boat out of irons. Do you know what the term means?"

"I'm suspecting it has nothing to do with the hot instrument that presses one's clothing or curls the hair."

This time, his smile did indeed appear, albeit brief. "You would be correct. 'In irons' refers to the state a boat is in when it has swung around to point into the wind. It's a state to which any sailing vessel, left to its own devices, will revert. Observe it. You won't go anywhere whilst in irons, because the wind is directly in front of you. A boat cannot sail straight into the wind."

"I see..."

"Do you feel the breeze on your cheek?" he asked. "If you don't, then turn your head until you find it. Where do you see the little waves on the water, and in what direction are they headed?"

"I feel the wind right here," she said, touching her nose.

"And the tiny waves?"

"Headed straight for us."

"Good. And what does that tell you?"

"That those little waves are being pushed by the wind, and thus, indicate its direction."

"Excellent! Now, turn your head to the right and turn it to the left, and observe the way it sounds in your ears when it strikes different parts of your face."

She did as he directed. He watched her closely, a devoted teacher, one who was in his element.

"You are very good at this, Mr. Lord. Who taught you how to sail?"

"Initially," he said offhandedly, "my father. And many others since then, including that best instructor, experience." He moved closer to her, leaning over her, and stretched his arm over her head to catch the boom just above that had brought her to such grief the day before. "Now, to get your boat out of irons, you must hold the boom over to the wind, like this. Watch."

She watched.

And saw the nose of the boat begin to track around,

and the light breeze begin to harden the little sail, which in turn pulled against the line in her hand, and a moment later the boat had begun to move and a little curl of water was happily gurgling beneath and alongside them and Mr. Lord was telling her to fall off, whatever that meant, just a bit, and leaning over her to place his hand over hers on the tiller, allowing her to feel the pulse of the little craft beneath it.

And feel it, Grace did.

But she also felt that hand covering her own, guiding hers, helping her to get the feel of the boat, heard him telling her to let out just a little bit of line so as to get more out of the sail, to be mindful of the family of swans so as not to disturb them.

"Look, we're doing it!" she said happily. "We're sailing!"

He grinned, let go of her hand, and settled back on the thwart. "Mind your course again, Lady Grace."

"Oh, right!"

"And remember, if you push the tiller to larboard, your boat will go to starboard. And vice versa. They are in reverse."

"Understood." She played with the tiller a bit, noting the quickness of the craft's response, and grinned, feeling a freedom in her newfound knowledge.

He was saying something else.

"So, did you grow up here?"

"What? Oh. Oh, no, I did not."

"Where, then?"

She shrugged. How to answer such a question? "Well, I guess you could say I started at Folkington Hall, since my father was the Earl. But he died early, so my memories of it are not very good."

"Watch your steering."

"What?"

"The boat is heading back into irons. Push the tiller away from the sail a bit. Yes, like that. Good."

"Why is it so hard to keep a boat on course?"

"Do you even have a course?"

She admitted that no, she did not.

"Find something on the opposite shore on which to aim. That rock on the beach, perhaps. If you have something to point at, 'twill make it easier to keep the boat true."

She nodded and moved the tiller until the bow was pointing at the rock. How easy it was to lose focus! How quick the boat was to take advantage of inattention, just as it had done with her yesterday.

"And then where?" he prodded.

"What?"

"We were talking about where you grew up."

"Oh, right. Well, after my father died, the title went to his younger brother, who had his own family, so Mama and I went to my grandparents' home in Surrey. Did you meet them yesterday? They were here. Mama's parents. We lived there for a while, then Mama met Sir Peter and married him and we went and lived at his home, until he was killed in battle. More heirs to supplant us, I'm afraid, so back to my grandparents' home in Surrey yet again."

"It must have been hard to call any one place home, having moved around so much."

"Indeed."

"And there was a third husband before your mother's new bridegroom?"

She looked at him, brows raised.

He flushed. "I'm sorry. That is none of my business."

She grinned, trying to put him at ease. "No need to apologize." And then, in a lowered, dramatic voice, "We don't talk about the third husband."

"I see."

"*Terrible* scandal."

He nodded gravely, but his eyes were warm, responding to the laughter in her voice. "I'll take your word for it."

"And now there's a fourth husband," she continued breezily, "and another new home. More staff to get to know, a new stepfather too, but at least he seems madly in love with Mama. I expect I'll be living here for the foreseeable future."

"Well, it doesn't look like such a bad place." His smile was tentative, as though he was unsure of her, unsure of what to say to her, feeling his way as he went along. "It seems like a beautiful home."

"It is, I suppose."

"Even if this pond here is rather—" a smile played at his mouth— "*dangerous*."

The way he drew out the word, making it teasingly ominous, made her laugh.

"*Dangerous*," she repeated in the same dramatic tone, her gaze meeting his.

"Dangerous. And you should stay out of it unless you have a sailor like me, to accompany you."

"Or Captain Ponsonby?"

His smile seemed to hang in place. The humor went out of it, and then the smile itself faded. It was a subtle shift, the change itself quick, but the brief, playful mood was lost and she immediately regretted it. He'd been droll, his company enjoyable as he'd begun to relax, and she'd gone and ruined it. Drat. *Drat!* The taciturn man was back, serious and stiff once more.

"Mind your steering again, Lady Grace."

"Oh, right." She pushed the long wooden bar to starboard, and the boat obliged.

They hummed along, the water chortling beneath the little boat. Her companion had gone quiet.

"And how about you?" she asked, trying to recapture the light mood. "Where are you from?"

"Hampshire, and prepare to come about. Unless you fancy hitting the shore."

"Come about?"

"Tack."

"How do I do that?"

"Start pulling in the mainsheet to bring the sail to the centerline. You'll push the tiller hard toward the sail, the bow will cross through the wind and she will turn."

"You make it sound easy."

"It is. Try it."

She pulled on the mainsheet, feeling the sail resisting her somewhat as she brought it in. It was hard to remember to keep the boat on course at the same time, but she managed, and then his hand was covering hers once more, guiding her, strong and competent.

"Now push the tiller over all the way, toward the sail. Yes, that's it. All the way. Keep going. Good."

The boat swung obediently across the wind, its bow tracing a graceful arc. The sail swung over to the other side and they were headed back across the lake, the shore falling away behind them.

"Look what we did!" Grace exclaimed, delighted with herself. "That was fun!"

"No, look what *you* did."

"Well, *you* told me what to do and how to do it, so therefore, it was a team effort!"

Her delight must have been infectious, as her teacher was tentatively smiling again.

"Team effort, then. But you're the captain of this vessel, and you've successfully tacked her. Well done."

His praise warmed her. He met her gaze and smiled, and Grace forgot all about Sheldon Ponsonby.

Until he and a few others wandered out of the house, some carrying their breakfasts or a morning beverage, a few laughing, a woman's voice rising above the rest.

The easy camaraderie she had been enjoying with her instructor fizzled, and nervousness took its place.

Distraction.

Two people were headed their way. One of them was Captain Ponsonby.

The sun was higher now, the wind picking up a bit, sweet, steady and contrite for the way it had treated her yesterday. Grace, flustered, tried to concentrate on her task. She managed to get the boat all the way to the other side of the lake yet again and to "come about" as Mr. Lord directed her in a manner that was actually quite smooth, though she did take a few seconds too long to trim the sail after the boat swung itself through the wind. Blame that on the fact that Captain Ponsonby was approaching, no doubt curious to see if she had improved her seamanship— lakemanship?— lakewomanship?— since yesterday afternoon.

"Mind the swans," her instructor said.

But Grace, distracted now, couldn't think. Captain Ponsonby was not alone, though it wasn't the beautiful blonde accompanying him this time but another officer; perhaps someone who'd arrived last night? The newcomer was dressed in the same dashing blue, white and gold uniform of the Royal Navy, but while the captain was munching a roll, the other man was sipping from a flask. Both were watching with interest.

"Ignore them," said her instructor.

"I can't."

"If you don't train yourself to ignore distractions, you will find yourself in the same sort of peril you encountered yesterday," he warned. "If not worse."

She nodded and jerked her gaze away from the newcomers, though not before seeing Captain Ponsonby take a seat on the sloping lawn so as to better watch her lesson, and suddenly Grace forgot everything she had just learned and found nothing in her head but blank nervousness and a rush of blood that brought the dampness out on her palms.

"Pay attention," Mr. Lord said tightly.

Grace tried.

The morning had a good breeze going now, and there just ahead were the swans, paddling directly out into their path with the three cygnets in their wake. Grace froze, and when her instructor told her a second time to pay attention and steer the boat to starboard, she pushed the tiller to starboard instead of the boat, forgetting that they were in reverse, and the boat went immediately to larboard—

And straight into the family of swans.

❧ 16 ❧

C haos ensued.

The female swan cried out in alarm, the cygnets scattered, and the cob came at them with wings beating and beak outstretched. Grace screamed, dropped the mainsheet and her grip on the tiller and stood up, trying to fend off the angry bird; her instructor grabbed her hand and yanked her back down into the boat before she could capsize it and spill them both into the pond, and the craft pitched and yawed crazily. The male swan attacked again and Mr. Lord gallantly fended it off, one arm coming up to thwart its blows, the other holding the boat steady, and then suddenly the bird stalked off and the boat was reeling drunkenly in the wind and Grace was holding a hand to her pounding heart.

From the shore came hooting jeers of laughter.

Horrified, Grace looked toward its source.

Captain Ponsonby and his friend were sitting on the grass near shore, Polly nearby and on her feet, hands pressed to her mouth. The captain looked torn between amusement and concern but his companion was slapping his knee and guffawing.

"I haven't had this much entertainment since I don't know when!" he cried, wiping at tears. "Honestly, Del, why fight the French when you have English swans to battle, eh?"

Mr. Lord stiffened, and the hint of lavender left his eyes to be replaced by something that made them look cold and very, very gray.

Grace saw Captain Ponsonby lay a hand on the other man's uniformed arm. "That's enough, James," he said.

But James was relentless. "If this is what the Royal Navy has come down to, pity the fate of our beloved England! I say, I haven't seen such a cock-up since Villeneuve succumbed to Nelson at Trafalgar!"

"You were not," said Mr. Lord icily, "at Trafalgar."

"And neither were you. Lady Grace! Why don't you allow a real sailor to teach you the proper rudiments of the art, eh?"

Captain Ponsonby yanked his companion close and cut his gaze to Mr. Lord. "Have a care, James, to whom you're speaking!"

Any patience remaining in Delmore Lord's eyes had fled. On the shore, Captain Ponsonby had gained his feet and was trying to pull the other man to his.

Mr. Lord took the tiller and the mainsheet, and promptly swung the boat toward shore.

"May I offer some advice?" Grace murmured, sensing the rising tension and hoping to defuse it.

"You may."

"A moment ago you told me to ignore Captain Ponsonby. I would suggest that you do the same with that odious man."

He said nothing, only continuing on that relentless course.

"Have I hit a nerve?" called Captain Ponsonby's friend, swigging from his flask and wiping his mouth with the back of a hand. "You already benefit from Sir Graham's favoritism, though one must wonder if it's because of ability or the fact that you're the little brother of his favorite captain. Would that we were all so fortunate!"

"Ignore him!" Grace said, putting a hand on her instructor's arm, which was rock beneath her fingers.

The other man wasn't backing down. "Will you enjoy his niece now, as well?"

Grace gasped, and saw Captain Ponsonby trying to steer his companion away. "Lieutenant Akers is foxed," he called with a nervous and placating gesture. "Pay him no mind, Del."

"Not foxed enough," Akers said, gaining his feet and in trying to keep his balance, shoving Captain Ponsonby aside. "But I'm getting there."

The boat nosed into the weeds, parted them, and hit the shore with a jolt.

Mr. Lord got out of the boat and pulled it farther up onto the shore, the muscles in his arms jumping, his face hard.

Captain Ponsonby tried again to get control of his friend. "I'll bring him into the house, Del," he said hastily. "No need for conflict here, really."

The smaller man pushed helplessly at him. "Unhand me, Captain. I do not need a child-minder."

"What you need is a good kick in the head," said Delmore Lord, reaching into the boat to help Grace out.

"What did you say?"

"You heard me."

"I should call you out for such an insult!"

Delmore Lord steadied Grace as she stepped out of the boat, making sure she did not get her feet wet. "Go right ahead. Nothing stopping you."

"I should! And I will."

"No, you shouldn't because it would be foolhardy on your part, and you won't, because you, sir—" Mr. Lord turned and leveled his gaze on the other man— "are a blustering coward."

The word hung in the air, ugly and shocking, and Akers stood there gaping, his face reddening with anger and his lips trembling with affront. He began to speak, thought better of it, and when he looked at Grace she saw the humiliation there, the rage, and a sudden violence in the man's eyes that made her instinctively want to crowd closer to her instructor as he yanked the boat fully up on the beach and tossed the bow rope around a nearby rock.

Akers found his voice. "What did you say?"

Mr. Lord straightened up. "I *said*, that you are a blustering coward. Do I need to repeat myself a third time?"

Grace's hand flew to her mouth. Her teacher moved toward the gaping aggressor, and Captain Ponsonby stepped suddenly between them.

"Now, now, gentlemen—"

His desperate attempt to prevent violence was a needless one.

At that moment the door to the house opened, Ned Falconer came flying across the lawn and in his wake, taking all the time in the world, was Sir Graham Falconer.

◆

"GOOD MORNING, GENTLEMAN," SAID THE ADMIRAL, smiling, but Del saw the cold glint in his superior's eyes, the assessing look he gave both himself and Akers, the way the little tightening of his mouth indicated his displeasure before he said genially, "Everything all right out here?"

"Yes, sir," Del said tersely.

"Aye, sir," repeated Akers, glaring at Del.

Sir Graham nodded to the little boat that Del and Grace had just vacated, giving his son permission to take it out onto the lake. "Good. Because I couldn't help but observe what was going on out here from the dining room. Given the propensity that naval officers seem to have for dueling, I won't have either of you engaging in such needless displays of foolhardiness." He looked at each man in turn. "Is that understood?"

Polly, watching this all with mute horror, had gone white.

It was Grace who broke the sudden tense silence. "Everything is fine, Uncle Gray. Mr. Lord was showing me how to sail a boat and this man here, well, he's had too much to drink so none of us are taking him seriously. Maybe it would be best if you bring him back into the house so he can sleep off the effects of too much rum."

"It was brandy, my lady," said Akers, bowing and nearly falling over. His mocking attempts at chivalry only earned a look of raw disgust from Mr. Lord, who turned away and stared hard out over the sparkling lake as though he could not suffer even looking at the other man.

"The admiral's right," said Captain Ponsonby, flashing a smile that found the pit of Grace's stomach and tweaked her nerves into a thrumming mire of confusion. "Best to get you to bed, James! Come along, let's go."

He snatched the flask from the man's hand and led him, still protesting, off toward the house.

Grace saw Mr. Lord's shoulders visibly relax. Sir Graham, however, was not mollified.

"What was that about, Del?"

"Bad blood between us, sir."

"Obviously."

"He has not changed since we served together aboard the old *Dancer*. In fact, he's only become worse. I cannot promise that my response will be as restrained the next time he insults me."

"There will be no next time. Maeve and I have decided that we've both had enough of silly sisters, stuffy houses, gossip, foolishness, and this lamentable house party."

Del said nothing.

"We have decided to spend the remainder of our stay up in Norfolk. It's been years since I last saw my former flag captain and I know you'd relish the chance to visit Colin and his family as well." Sir Graham grinned. "He is, after all, your brother."

Del nodded stiffly.

"I have asked Captain Ponsonby to transport us as he, too, owes his family there a visit. His sister Letitia is married to Tristan St. Aubyn, the Earl of Weybourne, is she not?"

"Aye, sir. And Weybourne is Colin's brother-in-law. He married Lady Ariadne St. Aubyn, the earl's sister."

"Complicated, all these family connections."

"Indeed."

"They raise horses now, I understand?"

"Yes, sir, they do."

"I love horses," Grace put in, gazing helplessly at Ponsonby's retreating back.

"Nasty, smelly creatures," Sir Graham said. "Give me a ship any day of the week over a foul-tempered beast who wants nothing more than to dump you on the ground or take off with your carriage while you cling to the damned thing for dear life."

"They are not as bad as all that, Uncle Gray."

"Even so, our time here is limited and I'll not waste it thumping and bumping in a cramped coach all the way up to Norfolk. We'll leave for Portsmouth tomorrow and travel by sea."

Grace felt a sudden panic. "I love ships, too," she added desperately, though she had never been aboard one in her entire two decades of life.

"Then I guess you should prepare to see one up close."

She stared up at her uncle, her mouth falling open in confusion.

"There's nothing here for you to do, what with your mother occupied with her latest husband. They deserve some time together. Hannah has declined the offer to visit Norfolk in favor of spending time with a friend at a nearby estate, but you are free, should you wish, to accompany us."

No separation from Captain Ponsonby then, and more time to make her case, to rectify damage, to try and win his heart.

She clasped her hands together. "Oh, Uncle Gray, I would love that. Thank you! *Thank you!*"

G race could hardly contain herself.

Escape from the dreary monotony of Ruscombe Hall and Mama and her new husband making eyes at each other. Escape from Nothing To Do. An adventure on a *real* boat where she might be able to demonstrate her newfound skills to Captain Ponsonby, and that real boat commanded by Captain Ponsonby himself, who would be blindingly handsome in full dress uniform and causing her heart to flip and flop in her chest like a fish gasping for air. She could just swoon with excitement!

It did not escape her, though, that her instructor didn't appear to share that excitement. A part of her knew why. She thought to say something, to thank him for the lesson, but he quickly excused himself and headed off to the house.

Captain Ponsonby left a few hours later for Portsmouth and Grace and Hannah were quick to start their packing, poor Polly, who was shared between them, lamenting the idea of being on a boat.

"I get seasick, milady."

"And how would you know that, Polly?" asked Hannah. "You grew up here. You've never been on a boat."

"Don't matter, I just know 'twill be awful."

"Oh, Polly, it will be fun! Think of all the dashing sailors you'll meet!" added Grace, thinking of one dashing sailor in particular and trying to picture him standing on deck in command of his frigate. "And once there, we'll get to see the Weybourne's famous Norfolk Thoroughbreds. You may not like boats, but no person in their right mind would pass up an opportunity like that!"

"I concur," Hannah said. "You couldn't pay me to get on a boat. No, you two can sail on up to Norfolk... I'm happy to be staying on *terra firma*!"

They took two coaches. One carried the Falconers, with Ned happily perched on the box and asking the driver all sorts of questions as his clever young mind sought to understand how teams of horses were driven. When they stopped for lunch at a coaching inn, he was given the chance to hold the reins and help drive the team around the yard— under heavy supervision, of course. Afterwards, everyone went inside for a repast of gammon, potatoes, hearty bread and a very nice pea soup. The second coach carried Grace and Polly, as well as the luggage. Delmore Lord and his manservant rode along on horses just outside, both heavily armed with pistols. Mr. Lord also had a sword, his face stony, his thoughts his own.

Watching him, Grace concluded that he was not the best rider in the world. He had a passable seat, but it was obvious that horsemanship was not something that came naturally to him and his demeanor when the animal got a little forward indicated unease. When they stopped to rest some time later, she invited him into the coach but he declined, saying the motion would make him queasy.

Grace had the distinct impression that it was an excuse.

But for what? Was he angry with her because of the mishap with the swans? Was he stewing over the frightful insults delivered by that odious man, Lieutenant Akers?

She watched him riding outside the coach, his face in shadow beneath his hat, only his hard lips and jaw, now properly shaved, catching the light from the sun above.

They stopped for the night at an inn and arrived in Portsmouth early the following afternoon. The mild weather back home had not followed them to the bustling naval port. Here, the air was cool and damp, heavy with salt, the harbor steeped in mist that looked much the color of Mr. Lord's eyes. Gulls screamed and called, mariners and seamen were everywhere, and the streets were full of carts and wagons and fancy vehicles carrying naval officers to and from their port duties. Heavy cloud hung suspended from a sky that yielded no blue, and as they got out of the coaches, with Mr. Lord coming himself to personally assist Grace and Polly down from theirs, her eyes lit upon the boats, ships and other vessels tied up at the wharves and anchored in the nearby reaches of the harbor, the masts of the tallest of them lost in mist.

"Which one is Captain Ponsonby's ship?" she asked him, unable to conceal her excitement.

"Anchored out in the roads. You can barely see her because of the mist."

"And the ship that you work on with my uncle — is that one here, too?"

"Yes, even farther out in the mist. You will not see her at all."

His manservant made a noise that sounded suspiciously like a guffaw, until a quelling glare from Mr. Lord silenced him.

The man turned away, smirking.

Confused, Grace looked at Mr. Lord, wondering why he was so stiff. So remote. So... *tight*. He passed the reins of his horse to a young groom who came running to assist them, all but dismissing her.

Grace glanced at Polly, raising her brows in question. The maid shrugged and then turned her attention on Mr. Lord's manservant who, at that moment, cast a glance over his shoulder and winked at the maid as he also gave his horse to the groom. Polly blushed wildly. Across the street, the door to an inn opened and out came Captain Ponsonby, polished and handsome, his smile as bright and shining as the buttons of his smart blue naval coat.

Grace's jaw dropped. Her heart pounded in her chest. She stood trying not to gape as he greeted the admiral and his family, for he was blindingly handsome in his uniform and he was now moving toward *her*.

And smiling.

Ohhh! He's looking at me. Me! Looking at me as though he actually sees me!

"Lady Grace." He took and bowed over her hand. Grace's heart skipped a beat and she glanced at Mr. Lord, hoping to share her excitement with her co-conspirator. He nodded tightly to acknowledge their small victory and turned away as Ned went running to him, excitedly babbling about the ships in the harbor.

Grace looked at him and frowned. Poor man. He must be sore from riding. No wonder he looked so unhappy.

But she was anything but unhappy. Captain Ponsonby was standing there right in front of her talking to her uncle, he had noticed her with warmth and interest, and she was suddenly glad she'd chosen her favorite nankin carriage dress for the journey. It was accented by a jaunty azure scarf with a white-butterfly print— a gift from her mother— tied at the junction of her collarbones. It complimented her eyes. Or so Mama said. Did she look all right? Would the Captain think so?

"The George is serving a delicious kidney pie for

lunch," Ponsonby said cheerfully. "And the gravy is enough to melt it in your mouth. Fresh bread right out of the oven as well. You must all be quite famished."

Hearty murmurs of assent.

Mr. Lord had moved closer to the water, his arm around Ned's shoulders as he pointed to something out in the gray, foggy harbor. Grace watched him for a moment, and then Captain Ponsonby was there at her side, offering an arm.

"Lady Grace," he said warmly. "Shall we?"

She blushed with delight and gave him what she hoped was a demure but dazzling smile. "Thank you, Captain."

Suddenly breathless, she slid her gloved fingers into the crook of his arm and allowed him to escort her and their party across the cobblestones and toward the building from which he'd emerged, Polly walking just behind her and no doubt worrying about the upcoming sea voyage. Sir Graham cradled the baby in the crook of his arm and Lady Falconer held tightly to the little hands of each daughter, both of whom were clamoring for kidney pie and speculating what the pudding might be. Ned raced past, nearly getting mowed down by a horse pulling a cart of produce before an admonition from his father and a shouted curse from the driver caused him to slow his pace.

"Sorry, Papa!"

Through her own euphoria Grace saw her uncle and aunt exchange a private smile, and she realized the admiral was relieved to be returned to his element.

They continued on toward the inn.

Forgotten, Del stayed behind for a bit, purposely giving them distance. He made idle chatter with the drivers as they waited for ostlers to come and take the teams, but his gaze went to the vibrant and pretty young woman clinging to Sheldon Ponsonby's arm as though it were a lifeline.

He watched her go, laughing and looking up at the captain, his presence already forgotten, and the sensitive Irish heart that beat so woefully in his chest suddenly throbbed with unbearable pain.

She looked back at him and he forced a smile and gave her a little wave.

He only prayed he could keep up the pretense that he was happy for her.

◆

TO GRACE'S EYES, THE FRIGATE WAS IMMENSE.

They had enjoyed a hearty lunch that was every bit as delicious as Captain Ponsonby had promised it would be and she had passed the hour without shedding any hairs into the captain's food, saying anything she'd instantly regretted, or otherwise embarrassing herself in any way.

Huzzah for small victories! And now they were all being rowed out to Captain Ponsonby's gallant ship, *Mars* to make the short journey up to Norfolk.

The ship got bigger and bigger as they approached and on the thwart beside her, poor Polly grew whiter and whiter. Grace began to regret the decision to bring her; the poor maid's distress and fear were palpable, and she began to worry about her.

"Are you well, Polly?" she whispered.

"Oh, yes, milady, I'll be fine," she whispered, with a wan smile. "Don't like this much, I don't. But it won't be for long now, will it?"

"Supposedly just a short sail around the coast and up to Norfolk. We'll be fine."

Polly nodded jerkily, and touching her hand to reassure her, Grace watched in excitement as the sailors hooked on to what Ned, giving her a running commentary about ship-parts, said were the "chains." Then, one by one, the men climbed aboard with ease, ascending strips of wood set into the tumblehome (according to Ned) with quick agility. On the deck high above, she heard shrill piercing whistles as the captain and her uncle went aboard, and half-heard Ned saying that was part of the navy's ceremonial greeting to an officer boarding a ship. Grace was still thinking about the tumblehome and thinking it could just as easily be called the side, or the hull, or even the wall, because from her vantage point in the small boat, that was exactly what it looked like as she peered up at the ship towering above her.

A wall.

Steep and painted in black and yellow, the snouts of cannons— guns, Ned told her— poked out in a menacing line all along its deck above.

It was a beautiful but intimidating thing, the ship, and she suddenly felt a bit of poor Polly's unease.

What mishaps await me this time? Because I know, I just know, it'll be something.

She and Polly were each hauled up this wall— or rather, tumblehome— in a contraption of ropes by some brawny-armed tars on the deck above, one of whom winked at Polly and caused her to blush wildly beneath her bonnet when her feet were finally on the deck. It did not escape Grace's notice that while Lady Falconer sent her youngest children and their nanny up via the rope contraption, she herself derided it; instead, she pulled her skirts to one side, looped them over her arm, and clambered up the ship's side as nimbly as did the men.

Well, of course. A decade ago, she had been a formidable pirate. Queen of the Caribbean, if tales were to be believed and Grace, watching her, believed every one of them.

Ned also took the sailor's route onto the ship and so did Delmore Lord, whose stony expression had not softened in the slightest. In fact, now that they were all aboard, he seemed even more out of sorts.

"Relax, Del," she heard her uncle tell him.

Mr. Lord murmured something that Grace didn't catch and went to the side, there to look broodingly out over the gray harbor. Out in the distance, bands of rain showed as vertical fans of slate stabbing down out of the clouds over the Channel. Behind her, Grace heard Captain Ponsonby issuing commands to sailors and decided to find an out-of-the-way spot where she could sit and watch him and savor her recent memories. The sight of him coming out of the coaching inn in his splendid uniform. The sound of his voice as they'd taken their lunch, his chivalrous attention to her, and the feeling she'd had in her chest every time he'd turned to her and spoken.

Such sweet memories! And surely, there were better ones yet to come.

But there was something about Mr. Lord that was troubling her, and every time she tried to lose herself in thoughts of Captain Ponsonby, she found herself wondering what ailed Mr. Lord.

Soon enough, those daydreams were replaced with concern for her sailing instructor. He had retreated away from everyone else and now stood leaning his elbows against the rail, his hands dangling over the gray and choppy water far below. One of them held his hat and now the wind moved through his hair, which looked very black in the day's gloom, the dampness in the air causing it to curl in thick, tight tendrils that clung to his jaw. As though sensing her perusal, he raked a hand through it, smoothing it back, and turned to look at her.

She smiled, hoping to soften the reality that she'd been staring after him in concern.

"Lady Grace. Let us hope we have an agreeable passage up to Norfolk."

She walked over to him. "Is something amiss, Mr. Lord?"

"I should hope not."

"You seem troubled. Out of sorts. If it's about the swans, I'm so sorry I embarrassed you in front of the others... you were a fine teacher and I learned so very much. And," she added hopefully, "our plan worked, just as I'd hoped. Did you see that Captain Ponsonby himself escorted me to the waterfront?"

"I did."

"If it weren't for you, he'd never have even noticed me."

"He'd have noticed you."

Grace frowned. "What is wrong, Mr. Lord?"

"Nothing that can be fixed," he said evasively. "But it is of no matter, and not worth discussing."

She eyed him narrowly, cocking her head slightly to one side.

"Not worth discussing," she repeated softly.

He glanced down at her briefly, and then away over the water as though it pained him to look at her. A muscle twitched in his jaw, and she remembered that jaw beneath her lips when she'd impulsively stood on tiptoe to plant a kiss upon it in gratitude for saving her life.

She remembered how it had felt. The hard muscle beneath, the faint harsh stubble of whisker against her lips. It was all she could do not to give in to impulse right now, to reach up and smooth the hardness away, to ease the pain in those clear gray eyes, but of course, gently-bred young ladies didn't do those sorts of things and so, she didn't.

Instead, she ventured, "Are you not looking forward to seeing your family in Norfolk?"

"I can't wait," he said honestly. "In fact—"

"Captain Lord! Captain Lord! Look! The mist is parting off to windward and you can see *Orion*!"

Grace glanced from Ned, running headlong toward them, and to her companion in confusion. "*Captain* Lord?"

The boy froze, open-mouthed, and began to redden. One small hand went to his mouth.

But Grace was staring at the man beside her.

"Did he just call you *Captain* Lord?"

Her companion's smile grew more pained. "Yes. You heard the boy correctly."

Grace stared at him. "You mean you're not a... clerk for my uncle? Or one of his sailors? I thought you worked for Uncle Gray!"

"I do work for the admiral."

"Your anonymity is up, Del," said Sir Graham, grinning as he walked past. "Might as well face it."

"*Captain?*"

The man beside her looked vastly uncomfortable, but Grace persisted.

"If you're a captain, then... which one is *your* ship?"

He turned his head in the direction of the wind. The mists continued to part and the ghostly forms of vessels out in the harbor took on shape. Small, single-masted sloops. Double-masted schooners and brigs. Frigates, like the one she found herself on, traders, ships of the line, an East Indiaman just weighing anchor, pilot boats and hoys, dinghies and a prison ship and there, far out in the water, the parting mists sharpening its outline as it was revealed, a massive vessel that dwarfed everything else in the harbor, a ship of many decks and row upon row of guns, with sides painted in a black and yellow checkerboard pattern and masts that reached all the way up to Heaven itself.

Delmore Lord smiled tightly and gave a little nod to the emerging leviathan.

"That one."

❧ 18 ❧

That one.

Grace stared at it, for it was easily the largest, mightiest vessel in the emerging harbor, the tallest, the most commanding, the most impressive, the one to which any schoolboy would have proudly pointed when asked which ship he thought represented the mighty splendor of Britannia herself.

That one.

"Wait," Grace said slowly. "Ned just called you *captain*. Captains command ships, and you just indicated that— that massive *boat* out there is *your* ship. Which leads me to conclude that you are the captain of that ship."

"I am," he said tightly.

"But—"

"Captain Lord didn't want to tell you because he was trying to have a nice, quiet holiday in England without any fuss or fanfare," Ned volunteered, trying to make amends for spoiling the secret in his excitement. "It's why he's not in uniform, but I can assure you he has one. He has several, in fact, but he chose to dress as a civilian so he could relax because everyone, Papa included, thinks he's needed to do just that." And then, in an aside, "Plus, my uncle Connor implied that he's rigid, so I'm sure he was trying to allay that accusation, is that not so, Captain Lord?"

The expression of pain that Grace had noted earlier faded into something that looked to be a mixture of amusement, dismay, irritation and embarrassment.

"Ned," he said slowly, "Why don't you go and help your mother with little Anne and Mary. They're wandering perilously close to the side."

"Aye, sir!"

"*Sir?*" Grace said, the shock of this revelation fading, only to be replaced by the feeling that someone had just punched her in the stomach.

"The admiral's son already fancies himself to be part of the Navy," Mr.— *no, make that* Captain— Lord said. "Though it'll be a few more years before he can think about being a midshipman and making his dreams a reality."

Feeling was flooding in, overwhelming Grace.

"You didn't tell me you were a captain."

"Your uncle's flag captain, if I must be honest."

"You didn't tell me you hold such rank!"

"I saw no reason to."

"You didn't tell me you commanded such a massive ship!"

"An admiral's flagship is never an insignificant vessel in either size or firepower."

"You let me believe you were a sailor, teaching me to sail a boat in a pond... oh, I am absolutely, positively mortified!"

"I *am* a sailor. And I do not regret the use of my time while at Ruscombe Hall." His steady gray gaze caught hers, and he lifted a dark brow. "Do you?"

"Well no, but I feel like a fool!"

"Why?"

"If I'd known that you commanded that— that— *ship* out there, I would have died of humiliation, knowing someone of such importance and rank was showing me how to work a sailboat in a tiny pond. Oh!"

He shrugged. "The principles of sailing remain the same."

"*Oh!*"

"From what direction, Lady Grace, is the wind coming from!"

"You are making sport of me!"

"No, merely ensuring that you remembered something of our lesson."

"I don't know, it's coming from *that* way," she snapped, emphasizing the *that*. "And because I can't see the sun for all this mist, I can't give you a better answer than that. I don't want to give you a better answer than that. I can't believe you allowed me to believe you were something you're not!"

Captain Lord's cool gray eyes glinted with affront. "I did nothing of the sort."

Lady Falconer was approaching, a struggling toddler pulling at each hand. She was grinning widely. "Del, are you upsetting the lady?"

"Not intentionally."

"He just told me he's Uncle Gray's flag captain! That he commands that massive ship out there in the harbor! Please Aunt Maeve, tell me that is not true, because I feel like the butt of a terrible joke!"

Her eyes danced with mischief. "'Twould be a lie if I told you it wasn't true."

"Did everyone know except me?"

"No, not everyone. In fact, most did *not* know, at least, not at the wedding. Those that did and said nothing were simply abiding by Captain Lord's request to enjoy some anonymity while off the ship. You mustn't be angry with him. My brother Connor accused him of being stuffy and unbending and worked so hard to get him to relax, to forget his cares and responsibilities for even a short time. Del tried to do just that during this trip." She turned to him and smiled. "And were you successful, Del?"

"Aside from an unplanned swim in a pond that stank of mud and goose droppings, yes, Lady Falconer, I daresay I was."

"So there you go," Maeve said cheerfully. And then, leaning down so that only Grace could hear her, she whispered, "And he's a far better catch than Captain Ponsonby will ever be. Mark me on that."

⚓

LIEUTENANT JAMES AKERS WAS ON THE QUARTERDECK when Captain Ponsonby returned to his ship. He had guests with him. The Falconer family. Lady Grace Fairchild, who was rumored to be quite heavily dowered. And that stuffy prig, Delmore Lord.

The sight of the man made Akers crave a bottle.

They had known each other since Eton, had been together on the old *Dancer*. Even then, Delmore Lord had been insufferable. His mannerisms, his cultivated speech, his naval pedigree going back generations and his lofty, far-reaching aspirations— aspirations that were quite natural to him, aspirations he'd taken for granted— had been an affront to Akers, the only child of a wealthy printer who'd made his fortune selling salacious gossip about the *ton* and other self-important people.

Not exactly a noble pedigree to be sure, and the other young gentleman-officers— naval elite or British aristocrats, all of them— let him know it.

They had never accepted him, leaving him to his own devices and bitter loneliness which, in hindsight, had probably been a good thing. Easier to conceal his secrets that way, really. He knew it at the time, and he knew it now, but that didn't erase the pain he'd felt then nor the resentment that he spent a good part of his free time trying to drown in a bottle, now. They'd looked down upon his family, his father's occupation, even the money that had sent him to sea.

He was not their equal, he did not have birth and breeding to aid him, and Akers, a master at studying facial expressions and a self-proclaimed expert on reading them, knew, just *knew*, that Delmore Lord thought as highly of himself now as he did all those years ago aboard *Dancer*.

And he despised him for it.

But that was nothing compared to the hatred he felt for Lady Grace Fairchild.

Because at the moment, the young woman was gazing with unabashed infatuation at Captain Ponsonby.

Akers clenched his fists.

He's mine, you simpering bitch. You'll never have him if I have anything to say about it.

Yes, his history with Delmore Lord went back a long time, but so did his history with Sheldon Ponsonby. Both went all the way back to Eton, in fact. James had been a small, slight boy, pimpled and shy, and his diminutive physique along with a pedigree that his schoolmates considered lacking, had marked him for abuse from the moment he'd set foot on the school's hallowed grounds.

He remembered the day as if it were yesterday. He, a new boy in a new school, an outsider who would never be accepted. On that particular afternoon, one of them had whipped an egg at him. It caught the back of his head, splattered, and dripped its sticky yellow mess down his neck and onto his shirt. Someone else had come up behind him and kicked him behind the knees, felling him, and as the jeering laughter of the mob had roared out around him, another boy had stepped in. He'd been tall, blond and confident, and instead of joining the others in their abuse, he'd pushed through them, walked up to Akers, and extended a hand down to help him up.

They had become friends, then, and that was the last time that Akers had ever suffered torment from his peers. Eventually, Ponsonby followed his family's calling to the sea, and when he invited Akers to accompany him, there'd never been any question that he would go.

Ponsonby, of course, had advanced faster than Akers, but even now his friend and captain protected him, encouraged him, and at some point, he would support Akers's own quest for a command of his own.

And Akers wasn't so sure he wanted to leave.

If he had his own way, he'd follow Ponsonby to the ends of the earth, and clear every forest, move every rock, part every sea for this man who had reached a hand down to help him up on that long ago day... literally and figuratively.

Now, he watched Ponsonby conversing with Sir Graham and for not the first time, Akers damned the admiral for choosing the wrong man to be his flag captain. He should have picked Ponsonby, who was brave and dashing, not cautious and dull like Lord. No, no one could fault his loyalty to his commanding officer. And if Lady Grace ever won him, Ponsonby feared that the great friendship he had with his captain would be no more.

He would have a new best friend in a wife.

His attention would belong to *her*.

The handsome Sheldon Ponsonby would never belong to James Akers. That was an impossibility.

But if Akers had anything to say about it, he'd never belong to Lady Grace Fairchild, either.

Lady Falconer.

❧ 19 ❧

"We should be getting underway shortly," Lady
Falconer said, helping little Anne to climb up
on one of the frigate's big guns. The child, her hair already as red as her mother's, broke into a huge grin and
jumped clumsily up and down on the expanse of iron,
her balance quite steady despite her mother's support.

"Gun go *boom*, Mama!"

Mary, frowning as she stared enviously at her twin,
crowded close, her little face already starting to redden
with the approach of a coming tantrum. Seeing it, Ned
picked her up and set her atop a neighboring gun where
her frown instantly transformed itself into an adorable
smile of baby teeth and joy.

"Boom!" she echoed.

"Will Papa command Captain Ponsonby to fire the
guns for them once we get underway?" Ned asked his
mother. "Because if he doesn't, it's going to be a long
voyage, to say the least."

Their mother sighed. "That is up to the captain."

Grace looked at the cannon on which each child
stood, great, long-nosed instruments of death and destruction. They looked quite harmless at the moment,
sitting in their trucks with their muzzles pointed out
over the harbor as if searching for an invisible enemy.

"Why such a fascination for cannon?" she asked Lady Falconer.

"Guns," Ned corrected, with a grin. "A cannon aboard a ship is called a gun."

"Oh," said Grace. "Right. *Guns*."

Grace wondered how many *guns* Captain Lord's ship had, and her gaze inadvertently swung to the huge warship that continued to reveal itself as the day brightened and the fog thinned. Still, no end to its masts despite the parting of the mist.

Just how big was the thing, anyhow?

"But to answer your question," Ned put in, "Captain Lord had his crew fire *Orion*'s guns a few times on the Atlantic crossing expressly for the entertainment of my sisters. I'm afraid they've developed a taste for the noise, the reverberation, the smoke and the excitement."

"Smells good," said little Anne.

Gracie put a tiny fist to her chest and thumped it. "Feels good in *here*," she added.

Privately, Grace wondered if the Falconers practiced pretend swordfights instead of the activities most normal families used as entertainment, such as charades. Card games. Singing. The learning of an instrument.

She wouldn't doubt it.

And speaking of *Orion*, where had its *captain* gone to?

She wanted to remain angry with him. And perhaps she could have maintained her fury if he or the Falconers had found amusement at the joke that they had all been in on, and which had caused her such surprise and mortification. But they hadn't seen it as a joke. And neither, apparently, did Captain Lord. It wasn't as if any of them had intentionally set out to make her look foolish for not knowing. And what did Captain Lord owe her, anyhow? Maybe, just maybe, the man really *had* just wanted to lay low and be absolved of all the responsibilities that went with his identity for even a short time. Certainly, looking at how busy Captain Ponsonby had become since they'd all boarded the ship, it was not hard to imagine how exhaustive command must be, and since Captain Lord's ship was countless times bigger than the one on which she found herself, it was reasonable to assume that commanding it carried many times the responsibility as well.

Her anger softened.

She had overcome past humiliations by not taking herself so seriously, and finding ways to laugh at herself when all was said and done. Because if you were the one laughing at yourself, it rather dulled the urge for others to do so instead.

Really, was this any different?

She looked around for Captain Lord. He had retreated to the rail some distance away, a remote, lonely figure who was gazing out over the water. Grace made her excuses and went to him.

"Captain Lord." She offered a smile, allowing her eyes to sparkle with forgiveness.

"Lady Grace." He slanted her a look she couldn't quite interpret. "I thought you were cross with me."

"I am." She joined him at the rail and looked down at the gray water so far below. "But being cross isn't my normal state of mind. A waste of energy to be angry at someone, really, though I did feel quite foolish, being the only one who didn't know your rank or who you really were when everyone else, it seems, did." She smiled when she saw him beginning to frown. "But I forgive you."

"Forgiveness accepted."

"But of course, that means that for me to forgive you, you probably should have given me an apology first. Otherwise the forgiveness doesn't really count."

"That is a very bizarre and confounded way of looking at the matter, Lady Grace."

"Is it?"

"Well, yes."

"It makes perfect sense to me. I have forgiven you for not apologizing to me as well as deceiving me."

"And I apologize to you, for the fact that I have no idea what you're talking about or how to interpret it."

"You are forgiven."

Del looked down and over at her, at her earnest face with its dark brows, its pert little nose and innocent mouth, and in that moment he saw the humor in those big blue eyes and realized she was playing with him.

He wasn't quite sure how to respond. He opened his mouth but nothing came out, and he felt suddenly rather witless as well as useless here on Ponsonby's ship as a passenger, with his admiral's flag flying from Ponsonby's command instead of his own. Where he had no role, really, except to help this beautiful, self-deprecating and helplessly funny young woman find a way to catch the eye of this ship's commander.

The idea of her succeeding brought him sudden pain.

I can't wait to get to Norfolk.

To get away from them both.

Ironic, wasn't it. He a naval captain, a senior officer whose home was largely the sea. He, a man who'd been all but raised on ships.

He a man who couldn't wait to get back on land where his current insignificance, at least, would have an excuse.

And he himself would have a respite from a task which was growing increasingly difficult, increasingly painful, and increasingly hard to assist toward its imagined outcome.

"Well, I'll leave you to your musings," she said, her

eyes dancing. "But I hope we can continue my education as a mariner-in-training while we're aboard ship."

He inclined his head. "It would be an honor, Lady Grace."

She gave him a smile that completely melted him. Then she moved off, heading back to his admiral's family and never knowing that his eyes— and his heart — followed her.

GRACE HAD NEVER SEEN, LET ALONE BEEN ON A warship. She stayed largely out of the way as Captain Ponsonby issued a barrage of commands that resulted in things she didn't know much about. Sailors going to the great contraption that turned round and round and brought the anchor up. Sailors going up the tapering crosshatched ropes that led up the masts, moving out along the yards (she knew they were yards because Ned himself came over to tell her) to release whatever it was called that held the sails furled. So many terms! So much to remember! Sailors bustling to and fro, Uncle Gray standing quietly near Captain Ponsonby but doing nothing to interfere with the business of running the ship, his two daughters squealing with excitement, Ned offering a running commentary about what was happening that had Grace thoroughly confused, in part because she was listening to none of it and instead, watching the figure she'd left behind at the rail.

Captain Lord kept himself apart, seemingly uninterested in the way Captain Ponsonby conducted the business of getting his own ship underway, his thoughts his own as he gazed out over the gray and misty harbor.

Grace found her eye drawn to him, her mind pondering what he was thinking about, and then wondering why she was thinking about Delmore Lord instead of watching Sheldon Ponsonby who was in all his glory, when suddenly a sailor up in the bows yelled, "Anchors aweigh!" The ship lurched and swayed, a sensation that immediately transferred itself to her stomach.

Oh, no.

Some of the smaller sails were down and drawing, and one of the bigger ones on the foremast as well. Grace had no idea what they were called despite the fact she must have asked Ned three times, and despite her resolution to learn as much about the working of the ship as possible she suddenly didn't care so much about any of it.

I don't feel well.

She took a deep breath of the damp salt air and let it out. Polly had come up from below and was sitting in a chair near Lady Falconer, who had an excited, squealing twin on each knee. Her maid was looking toward the waist of the ship, where Captain Lord's manservant had busied himself with the ship's company; he glanced up, caught Polly's eye, and raised his hat to her. Polly blushed prettily. They were starting to make way now. Grace couldn't yet feel any motion, but when she cast her gaze toward the shoreline, or a distant vessel against that shoreline, she could see the movement.

A shadow fell over her and she turned to find Captain Lord there.

"What do you think?" she asked, trying to get her mind off her suddenly queasy stomach. "Is Captain Ponsonby doing a good job of getting his ship underway?"

"Unless he hits something or goes aground, I cannot fault him."

"This is all rather exciting. I hope I'm teachable when it comes to the names of the many parts and practices of a ship. My memory is already overwhelmed. And I'm confused."

"About what?"

"Lots of things. To start with, why do the sails on that mast— what is it called?"

"The mainmast."

"Right, the mainmast. Why do those sails look different from the one aboard our little boat back at the lake?"

"These are square-rigged. The one on our boat was fore-and-aft rigged. Different setup."

"These look far more complicated."

"Same principle," he said.

Behind him, she could see Captain Ponsonby near the wheel, standing with the admiral and talking. Unbidden, Grace's gaze went back to Captain Lord.

He really is rather a handsome man.

Now, where did that thought come from?

The ship was picking up speed now, the massive warship that the man beside her supposedly commanded, growing larger as they headed toward it. She saw a look of fond longing move briefly over his face.

They would be passing it soon. As they approached, it grew and grew until it dwarfed the ship that she stood on. There were plenty of people aboard it, too. She could see moving figures and people waving wildly as they sailed past, could hear a great roaring cheer coming from it.

She glanced at Sir Graham on the quarterdeck. He raised his hat to them, and then Grace jumped as a gun fired a salute from the massive warship, echoing over the water in a cloud of smoke and rolling thunder.

The Falconer twins, restrained by Polly as their mother went to say something to her husband, squealed with excitement.

It seemed to take forever to sail past the great warship. The parting mists had still not found the top of its lofty masts, and Grace felt small and insignificant as they moved past the many rows of open gun ports and looked up, up, up to see the figures waving from the decks so high above them. She turned her head to look at Delmore Lord. It wasn't hard to imagine him commanding such a mighty vessel, and it occurred to her for the second time in as many minutes, that he must cut a fine figure indeed in his naval uniform.

As fine as Captain Ponsonby.

Maybe finer...

And then they were past HMS *Orion* and into the outer reaches of the harbor, and the long rolling swells coming in from the English Channel found them.

"Captain Ponzy! Fire the guns!" shrieked little Anne Falconer.

He, still in conversation with the admiral on the quarterdeck, didn't hear the children but Delmore Lord did. He looked pained.

"Captain Lord! Make him fire the guns!" howled her twin, Mary.

"Yes, we want to hear them go boom!"

"Please, Captain Lord!"

Delmore Lord smiled, then, something he did not seem wont to do, and knelt down to the children's level. "This is not my ship, girls," he said quietly. "But perhaps once we get out in open sea, Captain Ponsonby will fire the guns."

"Won't sound as good as *Orion*'s," Ned put in.

"I want to hear them *now*!"

Lady Falconer was returning, no doubt intending to take control of the situation, but Grace was no longer paying attention to the rising drama. The deck beneath her feet was moving up and down and tilted somewhat to her left, and she was beginning to feel dizzy. She turned her back on the Falconers and went to the rail and there, dug her fingers into the smooth wood, sucking deep breaths into her lungs and fighting down a rising sense of panic.

She shut her eyes. That made it worse.

Oh, dear God.

A presence at her shoulder once again. She looked up, expecting Captain Lord, but no, of all people it was *him*.

Captain Ponsonby.

"Lady Grace." His blinding white smile reached all the way up to his eyes and made them crinkle. "My admiral tells me you've never been aboard a ship before. Would you like a turn around the decks with me?"

Grace could only stare at him. This was the moment she'd been waiting for. The moment she had dreamed of, the moment when this very man finally made room in his own world for her.

She opened her mouth to reply—

And vomited the lunch he had so praised all over his clean white breeches, his shiny black shoes, and their perfectly shined buckles.

❧ 20 ❧

He leaped backwards as though he'd been struck.

"Ohhhh," she cried in abject humiliation, wiping helplessly at her mouth, feeling another wave of nausea already rising in her throat as Captain Ponsonby went green, muttered a hasty "I beg your pardon," and retreated. Through a spinning dizziness she watched him flee for the comparative safety of his quarterdeck, leaving her all alone in her misery.

The tears came. Her head swam and her knees grew weak and droplets of sweat popped out on her forehead as she fought another coming wave.

"Lady Grace."

She looked up through her tears and there was Captain Lord. He reached into the pocket of his tailcoat and extracted a clean white handkerchief and was just about to hand it to her when she clapped a hand over her mouth and ran to the rail, clenching her teeth against the rising vomit, her senses swimming.

She felt his hand upon her own where it rested upon the smooth wood. His tall presence beside her was soothing and she, dizzy and ill, found herself leaning into it.

"I don't want to be sick," she choked out, the tears rolling down her face. "I want to be able to *do* this."

The hand he'd laid over her own moved to her back, strong, reassuring. He leaned down to her. "Let it come out," he murmured for her ears alone. "You'll feel better."

"Yes, and you'll bolt, too, won't you?"

"No."

And here it came. Her head swimming, the contents of her stomach came barreling out of her mouth and nostrils with as much force as she suspected the nearby cannon would spew when called to war, and she shut her eyes, unwilling and unable to watch the wind take it and send it down and out over the sea.

Captain Lord was rubbing her back.

"I can't believe I'm seasick," she choked out, swiping at her tears, her sweating face. "My uncle is an admiral. I thought I had seafarer's blood."

"You may have seafarer's blood, but you have a land-lubber's stomach," he said kindly. "Though did you know, Lady Grace, that even the great Lord Nelson suffered from seasickness?"

"Did he really?"

Another wave of nausea hit her and miserably, she retched over the side. And there was Captain Lord again, the handkerchief in his hand, and he was tenderly wiping her chin, the corner of her mouth, unflinching, patient and caring when the man of her dreams had fled in horror and disgust.

Something lurched in her heart.

Her tears became something more and took on a different meaning. One of guilt and gratitude and realization. Of grief, even, as she mourned her idea of what she'd thought Ponsonby to be versus what he actually was.

"I need to go below," she said weakly. "I wish to lie down."

"You may feel better if you stay up here in the fresh air. But if you wish to go to your cabin, I'll take you."

She nodded, and clutched his arm when he offered it. The muscles beneath were rock-hard and strong and she clung to him, hanging her head, unable to look toward the quarterdeck where Captain Ponsonby was no doubt trying to clean his shoes. Together, they headed toward the hatch, Grace moaning in misery and struggling to stay on her feet, the motion of the ship sending her repeatedly stumbling and falling into the solid strength of the man who walked beside her, the man who gallantly adjusted his pace to accommodate her own, the man who uncomplainingly allowed her to lean heavily on him as they slowly made their way to the hatch.

"Del? Is Grace all right?"

Aunt Maeve's voice. Aunt Maeve the pirate queen, who had probably never been seasick a day in her life.

"A little *mal de mer*, nothing more. I'm taking her to her cabin."

"She'll feel better topside, you know."

"I just want to lie down," Grace moaned, grateful for his hard strength.

Somehow, he got her down the hatch and into the soothing gloom below decks and immediately, Grace knew both he and her aunt were correct. Down here in the close confines of the ship, the motion was worse. And the smells... bilge and unwashed bodies, vinegar and salt and a host of other odors, some of them noxious, some of them not, none of them doing a thing to alleviate her misery. She stumbled and almost fell and it was then that Captain Lord, without warning, without permission, scooped her up in his strong arms. She was too sick to protest, too weak to care, and lay nestled against his chest as he carried her past several small cabins and then, finally, to what amounted to little more than a cubbyhole.

Her cabin, which some junior officer must have given up for her comfort.

Inside was a narrow bunk built against the curve of the hull, a tiny writing desk, and her trunk which someone had already brought aboard. Grace looked at it all and her world swam dizzyingly, and she turned her sweating face against Captain Lord's chest once again.

"I want to die," she mumbled, into the clean white linen of his shirt.

"I know."

"I vomited all over him. Over his clothes. His shoes."

"You've laughed about your other disasters. And someday you'll laugh about this one, too."

"Will I?"

"You will."

"I've never felt so wretched in my entire life."

"Not even when he found the hair in his soup?"

She heard the humor in his voice, and managed to respond with a wan smile. "Well, I think this is worse."

"And so it is. But you'll persevere. You're resilient and strong."

With gentle tenderness he lowered her to the bunk, removed her shoes, and drew the light blanket that was folded at the foot of the bed, up over her body. She curled in misery on the thin mattress, moaning.

"Would you like me to stay with you, Lady Grace?"

Grace shut her eyes against the rolling of the ship, the spinning in her head, the nausea and the sweating and the absolute horror of it all. She nodded in a little helpless gesture, grateful for his presence, too sick to wonder or care why Lady Falconer hadn't come down here to be with her or why she hadn't sent Polly. She heard Captain Lord draw the chair close to the bed and as she lay there clenched in a ball of misery, dizziness led to sleep and his hand came out to rest on her shoulder in wordless comfort.

She never knew.

But he, sitting there in the gloom beside her, the

girl's slim arm clammy beneath his fingers, her tears of embarrassment still wet upon her cheeks, was keenly aware of her. Of the softness of her breathing. Of the tangled beauty of her hair. Of the sweetness of her cheek and the tilt of her nose, and the dark sweep of her long, long lashes lying against her pale skin.

A fierce and violent wave of protectiveness suddenly overcame him.

She would be wasted on Ponsonby, whose intolerance for hairs in his soup and puke on his shoes was an embarrassment to manliness in general and chivalry in particular.

But he had pledged to help the girl net that undeserving lout, and he was a man of his word.

He looked wistfully upon her sleeping form and leaned his head against the bulkhead that separated this cabin from the next.

He could not have her, as her heart belonged to another.

But he could gaze upon her beauty until either Lady Falconer or Polly arrived, and he could dream.

He hoped that she, in her slumbers, was doing the same.

LADY FALCONER DID NOT ARRIVE, NOR DID SHE SEND Polly to rescue Del from any whispers of scandal that might've resulted from his actions in taking Grace below, let alone remaining there. Not that anyone on board the frigate would have cared, really. Ponsonby was more interested in showing off the smartness of his command to Sir Graham, Polly and Mr. Lord's manservant were making eyes at each other, and Maeve had her hands full with her children.

No, the Pirate Queen of the Caribbean was quite happy to leave Del right where he was.

Ned came wandering over to her. "Mama, shall I go find Cousin Grace and make sure she's all right?"

"No, Ned. She just needs to rest."

"But Captain Lord hasn't come back."

"I know."

"Do you think he needs any help?"

His mother smiled and ruffled his hair. "I'm sure he's doing just fine."

Ned nodded gravely and wandered off to talk with the helmsman. On the deck below, a lantern swung just outside the tiny cabin where Grace slept fitfully, and the man who had carried her there sat in the chair and worried, increasingly, about the propriety of it all. He lived his life according to protocol and the high standards of both an officer and a gentleman. He shouldn't be down here with her, all alone. Where was Lady Falconer? Her maid? Anyone?

He could not leave her.

To do so would be an even worse breach of the standards by which he conducted himself.

And so he sat there wishing someone would come to spell him, but also hoping that no one would, for it was bliss to sit here with her, to gaze upon her lovely face, listen to the little sighs she made in her sleep, fancy himself to be her great protector and yes, to be the owner of her sweet and generous heart.

He felt the ship change tack. The blanket slid a bit from her shoulders and he quietly pulled it back up, taking care not to wake her. But Grace only sighed, snuggled into the blanket, and lay still.

And dreamt.

Dreamt of that massive ship that was back in Portsmouth. The biggest, mightiest one in the harbor.

His ship.

"Take the wheel, Lady Grace."

They were at sea, but his ship wasn't cavorting like a frisky colt over the swells the way Ponsonby's did; no, *his* ship was a heavy, solid, sure-footed warrior, stately, steady and strong, comfortable and, to the extent that a ship could be, considerate. It wasn't trying to make her sick; it was trying to make her well. To make her seagoing experience a pleasant, even a happy one.

"Do you know which direction the wind comes from, Lady Grace?"

He was standing so close, and she felt her body responding to that nearness. He was as solid and strong and mighty as the vessel he commanded, resplendent in his smart blue and white uniform with the gold lacing, once more the patient teacher who'd taught her to navigate a little boat across a pond when she had no idea what he did.

What he was.

And this was no little boat, nor was it a pond.

"It's coming from ... from the south, Captain Lord."

"Very good," he murmured, and leaned down even further—

And kissed her.

Grace came awake with a start. Around her, she could hear the creaks and moans of seasoned wood, the sea sluicing past the hull outside, and there was Captain Lord still in the chair next to her. He was not dressed in a naval uniform, nor could not have kissed her. His head was tilted back against the bulkhead, his eyes were closed, and his arms were folded loosely across his chest. As though sensing her perusal of him, he opened his eyes.

I had the oddest dream, she wanted to say.

But no. She would not make him uncomfortable by sharing it.

And yet the dream still clung to her, heavy, vivid and as warm and cozy as the blanket that covered her shoulders. She wondered at it. Why this man had been in the dream, and not Captain Ponsonby. Why in the dream he, not Captain Ponsonby, had kissed her.

And why she desperately resented the fact that she had woken up from it, just when he— not Captain Ponsonby— had been kissing her.

"Are you feeling better, Lady Grace?" he asked.

She sat up. There was no natural light down here save for what a swinging lantern just outside this small space offered, and in the close gloom, her companion was within touching distance. She flushed, still remembering the dream. She must be addled. It had to be the seasickness.

"Well, I don't feel as dizzy," she said, and tentatively sat up.

She swayed and his hand shot out, catching her. He moved from the chair to the bunk, and she leaned against him in gratitude.

"Thank you, Captain Lord," she murmured, and looked up at him.

His gaze was intent, his face very close. His head began to lower to hers. For a brief moment, she thought... hoped... that maybe he might kiss her, but then he gave a start and jerked back, as though suddenly remembering himself. He cleared his throat and moved away, and Grace figured she had imagined it all. Read more into the moment than was actually there.

Of course she had. The world was still swimming. She didn't trust anything she felt or saw at the moment, let alone thought.

Yes, she'd imagined it all.

"Are you well enough that I can leave you for a few moments?" he asked.

"I suppose I have to be." She mustered a reassuring smile, still mulling over that odd moment where something had almost happened, though what that *something* was, she still wasn't sure. "You have been very kind to stay with me all this time. I feel a bit guilty, and certainly very grateful. I won't make any more demands on your time, Captain."

"You misunderstand. I merely wish to find my trunk, wherever my coxswain put it, as I keep a generous supply of ginger there. I think it'll settle your stomach."

"Do you get seasick too, then?"

His grin was tentative, fleeting. "No. I just like the taste of ginger." He stood up, filling the small space with his height. "I'll be back shortly. Stay here, and don't try to move around."

He left, and she was alone. The space suddenly felt small and lonely without him, and she sat up on the small bunk, clearing a strand of hair from her forehead and clutching the blanket around herself.

That dream.

Oh, what of it? And why?

And why had it felt so *right*?

She sat leaning against the curve of the hull, weak but no longer quite as dizzy. Presently, she heard voices and there was Polly, rushing toward her with Captain Lord and Ned right behind.

"Milady! Can I get you something to drink? Some water, perhaps?"

But Grace's gaze found Captain Lord's. "That would be nice, Polly. But what I would really like is what Captain Lord went to find for me. Ginger. Because this is my first sea voyage, and I'm determined not to spend it down here being sick."

He gave her a private little half-smile in acknowledgement of her resolve, and produced a small jar from his coat pocket. Polly went to fetch some water, Ned vowed to teach her some tricks to keep from feeling sick, and before the hour was out, Grace was on her feet and allowing both the boy and the man to help her back up the hatch and to the deck above.

It *was* her first sea voyage.

She was not going to waste it.

❧ 21 ❧

They headed east and the weather got dirty, forcing Ponsonby to keep the frigate well off shore in order to maintain plenty of sea room between his command and England's southern coastline. Dover's white cliffs were visible in the distance, the sea thrashing against their base in curls of fury, and as they cleared Ramsgate they saw, far to the east, a French corvette that quickly turned tail and ran at sight of the English frigate. Del figured that Ponsonby would have liked to impress their admiral by giving chase, but the enemy vessel was quickly lost to the mists and the frigate continued on her way.

The weather cleared and the Falconer girls grew bored and Captain Ponsonby did not offer to fire the guns for their benefit— which brought Ned straight to Del. The flag captain had reluctantly given up the care of his patient to her maid, and was now relaxing on deck reading a book.

Or trying to.

A movement caught his eye. Lady Grace was back on deck, and there she stood in the wind, pale and wan and even a little triumphant.

He tried not to look at her.

Tried to give his attention to the boy.

"He's not half as nice nor half as accommodating as *you* are, Captain Lord," Ned was complaining, his mouth mulish and his arms crossed indignantly over his chest. "He's trying so hard to impress Papa that he's not even thinking about making the twins happy!"

Del's gaze flickered again to Lady Grace. He watched her progress to the rail, ready to leap to his feet and assist her if she looked as though she were unsteady. "Well, Ned, he doesn't have children of his own... surely, it doesn't occur to him what children might like."

"You don't have children either, but *you* know!"

Del couldn't help a tight smile. "I also had several thousand miles of boredom on an Atlantic crossing. Captain Ponsonby only has to get us from Portsmouth to King's Lynn. By the time it might occur to him to entertain your sisters, we'll be there."

"You know as well as I do, sir, that it *won't* occur to him!"

"Perhaps not, but we'll be there soon enough and then they will have horses to entertain them. Lots of them, as I understand it."

"Boring," the boy muttered, and stalked off.

Del returned to his book. It was a treatise on naval tactics and sea maneuvers and at any other time he might have found it engrossing. But not now. Not with Lady Grace up on deck, one hand coming up to clear a tendril of misbehaving hair from her eyes and then shading it from the sun. She was looking for something.

Ponsonby, Del thought sourly.

But no, that peacock was in plain sight up on his quarterdeck, and the girl's roving gaze had found and passed over him. She was clearly looking for something or someone else. She spied Del in his chair and to his surprise he realized, by her sudden smile and the way she started toward him that he, not Ponsonby, was the target of her attention.

Delight, quickly tamped down, swept through him.

He knew better than to get his hopes up. She was only being kind, and probably coming over to thank him for caring for her when she'd grown ill.

Unsteadily, her balance corrected with a lurch to the right and a sudden one to the left, she continued in his direction. Immediately, Del got to his feet and offered her his chair.

"Are you feeling better, Lady Grace?" he asked courteously.

"I am. The ginger you gave me helped settle my stomach, and I'm not feeling dizzy anymore." Her quick, infectious smile appeared. "In fact, I'm actually rather hungry."

"Some people just need adjusting. Others never get over seasickness. I'm heartened to see that you appear to fall into the former category, which bodes well for the rest of this rather short voyage."

She sat down in the chair he'd offered. "Will you join me?" she asked. "We need to discuss... tactics."

"Tactics?"

She cut her gaze to Ponsonby and back, her eyes dancing.

"Oh. Right."

Young Ned was nearby. "I'll get you a chair, sir!" He ran off, only to return a few moments later with one which he placed very close to Lady Grace's.

Del carefully slid the chair away to a more respectable distance and sat down, putting the book on the deck near his foot. By habit, he glanced up at the pennant and the trim of the sails and to his chagrin, found nothing with which he might fault his rival.

Rival?

There, he'd said it.

Or rather, thought it.

For all the good it does you, his mind said. *To her, you are*

149

nothing but a casual friend whose sole purpose is to help her catch the man of her dreams. And you are not that man.

His gaze went to the quarterdeck, part of him hoping, for her sake, that Ponsonby was watching. But he was immersed in conversation with the equally insufferable James Akers.

And Akers was glaring daggers at him and Lady Grace.

What a convolution. The lady pining after Ponsonby, both he and Akers pining after the lady. Del coldly met Akers stare until the other man looked away. He made a mental note to keep an eye on the lieutenant. He had never trusted him.

"So, Captain Lord," Lady Grace was saying. "I have, unfortunately, managed to repel him twice now. First with the Soup Incident and now with the Seasickness one. As a man, do you think I have any chance whatsoever to catch his interest?" She put her hands between her knees and peered at him, smiling, but he could see the desperate hope hidden beneath that cheerful demeanor.

He thought carefully about how he should respond. Ponsonby's squeamishness was not, he felt, becoming of a naval officer. He would like to say as much, but he did not have it in his heart to dash her hopes, nor to appear as churlish as he felt.

"Give him time," he said, somewhat evasively.

"I don't have time!"

"Perhaps when we get to Norfolk, opportunities will present themselves where he'll notice you in the ways you desire," Del said, lamely. *Like the sparkle in your eye and the beauty of your face, the kindness of your heart and the way you make a man feel all light and happy just by being near him.*

Sunlight broke through the clouds and brightened Lady Grace's bonnet. The wind caught its ribbons and she threw back her head to feel both sun and wind on her face, exposing the line of her throat. Del's finger itched to trace that line, to feel its softness.

She brought her head down and caught him looking at her like a love-struck puppy.

And smiled.

"I hope you're right," she said.

"I hope I'm not."

"And why do you say that?"

"Well, if you've driven off your quarry with hairs and an upset stomach, perhaps that leaves me room to convince you that I suffer from no such squeamishness."

"*Captain Lord!*" Her eyes were sparkling.

His lips twitched at her exaggerated affront. "Did I actually say that?"

"You did!"

"Well now, should I apologize?"

"Whatever for?"

"Seems to me you have enough on your plate, without adding to everything you have to digest right now."

"Don't use the word *plate*. Or *digest*. Unless you've got more ginger to give me."

Her laughing gaze met his, and held. He felt his smile growing, and marveled at how naturally the flirtation had come to him when he was normally so stiff, so unwilling to even put a toe across the bounds of propriety, when he habitually kept his thoughts and his heart so... contained.

But she didn't seem to mind.

In fact, there were twin spots of color in her cheeks, and she appeared to be as comfortable in his company as he felt in hers.

"However," he said with forced graveness, "I usually am."

"Usually what?"

"Right. Which means that your captain will not let a hair or an accident involving his shoe stop him from pursuing the most enchanting and beautiful woman that England has yet to produce."

She turned in her chair to look at him. "Why aren't you married, Captain Lord?"

"Well, now, I—"

"The truth."

He drew a breath, rubbed at the corner of his eye, and by habit, gazed up at the sails, checking their draw. "The truth is, Lady Grace, I haven't met the right woman. I keep thinking I've met her, but she always seems to choose another. And so I've stopped trying."

"That is sad."

"Don't feel bad. The right one will come along." He shrugged and smiled, not wanting to spoil things for her. "Someday."

"She will be a very fortunate young lady. I do think I'm a little bit envious."

"No you're not." He forced himself to grin. "You've got your sights firmly set on Ponsonby."

She ignored that with a little shake of her head. "But you are an interesting person. And you have endless patience, both with my little cousins and surely toward life itself. I mean, you must, being Uncle Gray's flag captain. I can't imagine the things you have seen and done. Have you been to lots of places, Captain Lord?"

"In England?"

"Around the world."

"I spent time in duty off the coast of North America. I've seen almost all of the West Indies, a bit of the Orient, and more of the French coastline than I'd care to remember, given the endless monotony of patrolling it."

"And is the Caribbean really as blue as they say it is?"

"Bluer. Times ten."

"Oh, how I should like to see it some day!"

"But it's not really blue. It's more green, actually. Or a perfect blend of them both. You can see the bottom, even if it's eight, ten fathoms down, as though it's no more than a few feet away. The water is that clear."

"Oh!"

"And there are all kinds of colorful fish, and coral. It is quite beautiful there, though also very hot."

"Are you eager to get back?"

He shrugged. "I go where your uncle directs me to take him."

"Have you ever seen gold from a Spanish shipwreck?"

"No."

"Ever had a parrot sit on your shoulder?"

"No."

"Ever seen a pirate?"

Del cut his gaze to Lady Falconer. "Yes."

She saw where he was looking, and laughed. "And now tamed by my uncle, by all accounts."

"I would not bet on that."

She looked at him and cocked her head in that charming, birdlike little way she had. "Do you know, Captain Lord, I think perhaps you should not have told me you'd swoop in and try for me if Captain Ponsonby were out of the picture. Because now I'm wondering if you were serious."

He said nothing.

"*Were* you serious?"

He looked at her, the confusion and despair and indecision in her earnest gaze, and realized an admission would only complicate things for her. It would muddy the waters, push their developing friendship in a direction that quite likely would end it. Women were like that. Hadn't his own sister once told him that it was all but impossible for a lady to be mere friends with a man? That the man almost always developed feelings for her, which then got in the way of the friendship itself since the woman, expecting and wanting nothing more from the man than that friendship, was then forced to end it for the sake of his besotted heart? A besotted heart that always yearned for more than she was able to give?

No. He would not do that to her.

Or, to himself.

But she was still looking at him, awaiting an answer. And Del made a little noise of amusement, shrugged, and gave her a wide and reassuring grin. "Of course not," he said dismissively, hoping she couldn't see behind his false smile. "I'm just trying to get your mind off your worries. I'm sure that your Captain Ponsonby is unaffected by a little splash on his shoe."

"You're certain?"

"Quite."

Their gazes met, and something moved between them— invisible, indiscernible, *there*. Del felt it as a frisson of warmth that passed like lightning through every cell in his body. She must have felt it too, as she colored deeply and looked down. The moment, short as it was, turned suddenly awkward. Del didn't know what to say. What to do. He cleared his throat and made to rise.

Her hand came out, her fingers on his wrist.

"Stay with me, Captain Lord."

He began to sit back down.

And at that moment Sheldon Ponsonby, his handsome face sporting the smile that had conquered the hearts of England's fairer sex wherever he'd gone, came toward them and the moment was lost.

"Lady Grace. Would you do me the honor of taking a turn around the deck with me?"

He offered her an arm and raised her to her feet. She glanced at Del and he nodded, grinned, and mouthed an *I told you so*. The grin immediately faded as they moved away, and Del was left sitting there all by himself, forgotten.

He watched them go, feeling as though he'd been punched in the stomach.

She did not look back.

With a heavy sigh, he retrieved his book and tried to pick up where he'd left off.

But the words, so interesting just minutes before, no longer meant anything.

⚓

CAPTAIN PONSONBY'S ELBOW WAS HARD AND muscular beneath his uniform sleeve, and giddy with excitement, terrified that fate would find some new way to sabotage her hopes and dreams, and most of all just plain confused about the conflict rising within her, Grace allowed him to guide her forward.

She heard him talking about the guns— how quickly they could fire, how far they could hurl a ball, how much each one weighed— and her mind didn't quite hear him because she was still thinking of the moment she'd just shared with Captain Lord. A moment of quiet friendship that had suddenly been so much more, a breaking-through of a desire that she'd been increasingly aware of but unwilling, or perhaps afraid, to acknowledge let alone address, and his startling words. Words which he'd retracted under the excuse of teasing her, an excuse she sensed with all the intuition of her soul, was just that.

An excuse.

Words. And he had said them.

She could not get their recent interaction out of her mind. Could not get his words out of her mind. Could not get *him* out of her mind.

And everything inside her felt suddenly hollow.

I would have liked to stay there with Captain Lord, her heart said. *I was enjoying that conversation. I was enjoying his company*.

But look! It is Captain Ponsonby's arm that you're on. You've been dreaming of this moment forever! replied her head.

And yet the easy laughter she'd shared with Captain Lord, the slow thawing of his rigid exterior, the cautious smile and his brief foray into flirting with her—

All gone up like vapors in the sun the moment Captain Ponsonby had appeared.

Her escort, the dazzling man of her dreams, was still going on about guns.

"Will you fire them for the Falconer children?" she asked suddenly.

"I beg your pardon?"

"Little Anne and Mary. They are apparently quite enamored of guns. I overheard them begging their mother to ask you to fire them."

Captain Ponsonby looked perplexed. "And why would I do that? It seems like an unnecessary waste of powder and resources, firing guns for the entertainment of children."

Something moved unpleasantly in her gut, and Grace realized it wasn't seasickness. It was something more than disappointment but less than anger. Either way, it did not feel good.

"They are your admiral's children, are they not?" she asked, smiling to mask that disappointment for suddenly, Captain Ponsonby wasn't shining quite so brightly.

"They are, but I am not going to fire guns for no reason at all. What if there's a French warship about and I call attention to it with such foolishness? No, my lady. Not a wise idea. Who ever would do such a thing, I wonder?"

"Captain Lord," she said, almost defiantly.

"Did he, now?" Ponsonby's brows rose, and his perfect and handsome face registered disbelief.

"That is what young Ned Falconer told me."

Her escort shrugged and made a dismissive little motion with his hand. "I'm sure he only did so at Sir Graham's directive, and given the endless monotony of a sea crossing, they were all probably quite starved for entertainment. Either way, if Captain Lord wishes to turn a warship into a circus show for the benefit of children, that is his prerogative." The captain flicked a bit of spray off the barrel of one of the guns. "As for me, I will save my vessel's resources for when it really matters. Shall we continue on, my lady?"

"Yes," she said a bit numbly, and turning her head she saw Delmore Lord quite a distance behind her now, his tall form filling the chair, his head with its noble nose and unruly dark hair curling out from beneath his hat, bent in perusal of his book.

Delmore Lord, who appeared to like children much more than Captain Ponsonby did.

Delmore Lord, who didn't think that firing guns and expending powder was a waste of his vessel's resources at all.

Delmore Lord, sitting all alone back there with an empty chair beside him.

Lady Grace Fairchild looked at that empty chair and something stirred painfully within her heart.

That chair shouldn't be empty.

I should still be sitting in it. Beside him.

"And this," Captain Ponsonby continued, sweeping his arm forwards, "is the waist of the ship, where the ship's boat is kept along with spare spars. It's the place where the men..."

His voice droned on, but Lady Grace Fairchild was no longer paying attention.

She could not get that empty chair out of her mind.

SHE WASN'T THE ONLY ONE WHOSE HEART WAS churning.

Lieutenant James Akers stood near the helm, his eyes hard with anger. He had watched his captain frowning as he'd spied Lady Grace occupying the chair beside Delmore Lord, and telling James to assume the quarterdeck, had headed over to the pair.

Akers knew his captain well enough to know that Ponsonby did not welcome challenges to the things he took for granted, including the hearts of the women that came in and out of his life and who salivated after him like bitches in heat. He would not tolerate competition, especially from a dead bore like Captain Lord.

Damn that chit, Akers thought savagely.

Though he was in possession of both, he didn't need good ears or eyesight to hear the words that passed between them or see the joyous smile that broke out on the girl's face when Ponsonby offered his elbow. He'd hoped she'd decline him, prove herself immune to him when every other woman Ponsonby ever encountered could not resist him. He'd hoped she'd stay there with Captain Lord, but why would she? The flag captain was stiffer than a stick, lacking the easy, confident charm and sheer charisma that was so much a part of Sheldon Ponsonby. She was probably grateful to be rescued. Grateful to get away from the company of such a snoozer. Still, such rationalization did nothing to temper Akers's jealousy, his anger that his captain was bestowing such attention on another. Someone who hadn't known him as long as he, James Akers had done, someone who would never be as loyal, as devoted, as steadfast as he had been to the very best man in the world. A man who had plucked him from abuse and torment all those years ago, befriended him, continued to care about him even now.

No, Akers was not willing to share.

Or see one iota of Ponsonby's attention transfer itself to some silly bit of fluff who would not only break his heart, but take Ponsonby away from him. Because unlike the many other women the captain had shown favor to over the years, Lady Grace presented a real and serious threat, and there was no denying it.

Fear, not unlike what he'd felt that long ago day at Eton, suddenly chilled him. Where would he be if Ponsonby wed the chit? Would Ponsonby care about him anymore with a wife and surely children, to occupy his time and interests? Who would protect him from his well-bred peers, the very unfairness of the system?

Nobody.

He would be alone.

Alone. Just like he'd been all those years ago at Eton before Ponsonby had reached a hand down to help him.

Akers clenched his fists, wishing there was something he could hit.

Nearby, the sailing master murmured something to the helmsman. Both laughed.

Akers rounded on them. "What was that?"

"Oh, nothing, sir. We just noticed how *interesting* the young lady became to the captain once he learned she's got a big dowry."

"And what business is that of yours?"

"Well, we heard talk, and—"

"You heard talk! *Talk!* You'll speak no more of it, nor gossip about matters you know nothing about. Is that understood? *Is it?*"

"Aye, sir," said the helmsman, touching his forelock, but his eyes had gone sullen and Akers, tormented by thoughts of what the man might be thinking, was suddenly filled with anxiety and rage.

He shot a last warning glare at Nickerson then went to the rail. No wonder Ponsonby had come fully about when it came to Lady Grace Fairchild. It wasn't just Ponsonby's pride trying to usurp and defeat a perceived rival. Oh, no. It was a more disturbing reality. A more terrifying one. Lady Grace Fairchild was a pretty young woman with a heavy dowry and a family connection to a powerful admiral. What more could an ambitious and career-minded officer want in a wife?

He determined to find a way to remove her before she could become even more of a threat to his friendship with Ponsonby.

Because Sheldon Ponsonby was *his*. *His* friend, *his* captain, *his* protector.

And James Akers always kept what belonged to him.

❧ 22 ❧

Grace spent a restless night in the tiny cubbyhole of a cabin, sharing the space with Polly, and neither of them got much sleep. Polly made some chatter about the sea voyage, voicing her gratitude that she hadn't yet been seasick and oh, didn't Captain Lord's manservant cut a handsome figure? As Grace had tossed and turned in the darkness, Polly had confessed that she had taken the trouble to learn the man's name. "Jimmy Thorne, milady. And he's Captain Lord's coxswain."

"What is that?"

"Don't know, milady. I'm still learning all this seafaring stuff, just like you. But I'll find out, I will!"

In the morning they were off Norfolk and well into the North Sea. Pushed along by a brisk westerly they followed the coast, changed tack and by early afternoon were in The Wash, their destination the bustling seaport of King's Lynn.

Captain Ponsonby had a spring in his step and was all smiles. His cheerful demeanor helped her forget his reaction when Grace had cast up her accounts all over his shoes the day before. And that conversation they'd had, where he'd expressed contempt for the idea of firing his guns for the benefit of children... that too seemed distant as well, as did her disappointment with him.

He'd probably been in a bad mood. Or perhaps he didn't care for a landlubber suggesting what he should do. Either way, that had been yesterday and today was today. She would think no more of it and instead, recklessly stuffed it to the back of her mind and bade it to stay there.

Not that there weren't other concerns. Yes, he'd given her a tour of the decks yesterday and she, enamored of being in his presence, had absorbed little of what he'd said. Oh, gun and sail and wind had come out of the conversation, and he had dutifully inquired about her health following her bout with *mal de mer*, but he never crossed the line from proper host to flirtatious potential suitor, and that had Grace more than a little worried.

She mentioned it to Captain Lord, her chosen confidante.

"I don't believe he really thinks all that much of me," she lamented as the frigate, her mainsail and foresail already doused, began to lose way as it nosed farther and farther into The Wash. She looked wistfully at Captain Ponsonby as he directed operations from his quarterdeck. "And now I suppose he will stay here with the ship."

"Perhaps absence will make his heart grow fonder."

"Perhaps absence will make his heart grow forgetful."

"I think you're worrying too much."

"What can I do, Captain Lord?"

"You could find a way to get him ashore."

"How?"

He shrugged. "Well, you could ask Sir Graham to suggest to him that he take the opportunity to visit his sister. After all, the former Letitia Ponsonby is married to Lord Weybourne and they live near my brother and his family. That would score points with Ponsonby, should he find out that you advocated for him."

"What a great idea!"

Del just shrugged again. *More the fool am I*, he thought. But it was hopeless, anyhow. It always had been. Lady Grace's attention was quite firmly on his charismatic blond rival. She saw nobody else.

Certainly not him.

Swallowing his bile over it, he watched her move toward Sir Graham who was relaxing with his family some distance away, and have a word with him. Saw his admiral nod and, a moment later, beckon a midshipman to him who was quickly dispatched to the helm to inform Ponsonby of his decision.

So much for that, Del thought, in defeat. He moved to the rail and stared down at the water, hearing the commands from forward as the anchor party prepared to drop the hook.

He took off his hat, raked his hands through his unruly curls, and gazed unseeingly at the low, flat marshes that surrounded the estuary. The houses and chimney pots of nearby King's Lynn were in shadow beneath passing clouds, the air thick with salt and the smell of the marshes. A tern flew past, its long elegant wings carving a path through the sky. Del looked away, and back down into the water below.

His heart hurt. He had tried to guard it, tried to keep it safely contained in its little box and once again, he had failed. His attraction to Lady Grace was no different from what he'd felt for Rhiannon Evans, and he cursed himself for allowing himself to be vulnerable yet again. But no. This was worse. Worse, because what he felt for Lady Grace far surpassed what he'd felt for Rhiannon Evans, eclipsed it, even. And why not? Rhiannon had never involved him in a plot, never spent any significant time with him, never asked him about his life with any real interest, and his admiration for her had been from afar. She had chosen another, just as Lady Grace had done, and by now he should have known better. But loneliness did that to a person, didn't it? Especially when paired with imagination and want. He was starved for female companionship, he wanted to start a family of his own, and he felt increasingly left behind, watching his peers all take wives while he seemed to be unlucky in love.

"Captain Lord?"

"What can I do for you, Ned?"

The youngster's lower lip stuck out and he looked as defeated as Del felt. "I don't want to go spend a week at some dumb horse farm with a bunch of people I don't know. I'm sorry, I know that Colin Lord is your older brother, and that he was Papa's flag captain at one time, just like you are... but how boring is that all going to be? I want to stay here, aboard a ship."

"We'll find something to do," Del offered lamely, and wondered much the same thing.

"What? I'm sure I'll end up having to watch Mary and Anne and keep them out of trouble. Mama is busy with the baby. At least at Ruscombe Hall, they had a pond with a boat in it."

"Well, as I understand it, this horse farm is near the sea... perhaps we can find someone with a boat so can make our escape for a few hours."

"Don't tell me you're not looking forward to this either?"

Del allowed himself the tiniest of grins. "I would never tell you that."

One corner of the boy's mouth turned up in a knowing smile. He nodded, mollified. Then, modeling the ways of his father's flag captain, he straightened his spine and adopted the same pensive pose, hands clasped behind his back and his thoughts his own as they both watched the anchor splash down into the harbor. Around them, the frigate bustled with sudden commands and activity. A boat was let down. Sailors rigged a bosun's chair for the women. A side party was mustered, and the shrill call of pipes rent the air as the admiral left the ship. Lady Falconer, as nimble as any British tar, followed him and with a little nod from Del, Ned did too, shunning the "girls' way down," as he put it, that was the rope sling.

The shunned contraption, however, was in full use. The Falconer's nanny, the babe wrapped tightly in her arms, was next, and then the twins, both of whom loudly protested such an undignified exit from the ship when their parents and brother had taken the "real" way off. Grace, dubiously eyeing the rope sling, was next to go. Del, still at the rail, curled his fingers into his palms and watched the sailors' actions with a critical eye. He was just about to step forward to help her when Akers brushed past him, rudely bumping his shoulder.

"Beg your pardon, *sir*," the lieutenant said, barely glancing at him. "Captain asked me to assist the lady."

"Are you so damned clumsy that you can't walk a straight line from the quarterdeck to the side without knocking into a person, Akers?"

Akers gave him a nasty glare. "No, sir, but from my observations the lady is, and my captain doesn't want her to come to any mischief."

Del felt a muscle twitch in his jaw. He could make an issue of it if he wanted, but this was not his ship nor his lieutenant, and he was not so hot-headed that he would chastise the man over the incident or the blatant disrespect he was displaying to a superior officer.

Akers went to the side, purposely turning his back to Del in unspoken insult as he helped get Lady Grace into the sling, then scrambled down the side to the waiting boat. There, the Falconers had already found seats. The girl was hoisted up and out, her gloved hands gripping the ropes, her smile a bit strained as she looked down at her feet swinging out over the water so far below. A gust of wind batted at the hem of her skirts and wrapped it around her ankles, defining their slim perfection. Del's throat went dry. He watched her for a moment and turned abruptly for the entry port so that he could be in the boat when she arrived there.

It was a relief to be off Ponsonby's command and into the smaller vessel. Akers was already there, looking up at Lady Grace as she was lowered down. There was something in his eyes that Del didn't like. Something sinister. Something hard. Something ugly.

That one bears watching, he reminded himself, and took a position so that he would be the one to assist the lady, not Akers.

The bosun's chair and its precious cargo reached the boat. The girl's cheeks were flushed a pretty pink, her eyes sparkling. Del took a firm grasp of her arm to steady her as she was released from the sling and helped settle her onto a thwart, choosing a spot near the bow where she'd be out of the way of the oarsmen.

He could feel Akers's gaze burning a hole in his back.

"Oh, Captain Lord!" She tilted her head back, shading her eyes from the emerging sun as it found its way past the brim of her bonnet and struck her in the face. "This is going to be great fun!" And then, leaning closer, so close that her shoulder brushed his own and he caught the tantalizing essence of lavender and soap, and even the sweet scent of her skin, she whispered, "When do you think Captain Ponsonby will be joining us?"

"As soon as he secures his ship, I should think."

She was quiet for a moment. And then: "You don't like Captain Ponsonby very much, do you?"

"Why would you say that?"

She shrugged. "When I say his name, you tense up and your face changes. It's quite noticeable, really, though you probably don't realize it. Did something happen between the two of you at some point, to make you dislike him?"

"Captain Ponsonby is a fine man," he said tightly.

"That's not what I asked."

"And I am not one to speak ill of another officer." *Even if I'm more than a wee bit jealous, as Mama would say.*

She studied him for a moment, her head slightly cocked to one side, her eyes beginning to sparkle and the corners of her mouth lifting in that way that, indeed, made him "tense up." It meant that she was noticing something. Something about him.

He decided to deflect whatever was about to come out of that pretty bowed mouth that everything about him wanted to kiss senseless.

"So," he said briskly, "Are you feeling quite restored to health, Lady Grace?"

She regarded him for a long, thoughtful moment longer, and then something in her eyes changed. The sparkle went out of them and a shadow moved across her fine blue irises. A flash of pity. Sorrow. Despair. He couldn't quite pin it down.

But Grace knew exactly what she was feeling.

Sympathy. Regret. And a shattering realization.

Captain Lord was jealous.

Not of Sheldon Ponsonby himself, but the fact that he was the one who owned her heart. And he had meant every word of the flirtatious things he'd so quickly denounced, indeed even brushed off, the previous day.

The knowledge sobered her, complicating the situation and stealing the joy out of what had been shaping up to be a fine and greatly-anticipated afternoon.

I must not flirt with him. I must pull back, pull back even from my friendship with him, as he's only getting ideas that will lead to his own heartbreak. He is kind and gallant and good. I can't do that to him.

The boat began to move. Her gaze moved to the

smartly-dressed oarsmen with their jaunty hats and ker-
chiefs, their arms all moving in unison as their powerful
strokes sped the boat to shore. Water slid past them,
the bow slicing through the gentle swells and every so
often sending spray up into the boat. Her skirts were
suddenly wet. Captain Lord took off his coat and offered it to her with a word that she should cover her lap
with it.

She declined.

There was the landing growing closer, now rising
above them, its slippery wooden stairs ascending from
the water.

Shouted commands. Akers trying to impress Sir
Graham with the smart precision of his oarsmen. One
of the twins starting a war with the other one (Grace
could not tell them apart very well) about who would
get to go up first. Ned trying to mediate before relin-
quishing the task to the nanny. The nanny also failing,
until Maeve Falconer herself had a word with the two,
which cut short the rising argument but did nothing to
quell the glares of promised retribution between the
two combatants. The boat was made secure, bobbing in
the swells. Grace could smell the mix of salt and mud
and briny dankness, of wood that never had the chance
to dry, and on the breeze, the scent of a working ship-
yard — tar and lumber, paint and hemp.

Sir Graham, one of the twins tucked securely under
his arm, went up the steps. His wife followed him,
holding the baby. The other twin hooked her little arms
around Ned's neck, and riding piggyback up the stairs,
stuck her tongue out at her sister as they reached
the top.

"That's not *faaaaair*!" screamed the one her father
had carried up.

"It is too, *you* got to go first so *I* got a piggyback!"

"Papa, I want a piggyback! If she had one, I get to
have one!"

"You can't!"

"*Papaaa!*"

Grace stole a glance at Captain Lord. He had looked away so that his admiral, trying in desperation to ward off yet another fight, would not see his helpless grin.

Grace caught his eye and returned the grin.

Yes, Captain Lord liked children.

The fight above them escalated, and Captain Lord's strong, muscular hand came up to push helplessly at his mouth, as though trying to wipe away his rising humor.

"We might as well go up and give your uncle some reinforcements," he said. "The insult to young Mary will not be soon forgotten."

Indeed, young Mary's indignant shrieks were drowning out the screams of the gulls now wheeling above.

"I don't know what the two of you are laughing about," snapped Akers, just behind them. "That racket is giving me a headache. A most hideous display of spoiled indulgence, if you ask me!"

"Nobody did ask you," Captain Lord snapped back, and reached a hand out to Grace.

The stairs leading out of the water were too narrow for him to accompany her up them. He bade her to sit still and climbed over the gunwale, taking care to keep his shoes from the water swirling on the lowest step. Already, the incoming tide was swallowing the strip of wood and reaching for the next one.

Grace watched him go. Sat patiently as he helped Polly out of the boat and up the stairs. She felt the enmity radiating from Lieutenant Akers, the sullen contempt in which his oarsmen held him. She could just see Akers out of the corner of her eye. His narrow face was pinched, his lips cast in a perpetual sneer. But Captain Lord was above her now, reaching down to help her up the steps. Grace stood up, her balance unsteady, and took his outstretched hand, feeling it firmly clasp hers.

She allowed him to steady her, and as she took that long step from the boat and over the gunwale and onto the pier, trying vainly to keep her balance, it happened.

A tugging, the sound of a sharp, rending tear, and then a sudden release. Cool air swept up the back of her legs and she lurched upwards into Captain Lord's arms. She heard a cry of horror and realized it was coming from her own mouth.

"Oh!!!"

The gown had snagged on something, and everything she owned from her ankles to her upper thighs was suddenly bared to the grinning tars in the boat below.

D el immediately saw what had happened.

As he'd reached down and grasped Lady Grace's small, gloved hand, as he'd held her steady as she'd been about to step from the boat to the stairs, her skirts had caught on something in the boat.

He was quick to act. Quick to get her safely onto the narrow step below him, quick to doff his coat, quick to let his mariner's sharp gaze sweep the thwarts, the hull, to see what she might have caught her hem on.

Nothing.

He glared hard at the tars in the boat, one or two of whom were smirking; to a man, they all turned away, recognizing his authority.

And then his gaze settled on Akers.

Akers, who returned his stare with mocking triumph.

Beside him, Lady Grace crowded close, desperate to preserve what was left of her pride and modesty. Del covered her with his coat, his temples pounding with building fury. He may not have seen what had happened to the lady's gown as she'd moved to join him on the stairs, but Captain Delmore Lord was half-Irish, and he had feelings about things. Feelings that were, almost always, correct.

And as he looked at Akers's barely-contained smirk, Del suddenly knew what the man had done.

He saw the raging contempt there. The loathing. And he knew.

To her credit, Lady Grace managed to keep her head high, and despite the humiliation of the moment, bravely attempted to joke about it.

"There I go again, always so clumsy! How you must tire of me, Captain Lord!"

But Del barely heard her. He was thinking of Akers and his oarsmen and knowing that each and every one of them was savoring the memory of Lady Grace's legs suddenly revealed to their prurient stares.

All of them except Akers whose tastes, Del also intuited, did not run toward women at all.

Rage filled him. He wanted to wrap the girl in his arms and carry her away from all humiliation, insults, indignation. He wanted to protect her against everything the world and the more base creatures who inhabited it, threw at her. And clumsy or not, he wanted to protect her against herself.

Mostly, though, he wanted to put his fist into Akers's face with force enough to break every tooth in his head.

He took a firm hold of the girl's elbow as they traversed the wet and slippery stairs. She looked small and lost within his coat.

Sir Graham was waiting at the landing.

Frowning.

An unhappy admiral was never a good thing. But Del would not share his suspicions about what Akers had done, quite so publicly.

"What just happened, Del?"

"The lady caught her dress on something in the boat, sir."

Sir Graham's frown deepened.

"Grace?"

"I don't know, Uncle Gray. But Captain Lord was quick to lend me his coat. It's all right. I'm decently covered, and all in one piece."

The admiral's eyes, the same deep azure as his niece's, went to Del's and held. Hard.

What happened down there?

I don't know, sir. But I will do my best to find out.

The admiral's sharp gaze moved to the boat and its occupants, and narrowed. Akers, preparing his men to head back to the frigate, did not see that hard perusal, but Del did.

Vice Admiral Sir Graham Falconer didn't have an Irish bone in his body.

But even he had intuited that something wasn't quite right here, that Akers was somehow involved.

The admiral looked back at his flag captain.

"Keep an eye on things. A close eye," he said flatly.

"Aye, sir. You can depend on it."

⚓

FOLLOWING THE HORRIFYING INCIDENT WITH HER gown, it had taken every ounce of Grace's courage to maintain her composure, and as they all waited to get into the coaches that would take them out to Burnham and the horse farm owned by Captain Lord's brother Colin and his wife Ariadne, she had time to wonder, indeed, just what *had* happened back there.

She was prone to accidents that resulted in embarrassment.

She was prone to mishaps that resulted in mortification.

But this... this had been something more, and her suspicions were confirmed by Captain Lord's entire demeanor.

He was sullen, preoccupied and brooding. His jaw was tense, the line of his mouth, hard. He smiled when he addressed her, but she sensed a bristling and danger-ously contained fury within him and a remoteness that did not invite conversation.

Their trunks arrived on the shoulders of several burly seamen. Captain Ponsonby was with them, looking no less diminished without a quarterdeck under his feet. Lieutenant Akers immediately left them to join his captain, occasionally directing a subtle smirk in Grace's direction that confused her all the more. An ostler brought a pair of horses, both tacked up and ready to go. The admiral and his family, the twins making faces at each other behind their mother's back, lined up to get into the first coach. Word had spread of their arrival and a crowd of townspeople had gathered, their faces curious and excited. Sailors and fishermen, artisans, shopkeepers and vendors, respectable wives and daughters, even children— all of them were eager to catch a glimpse of Sir Graham Falconer, one of Eng-land's heroes. Grace could not help feeling a certain pride in her uncle. In Captain Ponsonby as well, who was at his radiant and compelling best as he raised his hat to acknowledge the crowd's excitement and praise. And then she looked at Captain Lord standing silently nearby, his civilian clothing making him invisible, in-significant, to the onlookers.

How must he feel to be so overlooked?

Was he a hero, too?

Indignation seized her. Of course he was a hero! *Her* hero! An overwhelming wave of protectiveness rose within her. Whatever he might've done for England mattered little compared to what he had done for *her*.

He saved my life. Certainly once, maybe even twice.

She adjusted Captain Lord's tailcoat around herself, grateful that it afforded her decency, if not proper fash-ion. As soon as they got to their destination, she would change into a fresh gown.

The first coach rattled off, carrying the Falconers.

She moved with Polly to the second one, sucking the heavy salt air deeply into her lungs as it drove in off the nearby marshes. Captain Ponsonby and Lieutenant Akers were already astride the two horses. Funny, Grace mused, she'd been so engaged in pondering Captain Lord that she hadn't even thought to watch Ponsonby swing up into the saddle. Now, he made a splendid sight as the bay mare pranced beneath him, tossing her head and eager to be off.

Their coach awaited. The team sweated in the sun, their tails swishing at flies, their pungent odor familiar and sweet. The steps were let down, and Captain Lord offered his elbow. Grace was glad it was a mild day, for he was now in shirt and waistcoat and she would not have wanted him to be cold because of her. She tried not to notice how dark his overly-long, wildly curling hair looked against his white shirt and necktie, how neat and precise he was in his dressing. There was something solid and reassuring about him, as though he were a man that a loose end would never dare trouble, a man whose natural competence was something that he, and perhaps those who knew him well, took for granted. A reassuring discipline. All in its place.

Right now, still a bit shaken from her incident in the boat, Grace was grateful for that natural competence. Grateful for the fact he positioned himself behind her, blocking her mortifying dishabille from others.

Grateful for *him*.

And to him.

She settled herself on the squab and waited while he handed Polly up to join her. Then he ducked in, taking the seat opposite, and closed the door.

That pleased Grace.

"No horse for you?" she asked chidingly, trying to soften the tension that clung to him. The anger she couldn't understand.

"No."

She couldn't blame him. He was not the accomplished horseman that Ponsonby was. Perhaps he didn't want to suffer the inevitable comparison to a man he already seemed to despise.

He took off his hat and laid it in his lap. The confines of the coach were suddenly quite small, and Captain Lord seemed to fill almost all of it. His long legs intruded into the area her own occupied, though he tried to minimize their impact by slanting them off to one side. He cast his gaze out the window as they waited for the coach to get underway.

Polly caught her eye. She, too, noticed his dark and dangerous mood and quietly shook her head in warning.

Best to leave him alone, milady.

Grace ignored the silent advice. "Are you all right, Captain Lord?" she asked softly.

He gaze swung from the window and to her, his gray eyes coming into focus and back to the moment. They were hard. Cold. Unsmiling. "Am *I* all right?" he asked harshly.

"Well yes, you."

"You are a kind soul to show such concern for my welfare when it's yours that has suffered a grievous insult!"

"My welfare is quite fine. It's my gown that has suffered the insult."

He said nothing and just returned his glare to the marshes outside the window.

"However," Grace prompted, "you can ask me about my welfare if it will restore you to a better mood."

"I was not aware that you'd noticed my mood."

"I notice a lot of things, Captain Lord."

"So do I."

"What do you mean by that?"

"Nothing." His lips were clamped into a hard line, and she saw a muscle clench in his jaw. And then he turned the full force of those gray eyes upon her, eyes that were so chilled that the color had become like ice — crystalline and cold and hard— and she caught the controlled emotion in his voice.

"I failed you," he said with unbridled fury. "I should have done a better job at protecting you."

"Protecting me? From what, myself?" She grinned. "I have a history of accidents. You should know that by now."

He just looked at her, and she could not know that Del was thinking a lot of things, none of which he was inclined to say, none of which he was inclined to share, none of which were worth putting on her, a gently-bred lady who didn't need something more to worry about when he, as her self-appointed protector, should be worrying about them for her.

And doing something about it.

That was no accident, he wanted to retort. *It was deliberate sabotage and I'll be paying a visit to that despicable lout before the day is ended, mark my words.*

She was watching him, innocent and unaware. Waiting.

"Well?" she persisted. "Protecting me from what?"

"Everything. It can be treacherous, getting out of an unstable boat and onto stairs such as those."

"And you had a firm grip on me."

"And still you came to mishap."

"So my gown got caught on the oarlock or something. It's not such a big thing, is it?"

Del looked away, drumming his fingers on his kneecap in rising agitation.

"I didn't trip, nor did I fall into the sea, and here we are, safely on our way to this horse farm of your brother's." She looked at him in that characteristic, bird-like way she had, of leaning her head to one side and regarding him with eyes as bright as a sparrow's. "Is he very much like you, Captain Lord?"

"Are you trying to take my thoughts off what happened back there?"

She grinned. The coach tilted a bit as trunks were loaded, and he heard Jimmy Thorne loudly talking to the driver and volunteering his services against highwaymen, thieves and the like— no doubt for the sake of impressing Polly.

"I might be," she allowed. "Or, I might simply be wishing to learn more about your family, since we'll be spending time with them. Aunt Maeve says that your brother keeps lots of animals. I like animals. Especially cats. Well, that's not quite fair, because I like dogs, too. And horses. Your brother raises racehorses, does he not?"

"Yes, purported to be the fastest horses in the world."

"Oh! I wonder if I might ride one!"

Del shut his eyes and rubbed at his temple with two fingers.

"What?" she asked playfully.

"Given your propensity for mishap, I don't think that's a good idea. These are spirited animals, and—"

"Pah! I'm a confident rider with an excellent seat. Perhaps you might join me, Captain? Take me for a tour of this estate?"

"To be quite honest, Lady Grace, I've never been to my brother's home, so I'm not sure I'm the best person to show you around it. I was at sea when he married and moved to Norfolk. I've not been back to England in some years. I haven't even met his wife or children. It will be good to see Colin again, but I'd also like to visit my parents and sisters in Hampshire before we head back to Barbados."

At the mention of Barbados, something in her face fell. It was ever so slight, but Del noticed it.

She gave him no time to ponder it. Immediately she

was right back to her perky, chipper self. "Your parents live in Hampshire?"

"Yes."

"Have they always?"

"For the most part. My father is a retired admiral so he was off at sea a lot, but the family pile is near Hambledon, in the downs."

"Did you grow up there?"

"I did. Partially at least, as I've reached an age where I can say that the first half of my life was spent at home and the second half at sea, in almost equal proportions."

"And how old *are* you?"

Despite the righteous anger he felt on her behalf, he felt himself softening. It was impossible to be in a bad mood with Lady Grace around. Impossible to resist her attempts to pull him out of that bad mood. Now, a smile tugged at his mouth, and he was helpless to prevent it.

"You're asking my age?"

Her eyes were sparkling. "I am."

"I'd be crucified if I asked that question of a lady."

"Well, you're not a lady, so I can ask it. Besides, I don't mind if you ask my age. In fact, I'll spare you the trouble. I've recently celebrated my twenty-first birthday. Your turn."

"Twenty-nine."

"Oh!"

"Oh?"

"I, um, thought you were... older, that's all."

"Milady!" Polly gasped.

Older? "And why do you say that?" Del asked rather stiffly, trying to staunch the bleeding wound she had just rent in his vanity.

"Because you are so very, *very* serious. As if you wear the weight of the world on your shoulders. It makes you seem much older, really."

He blinked, not quite expecting that.

"Would you agree?"

"Well, I—"

"Polly, what do you think?"

"Oh, milady, I couldn't begin to offer an opinion."

Del tugged at his mouth, at the helpless grin that lurked there. "I will concede a victory," he said slowly, "But *do* give me a bit of leeway. My father had certain expectations of his sons, and both he and the Navy were strict disciplinarians. When one has a large ship to oversee, and the safety and welfare of everyone aboard it including the admiral, rests on one's shoulders, there's not much room for frivolity."

"Oh, I'm not advocating for frivolity," she said brightly and with a little flutter of her hand. "That would be most unbecoming in a man, let alone a naval officer. But I might have to find some ways to get you to... well, to relax, just a bit," she mused, tapping a finger against her mouth while allowing her eyes to sparkle with a sudden impishness as her gaze lifted to his. Her voice gentled. "It's not good to take yourself so seriously, you know. Life becomes much more interesting and fun when you do not."

He pondered that, still oddly relieved that it was his demeanor that had aged him in her eyes, not his looks.

"Well," he said, "That is good to hear, then. I was about to start checking for gray hairs."

She laughed. Despite himself he allowed a little smile as well, and something moved between them, warm and intimate and impossible to ignore. She blushed and looked down. He remained gazing at her for another moment, admiring the curve of her cheek, the way her fine blue eyes had shone as she'd playfully flirted with him and drawn him out of his bad mood.

She looked up then, caught him gazing at her with fondness and admiration, and this time, did not look away.

"Well," she finally said, holding his gaze. "I got you smiling again."

"So you did."

A moment later the vehicle dipped as both Jimmy Thorne and the driver clambered aboard. He clucked to his team, the coach gave a sudden jolt and began to move.

They were on their way.

❧ 24 ❧

So she'd thought of him as *old*.

Old!

Just how *old* did his demeanor make him appear? To her? To others? Had Connor Merrick been right all along after all? Connor who'd worked hard to get him to "live a little," mocking his strict adherence to protocol, uniform code, the expectations of a Royal Navy officer?

Connor who, having worn Del down and found a hole in his rigid comportment one hot and sweltering Caribbean afternoon when the idea had finally become too delicious to resist, finally convinced him to climb the schooner *Kestrel*'s rigging and take turns leaping into the sea just for fun?

Fun.

Fun?

He pondered that. And wondered if "fun" and "old" were compatible, and if the removal of the former from one's life produced the latter, because he certainly wasn't in the business of seeking "fun."

But...

Old?

How old might Lady Grace have thought him to be if he didn't carry such a heavy weight of responsibility, if he were not modeling everything he'd been groomed to believe an officer should be? If he, like Connor, behaved with unfettered abandon?

And had *fun*?

That afternoon when Connor had challenged him to leap from the rigging seemed like another lifetime ago. Indeed, it had only been several months.

Two people now, who were advising him to... to what? Go soft? Behave like a young lad? A man without responsibilities?

What, exactly, did they mean?

He sat there wondering whether he should be grateful for this mutual observation or irritated, and directed his gaze out the window so as to give his thoughts free rein to decide.

And saw Akers.

Irritation won, and he forgot about any fleeting inclinations to improve himself.

Just outside, Akers was on a chestnut gelding and chatting to Ponsonby. They were laughing at something, sitting their horses with an ease that Del knew he lacked. Anger chewed at the ends of his carefully cultivated aplomb. He turned away, the good mood that Lady Grace had coaxed from him too fragile to withstand the sight of that sniveling little snot just outside. It had taken everything he had not to confront Akers right there on the landing after Lady Grace had been so unforgivably humiliated. But to accuse the man, to call him out in front of an audience that included the victim herself, would cause the kind of scene that Del did not wish to make.

He was patient.

He would deal with this matter at the right time and place.

His chance finally came when the procession neared Burnham Thorpe, birthplace of the famous Lord Nelson whose acquaintance Del had never had the great fortune to make. It was also the family seat of the

Earl of Weybourne whose newly-wedded wife, Letitia, was the sister of Captain Ponsonby himself.

The countess was working a frisky adolescent colt on a longe line, and when she saw them coming, she hurried toward them, the colt in tow. She was vivacious and bright and invited them all in for refreshment but Sir Graham, cooped up in a hot, noisy coach with the twins fighting over who would be the first to ride one of the famous Norfolk Thoroughbreds, was eager to be on his way.

"We'll come by for a proper visit before we leave, I promise you," he said kindly.

But it was obviously the last stop for Ponsonby. He dismounted, exchanged a few words with the admiral through the open window and leading his horse, headed down the drive with his sister, laughing with her as Akers, still mounted, followed just behind.

Del's cool gray eyes missed little, and even from inside the coach he saw the angle of Akers head and knew the lieutenant's gaze was lingering after Ponsonby as his superior walked in front of him.

Del reached for the door handle.

"Captain Lord?"

"I'll be but a moment, Lady Grace."

He opened the door, stepped down, and strode briskly toward the retreating trio. None were aware of Del's swift approach from behind.

"Lieutenant Akers," Del said coldly. "A word with you in private, if you please."

The lieutenant turned and just looked at him, one brow raised, the corner of his mouth turning up in a faint sneer. "Did I forget something, *Captain?*"

"No, but I did."

Ponsonby and the countess had paused as well. The captain's face registered confusion but being a gentleman, he allowed Del the moment he requested without questioning it. Del stalked to the shade of a nearby sycamore, drawing Akers well out of earshot of the others. There, he turned to face the man, who was quick to get in the first word.

"I do not understand why, *sir*, you must lead me all the way over to this spot when whatever it is you have forgotten, could have been conveyed to me earlier. Why, to go to such measures to—"

"I saw what you did to Lady Grace and her gown."

The words were delivered with the cold challenge of a drawn sword, and something in Akers's face changed. A momentary panic, of alarm even, and then the smiling facade moved in once more.

"And just what do you think you saw?"

"You stepped on her hem when she was about to get out of the boat. You did it on purpose, to humiliate her in front of Ponsonby and to possibly cause an accident."

"And why would I do that?"

"Do I really need to spell it out for you?"

"Perhaps you should."

Del stared at him coldly. "You perceive Lady Grace as a threat, don't you?"

Akers blinked. Then his face suffused with color, a scarlet that was on the verge of going purple, and sweat stood out at the roots of his hair.

"What—what madness!"

"Is it?"

Akers's hand dropped to his sword, and he struggled to maintain his air of ennui. His voice became high with fury. "Your eyes deceive you, Captain Lord. And your tongue, unless it delivers an apology for not one but now two insults, will be your undoing."

"Let us not waste words, then. My second will be calling upon yours later this evening."

"And he will find him right here where we're standing."

Del did not bow to the other man, nor was that courtesy afforded him. He simply turned his back and walked away. By the time he got back into the coach, he was relaxed and smiling.

"What did you say to Lieutenant Akers?" Lady Grace asked, her blue eyes wide with confusion.

"I was merely confirming a breakfast date with the fellow," Del said, and turned his gaze back to the distant pastures as the driver chirped to the team and the coach got underway once more.

THE BREEZE OFF THE NEARBY MARSHES WAS A RESPITE from the day's heat, carrying the scent of salt and sea grass, and it blew gaily threw the open windows of the coach. Grace had not been raised near the sea though she had once visited it, and she found the odor heady and exhilarating. She leaned close to the window and closing her eyes in bliss, inhaled deeply.

"I could never get tired of this smell," she said happily.

She was keenly aware of Captain Lord on the seat opposite her... and so was every cell in her body. Strange, that, when the prickly tingles she felt at his nearness were ones she'd expected to feel with Captain Ponsonby. Indeed, she'd watched the handsome blond naval officer walking off with his lieutenant and Lady Weybourne, but the hollow emptiness she'd expected to feel at his departure had been curiously late in coming.

In fact, it hadn't come at all.

But there was Captain Lord on the seat across from her. His manner, while polite and cordial, seemed withdrawn, as though he had a lot on his mind. He was looking out the window, watching the fields and hedgerows as they passed them by, the distant blue line of the North Sea as they crested a rise. Though he had one wrist draped over his knee, the other resting along the seat back, the tension that had clung to him earlier had returned.

"Captain Lord?"

"Yes, Lady Grace?"

"Are you feeling quite well?"

He seemed to come back to himself and smiled a little. "I confess that I find coach travel rather tedious."

"You're not seasick— coach-sick?— I hope?"

His smile spread, became genuine. "No, of course not. And current company makes the journey quite enjoyable even if the endless swaying and rocking does not."

"That is a sweet thing to say," she said, meeting his eyes with a little grin of her own.

Again, that flash of heat. Of *connection*. Her nipples tingled and she folded her arms across her chest to contain the feeling, surprised and a little shocked.

Did he feel that same odd connection?

Could he know that she did?

But he had looked away, returning his attention to the fields and green meadows passing outside. Grace studied the faint indentations beneath his cheekbones, the muscles in his jaw, the hard sculpt of his lips. She wondered what he looked like in a uniform. Navy blue... it would complement his cool gray eyes. Gold epaulets on those proud shoulders, the tails of his uniform coat emphasizing his physique, snug white breeches showing off the length and musculature of his legs.

Really, her mind shouldn't be going in such directions.

You should be reserving such thoughts for Captain Ponsonby. After all, he's the one you fantasize about. The one you hope and plan to marry.

But she wasn't fantasizing about Captain Ponsonby.

She was fantasizing about Captain Lord.

They were crossing a small river now, moving through a village. Captain Lord remained silent. Even

Polly, sitting beside her, cut her eyes to the captain and back to Grace, silently questioning the tension.

Grace shrugged and cleared her throat.

"Are you looking forward to seeing your brother, Captain Lord? Meeting his family?"

"I am indeed. It's been a long time. Too long."

"Have you ever seen one of these Norfolk Thoroughbreds they raise?"

"I have not."

He returned his attention to the passing landscape, withdrawing into that contemplative place from which she'd temporarily been able to draw him, thinking his own thoughts once more. Maybe it was best to leave him with whatever so occupied his mind. Still, she wondered what was bothering him so.

Wished she could reclaim the easy companionship they'd enjoyed before.

Sighing, she leaned back against the squab and forced her own attention out the window. Best not to think about Captain Lord. About his nearness. His very *presence*. She looked at the manicured fields with their trimmed hedgerows, a kestrel hovering above waving grasses. At the blue, blue sky that spread high above the landscape, the thick cottony clouds that rolled across it, pushed along by delicious summer breezes. The land was flat here, the soil sandier than she was used to seeing, the air sweet and fragrant with the scent of grasses and flowers. More gently rolling pastures and a little stone church, brick and stone houses and the flat Norfolk marshes beyond. Another field, low and rolling, and neat white fencing that stretched off into the distance. And there, horses, their tails flicking as they grazed. Beautiful horses with gleaming coats and long, long legs under powerfully muscled haunches. Beyond them, a manor house slumbered in the sunshine. The coach began to slow and moments later, they were turning down a drive that paralleled the western side of the enclosed pasture.

The horses within it lifted their heads, pricked their ears and watched them. Several came galloping up to the fence, trotting alongside it with necks arched and tails high as they kept pace with the coaches, exchanging friendly whinnies with the steeds that pulled them.

"Are those the famous Norfolk thoroughbreds, milady?" asked Polly, peering out the window.

"I don't know," Grace answered. "I've never seen one. Captain Lord?"

He was looking, too. "I wouldn't know a thoroughbred, let alone a Norfolk one, from a Shetland pony."

She laughed. "I guess you're probably not the best person to invite out for a ride to explore the local countryside."

"Not a ride, but a walk would do nicely."

"That's boring," Grace said, and grinned.

A smile played at the corner of his mouth. His eyes were warm again, as though he had resolved whatever had been so heavily on his mind. "I have found, Lady Grace, that when you are involved, nothing is boring."

"Hairs in soups and spills in ponds and tears in dresses and all that?"

"All that. And let's hope there is nothing more."

J ust outside the window two horses trotted along the fence-line, keeping pace with them. And then the wheels of the coach were crunching on gravel and they were pulling up in front of a fine home of sun-washed brick. It was a charming house, with ivy crawling up its walls, fat red roses blooming under tall leaden windows and gables in its slate roof. Several black and russet chickens scratched beneath one of the rose bushes, then settled into the dirt, fluffing it over their feathers.

"My brother seems to have done quite well for himself," Captain Lord said, smiling. "Even if he did leave the Navy to become a veterinarian."

"A what?"

"Animal doctor. And he's very good at it, I'm told. His patients adore him."

"I look forward to meeting him. And, your family. What a beautiful home!"

"Yes, it is," he mused, studying it from the window.

"You've never been here?"

"First time."

"How exciting!"

The coach rolled to a stop. Captain Lord got out, quickly turning to help Grace and Polly down. Grace was embarrassingly aware of her dishabille as she prepared to meet these perfect strangers and determined to hold her head high. She was grateful for Captain Lord's coat and steeled her resolve, ready to respond to raised eyebrows or anyone who might question such an odd fashion with a laugh to cover her mortification— after all, she was well-used to being mortified— and an explanation that she was trying the newest style from London. Or Paris. Or the wilds of the Americas. Or... well, she would think of something, wouldn't she?

She always did.

Just ahead of them, Sir Graham was already out of the carriage, the twins pulling impatiently at his hands in an attempt to get to the two horses whose dark eyes watched them with curiosity. One had its neck over the fence, stretching to get closer. And then the door to the manor house opened and a pack of dogs poured out, all racing to meet them.

"Doggies!" cried little Mary, and would have run right toward them if her father hadn't had a good grip on her.

"I want doggies!" yelled Anne, not to be outdone, and suddenly both girls were howling, their cries to be set free rising over the dogs' frenzied barking as the canines attacked the twins with slobbery kisses.

"Papa, I want to play with them!" cried Mary, going red in the face as she struggled against her father's grip. "Let me go!"

As the twins' shrieks began to drown out even the dogs' barking, it was young Ned who came over to where Grace, Polly and Captain Lord stood and said wryly, "I daresay Papa's hopes for a relaxing visit are doomed."

Anne and Mary were now both sitting on the ground, faces red, tiny feet planted against their father's shoes as they stretched and pulled and writhed in their attempts to get loose.

"I want to play with doggies!"

"I get the white one!"

"*I* want the white one!"

"I asked first!"

"That's not *faaaaair*!"

A man appeared in the doorway, put his fingers to his mouth and gave a shrill whistle.

"*Bow! Marcus! Nelson! Come!*"

His voice was full of authority. Immediately the dogs left off their wild greeting and raced back to him, winding themselves around his ankles before sitting obediently at his feet, tongues lolling as they gazed up at him in adoration.

The twins screamed in protest.

"Papa, he took our doggies!"

"I want them back!"

"I'm still getting the white one! Tell Mary she can't have the white one, it's *mine*!"

Ned cupped a hand to the side of his mouth, cut his eyes to the man who'd ordered obedience from the dogs, and stood on tiptoe to better reach Captain Lord's ear. "I wonder if he can perform that trick on my sisters."

Captain Lord let out a helpless guffaw before quickly recovering his aplomb.

Sir Graham was beginning to reach the end of his patience. And then Lady Falconer was out of the coach and marching to the rescue, yanking each screeching, red-faced young lady to her feet and giving them The Look.

Instantly the children quieted, as obedient to the former Pirate Queen of the Caribbean as the dogs were to their master.

"That is *enough*."

And it was all she needed to say.

Sir Graham let out his breath, put his fingers to his temple in relief, and turned, a grin lighting up his handsome face as the man with the dogs approached. He was tall and blond and wore little wire-framed spectacles, and he walked with a decided, hitching limp.

"Sir Graham! Lady Falconer! It is *ever* so good to see you again. Welcome to our home."

"To hell with the damned Sir This and Lady That," snapped Maeve Falconer, and releasing the twins, embraced the man in a ferocious hug that forced the formality from his bearing and released the dogs from their invisible hold. They immediately set to barking and jumping up at the new arrivals and to add to the clamor, the door to the house opened yet again and two little boys came running out. In their wake was a petite woman with bright red-gold hair dressed in a riding habit and boots. She had dark, lively eyes that danced with delight as she hurried forward to join them.

"Colin," the admiral said warmly, as his wife stepped back from the greeting and allowed him the chance to make his own. He extended a hand. "I say, it's damned good to see you again after so many years. How've you been, eh? Life treating you well?" He pulled little Mary up from the grass, where she lay giggling as the long pink tongue of one of the dogs swept her face and its tail beat at Anne's chin while the child, shrieking in delight, tried in vain to grab it. "I hope you don't regret a Falconer onslaught! And it is an honor to finally meet you, Lady Ariadne," he said, bowing deeply to the woman as Colin quickly made introductions. "I can see that you've taken very good care of my old flag captain."

"The famous Sir Graham! The honor is mine, surely."

The admiral beckoned his son forward. "You remember Ned here, don't you, Colin? Hard to believe he was just a baby when you last saw him."

"Hello, Captain Lord," said Ned, drawing himself up to his full height.

"Ned! My, but how you've grown!" He laid a hand on

the boy's shoulder. "And please, it's Mr. Lord, now. I'm no longer a captain in His Majesty's Navy. I heal animals now. Dogs and cats and horses and pretty much everything else."

"Horses!" squealed one of the twins, and bolted toward the nearby fence, nearly reaching it before Ned could grab her.

"I want to ride the horsie!"

"I get to go first!"

"I daresay you've got your hands full, sir," said Colin Lord, with a twinkle in his eye. "A spirited duo, those two!"

"Aye, the minute one turns his back, they're in trouble."

Colin Lord watched with amusement and took the hands of the two children who were quietly watching the twins with something like horror. "And here are our boys, Jonathan and Aaron who will be, I'm sure, quite happy to lead them into even more of it." He smoothed the bright hair of the youngest, who looked pale and tired. "Poor Aaron has a cold, so he's a bit out of sorts. You know how it is with children. They seem to catch everything that makes the rounds, don't they?"

The initial greetings complete, the small party moved to where Grace, Polly and Captain Lord stood patiently waiting beside their carriage. Grace tensed, painfully aware of her dishabille and grateful for the captain's coat that covered it.

"Del!" The tall blond man's eyes warmed with unfettered joy, crinkling at the corners behind his spectacles. "It is *so* very good to see you after so many years."

"Hello, Colin."

The two began to formally shake hands, and then the older drew the younger into his embrace and slapped him affectionately on the back. "I almost didn't recognize you out of uniform. Why, I'm surprised you even *own* civilian clothes!"

194

"You can blame your cousin Connor for that," Sir Graham said, coming over to join them. "He was the one who finally got Del here to relax a bit. I'm sure he's itching to be back in full rig though!" He took Grace's hand. "Colin, Lady Ariadne, this is my niece, Lady Grace Fairchild. I thought it fitting to get her away from my sister for a few days. Nothing more oppressive than a mother enjoying the early days of her nuptials, even if it is the fifth time she's tied the knot."

"Fourth," said Del, hands clasped dutifully behind his back.

Colin beckoned his two boys over and introduced them to the newcomers. Their eyes widened as they met their Uncle Delmore for the first time as though trying, and failing, to envision him in a naval uniform. Behind them, the twins were reaching through the fence to touch the horses and seeing it, Lady Ariadne sent her sons to go supervise them.

"They are gentle, but I do worry about little fingers," she explained. "Perhaps they'll enjoy a ride on our old pony, Thunder. He'll keep them safe." She turned to study the two brothers. "My goodness, it's hard to believe you two are siblings!"

"You'd never know it, would you?" Grace concurred. "Though they *do* both have the same eyes and are of similar height."

"And that, along with a love for the sea, is where those similarities end," said Colin, leaning down to scratch the ear of one of the dogs, now sitting on his foot. "I take after our father in coloring, as do our sisters. Del is the only one of us to inherit our mother's looks."

"And hair," Captain Lord said somewhat resignedly.

"It's the Irish blood," said his older brother. "Has to come out somewhere."

The other two dogs ran over to join the one sitting on Colin's foot, bumping against his knees as they got carried away in their play with the giggling Falconer twins, who'd left the horses to follow them. Colin reached down to seize the collar of the biggest one, a white-and-brown-ticked gun dog whose exuberance with the girls he was obviously worried about. "Easy there, Marcus. You don't want to knock them over."

"Don't worry sir, they bounce," said Ned, spotting his sisters' frowns as their host held the dog back.

"Aye, let him go, Colin," added Sir Graham. "They're having fun." And then, in a lower voice, "We don't have a dog of our own, though I suspect that after this visit that will be the next thing these two will want."

"Oh, Papa! Can we get a doggie?"

"Yes, can we?"

"I asked first, so it will be my dog!"

"Mama! Mama, she can't have the dog, I want it!"

"I asked first!"

"I'm the one he licked first so I should get the dog, obviously they like me better than you!"

"*Papaaaa!*"

Vice Admiral Sir Graham Falconer, Knight of the Bath, Hero of England, and once part of Nelson's famous Band of Brothers, made a V of his fingers and pressed them helplessly against his forehead as the fight ramped up and the noise became deafening.

"I think it's time we go inside for refreshments," Lady Ariadne said cheerfully, and grinning, led the procession toward the house.

❧ 26 ❧

S ervants tended to their trunks and a groom came to take the horses. Jimmy Thorne vaulted down from the box, plucked a yellow dandelion from the verge and gallantly presented it to Polly before heading off with the driver to partake in offered refreshments in the kitchen. Once again Captain Lord offered his arm, forcing Grace to pause for a moment so that they could bring up the rear.

She looked up at him and cocked her head, wondering why he had chosen to tail the others. He just smiled and glanced at his own coat, still covering her.

Of course. He didn't want anyone walking behind her, where her torn gown would be obvious and cause her even more embarrassment.

Gratitude swept her. Was there no end to this man's thoughtfulness?

They climbed the steps and found themselves in a cool and shadowy entranceway. Hats and coats were taken, more pleasantries exchanged, the Falconer nanny taking the baby upstairs for a change and a nap. Grace had further opportunity to subtly compare the two siblings. Their features were similar, but Colin had a kind, relaxed gentleness about him whereas his younger brother was reserved and somewhat stiff. But as Lady

Ariadne had noted, both had the same eyes and both were tall, broad across the shoulders and lean through the torso. It was not hard to imagine either of them standing on the quarterdeck of Sir Graham's mighty flagship, commanding hundreds of men.

Grace sent Polly to unpack their trunks and gave her the afternoon off, knowing it was likely to be spent with the roguish Jimmy Thorne. Little Jonathan Lord and his brother Aaron, sniffling, shyly invited their boisterous young cousins out to see the horses though Ned, yawning, declined to join them. Shrieking in excitement the children raced outside, taking chaos with them, and the adults made their way to a small parlor. There, open windows let in a cooling breeze from the not-so-distant sea, and potted plants bloomed on deep windowsills. The walls were papered with yellow silk, and above a marbled fireplace mantel hung a painting of a proud bay stallion.

"Peace and quiet at last," Sir Graham said, accepting a glass of brandy from his host as he settled himself on a damask settee. "I'm told I'm supposed to relax when on holiday, but God help me, I'm having the devil of a time doing it!"

A servant came in with tea and elegant little cakes. Grace took a cup and sipped it slowly. Talk droned on around her, of the weather, of children, of boats and horses and the Royal Navy. She was only half-listening because her thoughts were on her odd garb, and finding a way to politely excuse herself so she could go change. She didn't wish to appear rude. Her distress must have shown because once again, it was Captain Lord who came to her rescue.

He caught her eye and indicated his coat, still covering her, and then raised a finger as though to point upstairs, his brows raised.

She nodded briskly.

"Colin, Ariadne... Lady Grace here has had rather a

trying day, and I daresay she might like to go upstairs and rest for a little while. Will you excuse her?"

Grace shot him a grateful smile and mouthed her thoughts.

Thank you.

"Of course," their hostess said. "Come, my dear. I'll show you to your rooms. You've had a long journey, haven't you?"

"Yes, and I was seasick, too. But Captain Lord gave me something that made me feel better."

"Did he, now?" And then, lowering her voice and eyes twinkling, "Such a kind and thoughtful man, just like his brother. Come along. Plenty of time for us all to get to know each other after you've had some rest."

"I'll join you," said Maeve Falconer, finishing her tea and getting to her feet. "Best to check on the baby as well as the twins, wherever they've gone. I hope they don't turn your household upside down. They were in rare form this morning."

"Not so rare," said Sir Graham under his breath.

Maeve shot him the same *Look* she'd bestowed on her daughters, but her lips were twitching.

The admiral laughed and blew her a kiss.

The men rose to their feet as the women headed for the door. Del watched as they exited, thinking that Colin had chosen a spirited and perfect match in Lady Ariadne. He looked forward to getting to know his brother's family and spending time with his two little nephews. Grace was the last one through the door and there, she turned and looked over her shoulder, her eyes finding his. He smiled. She smiled back and nodded. She turned and followed the others, and his gaze lingered on her until she was out of sight. It was only after the women were gone that he finally relaxed. He was not one to imbibe but the day's events demanded it, and he accepted a glass of brandy when it was offered.

Sir Graham looked at him in surprise.

"Right. You're tighter than a strained backstay. What is it?"

Del glanced at Ned, who remained in a nearby chair. The energy had gone out of the boy and his face looked wan. Given the maturity he had for his years, he was too old to go to the nursery.

And too young for the unguarded conversation of adults.

"Ned, would you like to go outside and meet the horses?" Colin asked, seeing his brother's hesitation. "That one in the painting there above the fireplace is Shareb-er-rehh. He's famous."

"I'm afraid I've never heard of him, sir."

"Well now," said Colin, kindly, "he's never heard of you, either, but I'm sure that once you meet him you'll never forget him. And vice versa."

"Actually, Capt— I mean, Mr. Lord, I'd rather find a place to rest for a bit. But after I've done so, I would love to meet your horse."

"Mitchell here will show you to your room, then," said Colin, indicating a footman who stood nearby. The boy got to his feet, and followed the servant upstairs.

Once he was gone, Colin spoke. "Your son does you great credit, Sir Graham. And unless I miss my guess, he's inherited his mother's gift. There's something special about him, isn't there?"

"Aye, Colin. He may have the Sight, he may not. But he's intuitive in ways most of us aren't, and he's had some dreams that are damned uncanny. Nearly lost him this past winter. Malaria... it was your cousin Connor who, along with Del here, took one of my ships and in the middle of a raging hurricane, sailed off into the teeth of it to bring back the anecdote." He looked at his flag captain. "Bravest damned thing I've ever seen and I've seen plenty of brave things over the years. I owe him and your brother here my eternal gratitude for saving my boy."

Del took a sip of his brandy and looked down, faintly embarrassed. He loved Ned as much as if the boy were his own son, and there was nothing he wouldn't do for him, even if he would prefer to forget that hellish mission on which Connor had led them to get the Jesuit's bark that had saved the boy's life.

From outside came the song of a warbler, drifting in through the open windows.

"Right. So what's troubling you, Del?" asked the admiral, with a penetrating glance at his flag captain.

Del, who'd been savoring the brandy he still held in his mouth, swallowed it. He steadied the glass on his knee and looked his superior in the eye. "Lieutenant Akers stepped on Lady Grace's gown as she moved to get out of the boat. I saw it with my own eyes, and it was deliberate."

"You don't say!"

"I wouldn't make up nor exaggerate a matter of such grave importance, sir."

"Surely it was an accident—"

"It was no accident. I saw what happened, all of it. As she stepped from the boat, he put his foot down on the hem of her gown. It's why it tore. And he was smiling, the bastard. He thought he got away with it but I saw what he did, and every tar in that boat saw things they had *no* business seeing!" Del took a steadying breath, trying to keep his anger under control, and put the glass on a nearby table before his clenched fingers could break it. "I caught up to the blackguard when we stopped to let Ponsonby out, and the matter will be settled at dawn."

"Bloody hell, Del," said the Colin, alarmed.

"What would you have me do? The lady's modesty and honor were compromised," he snapped back. "As a gentleman it's my duty to defend them both!"

"This makes no sense to me whatsoever," Sir Graham said. "Why would he even do such a thing?"

"Is it not obvious?"

The admiral raised his shoulders in a blank shrug.

"The man perceives your niece as a threat. He's a—" he swore, then lowered his voice and blurted, "—he's in love with Ponsonby."

"*What?!*"

"And that's his own damned business, but it becomes mine when he attempts harm to a woman I consider to be under my care!"

"Easy, Del," said Sir Graham, putting down his glass. "We'll find another way out of this."

"There is no other way out of this."

"There has to be."

"There isn't."

Sir Graham swore beneath his breath and got to his feet. "A duel. A damned duel. I swear, this so-called *holiday* has been fraught with more stress than a visit to the First Lord of the bloody Admiralty."

"The challenge has been made and accepted. I will defend your niece's honor and fight the duel."

"You've never fought a duel in your damned life."

"I fight a duel every time I take *Orion* out to sea and face the chance of meeting up with a French adversary. Is a lady's honor no less important than that of Britannia herself?"

The admiral put his forehead in his hand and began to knead his temples. Then he picked up his brandy and drained the glass in one swallow before getting to his feet and going to the window, there to stand looking out over the flat green pastures and the sea in the distance.

"I'll be your second," Colin said quietly. "I think Sir Graham should sleep in tomorrow. This trip has been taxing for him, I think."

The admiral turned. "Damn your eyes, both of you. You treat me as if I'm an old man!"

The two brothers just looked at each other.

"We'll be back in time for breakfast, I'm sure," soothed Colin, who knew his old superior well. "Why, by the time you wake, the matter will have been dealt with."

The words were just that. Words. As gentlemen, all three of them knew that Del had done the only thing he could do, and that there was no way out of this.

"*I'll* be your second," the admiral finally said with resignation. "Tell me the details so I can meet with Akers' man and arrange a spot to conduct this wretched affair. Colin, you can stand in for the surgeon."

❧ 27 ❧

D el retreated to his room to freshen up. He was
just changing into a new shirt when he happened
to look out the window and down onto the lawn
outside.

There was Lady Grace, moving across the freshly-
mown grass toward an outlying barn. Ned was with her,
and the two were laughing.

So much for any late-day naps the two might've
taken, he thought wryly. Though to be fair, a good hour
had passed since they'd all parted following refreshments.

He had intended to spend what remained of the afternoon reading Scripture. Preparing one's soul for the
afterlife was never a bad idea, especially on the eve of a
duel where anything could happen, and the beautiful
words of the 139th Psalm, his favorite, called to him.
Words of comfort and majesty, assurance and divine
omniscience. Words that he knew by heart, but which
spoke to him differently every time he pondered them.
He got the old leather Bible from his trunk, leafed
through the well-worn pages, and began to read.

O Lord, thou hast searched me, and known me.

Outside, their laughter drifted up, his childish, hers
as pure as morning sunshine.

Thou knowest my downsitting and mine uprising, thou understandest my thought afar off. Thou compassest my path and my lying down, and art acquainted with all my ways. For there is not a word in my tongue, but, lo, O Lord, thou knowest it altogether.

Del put a finger in his ear and tried to block out their laughter.

My substance was not hid from thee, when I was made in secret, and curiously wrought in the lowest parts of the earth.

Thine eyes did see my substance, yet being unperfect; and in thy book all my members were written, which in continuance were fashioned, when as yet there was none of them.

His days had all been written. His life had been known to his Creator before he'd even come red-faced and squalling into this huge and uncertain world and begun to live it. This life that brought him joys and triumphs, questions and answers, pain and grief, and surprise and confusion but so far, had not brought him someone to love.

Would it ever?

In thy book all my members were written.

Again, the merry notes of her laughter.

Was she, Lady Grace Fairchild, written into his own Book of Life before either of them had even been born?

And if she were, what was he doing up here all alone, all but handing her over to Sheldon Ponsonby when God Himself might have other plans?

Del didn't know what God's plans were.

But he did feel a sudden and irresistible urge to close the old book, pick up his hat, and go down there and join them.

⚓

THE BARN WAS BLESSEDLY COOL.

She and Ned were poking about its interior, hoping to find the great Shareb-er-Rehh, but aside from a trio of empty stalls laid with fresh straw, the building was empty.

"Perhaps they're all out to pasture?" Ned speculated. "I'm sure I can find this horse. There's a painting of him above a fireplace back in the house. He's bay, with a big bold blaze."

"That would describe any number of horses, I should think."

"Well, I bet I can recognize him. Let's go look outside. Besides, there's nothing in here."

Actually, there was.

Delmore Lord stood there in the entranceway, silhouetted by the late afternoon light. Grace's eyes, accustomed to the gloom within the old barn, could not make out any details save for his outline. She was struck by how tall he was, framed by the space of the open door and the bright sunshine outside.

"I hope I'm not interrupting?" he said.

"Oh, no, of course not. We were just trying to find this famous racehorse. Have you ever seen him, Captain Lord?"

He moved fully into the barn, his hat in his hand. "No, I confess I haven't. But I can help you both look for him, if you wish."

"I would like that," Grace said happily. "Ned?"

"We need all the help we can get. But it's hot outside, and the sun's bothering me. I'm just going to run back to the house and get my hat. I'll be right back!"

The boy hustled out of the barn, shutting the door behind them and plunging them into deeper gloom. The only light came from thick windows set with cobwebs and spiders' nests, high up in each stall.

"Well," said Lady Grace. "Good to see you smiling again, my friend."

"Hmph. *Friend.*"

She tilted her head and grinned up at him. "You say that as if it's an accusation."

"Well, it is, actually. Who wants to be the mere *friend* of a beautiful woman? You can't blame me for wishing you thought of me as more than that, but alas, the die is cast so I'll take whatever meager scraps you throw my way."

Grace laughed, enjoying the flirtation "Why, Captain Lord! You have a poetic side of you I'd never have imagined!"

"There are lots of things about me you may never have imagined, but since you're not rejecting my compliments, allow me to pay you another. You look quite ravishing in blue. I daresay it's your color."

"I can imagine that it's *your* color as well, given the Royal Navy uniform I've yet to see you in, though you seem adverse to wearing it in your civilian identity."

"Perhaps that is because I really don't *have* a civilian identity?"

"I should like to see you in uniform someday."

"Not likely, unless we meet at a naval gathering somewhere. But ah, never mind. I forget myself. My mood is a strange one this afternoon, and my tongue seems to have a mind of its own."

"Then don't govern it. Your lack of restraint is refreshing."

"Is it?"

"It is."

"Don't marry Ponsonby."

"What?"

"Marry me, instead."

"*Captain Lord!*"

"Have I made you uncomfortable? I do apologize."

"You haven't made me uncomfortable, it's just that—"

"Do you want me to take back what I just said? Forget I ever uttered such words of—" he grinned and laid a dramatic hand over his heart— "covetous devotion? No, don't answer that, as I don't believe I can take them back, nor will I."

She laughed harder, her eyes now sparkling, appreciating this playful side of him that he had never allowed her to see much of. "If you take them back, I'll be annoyed. So don't. I know you're just joking, and that you really *do* wish to see me accomplish my goal of marrying Ponsonby. But whatever has got into you? It's not like you to be so unreserved. So carefree. You're usually much..."

"Stuffier?"

"I would use a kinder word, actually."

He shrugged and said cheerfully, "Well, one never knows what life will bring, do they? A person might be here one day and gone the next, so might as well say what needs to be said and blast the consequences. Besides, it's a fine day, with even finer company, and I don't feel inclined to be *stuffy*."

She looked closely at him, her eyes narrowing. There was something dark beneath his breezy words and cavalier manner. Something he was hiding.

"Here one day and gone the next? And what is that supposed to mean?"

"Only that if there's something on your mind, it's best to say it while there's still time. Better to regret it in the here-and-now than in the here-and-after, when the opportunity for such utterances is then lost."

She cocked her head, her frown deepening. "You are correct. You *are* in a strange mood this afternoon, Captain Lord. I'm worried about you."

"Have I failed so dreadfully in my attempts to flirt with you? Drat."

"Why are you going on about life's uncertainties and waxing philosophical, speaking so oddly, as if you're to —" she made a helpless little gesture with her hands— "I don't know, die tomorrow?"

"And if I *were* to die tomorrow, would you miss me? Grieve me?"

"What*ever* are you going on about?"

"Answer me, if you will."

He was no longer flirting with her, no longer playful, and the intent seriousness of the question unnerved her. She put a hand on his sleeve to convince him of her earnestness. "Of course I'd miss you. Mourn you. Grieve you, terribly. You are, after all, my friend."

Friend.

He bit his lip, his face reflecting an emotion she couldn't understand, and then he closed his eyes and pulled back, looking quite stricken.

"We should go," he said stiffly. "It's not proper for us to be alone in here. I would see no harm come to your reputation."

"But—"

"I was wrong to come out here. To flirt with you like that when you love someone else. It was unfair, but sometimes a man can't help himself. Come, let's go."

"But—"

He shook his head and just offered his arm. Feeling confused and deflated, she took it. Together they moved wordlessly to the door—

And found it locked.

"What the devil?"

The captain pulled on it, frowning. He tried the latch. Jiggled it. Rattled it and swore beneath his breath and finally sighed and leaned against the cobwebby wooden wall. "Ned. I should've known."

"Known what?"

"That boy has been raised in the Caribbean. The sun wasn't bothering him and he didn't need a hat. It was an excuse. He locked us in here."

"What?" Grace's eyes widened. "Why would he do that?"

Captain Lord just looked at her and raised a brow.

"Maybe because he, too, would like to see us be more than just *friends*."

"He wouldn't do that."

"Oh yes, he would." Del tried the door again. It was solidly locked.

"Please tell me you won't say anything to his parents. He's just a boy."

"Of course I won't."

"So now what do we do?"

"We either wait for him to return, I kick the door down—"

"Oooh! How romantic!"

"Or I hoist myself out one of these windows, come around the other side to the door and let you out."

"That seems to be the most reasonable option."

They stood there in the gloom for a long moment. Captain Lord looked at her, and again she saw that conflicting emotion in his face and realized, right down to the very roots of her soul, that his flirtation had been dead serious, that his offer of marriage had been dead serious, that what she saw in his face was pure unmitigated desire and he wanted her with an intensity that made her dizzy just thinking about it.

Her mouth went dry.

She swayed toward him, and he put a hand up, stopping her. He stepped back. His eyes were fierce.

"Don't. You'll hate yourself."

And then he turned on his heel, headed for the window, hoisted himself up on the sill and disappeared. And when the door to the barn opened ten minutes later, it wasn't Captain Lord who stood there, but her maid, Polly.

"Mr. Thorne said you'd locked yourself in the barn and needed to be let out. Are you all right, milady?"

Of course. Ever the gentleman, ever conscious of propriety and a lady's reputation, Captain Lord had made damned sure he had sent someone safe to rescue her.

"Yes, Polly," she said with a heavy heart. "I am fine."

A DUEL.

The three men might have intended to keep the matter quiet but Mitchell, who'd overheard their conversation as he'd returned to his post, had paused just outside the door and listened. He heard enough of it to glean the details of when, where and speculatively, how.

He'd wasted no time telling the other servants when they took their tea late that afternoon, and by the end of the evening every person in the house knew of it.

Including Grace.

Polly told her as she was brushing out her mistress's long dark hair for bed. After the maid left, Grace lay in the darkness, staring up at the canopy above her head. Sleep evaded her.

Duels. They were commonplace, she knew.

And she also knew that not everyone survived them.

Captain Lord was doing this for her. Now, she knew why he'd been so distant and tense as they'd traveled out from King's Lynn. Now, she knew the reason for his odd behavior, his cavalier and almost morbid philosophical musings, his reckless flirtation that was so out of character for him out in the barn. Guilt assailed her. She didn't want anyone fighting a duel over her, no matter what might— or might not— have happened.

Surely, her gown had merely caught on the oarlock.

Hadn't it?

She turned over onto her side, staring through the parted bed hangings and out the open window. A cool night breeze moved through the room, bringing with it the scent of pastures, horses and the sea.

Sleep would not come.

Grace flipped onto her stomach and shoving aside her pillow, lay her cheek against the sheets. They were crisp and clean and smelled of lavender. The essence was supposed to be soothing, relaxing, but as she lay there with eyes wide open in the darkness, Grace knew that no lavender or anything else was going to allow her to rest this night.

And really, she had no right to rest, given that by this time tomorrow night the kind and gallant Captain Lord might very well be dead.

All because of me.

She got up. Her soft white cotton nightgown all but glowed in the darkness, and she found a wrap and cinched it tightly around her waist. What she was about to do went against every rule of decency and morality, but neither virtue were worth more than a man's life.

A life she was determined would not end because of her.

She pulled open her door and on silent feet, moved down the hall to the room that Polly had told her was Captain Lord's own.

She had only hours to stop this.

And she would.

DEL DID NOT SHARE GRACE'S WORRY.

At the same moment that she hovered outside his door, lower lip sucked between her teeth and her skin prickling with anxiety as she gathered the courage to gently knock, to enter if need be, and put a stop to what she saw as madness, he lay sound asleep in his bed.

He slept the rest of a man who had no cares, but in the dark nothingness of his slumber he sighed, turned over, pushed the sheet off his shoulder and began to dream.

It had been decades since Gráinne had visited him, and in those years he had quite forgotten that she had ever even come to him through the door of his sleeping mind. His adult self would discount that long ago visit as a childhood fantasy, of nonsense born of too many stories and a little boy's overactive imagination.

But the fierce, dark-haired woman who visited him tonight was no product of a childhood fantasy or a little boy's overactive imagination, for that little boy was no longer a child.

"Hello, Captain," she said fondly, her voice rough, husky and strong. All those years ago, she had stood on the deck of a primitive ship, the wind in her hair, the salt spray on her cheeks. Tonight, she sat on the far end of his bed, her legs off to the side. There was nothing diminutive about her. Nothing feminine in the traditional sense, for while she wore some sort of woolen gown that laced across the bodice, a wide leather sword-belt hung from her waist and her fingertips were stained with gunpowder. She might be sitting on the edge of his bed instead of commanding a galley but she was still vibrant, wild and alive, and around her neck was the ancient cross that had so enchanted them all as children.

"Hello... Grandmother," he said, greeting her in Irish.

She laughed. "All these years in the Royal Navy and you still run true to your blood."

"My blood is as much English as it is Irish," he said, this time in English.

She made a dismissive motion with her hand and leaned toward him. "Bah! I don't recognize that part and neither should you, but that's not why I'm here."

"Why *are* you here?

""Don't you know?"

"All I know is that this is an odd dream for me to be having on the eve of a duel that might end in my death."

She laughed again. "That worries me as much as it

worries you, that is, not at all. And you don't think I'm just a dream, do you?"

"You have to be. Our branch of the family didn't inherit the Sight, like my cousin Maeve's did."

"They have the Sight. You, dear son, have me. And I'm tired of seeing you suffer the pain of a broken heart while those around you find love. Enough of that! You'll hear a knocking at your door soon, and you're to answer it."

"A knocking on my door?"

She got up. "That's what I said."

Her image was fading into the sound of wind and waves, of crashing surf, and Del sat up in bed, looking toward the open window for a sea that was not there. But he did hear a faint knocking.

I'm losing my mind.

It's just a dream, brought on by concern about tomorrow.

But he *wasn't* concerned about tomorrow. Indignant about the way Lady Grace had been treated, but not concerned. Angry that a good night's sleep was being interrupted by this nonsense, but not concerned. Impatient to get the matter over with— but not concerned.

At all.

The faint knocking was surely part of the dream as well. Ignoring it, Del pulled the light blanket back up over his shoulder, nestled down into the pillow, sighed and tried to go back to sleep.

Couldn't.

Because the knocking wasn't stopping. It was getting louder.

"Captain Lord?"

He cracked open an eye and stared into the darkness, tensing, every sense on sudden alert. This voice was not his ancestor. Oh, no.

"Captain Lord!"

He bolted upright in bed, alarmed, for if she were seen out there and word got back to his brother and his sister-in-law, surely they'd think ill of her. He didn't want anyone thinking ill of her. No one. He'd been lucky he'd managed to get her safely from the barn back to the house via Jimmy Thorne and Polly after that... that exchange, with no one the wiser. An exchange that should never have occurred.

What had he been thinking?

"Captain Lord?"

What the blue devil was she doing out there?

He lunged from the bed. On bare feet, he grabbed his trousers, stepped into them as he padded across the room, stuffed his shirt into the waistband and yanked open the door.

And let out an expletive as a body fell into his room.

"Oh!"

"*Lady Grace!*"

She got to her feet. "Captain Lord, I *must* speak with you—"

He shot a glance down the hall, grabbed her wrist and instinctively yanked her inside, kicking the door shut behind her. Her face was a pale moon just inches from his, her head pressed against the wall, her dark hair flowing over white shoulders and her eyes huge in the heavy gloom. He loomed over her, furious.

"*What* are you doing here? Are you mad?"

"I came here to stop you from fighting that duel!" She drew herself up, bravely tilting her head back so she could meet his gaze. "And yes, every person in this house is aware of it, so don't look surprised that I know what you're intending to do. I've never had anyone fight a duel over me and I'm not going to allow you to be the first, especially over something so stupid."

"You regard the defense of your honor as *stupid?*"

"I regard your life far more than I do my honor!"

"If anyone finds you here—"

"Nobody's going to find me here, and stop acting so, so *priggish*—"

"For God's sake, lower your voice!"

"I won't let you fight a duel over me, Captain Lord, I just w—"

His mouth silenced her and it happened, just like that. Just like it had been intended to happen since Del had first set eyes on his admiral's niece and it happened without thought, without intent, without planning and totally without remorse. He kissed her. His lips came down hard against hers and every bit of restraint he owned went out the window with the warm air that still lingered from the day, and her arms came up to wind around his neck, her body pressing itself to his with reckless abandon, and he was lost. Utterly lost. He slid a hand behind her head and drew her closer, deepening the kiss. He felt her hair tumbling over his knuckles. The shy touch of her tongue, the sweet taste of her lips invading his senses. She made a little noise of assent, and everything from his waist down caught fire as though someone had thrown a bomb into the powder keg that was his loins.

Damn.

Damn!

What on earth was he thinking?

He drew back, utterly shocked at his loss of restraint, his heart hammering in his ears.

"I *beg* your pardon!"

She looked up at him, speechless and blinking. She looked stunned. Confused. He took a step backward, away from her, before he could lose control of himself and kiss her again.

Still, she said nothing. Her fingers came up to touch her mouth. She slowly let her hand drop. Passed her tongue over her lips and took a deep and steadying breath before looking up at him.

"Don't be sorry," she whispered. "I'm not."

"You were saving that for Ponsonby," he said rather more harshly than he intended.

"I... I don't know as if I were."

He swallowed hard. "You need to leave. Now."

She remained where she was for a long moment.

"*Now.*"

She nodded. Her eyes were huge in her pale face. Her hand went to the door. He could see it shaking. She looked dazed, as if someone had struck her a mortal blow, and then she pushed it open, turned to look back at him for a long moment, and slipped out into the darkness.

CLUTCHING HER ROBE TO HERSELF, GRACE LET THE door shut behind her and stood there in the darkness, her heart pounding. She could barely breathe. Her blood was humming through her veins. Her lips were on fire, the back of her head still ached for the cradle of his palm, and parts of herself that weren't mentionable in polite company were letting her know, very loudly, that they existed.

She leaned back against his door and stared into the gloom.

What had happened back there?

What, she thought, putting two fingers to her heart as though she could plumb its depths, *was happening in* here?

She remained unmoving for a long moment, shaken, not trusting her feet to carry her back to her own bed. The empty hallway stretched out in the darkness. Her aunt and uncle were somewhere nearby and if Aunt Maeve happened to be up feeding the baby, she might have heard their low voices and be on her way to investigate. Grace had caused enough scenes in the past few days. She would not add another disgrace to her growing list of embarrassments, or get Captain Lord into more trouble for having to defend her from something else.

Oh, what is happening to me?

It's Sheldon Ponsonby I love!

But Captain Lord had just kissed her. He had kissed her with the passion of a strong and virile man. He had kissed her until her head swam and her body went up in flames and her very toes had tingled. That had been no sweet kiss between two mere friends. It had been no shy exploration, no hesitant coming-together, but a kiss that had meant business.

And Grace wasn't quite sure what she felt about it.

What she even *ought* to feel about it.

Go to bed, her mind told her. *There's plenty of time to think about this in the morning. It was probably just a one-off, an accident, the result of a long and exhaustive day where both of you forgot yourselves. Captain Lord was caught in the moment and so were you. Go to bed. Get some sleep. Because if you intend to do anything about this duel, you'll need to be awake in time to stop it.*

Yes. Good idea, all of it.

She opened her door, slipped inside, and crept back to her bed.

Somewhere in the distance, a clock ticked away the hours 'til dawn. She pulled the sheet up to her chin and lay staring up into the darkness.

But sleep, after what had just occurred on the other side of the hall, was out of the question.

DESIREE HOLDEN

❧ 28 ❧

S he was not insomnia's only victim.

On the other side of the door, Del had stalked back to bed, slid beneath the sheets, and also lay awake. He cursed himself for his boorish behavior. For losing control of himself.

If she hated him, he would not blame her.

I should not have kissed her. I should not have claimed what's not mine, should not have behaved like an unbridled stallion, but damn it, I'm glad that I did because that's probably the one and only time I'll ever get to claim such a prize.

A kiss. No damned crime.

There was only so much a man could take.

He turned over and stared at the wall. At the darkened window, open to the night outside. He tossed. He turned. He sighed and punched the pillow and flung himself back on his opposite side. Eventually his eyes drifted shut and his torments ceased. He slept. His Irish ancestress did not return to trouble him. His brain, exhausted by constant thinking of, and exposure to a woman he could not have, fell quiet. He did not dream, did not stir, and awoke an hour before dawn.

He lay there in the heavy gloom, his eyeballs aching with fatigue. There was no need to reach for his pocket watch to confirm the time. He did not have the Sight, but he did have an uncanny ability to sense the hour, even down to the minute give or take ten of them, and he sat up, rubbing his eyes and feeling heavy and dull and unrested.

Grace O'Malley.

Had he dreamed the whole damned thing? His formidable ancestress? The knocking on the door? The events that had followed?

Lady Grace Fairchild.

No. He hadn't dreamt it. He hadn't dreamt *any* of it.

His window was open to the night. A light rain was falling, and even the birds had not yet begun to chirp. Del lit a candle from the tinderbox, set it down near the washstand, and by the faint flicker of light, scrubbed the sand from his tired eyes and the skin from his face in an attempt to wake up. Aboard ship, Jimmy Thorne would be coming in to shave him. His coxswain was likely still asleep somewhere and no doubt dreaming of Polly, and Del was not of a mind to lament his absence. He could shave his own damned jaw.

He found the razor, lathered, and with bleary eyes, proceeded to neaten himself up for the coming contest of honor. The razor scraped over the night's bristle. He rhythmically wiped the blade with a towel, scraped some more. It was hard to see in the dim light, and passing his fingers over his jaw, he was finally satisfied that he'd done a passable job under the circumstances. He toweled his face and ran a comb through his hair. It caught on a thick spiral curl, which snarled and refused to budge. Cursing his hair — as he did every morning — Del put the comb down and used his fingers to tease out the tangle. One spiraling kink stood all but straight up from his head. He tried to smooth it down. It resisted and sprang up yet again. Sighing, he picked up his hat and slammed it down on the unruly lock, ending the battle.

His stomach growled.

I kissed her. I can't believe I did that.

He began to gather up his clothes.

I bloody kissed her.

He dressed quickly and in silence. It would be pistols, and he chose a black silk shirt so as to lessen his profile... and to hide any blood he might be unlucky enough to shed. His fingers did not shake as he did up the buttons of his waistcoat, nor should they — he was an admiral's flag captain, for heaven's sake. He had faced worse than the likely poor aim and trembling hand of a nervous lieutenant who was probably even now emptying his runny bowels into a chamber pot.

On the eastern horizon, pale gray light began to glow atop the pastures. Outside, a blackbird began to call.

I kissed her.

Del buckled on his sword belt, blew out the candle and stalked to the door.

And so he had. He might die today, so he might as well stop regretting it.

⚓

ACROSS THE HALL, GRACE WAS ALSO UP.

She had not slept well. Perhaps, she mused, she might not have even slept at all. In the growing light of day, the kiss she'd shared with Captain Lord seemed distant. Unreal. As though it hadn't actually even happened. And yet the scent of his cologne still lingered in her nostrils. The feel of his mouth was branded against her own. She recounted the way her nipples had ached and her private places had warmed and how she'd felt so very *small* against his powerful body as she'd wrapped her arms around his neck and pressed herself against him and knew, with a mixture of delight and confusion, excitement and despair, that she hadn't dreamed any of it.

He kissed me!

She got up and pulled the blanket from her bed. Clutching it around her shoulders, she curled up on the damask-covered chair near the window and tried to think.

It was still dark beyond the thick glass pane, but she could see details emerging ever so faintly outside... the long, broad Norfolk pastures, all but indistinguishable against the sky. Horse fencing just becoming visible. Another degree of light... trees beginning to take shape.

Was today the day that a man would lose his life because of her?

A gallant, upstanding man who had noticed her, who cared about her, who zealously guarded her dignity and her life when the man she wanted— or thought she wanted— was nowhere to be found?

There was a slight knock on her door, and Grace jumped.

It opened and there was Polly, holding a candle. It glowed softly against her young face.

"Good morning, milady," she said. "I thought you'd be up."

"I can't sleep knowing what's about to happen."

"Nothing's going to happen. Men duel all the time, they do."

"Men die in duels all the time, too."

"Best not to think that way, milady. Thinking it might make it happen."

"I have to stop this."

The maid set the candlestick down and went to the wardrobe. "There's nothing you can do about it. 'Tis unwise to interfere in the business of men. Let them go fire a shot or two each, satisfy their honor, and Captain Lord'll be home for breakfast."

"Is that what Mr. Thorne thinks?"

Polly had the good grace to blush.

Grace pulled off the blanket and got to her feet. She

began to pace. "I could go to the duel and pretend to swoon. If Captain Lord cares about me, he'll be more attentive to my supposed plight than he would be to the duel itself and that would stop it."

"Might also get him killed, distracting him so."

"Then I'm going to my Aunt Maeve. She can get my uncle to stop it."

"They're gentlemen. They can't stop it. Not once a man's honor's been challenged."

"I don't understand men!"

"Well, they don't understand us either, and as long as the good Lord has a few mysteries left in the world for humans to solve, I figure that can't be all bad." She opened the wardrobe and turning, held up a pretty cream gown with little cap sleeves tied with blue ribbons.

"Not that, Polly. My riding habit, I think. I need something more... more functional."

"This one?"

Somewhere out in the corridor, a door opened and thumped shut. Another. Masculine voices in low conversation as someone moved past their door, another door opening and closing.

The voices were receding.

Dear God. It was happening.

Now.

Panicking, Grace burst into action and grabbed the habit from her maid.

"Lady Grace?"

"Oh, do help me, Polly! There's no time to lose, they're already on their way! She glanced with mounting despair out the window, where morning's gray light was bringing definition to the world outside, and all but plunged herself into her clothes before seizing the maid's arm and racing with her toward the door. "Come, hurry! Captain Lord's life may well depend upon it!"

❈ 29 ❈

At about the time Grace went running to Lady
Falconer for help, a coach carrying three men left
the courtyard in front of the stables and wheeled its
way down the drive, through the sleepy village of
Burnham Thorpe and past the church and rectory
where the famous Lord Nelson had been born and
raised. Cocks were crowing and the scent of rain, which
had let off for the moment, hung in the air. The sun
wanted no part of the coming contest and hid its face
behind a low, roiling cloud bank before disappearing altogether. To the west the sky was dark, the wind
starting to kick up as the weather moved closer.

Nobody spoke. Sir Graham was silent and moody,
and the dark circles under his handsome blue eyes testi-
fied to a restless night. Colin seemed marginally more
cheerful, but he'd discreetly tucked the wooden box
that was his surgical kit beneath the seat, a fact that
wasn't beyond the notice of his younger brother. He
made idle talk, but the words seemed out of place in
the dark and silent coach, and eventually he gave up
altogether.

The vehicle rocked and rattled, pitching and yawing
like a frigate buffeted by a beam sea as its wheels found

well-used ruts and then bounced back out of them again.

Del just looked out the window, his face pensive. His eyes and the mind behind them were focused far beyond the spots of rain that began to hit the glass. Far beyond the flat misty pastures beyond, far beyond the heavy gray line of the distant sea, even, and on a kiss that had rocked him to his core. A woman who loved someone else.

"Doing all right, Del?"

Sir Graham's low voice brought him back to himself. "Just another day, Sir Graham."

"You still prefer pistols?"

"Yes, sir."

His stomach growled. Sir Graham frowned.

"Didn't you eat anything before you left the house?"

Del shrugged and looked away. "Hunger will keep me sharp."

Rain was falling in earnest now, leaving long streaks on the window. A gust buffeted the coach.

"Damn the rain," Del muttered. "I've no wish to get my trousers muddy."

Sir Graham just arched a brow, shook his head, and looked away. "Your fastidiousness has no place at the moment. Just get this damned affair over with as soon as it's feasible so we can put it behind us all."

"My intentions, sir."

The coach was turning, going down a long narrow track bracketed by hedgerows, and then they were in a clearing. A small brook ran alongside the track and beyond it, a stand of oak. A conveyance stood beneath them, waiting. As they approached, its door opened to emit James Akers and his second, a man in a marine's uniform who must have been hastily summoned from Ponsonby's ship. Leaving Akers standing in the lee of the vehicle against the rain, the marine approached.

Sir Graham had his hand on the door handle. "You sure you want to go through with this?"

"I will not revoke my charges against that blackguard."

The admiral sighed, nodded, and picking up the fine case of dueling pistols he had brought, let himself out of the vehicle to go meet Akers' second.

Colin had been so quiet that Del had almost forgotten he was even there, so lost in thought was he.

"You must be quite fond of the girl," his brother said.

Del turned from watching Sir Graham, now opening the case so that Akers' second could inspect the weapons within. "For all the good it does me. She's in love with another."

"And why isn't *he* here defending her honor?"

"He did not witness what I did. Therefore, he has no charge to bring."

"I see," Colin said, nodding slowly. And now Sir Graham was coming back, his face grim.

"Akers will not apologize, so this affair will proceed," he muttered. "Let's go."

Del stepped down from the coach, Colin right behind him with his surgical kit. Del ignored its implications, as well as the thought of what creatures the instruments it contained had last been used on.

He didn't want to know.

Both combatants removed their hats and handed them to their seconds. For the first time, Del felt a momentary twinge of... something. Not quite nervousness, nor was it alarm, but something related to both that left his mouth dry.

Sir Graham, sensing it, offered Del a quick sip from a flask. It was brandy, smooth and bracing. Del allowed himself one swallow. No more.

"The challenger chooses his distance, the challenged chooses his ground," said the marine, a portly young man with sleepy blue eyes and reddened hands. He must have won the privilege of starting the duel. Faced with an admiral, he appeared nervous but efficient, and had a grandiosity about him that indicated he was quite enjoying his role. "We will follow the rules of the *code duello*, of course."

His voice droned on. Del smoothed a speck of white dust— actually, it was dog hair, no surprise given how many of them lived in his brother's house— from his black silk shirt and chanced a look at his opponent. Akers, his mouth tight, was pushing the toe of his shoe against the ground as the seconds spoke in turn. He would not meet Del's eyes, but kept his gaze downcast and on his toe as it worried and unearthed a tuft of damp grass.

The rain was coming down hard now. The great branches of the oak above offered some protection against the growing deluge, but the rain was now splattered across the lenses of Colin's spectacles and Del, having been handed his pistol after the weapons were loaded, put it under his forearm so as to keep the powder dry.

Only then did Akers look up, and in his pale and strained face, Del saw something amounting to terror.

He felt pity. Almost.

And then he remembered that same toe coming down on Lady Grace's hem, and the pity was lost to a cold fury.

There would be no advantage with sun behind anyone and in an opponent's eyes. There would be no advantage of ground, though Del was offered the choice of where to stand. He put a hand over the lock of the pistol, balancing the weapon in his hand, getting the feel of it.

"Take your positions, gentlemen. You will stand back to back, proceed twenty paces to your marks, and fire at will."

Del stood there, his hand over his pistol to keep the powder dry. At his back, he could feel the raw terror of his opponent, and that concerned him more than if Akers had been confident. Terror might mean the man would be more interested in self-preservation than avenging his bruised honor, though it might also mean his hand would be shaking so badly he might miss his aim entirely.

"Are you ready, gentlemen? When I drop this handkerchief, you may begin your paces."

Del flexed his shoulders. A whiff of Akers' sweat caught him and he wrinkled his nose in distaste. He turned his head, fixed his gaze off beyond the stand of oaks, and there, saw color.

Not the green of grassy pastures, not the rich browns of soil, but a smart periwinkle-blue riding habit.

Lady Grace.

He shut his eyes and swore.

The handkerchief dropped.

❧ 30 ❧

Lieutenant Akers was shaking so hard he could barely breathe. When the white scrap of fabric dropped, only to be pounded by rain toward the ground, he all but ran to the mark, desperate to get there first, desperate to fire in what he now knew, having seen the cold fury on Captain Lord's face, would be his only self-defense.

For not the first time, he wondered how he'd become involved in this dreadful affair with a man who was rumored to be very exacting, very self-governed, and when provoked, very dangerous.

And it wasn't even Delmore Lord that Akers had an issue with— it was that hussy, Lady Grace Fairchild.

But all these thoughts flashed through his head with the fleeting speed of the shot he intended to discharge, and he ran to the mark, whirled, brought his pistol up just as his opponent was starting to turn— and fired.

Behind the pungent cloud of blue-gray smoke, he saw Lord flinch, but the man didn't go down. And now he raised his arm, brought it up to sight all the way down its length, and then, quite deliberately, aimed high and fired into the tree branch above Akers' head.

Akers stood there feeling sick, his heart hammering so hard in his chest that he thought he was going to cast up his accounts right then and there. Through a haze of relief and yes, even guilt for his unfair rush to the mark, let alone Delmore Lord's deliberate sparing of his life, he heard the seconds asking if honor had been satisfied. His own voice came from his mouth, detached, and through the now-driving rain that hammered the earth all around them, he saw Lady Grace Fairchild herself emerge from the shelter of the trees and wondered where she had come from. Blood was dripping from Captain Lord's arm but he seemed oblivious to it, even as the girl ran to him with a cry of dismay and the blond doctor who was, Akers had been told, Captain Lord's brother, grimly carried a wooden box toward the stricken man.

"Damnable rain, sir," said Donahue, the marine. "If it's all right by you, I'd like to get back to the ship and dry off."

Akers nodded his agreement, and as they headed toward the coach and stepped inside, he saw Delmore Lord turn his head and regard him.

The captain's mouth turned up ever so faintly in a little smile of malice. And Akers didn't need to hear what he was saying; it was clear enough in the man's cold gray eyes.

Mind what you do from here on out, Akers. Because I'll be watching you.

⚓

AS AKERS' CONVEYANCE MELTED OFF INTO THE RAIN, the horse lowering its head against the sudden deluge, Sir Graham made it all too clear that he did not welcome his niece's sudden appearance in what was supposed to be a private affair between gentlemen.

"What the *devil* are you doing here?" he exploded. "You could have been injured by a stray shot! You could have seen things you should never have seen! You could have distracted Captain Lord and caused him a fatal wound! Devil take it, Grace, what were you *thinking*?!"

Del had seen men sink like butter in the Caribbean sun under the admiral's wrath, had known naval officers who'd had seen death and destruction turn white when faced with it.

Instead, Grace just ignored him and reached for Del's arm.

"You're hurt," she said simply, her eyes shimmering with tears. And in that moment, Del would have gladly suffered a hundred such wounds in every extremity of his body if it meant that such a perfect woman would turn that worried face, that kind and gentle heart, those huge blue eyes, on him.

"'Tis merely a scratch," he said.

Colin was there, guiding him toward the base of the tree and out of the worst of the rain. "Take off your shirt, Del. Let me have a look at that."

"Here?"

"No, back in London, you fool. Of course, here. For God's sake, Del, you're bleeding."

Del glanced at Lady Grace.

"Take off your damned shirt, and do it now. That's an order," grumbled the admiral.

Del sighed and seizing the tails of the shirt, pulled it off over his head, leaving his torso bare to the rain, to the morning— and to Lady Grace's eyes.

Eyes that widened quite suddenly, though what was in them, Del couldn't quite read.

His attention had been caught by the bloodied flesh of his forearm.

The wound was worse than he'd anticipated, and now that it all but stared him in the face, he felt a swift hit of dizziness that passed as quickly as it came. Poor Lady Grace was not so disaffected; her hand went to her mouth in dismay, her cheeks lost all color, and without a word, she snatched the black silk shirt from

Del's hand and, using one sleeve, proceeded to tie a tourniquet just above his elbow.

As Colin set his case on the ground he happened to look up, and saw the girl deftly doing work that he'd been about to do, himself.

"Well," he said mildly, "It appears I have an able assistant." He pulled a flask from his bag and offered it to Del. "Here, drink this. Not all of it, though, as I've need of some. Do you want to do this here or in the coach?"

"Do what here? It's just a flesh wound."

"We'll know that after I have a look at it."

"He's still on his feet so he can bloody well walk to the coach," Sir Graham muttered. "No sense all of us standing out here in the rain."

"Really, sir, I would implore you to mind your language around a lady," Del said, and Sir Graham flushed darkly, muttered something unintelligible and turned away.

The young woman's gaze lifted and found Del's. The awkwardness he expected to feel after that impulsive kiss was absent. There was only concern there. Guilt, even. And seeing it only brought the temporary dizziness roaring back.

"Let's just do it here," Del said, thinking that the close and steamy confines of the coach were not a place he particularly wanted to be. Not with an irate admiral. Not with that same steamy, hot interior filled with the tinny scent of his own blood. No, he preferred the fresh air, and under the massive branch of the tree overhead, the shelter was quite acceptable. "But you, Lady Grace. Why don't you and your uncle take refuge in the coach. My brother is quite competent. He'll have me fixed up just fine."

"I will stay," she declared firmly.

Colin's gaze met Del's above the girl's head and Del saw the sudden twinkle in his brother's eyes.

"Sit down then, brother." he said. "If you faint, you won't have as far to fall."

"I don't *faint*," Del returned with righteous indignation. "And besides, the grass is wet."

But Lady Grace sat. Lady Grace had no worries about getting her lovely blue riding habit either wet or muddy, and as she looked up at Del and cocked her head, he sighed in defeat.

And sat.

Colin was pressing the flask on him again. Del drank and handed it back to his brother. Colin's strong, competent fingers were now against his forearm, and Del directed his gaze elsewhere. Sideways, to the rough, rain-stained bark of the oak that sheltered them. To Sir Graham standing against its massive trunk and gravely looking down at them. Up through the leafy branches to the clouds moving swiftly overhead. To the long, damp tendril of Lady Grace's hair that had escaped her hat and hung on her shoulder and trailed down to her bosom. He swallowed hard and shut his eyes. Around them the rain beat down, carried by a sudden wind that blew in from the sea, and he longed to retrieve his coat and put it over the girl's shoulders to protect her, but then Colin was pouring brandy over his raw flesh and the sensation caused him to suck in his breath and clamp his teeth down hard on the same language he'd just chastised his admiral for using.

"For God's sake, Colin!"

"Be still."

"Why are you wasting that by pouring it over my arm?"

"I have found it useful in preventing wounds from going bad. Now please. Let me do my work."

Del leaned his head back against the tree and shut his eyes. Rain dropped steadily from the leaves overhead, plopping against his forehead, his eyelashes, his cheeks. Damn, but his arm hurt. Hurt even more as

Colin's expert fingers began to probe it. Del clenched his teeth and opened his eyes. A raindrop hit him in the eyeball.

"Passed clean through," Colin pronounced, drawing back. He threaded a needle. "You're lucky. Especially after that blackguard rushed the mark and fired before you'd even had the chance to turn around. There's no honor in that. I'm tempted to call him out myself."

"You are correct, Mr. Lord! He didn't play fair at all!" Lady Grace added heatedly. "If I were a man, I'd go call him out myself!"

"If you were a man, your honor wouldn't have needed defending," Del put in.

"Yes, my *honor*. And for what absurd reason did you two even get into a duel over me, anyhow?"

"That is none of your concern."

Colin pinched his skin shut, pushed a needle through his skin, and Del bit down on a muffled curse.

"It is too my concern, since it was fought over me!"

The needle went in again, and Del felt the slippery slide of the thread through his skin. It was an unnerving feeling, and something must have shown on his face because Colin's voice was suddenly there, far away and then close, as though coming to him through a sea of murk.

"Holding up okay, brother?"

"Just get on with it. I want nothing more than a bath and a fresh change of clothes."

"D'you know what I want?" Lady Grace was saying, and she was so close that Del could smell the fragrance of her wet hair, feel the brush of her clothing as she adjusted her position beside him. He didn't resist the natural inclination of his body, and soon enough he was leaning against her, tentatively at first and then, when she did not move away, with abandon. He shut his eyes, taking what bliss he could.

Damn you, Ponsonby. Damn you to hell and back for having her heart.

"No clue," he said, in answer to her question.

"I want to go find that wretched man who did this to you and tell him just what I think of him!"

Colin was pulling another stitch through.

"You will do no such thing," Del said, trying to think of anything but the needle. "You'll say something to anger him and then we'll be right back out here fighting another duel this time tomorrow."

"Then I'll have my uncle punish him for what he did! Uncle Gray? You will punish him, won't you? *Won't you?*"

"Grace, I really think you should leave this affair to us."

"Leaving it to you three nearly got him killed! Oh, no, I won't let this stand. I'm going to tell everyone I know how cowardly that wretched man is and what he did! And I'm going to start the moment we get back!"

"It's over, Lady Grace. And trust me, I'll be— ouch! For heaven's sake, Colin, I'm not fabric in an embroidery hoop!"

"Almost done."

Del took another direct hit in the other eyeball from a drop of rain, and wiped his eye with the back of his wrist. He looked down at the wound with the needle and thread going in and out of it beneath his brother's bent head. His stomach swam and he cursed himself for his weakness. And then he felt it.

Her arm, lithe and strong, coming around his back to support him. Holding him close.

Colin, damn him, chose that very moment to finish up, and as he deftly tied off the last stitch and snipped it with a pair of scissors, that sweet little arm fell away and Del was suddenly cold and wet and miserable.

"There," Colin said at last. "All done." He wiped the needle with a cloth, stuck it through a spool of thread and returned them to the wooden case. "I think we should bandage that, though. Best to keep it clean and dry."

"It's fine," Del said, and got to his feet. He felt suddenly lightheaded and swayed, cursing himself for a second time.

"Are you all right, Captain Lord?" came Lady Grace's voice from what seemed to be far away.

"I'm fine. Just famished and in need of breakfast." He smiled to try and put her at ease, and reached down to help her up. Her fingers were wet and damp within his own, her hand dwarfed by his.

And then she untied his shirtsleeve from his arm and shaking the garment out, offered it to him, her eyes soft. Their gazes met. He felt the now-familiar slash of current pass between them that left him dry-mouthed and hungry for her, left him wanting to take her in his arms and kiss her senseless the way he'd done just hours before. She must have felt it too, as she blushed and looked away. Wordlessly, Del offered her his good arm. She took it, he covered her hand with his own to keep it dry, and together, the four of them walked back to the coach.

❦ 31 ❦

P onsonby was waiting for them when they returned to the house.

There he stood in the front hall, hat in his hand, dripping wet and the picture of alarm. He must have just arrived.

"I came just as soon as I heard about it," he said breathlessly. "Lady Grace! Are you all right?"

"Oh, Captain Ponsonby! Your colleague here has fought a duel over me, and I hope you'll have a word with your lieutenant on how he behaved! He rushed to the mark and turned before Captain Lord here even had a chance to do the same and thus had an unfair advantage, and—"

"That's enough, Grace," said the admiral. "Captain Ponsonby and I will discuss it. You must be hungry. We all are, I daresay. Ah, Lady Ariadne. Maeve, my dear. Thank God at least *two* of the females in this house saw fit to stay out of men's affairs though I'd like to know which one of you told Grace here where the duel was held, and how to get there."

Lady Falconer just smiled, her eyes gleaming.

"Breakfast, anyone?" asked Lady Ariadne, also smiling.

Running footsteps and then Ned appeared, his face

pale and anxious. Childlike, he ran straight to Captain Lord and then stopped, pulling himself up and proceeding with what he thought was measured calm. "Nobody died, I hope?"

"Nobody died," said Captain Lord who, to Grace's dismay, had retreated behind a wall of stiffness at sight of the other captain.

She tried to soften the sudden tension in the room.

"Captain Lord spared Lieutenant Akers' life," she babbled. "And this, after Lieutenant Akers shot him. If someone had shot me, I wouldn't have been so restrained! I would've shot him back! But Captain Lord fired high. I think that was very noble of him, don't you, Captain Ponsonby?"

"Rather frowned upon in the rules of the *code duello*, I daresay," he returned, and the atmosphere in the room went even colder as Captain Lord's eyes hardened and he swung to face the other man.

"You wish to be next, Ponsonby?"

"That's enough, both of you," snapped Sir Graham. "I'll hear no more on the matter from either one of you or anyone else." He bestowed a stern look at his niece. "And that includes you too, young lady."

"Why don't we all go to the dining room and have some breakfast," Lady Ariadne said cheerily. "Such a gloomy day, I'm sure some eggs and toast, pastry and a pot of tea will be just the thing."

"I have already broken my fast," said Captain Ponsonby, with a polite inclination of his head. "But I'll take some coffee, if I may."

"Why don't you go and take yourself off, instead?" snapped Captain Lord.

"I *beg* your pardon?"

"Del, what is the matter?"

"There is nothing the matter, Lady Falconer. Nothing at all. If you will all excuse me, I'll take breakfast up in my room. Good day, all of you."

He turned on his heel and stalked to the stairway, leaving Sir Graham frowning, Captain Ponsonby wondering what to do about the affront, and Grace exchanging a confused look with Lady Falconer.

The tension in the room softened at his disappearance.

"Yes, let's eat," said the admiral. "Dirty weather out there, not a good day to be out of doors."

Grace stood there for a moment as everyone began to file toward the dining room. Captain Ponsonby lingered behind and with a blinding smile, offered his arm to her. She took it, feeling suddenly uncertain.

Look! He is noticing me! Does it get any better than this?

But the triumphant voice was small and even a little desperate, and it was in her head, not her heart.

Is it possible that I don't care for Captain Ponsonby as much as I think I do?

The arm beneath her fingers was strong and muscled, hard and unyielding, and another man's arm flashed into her mind, the one belonging to the man who had just removed himself from their company and gone upstairs, the man who had tenderly covered her hand to keep it dry, the man who had fought a duel over her.

Fought a duel over her.

Grace's heart swam with confusion, and she felt a sudden overwhelming guilt.

He did all that for you, and yet here you are with Captain Ponsonby, your dream finally coming true.

Her other self answered back. *But Captain Lord knows how you feel about Captain Ponsonby. He agreed to help you win his heart. There's nothing to feel guilty about.*

They entered the dining room. Outside, the rain streaked against the windows and pale silver patches began to show amongst the dark scudding clouds. The room lightened and within the myriad colors of the sky outside, thin bits of blue began to show.

Captain Ponsonby pulled out her chair for her and seated her.

Took a spot beside her.

Grace was barely aware of the food being served, her appetite suddenly gone and her mouth too dry to swallow anything, anyhow. She took tea, sugaring it well, steadying her shaking hands by anchoring them around the hot porcelain. She pretended to engage in the conversation around her but inside, she wondered what Captain Lord was doing upstairs, if he was sinking into the hot bath he'd professed to want, if his arm hurt, and if he was thinking of her.

As she was of him.

She longed to go to him, to make sure he was all right, but Lady Ariadne was inviting them all out to the stables after breakfast so she could show them the famous Shareb-er-rehh, the clearing skies outside the window promised what looked to be a fine summer day after all, and Grace had no chance to make her escape.

BREAKFAST HAD FINISHED. HIS CRAVING FOR COFFEE satisfied, Sheldon Ponsonby stayed behind for a few moments as the others filed out of the room and headed for the stable.

He saw Lady Grace look back at him, her brow furrowed, and smiled at her in reassurance that all was well.

He waited until she'd gone and then hailed the admiral before he could join them.

"A word if I may, Sir Graham?"

"If it's about another damned duel, or the one that took place this morning, I don't want to hear it. But you'd damn well better have a word with Akers."

"I will, sir. But that's not what I wished to talk to you about."

Ned was lingering, pretending to be scrounging for a last pastry in an ill-concealed attempt to eavesdrop.

"Out with it, then."

"In private, if I may, sir?"

Sir Graham looked at his son. "Off with you, lad. We'll be along in a moment."

The boy nodded and left the room.

"Spill it, man." said the admiral. "What is this about?"

Sheldon drew himself up, smiling. "It is about Lady Grace," he said. "It has not escaped me, that she is exceptionally kind-hearted, brave, and of course, uncommonly beautiful. That she typifies the best of her sex. I am enchanted by her. There, I've admitted it."

Sir Graham just stared at him, his face inscrutable.

Pressing on, Sheldon Ponsonby blurted, "With your permission, sir, I would like to court her."

DEL HAD FINISHED HIS BATH, DRIED HIMSELF WITH A thick fluffy towel, dressed and sat down at his desk to compose a letter to his parents. Anything was better than staying here feeling his heart break into a million pieces over yet another woman he couldn't have, another woman who'd fallen for someone else, when a fierce knocking on his door caused him to put the quill down and look up.

"Who is it?"

"It's me, Ned. May I come in, sir?"

"Aye, come in."

The door opened, the boy slipped inside, and hastily shut the door behind him. "We have an emergency," he said gravely. "A *real* one."

"This whole damned holiday is an emergency. In fact, I was just writing to my parents to tell them I'll be leaving here immediately and heading down to Hampshire to visit them."

"Sir, this is serious."

Del raised a hand, raked it through his damp, freshly washed, and frizzing like a halo around the moon-hair, and shoved the curls off his forehead. "What is it?"

"I just overhead that awful Captain Ponsonby speaking to my father."

"He's not awful."

"Yes he is, and you think he's just as awful as I do."

"No, I do not."

"He asked Papa if he could court Lady Grace!"

"Right, then, he's bloody awful. Thank you, Ned. You may go, now."

"But sir! You have to do something!"

"What am I supposed to do? Your cousin came to me before we even left her mother's wedding to tell me she fancied herself in love with Ponsonby and asked if I might help her win his heart. It would seem as though I have accomplished that aim."

"That's not what you really want. I can tell!"

"Oh?" Del raised a brow. "What is it I really want?"

"Grace! You're in love with her!"

Del said nothing. He carefully wiped the pen off, put it in its brass holder, capped the bottle of ink.

"Funny, isn't it," he said at length, "that you, a young boy, have discerned that unhappy truth whereas the lady in question remains painfully oblivious to it."

"Is that why you're going to Hampshire?"

"Better that than the alternative, which is likely to be another duel." He folded the letter, sealed it with wax and signed it with his signet ring. "You may know me, Ned, as a man of restraint. Of protocol, rigorously defined and defended. But your cousin brings things out of me that are beyond my control, and it is not good for either of us that I remain here. I am only complicating things for her. Confusing her. You understand that, don't you?"

"I don't want you to go."

"We will meet back on *Orion* when it's time to return to Barbados. Which, given your father's obvious stress over this trip, is likely to be sooner rather than later. He's short of temper, unhappy, constrained. I fear for his health."

"I don't think my cousin will want you to go, either."

"Your cousin has got what she wanted. A handsome man with a fine reputation from a good family who will treat her with kindness and dignity. The man she'd set her sights on all along."

"You're all that and more, Captain Lord!"

Del stood up, his chest full and his arm throbbing beneath the sleeve. He blew out the candle and laid a hand on the boy's thin shoulder. "Someday, Ned, you will understand how the heart works. Or maybe, like the rest of us, you will not. But I do know this. We cannot order it to love someone it does not, nor can we order it to stop loving someone we can never have. Lady Grace will be happy. Let it go at that."

❦ 32 ❧

T he clouds were filing off to the east, and the sky they left behind was bright and clear and blue. The scent of the sea hung heavily on the freshly-scrubbed air and sunlight sparkled on the grass as the party, led by Lady Ariadne and accompanied by a trio of dogs, headed towards the stable to meet the famous Norfolk Thoroughbreds.

There was not a person in all of England who did not know of the legendary match race between Shareber-rehh and the devil horse, the indomitable Black Patrick, though four years had elapsed since the contest had proven Lady Ariadne's stallion much the fastest in all of England. And there in his paddock and grazing some distance away, stood a tall bay horse whose coat gleamed in the sun. His black tail swished at a fly and he appeared not to have a care in the world.

Lady Ariadne paused at the fence and called to the stallion. Immediately, his head shot up, his fine ears pricked, and kicking off his flight with a bucking leap, he came thundering across the pasture toward them.

"Hello, Shareb!" said his mistress, fondly pulling at his forelock before reaching into a basket and producing a pastry from the breakfast table. The horse took it from her palm, munching happily. She grinned and looked at her guests. "Please don't tell Colin," she said conspiratorially. "He doesn't approve of raspberry tarts as part of the equine diet."

Her husband, who'd hung back a bit to throw a ball to the three dogs, came up. His bad leg might have hindered him, but there was nothing wrong with his eyesight.

He slid a hand around his wife's waist. "I saw that," he chided.

She laughed. "I figured you would."

"What a splendid animal," said Lady Falconer, studying the stallion and stroking his broad, flat cheek. "How my mother would envy me this opportunity to see such a horse. She was passionate about them... why, we all learned to ride before we could even walk."

Nobody said anything, for Lady Falconer had lost her parents only a few months before. As though sensing her sudden pain, the stallion pushed his jaw against her hand and closed his eyes, just standing there in silent communion with her.

Grace, still on Captain Ponsonby's arm, exchanged a glance with her uncle. The sadness was there in his eyes, too.

She directed her gaze back to the horse. Aunt Maeve was correct. The famous Shareb-er-rehh was tall and well-muscled, with a large dark eye and a big white blaze that tumbled down his noble face. And now, as he pushed his chest against the fencing and hung his head over it, allowing the former pirate-queen to stroke his cheek, he opened that dark eye and settled it on Grace. She could lose herself in that mysterious orb, and she wondered if he could sense her pain and confusion as he so obviously seemed to sense Lady Falconer's grief.

Captain Ponsonby eyed the horse. "I suppose," he said tentatively, "that it's out of the question to borrow him for a ride? I would love to show Lady Grace here, some of the surrounding countryside."

The horse's ears went flat and he stepped back.

"Was it something I said?" asked the captain, with a nervous little laugh.

It was Colin Lord who cleared his throat and said quietly, "Shareb-er-rehh will allow no one on his back except for my wife. But there are other horses here, far gentler ones, that you're welcome to take out for a ride. Or even a drive, if you would rather."

"A drive would be quite nice," said Ponsonby, relieved to be saved from his sudden embarrassment. "Lady Grace? Would you care to accompany me?"

She sensed a sudden tension around her, as though Captain Ponsonby had made some sort of *faux pas* with his initial request— and deepened it by inviting her out for a drive. As though he were treading on ground that those around her would prefer he stayed off. Did they not like the man?

She cast a glance toward her uncle, who had been uncharacteristically silent. "Uncle Gray?"

There was something fleeting and pained in his eyes, but it was gone so fast she wondered if she'd imagined it. "Yes, you may, but do take either Ned or Polly with you for the sake of appearances."

"Of course," said Captain Ponsonby, answering for her and flashing his dazzling smile.

Grace smiled back. Excitement warred with something else in her gut, something that felt unpleasant and wrong. Very wrong. Wasn't this what she'd been waiting for? Something she'd been wanting all along?

Again she thought of the morning. Of Delmore Lord and his brave defense of her so-called honor, of the way he'd looked suddenly wan and ill as his brother had sewn up his wound and how she, Grace, had had an unexplainable urge to take him into her arms and hold him.

And she thought of the night before.

He kissed me.

And it felt so... so right.

"Lady Grace? Shall we go?"

"Yes, Captain Ponsonby." She swallowed against the sudden dry spot in the back of her throat. "I would like that very much."

⚜

FROM THE UPSTAIRS WINDOW OF HIS ROOM, DEL gazed down upon the small party as they headed toward the pasture.

He did not want to look. And if he were smart, he'd have yanked the drapes shut and denied himself the opportunity to further torture himself.

But Lady Grace was down there, her dark hair loosely caught up beneath a jaunty little hat, her body trim and lithe in that same blue riding habit. She was standing with the others; Sir Graham and Lady Falconer, Colin and Ariadne, several dogs and yes, that insufferable peacock, Ponsonby.

As Del watched, the man offered his arm to Grace, and smiling up at him, she took it.

A moment later their backs were turned and they were walking away toward the paddock, the gentle sway of the girl's hips and the sound of her laughter as it drifted up to him, causing something to catch in his chest and flame in his loins.

I am damned.

Damned and double-damned.

The kisses had meant nothing. The sparks between them meant nothing. He'd got his hopes up for nothing.

She had made her choice.

He called for Thorne and sent him to find out when the stage ran. He tidied up his room, a task another man might've left to his valet or a housekeeper. He, however, needed something to do and the small staff in his brother's employ surely had enough other things to contend with than cleaning up after yet another guest.

He felt invisible. He was used to feeling invisible.

Might as well wipe away any trace that he'd ever even been here and further that notion. Invisible people left no traces. There was no need to stay here, really, with the pain of Lady Grace's victory staring him in the face. And he had no desire to.

Jimmy Thorne returned just as Del, having pulled the sheets off the bed, was folding them and laying them in a neat pile on a chair. If he thought such an action was beneath the captain's station, he wisely kept his thoughts to himself.

"The stage down to London comes every afternoon just after one," the man said, frowning as he watched Del pull the coverlet back up over the bed and neaten it with military precision. "We can catch it at the inn in the village. Shall I procure tickets, sir?"

Del paused and in that moment, he heard Lady Grace's laughter from outside and the sound pierced his heart.

"Thank you," he said simply, and pulling out his purse, deposited some coin in the man's hand. "That would be most appreciated."

THORNE LEFT.

The room was silent and still. Echoing with emptiness. With the drapes shutting out the day outside, Del opened the desk once more, pulled out the quill from its brass case, uncapped the ink bottle, and put pen to paper.

"MY DEAR LADY GRACE,
I hope you will forgive me for my sudden departure, but it

*would appear that our efforts have yielded the prize you had
sought, and my services to that effect are no longer needed.*

*Our trip to England was never intended to be a lengthy
one, and as it has been some years since I've visited my parents,
I have decided to catch the afternoon stage and return to
Hampshire so that I might see them. I am sorry I did not get
the chance to say goodbye, but do know that I will forever
think of you with fondness and respect, and wish you and your
captain well. If you should ever have need of me, I will always
be honored to offer you my services.*

Your friend, always,
Capt. Lord

＊ 33 ＊

H ambledon, Hampshire, England.

DEIRDRE O'DEVIR LORD WAS A HANDSOME WOMAN of some years, and she was busy going over the week's meal plan with the housekeeper, Mrs. Adams, when the butler announced that they had a visitor whose identity he was asked, by the visitor himself, to keep secret.

"How odd!" said the Irishwoman, and tucking a long silver curl up into her hopelessly disheveled coiffure and twisting it around another strand to keep it there, left Mrs. Adams with the menu and headed toward the hall.

"Christian?" she poked her head into the library where her husband, his ankles propped on a leather footstool and a book in his hand, looked up. He was still as handsome as he'd been when she'd first met him all those years ago, as virile and commanding now as he was then, and she was glad that he'd finally retired from the Admiralty so she could have him all to herself. His gray eyes warmed when he saw her and he put the book down. "Is everything all right?"

"'Tis an unknown visitor who's come a-calling," she said. "Won't tell Mr. Adams who 'e is."

The admiral swung his legs from the stool, and got to his feet. His joints were increasingly stiff these days, especially when rain was in the air, and he vowed to add another half-mile to his afternoon walk in an attempt to loosen up. He'd be damned if he'd seize up like some of the other old coots his age. He may not be a young man, but he had plenty of fight left in him yet.

Arm in arm, the two of them walked from the library.

A figure, hauntingly familiar, stood in the gray light coming in through the tall, many-paned leaden windows. He had allowed Mr. Adams to take his hat and coat, and stood with his back to them looking out over the downs. For the briefest of seconds Deirdre thought she was looking at her brother Ruaidri, so alike was this young man's wildly curling black hair to that of her brother's, so proud and erect was his stance. And in the next second he turned, and she let out a happy shriek of excitement.

"Delmore!"

She ran to him and threw herself into his arms, laughing, the sharp edges of the bejeweled cross around her neck pressing into her flesh and his, molding her to her son, cementing their Irishness in this very English part of the world she had called her home for decades now. She hugged him with fierce abandon, and sudden tears filled her eyes and spilled down her cheeks. She grasped his shoulders and held him at arms' length, inspecting him with the thoroughness that only a mother could give.

"Ye're lookin' grand," she said fondly, perusing him. "But yer color's not good. Are ye feeling all right, my little laddie? Ye need to eat more, I think. I know ye've always been picky about yer food, and maybe coconuts and bananas are all Sir Graham has t' feed ye out there in Barbados, but ye're going t' waste away to nothing if ye don't pack some meat on those bones of yers!"

Her son laughed, a sound that warmed her heart because Del had always been her serious one. Even now she could see a deep pain in his eyes, a pain that made them almost purple, and her motherly heart wondered at the cause of it. But he was here, and there was plenty of time to not only feed him, but to learn and do something about whatever it was that had him looking so lost and forlorn.

"I can assure you, Mother, that we have more than coconuts and bananas to eat in Barbados. But I will admit to a certain craving for a good Irish stew. Preferably with that brown bread you always used to make when we were little."

His father formally extended a hand. "Delmore, son. It's good to have you home."

"Thank you, sir. It is good to be home."

"Not much to do around here now that I've retired from the Admiralty. I daresay, I'm bored out of my mind."

"And yer father cannot stand being bored," his mother chirped. "In fact, he's going t' write a book. 'Twill be about all the wonders of the world he's seen from the quarterdecks of various ships. He's even going t' illustrate it!"

"*Attempt* to illustrate it," said her husband, rather sheepishly. "I'm only just learning how to draw."

"You're more than proficient at anything you set your mind to," Del said, and meant it. He'd always felt somewhat stiff and uncomfortable around his father, as though he might never quite measure up to what his father expected of him, though there was no denying that the admiral was more relaxed than Del had ever seen him and privately, he decided that retirement must agree with him.

"Let me ring for tea," his mother said and off she bustled, humming. She had aged a bit since Del had last seen her, her hair grayer, her face more lined and her waist a bit thicker, but her effervescent spirit and earthy gentleness hadn't changed a bit. He looked forward to just... being here, in his childhood home, where he could relax with his family and put Lady Grace and her memory far behind him.

"So how are you keeping, Del?" asked his father, motioning toward the hall and the library beyond. "Sir Graham treating you all right?"

"Aye, sir, but being his flag captain is more demanding than I'd have thought it would be."

"He'll teach you well. I can't think of a finer mentor than one of Nelson's own. And if he's demanding, that's to your benefit, and you know it as well as I do."

"Of course," said Del, because it was unspoken knowledge between them that he, like his father before him, like his father before him— another Delmore, for whom he'd been named, much to his chagrin— had been admirals, and he was expected to follow the same path.

He strode with his father to the gold drawing room. His mother had always said she'd chosen the paper because it reminded her of the color of her husband's hair, and while the walls were still a pale, sunny gilt that was quite cheerful against the day's grayness, the draperies were new, the heavy fabric from the last century now replaced by a pale blue silk on which embroidered little birds flitted amongst green and yellow leaves. Above the fireplace mantel was a painting, poorly executed, of a ship of the line standing into what appeared to be Portsmouth Roads.

His mother reappeared, her boundless energy right along with her. "I see ye admiring that lovely work of art, Del! Doesn't it fit the room well? Yer father painted it last month. 'Twas his first piece, and I'm ever so proud of him."

Del put a hand over his helpless grin to hide it. The

painting was awful. He pitied the book that was about to bear the burden of his father's illustrations.

But then his heart softened. His austere father, always a perfectionist, always so very good at whatever he set his mind to, had found a challenge he had yet to master and Del figured that as long as his sire had something to strive toward, especially in retirement, his remaining years would be both rich and bountiful.

He went to his favorite old chair, relieved that it still wore the striped damask that he'd known as a child. As he sat, he felt a sudden wave of weakness.

"Are you well, my son?"

"I'm fine, Mother. Just—" he smiled wanly— "just hungry."

Tea was brought in, the steam rising from the same old floral porcelain pot he'd always known, the same little cups that his mother had always brought out for their best company. The hot brew splashed into the cups. He looked hopefully at the plate of refreshments as it was set down before them and his heart, so recently bruised, so heavily laden, filled with that special joy of homecoming, of being back where he belonged. For there was the same thick brown bread his mother had always made, cut up into little rectangles and spread with thick pats of rich yellow butter.

Del sipped his tea, but as he looked at the bread, sudden nausea assailed him. He thought of the back and forth sway of the coach all the way down from Norfolk and wondered if perhaps, now that he'd finally escaped such torment, this was the equivalent of seasickness. It certainly explained why his muscles ached, and why wouldn't they, trying to maintain his balance in such an unpredictable contraption? He lifted the teacup to his mouth. Heat flooded him from the inside out, leaving perspiration popping out on his forehead.

His mother was eyeing him critically. "Are you ill, Del?"

He set down the cup before his suddenly shaking hand could spill it. "I think I'm just out of sorts from the trip down from Norfolk," he said. "We went up to visit Colin and his family."

"How is he? Ariadne? The boys?"

"Happy. They're doing well for themselves."

I wonder what Lady Grace is doing at the moment. If she read my note with relief that I removed myself from a situation that would only cause her guilt and confusion. It was the right thing to do.

Wasn't it?

"We were there for Christmas," his father put in. "Had a wonderful time. Some nearby farmer brought a sick horse to your brother and he cured it when the farmer himself thought the poor creature needed to be shot and put out of its misery." He reached for his tea. "It broke my heart when he left the Navy, but he's as good an animal doctor as he was a naval officer. Got to admit, I'm proud of him."

"He wields a mean needle," Del said, willing his nausea away. "I got to stand in for one of his patients."

"What?"

"Oh, just a minor scratch."

By now, Ponsonby's probably already asked Sir Graham for her hand. By now, they've probably already set about getting the banns posted, planning her wedding trousseau, dreaming of their future together.

His brow was beginning to throb and he rubbed at it, feeling slick, clammy moisture that came away on his fingers.

"Del, ye don't look well a'tall," his mother said in sudden concern, putting her cup down. "Come, let's get ye settled into yer room. Ye need to rest."

"I'm fine, Mother." He reached again for his tea, paused, put it down, and pushed himself to his feet. As he did, the room revolved around him, and he grabbed at the back of the chair to keep himself steady. The pounding in his temples began to beat like a marine's drum, his heartbeat increasing right along with it and he feared, suddenly, that he was going to be sick.

He barely felt his father supporting him as they made their way up the stairs, heard his own voice coming from far away as he asked for a chamber pot before he could cast up his accounts all over the carpeting, felt nothing but the blissful embrace of the soft featherbed as he tumbled, fully clothed, onto its blessed expanse.

By the time his mother got his sweat-soaked shirt off him and gasped in horror at the red and puffy wound swelling beneath a row of stitches on his forearm, he was already unconscious.

"Jesus, Joseph n' Mary," she breathed, her hand going to her mouth. The face she turned up to her husband was white. "Christian? What is it?"

"I'm guessing it's blood poisoning," he said grimly.

His wife pressed both hands to her mouth. They exchanged glances, and looked again at the angry wound on their son's arm.

Both of them knew it was a certain death sentence.

"Del. *Del!*" his father demanded. "What has happened to you?"

But his son was already well past answering.

T he day was glorious, the curricle was open, the horse was fancy, and the man handling the ribbons was Captain Sheldon Ponsonby.

Grace sat beside him, pressed by necessity against him, really, as the seat was exceedingly narrow. They were on the flat, grassy course on which the Norfolk Thoroughbreds trained, the wheels gliding over the turf and occasionally hitting a bump that sent her knocking against her companion. The hedge to her left seemed to fly past in a blur, and she felt the wind on her cheeks, pulling at her hat-strings and playing with the folds of her skirts.

Lady Ariadne had invited some of the local gentry for an afternoon lawn party, and a small crowd was lounging in the center of the field. Spots of color marked the pretty gowns worn by the daughters of those same gentry, all of whom were glaring daggers at Grace for having the good fortune to be the current occupant of Captain Ponsonby's curricle, as well as attention.

By now, word had got round that he was formally courting her.

Yes, this day should have been the pinnacle of her joy, this jaunt in the curricle with the man of her dreams, a bigger-than-life memory to take out and re-live with sighs and smiles for every day of the rest of her life.

Should have been.

And on the surface, it was. She smiled happily up at her handsome suitor, felt the sweet summer breeze on her face and in her nostrils. Beneath the surface though, currents ran strong, tainting her joy and making what should have been a grand day, one of conflicting emotions.

And it was all because of Captain Lord.

He'd been gone less than a week, but she felt his absence in a profound and piercing way that troubled her. How shocked she'd been when she'd found his note beneath the door to her room. Even now she remembered her numbness at his sudden departure, which had felt like a blow to the stomach. Her anger. And finally her sorrow, which lingered still, and sent the only clouds scudding across what should have been a happy heart at the situation in which she currently found herself.

You didn't even say goodbye.

Did our friendship mean so little to you?

The pain at his defection was almost visceral, and she forced him from her mind. She would not let Captain Lord or anyone else, anything else, ruin this day that she had hoped for, longed for, all but prayed for, for so long.

And yet...

"Why so pensive, Lady Grace?"

"I'm sorry," she said with a smile meant to be reassuring. "I have a lot on my mind today."

"It's far too perfect of an afternoon to be troubling yourself with heavy thoughts." He clicked to the horse. "Are you enjoying yourself?"

"I am."

"I hope you're not frightened. Am I driving too fast? I'll slow down if you wish."

"No, it is fine."

"Are you cold? Hot? Getting too much sun?"

"No, I'm quite content, Captain." He looked genuinely concerned and she suddenly felt both guilty and irritated. "I'm sorry if I gave you that impression. I'm not frightened at all."

"Good to hear. Because after giving each of the Falconer and Lord children a ride, I feared the poor horse would be spent by the time it was your turn. I must say, if I could trade each of the turns that were wasted on a child for yet another one with you, I would be the happiest man alive today."

Grace's pasted-on-smile froze in place. "Wasted on a child?"

He had the good grace to redden. "I beg your pardon, poor choice of words on my part. What I meant to say, Lady Grace, is that I regret any moment spent with others when it could have been with you."

She felt a bristle of irritation. "That is very gallant, Captain, but I don't regret seeing the delight of each child who enjoyed a ride in your curricle. Why, it was surely the highlight of the day for each of them."

He steered the horse around a slight depression in the turf. "Well, maybe not for young Ned Falconer. Poor lad looks quite miserable, I daresay."

Grace glanced toward the grassy field, where Colin and Lady Ariadne, the Falconers, Lord and Lady Weybourne (the brother and sister-in-law of their hostess) and several neighboring families were abandoning their game of croquet to enjoy picnic baskets that footmen were setting down near blankets spread out over the grass. The admiral, looking peaceful and relaxed, was deep in conversation with Colin, their wives digging into the picnic baskets and handing food to eager children. Mary and Anne Falconer were chasing a butterfly, their high giggles and laughter floating on the wind. And sure enough, there was Ned.

The boy stood a distance apart from them, sullenly watching the curricle. Something about his face tugged at Grace's heartstrings, and she lifted a hand to wave to him.

He did not wave back. Instead he turned and walked away, heading back toward the house.

Grace frowned, and the day lost even more of its luster. What was troubling the boy?

"Pay him no mind," Captain Ponsonby said, laying a hand over her own. "He's a surly lad, that one."

"He is my little cousin, and he is not surly," Grace said, feeling another flash of irritation. And it wasn't just irritation. It was an unhappiness coming from a place she couldn't quite access, let alone understand.

What's the matter with you? You've wanted this for a long time, and now it's happening. Look! You're riding in an open curricle with the man of your dreams!

She watched the boy walking away.

If he's the man of my dreams, then why do I feel so flat and cold? Why do I feel this odd guilt, and why does being here with him seem so... so wrong?

Another face, with cool gray eyes and a too-serious mouth, wild black curls and broad shoulders. A friendship she didn't deserve, had never deserved. A man who had kissed her senseless in a darkened room and fought a duel on her behalf, who had come into her life and so quickly walked out of it without even a proper goodbye. A lump rose in her throat, and tears burned behind her eyes, and she suddenly realized why she felt such guilt at being with Sheldon Ponsonby.

You're not supposed to be with Captain Ponsonby.

Well, of course she was. He was handsome and kind and courteous. He was gentle with the horse, solicitous of her health, her comfort, her feelings. He was actually quite perfect.

You're just rattled because of Ned's strange behavior. You've got cold feet because you finally got what you wanted and you didn't expect it to happen so quickly. What is wrong with you, you ninny? Captain Ponsonby is a heartbeat from offering for you. It's what Mama had hoped for when she invited him to the wedding. What you had hoped for. Any woman would be proud to be on his arm!

"Well, if young master Ned is out of sorts, I'm sure he'll get over it soon enough," Captain Ponsonby said briskly. He leaned close to Grace, and she felt the brush of his lips against her temple.

Everything inside of her went cold, and she stiffened.

"I think I would like to go back now," she said, making a big pretense of smoothing her skirts. "I find myself ever so thirsty."

"A splendid idea," he said, and laid his palm over her kneecap for the briefest of moments before turning the horse in a wide circle, lowering the whip, and pulling back on the ribbons to ease the animal down to a walk. "I'll just cool him out as we walk back. Unless you are in a hurry?"

"The horse's welfare comes first," she said with a wan smile, and suddenly realized that Captain Ponsonby had slowed the horse not only for its own welfare, but to prolong the extent of their time together before joining the others.

Grace pressed her knees together, trying to maintain a narrower profile. She was beginning to feel an inexplicable panic. Especially when he stretched an arm along the back of the seat.

Soon enough, they were approaching the gathering, the Falconer twins rushing up to touch the horse. Movement caught her eye, and she turned her head to see a servant approaching, bearing a silver tray on which was a letter.

He made straight for Colin Lord. Their host took the letter, broke the seal and opened it. As Grace waited for Captain Ponsonby to help her down, she saw

Colin's face go white, saw him say something to Sir Graham and pass him the letter, saw the admiral lose his relaxed amiability and put out a hand to touch Colin's shoulder. Both men had got to their feet, their faces grave.

"Bad news, by the look of things," murmured Captain Ponsonby, jumping lightly down from the curricle. "I'm sure it's concerning the French. It's always concerning the French." He reached a hand up to help Grace down. "I hope I'm not getting sent back out on sea patrol. Not when I've just discovered the joy of your company, Lady Grace."

The admiral was saying something to Lady Falconer, and now heading toward them. Colin Lord was now hurrying in his odd, purposeful limp toward the house. A shadow had definitely come over the afternoon, and Grace felt a sudden tremor of dread.

She hurried to her uncle.

"What is it, Uncle Gray?"

"My flag captain," he said shortly. "He's developed blood poisoning from his wound and isn't expected to survive the week."

HE HANDED THE LETTER TO GRACE.

MY DEAREST COLIN,

I am sending this letter with the utmost urgency. Your brother arrived earlier today and is sick with a fever. He has a terrible wound on his arm and between the two, we fear blood poisoning. We have sent for the doctor, but I didn't want to waste any time in writing to you as you may wish to come immediately to say goodbye. I fear your brother won't last the week. If you have a person named Grace with you, please bring her along, as he is out of his head and calling for her. Godspeed.

Love, Mama

"POOR CHAP," SAID CAPTAIN PONSONBY, AS GRACE silently read the letter. "I hope they've found him a doctor who had the sense to amputate, only way to save a man's life after something like that."

Grace, stricken, couldn't move. She just stood there, trying to swallow, trying to reclaim the feel of the ground beneath her feet, the sound of her breath through her lungs, which had stopped and now hung, suspended, somewhere in her throat. She pressed the letter to her heart and blinked away the sudden tears.

"Lady Grace?"

It was Captain Ponsonby, his perfect brow furrowed, his hand coming out to take her own.

"This is all my fault," Grace whispered, her eyes flooding. "Oh, dear God..."

"You must not fret," said the captain. "It will not do your sensibilities any good to—"

"You don't understand!"

He blinked, confused, and in the next minute Grace had found her feet, and was running toward the house, passing Colin Lord and quickly catching up to Ned.

He turned as she came up behind him, breathing hard. Turned his head and picked up his pace.

"Ned!"

"I already know."

"Already know what?"

"That something bad has happened to Captain Lord."

"How can you know that?!"

"I just do. I know lots of things."

He continued his march toward the house, trying to put distance between them.

"Ned, please wait!"

He whirled then, and his face was red and angry, his

mouth mutinous. "You should never have accepted Captain Ponsonby's suit, Grace! You might as well have just cut Captain Lord's heart out of his chest and fed it to him. How could you do that to him? Why were you so cruel? And now he's probably dying, and it's all your fault!"

The boy's eyes blazed, then filled with tears.

"Oh, Ned..."

"He was in love with you, and you couldn't see it because you were so wrapped up in Captain Ponsonby. You broke his heart, you know. Why do you think he left? It was because he couldn't stay here and see the woman he loved fawning over another man!" The boy wiped angrily at his eye with the back of his knuckle. "I thought better of you, Grace. After all that he did for you!"

The boy turned and this time, he was no longer walking in the determined strides of the man he was trying so hard to be. He was running, a child once more, and in his wake Grace heard his sobs. He reached the door, tore it open, and fled into the house.

Grace stood there on the lawn. Colin Lord, the speckled gundog trotting at his heels, caught up to her.

"I assume you're going to Hampshire," she said, falling into step beside him.

"Immediately." He turned then, his kind and gentle eyes, so much like Captain Lord's, filled with pain. "I'm sorry to leave you all so suddenly, but he's my brother. The only brother I have." His gaze turned bleak. "I can only hope that I get there in time to say goodbye."

"I'm going with you."

He looked at her and nodded. "Good. I'd hoped you would. Let's pray we're not too late."

❧ 35 ❧

H e lay in this bed that had been his as a child, his muscles aching, his very bones on fire, his skin slick with sweat and his body shaking with cold beneath three heavy wool blankets. He rolled over, trying to get comfortable. Moved an arm. Moved it again, this time under his pillow in an attempt to support his aching head. Beyond the window, the Hampshire Downs stood like sentinels against the night, and eventually their glow was lost to the gloom and finally, backlit by stars.

His mother came in, wrung out a cloth in cold water, and tenderly bathed his brow. In the glow of the candle, her profile was serene and still breathtakingly beautiful.

"Sleep, my sweet little lad," she said in Irish. "Sleep, and let He who walked on the water itself, come and heal you."

But Del couldn't sleep, and eventually the glass she handed him contained the awful dram she used to bring when they were down sick as children, some wretched and familiar concoction of pure misery she'd learned from her people back in Ireland. There was alcohol in it, and something else. A sleeping potion, it was. Or a fast vessel toward an early grave if it didn't do the work it was meant to do. It tasted as bitterly foul as it had done when he was a boy but he didn't have the fight in him to resist it. He sipped it, managed to keep it down, sipped some more, and felt himself drifting off as he struggled to finish the last few swallows.

His mother took the glass and put it on the table beside the bed, and pulled the blanket up more fully over her son's broad, strong shoulders as he closed his eyes and finally settled on his side. Somewhere between sleep and the misery that was wakefulness, Del felt her softly stroking his back through the nightshirt, and his fierce, uncontrollable shaking lessened and finally stopped.

He drifted, his body hot, sweating, and then seized again by chills. The hand on his back, his shoulder. The touch, rhythmic and soothing, brought him comfort, and a peace that lulled him deeper into slumber. Above the ceiling, the several stories of the old house, the roof above, the stars in the heavens wheeled in their prescribed track, and sometime during this long, stately dance across the sky, he finally slept.

⚓

COLIN LORD, ACCOMPANIED BY LADY GRACE Fairchild and her maid Polly, took his own coach south toward Hampshire.

It was not pulled by the famous Norfolk Thoroughbreds but it made good time nonetheless, and the shadows were long and stretching across the great lawn, the Downs of Hampshire, when they finally arrived at his childhood home.

Tension now gripped his jaw, withered any predisposition toward idle conversation. He had brought his surgical kit and every medicine he thought might turn things around for his younger brother, though he doubted he could offer anything more than the local doctor would have come up with. But the question remained.

Did I do this to him?

He knew as well as anyone that even the slightest flesh wound could go putrid. That a seemingly innocent cut through the skin and muscle could spell the death of a man. He had cleaned the wound, fished out the bits of Del's sleeve, stitched it up tightly, admonished him to keep it bandaged and clean... what more could he have done?

His father met them at the door. "Colin," he said, a bit sheepishly. "Did you not get our second letter?"

"What second letter? We left Norfolk immediately after receiving the first. Please tell me we're not too late."

"You are not." The old admiral looked uncomfortable. Embarrassed. "Um, uh... thank you for coming. Do wish you'd gotten the second letter, though."

Colin searched his father's face, looking for news he wasn't prepared to hear. His relationship with the old admiral was... formal, for lack of any other word he could summon, and he knew there were still hard feelings and wounded pride following his court-martial out of the Royal Navy several years before. An eldest son in a proud tradition of naval officers didn't leave the Navy, willingly or otherwise, and he certainly didn't go on to become what most people considered to be little more than a farrier.

His occupation, he well knew, was in his father's eyes beneath him.

"How is he?"

"Asleep."

"And?"

"Colin!" There was his mother, rushing to meet him. For a moment, Colin froze, prepared for the worst. But her face did not look ravaged or tear-stained, which told him she was either in denial of Del's condition, or his brother still clung to life. What was going on here? Why were his parents behaving so strangely?

"Oh, my son, how I've missed ye! And ye've brought friends? Don't be rude now, let's have introductions!"

Colin hastily made them, and saw his parents exchange a private, knowing look that confused him all the more. But explanations would have to come later. He was desperate to see his brother. They all went into the house, Colin's leg bothering him after the many hours spent in the coach.

The day had been warm, the heat still lingering in the foyer, the sun lighting it up in an orange glow as it began to sink over the downs. A footman took his hat and coat. Colin did not recognize the young man. Another thing that had changed since he'd last been to his childhood home. The housekeeper took Polly off into the kitchen for refreshment.

"He's upstairs," said his mother. "The doctor has already come and gone for the day, but I hold with yer professional opinion far more than I do his."

"Mother, I am a veterinarian, not a physician."

"And ye brought yer case of instruments, so don't tell me ye didn't have hopes of tryin' yer own cure. Go on upstairs with ye. Lady Grace and I will take tea in the parlor while ye're having a look at him."

There was nothing intimidating about the Irishwoman but Grace, following her, could feel the unasked question weighing heavily in the air. And it was as they entered a room papered in gold and set with pretty damask chairs and a maid brought in a tray of tea, that Mrs. Lord asked it.

"So, Lady Grace, what's yer relationship t' my son?"

Grace flushed. She didn't even know where to start.

But she tried. She began with Captain Ponsonby

and her foolish attempts to impress him, and how Captain Lord had saved her from drowning, and how he'd gallantly agreed to help her learn how to sail in order to catch Ponsonby's eye. She told the Irishwoman of the friendship she and Delmore Lord had cultivated and how he had cared for her when she'd been seasick, and how he'd fought a duel over her honor. And while she did not mention the kiss, she told her how much he had come to mean to her, and of her guilt that he was upstairs dying because of her.

And it was there, with that one awful word, that Grace's composure began to crumble and the paralyzing grief she'd harbored since reading that awful letter finally gave way to the tears she was trying valiantly to contain. She bit down hard on her lip, hoping this kindly woman would not see the water flooding into her eyes.

"I do wish we hadn't been quite so hasty with that first letter. Would've saved ye a long trip and a bucket o' tears as well," Captain Lord's mother mused. She leaned forward to pour the tea and slid a cup to Grace, smiling a bit apologetically. She had eyes of a color somewhere between violet and purple, and the kind of manner that made a person feel understood instead of judged. "But what's done is done. Ye're here now, aren't ye?"

Grace nodded, unable to speak.

"And were you and my son successful at nettin' this Captain Ponsonby?"

"Yes," Grace whispered. She looked down. "Yes, we were."

Silence. Grace put her hands together and pressed them between her knees. She stared at her kneecaps beneath her gown, blinking. As she did, her vision finally blurred and her sinuses burned and she saw a teardrop fall upon the soft muslin.

Another.

There was a slight *clink* as Mrs. Lord put her cup down in its saucer. She said nothing for a long moment, giving Grace time to regain her composure.

"And now that ye have him, ye're not sure ye want him," she said gently.

Grace burst into tears and buried her face in her hands.

A moment later, she felt the warmth of the other woman's arm around her shoulders, her motherly concern. "There now, dearie," she said, her kind empathy so different from Grace's own mother's detached indifference, "'twill be all right. I've been around long enough that I know very well why ye came, and why ye're cryin'." She pressed a handkerchief into Grace's hand. "When Colin comes down, why don't ye go up and sit with Delmore for a while. He would like that, I'm sure."

"But he's so upstanding and proper, I can't imagine he'd approve of that."

"I can assure ye, love, he won't even know."

The implication was there. That Captain Lord was so sick, that he was past recognition of the rules of propriety, past knowing or caring whether Grace was there or not, and the reality of that fact hit Grace all over again.

She burst into fresh sobs, and buried her face in the handkerchief.

"Hush, child. Everything's going t' be fine."

Grace pressed the handkerchief to her eyeballs, weeping.

"I'm so sorry," she managed, between sobs. "You must think terribly of me... I'm just so... so confused."

"I know. And trust me, I understand. I was young and in love once, too. With a man who was supposed to be my enemy, a man I'd vowed t' kill for the wrongs he'd done t' me family. And then I went and married him, and he's given me the happiest years of me life." She held Grace close, her arm an anchor when Grace felt she was going to come apart. "Hearts are stubborn things, they are, and we can't tell 'em what direction they're supposed t' go in. 'Twill all work out, I promise. And here comes Colin. Dry yer tears, love, and I'll take ye upstairs."

36

H e was miserable.

Sleep provided a welcome escape from that misery and Del, lying on his stomach with his cheek pressed against the pillow, resisted the pull toward consciousness as he felt his mother's hand against his shoulder, her touch through the light blanket. Someone must have opened the window; he could feel the cool kiss of the summer evening against his bare shoulders, the nape of his neck. He tried to sink back down into oblivion. Instead, the pillow melded itself to his cheek, and he felt the ever-present ache in his head.

"Mother," he murmured, "please let me be."

She had always been a little hummingbird, a hoverer through every childhood cut, bruise and illness, and while the part of him that had once been that little boy treasured those memories, right now Del only wanted to sleep.

His mother didn't answer, though the light touch against his shoulder fell away. He shifted onto his side, trying to get comfortable. There was a scratchy spot in the pillow— probably dried mucus, he thought in disgust— and he moved his head away from it. Slid a hand under the pillow to support his cheekbone.

Wakefulness persisted.

Ohhhh, I feel like absolute shit.

He pushed himself to his side and dragged open his eyes.

The room was in darkness, save for the soft glow of a candle. He groaned, trying to orient himself. There was a figure sitting in a chair, her face beautiful in the candlelight.

Del blinked.

What the hell? He raised himself on one elbow and wiped at his eyes, feeling oddly disoriented, detached from his body. "Lady *Grace?*"

She smiled nervously. "Captain Lord."

"Am I dead, or just dreaming?"

"Neither, it would appear."

His mother had given him one of her cursed Irish drams to help him sleep. Now, the cobwebs that threaded his brain were a hindrance instead of a blessing. He struggled to make sense of the reality as opposed to the impossibility.

"If I'm imagining you to be here, I must be sicker than I thought."

He shut his eyes, determined to try and get back to sleep, because as delicious as this dream was, the painful reality was that Lady Grace belonged to another, that Lady Grace was far, far away in Norfolk, and that Lady Grace was only here as a figment of his fevered imagination.

But that figment was gently peeling back the blanket that covered his shoulder, denying him the sleep he so desperately sought. He felt fingers near the wound that Colin had sewn up with such confidence. *What the devil?* This dream was more real than it had any business being, and impatient with the dram that had brought it on instead of the sleep he craved, Del pulled his arm back, pushed himself up on the pillows and ran a hand through his disheveled curls.

The figment was still there.

Solid and warm and real.

"Lady Grace?" he said again, blinking. "What...?"

"I know. What am I doing here?"

"What *are* you doing here?"

"May I see your arm?"

Frowning, he offered it to her. Her fingers were sweet and light as she cradled his elbow in her palm and peered down at the wound, her brows drawn close with concentration, her hair falling over one shoulder and tickling his wrist. She looked up in confusion. "Why, I expected it to look so much worse."

"I have been living in a fog of my mother's doing for the past three days," he murmured. "You'll understand if I don't quite believe what I'm seeing."

She smiled and lowered his arm down to the sheet on which he lay. "I'm sure it must be confusing to wake up and find me here, but... well, I had to come."

"Why?"

"Because we received word that you were dying. And that you were... that you were asking for me." She flashed him a smile and then looked back at his wound, her eyes confused. "But your arm appears to be healing quite nicely."

"Well of course it is. My brother is thorough and competent."

"I thought that with blood poisoning, the flesh would be black and putrid."

"*Blood poisoning?*"

"Well, yes, that's what usually happens, is it not?"

"Dear God, I should hope it's not black and putrid!"

"It looks sore, but it's not black, and—" she lowered her nose to his skin, sniffing it— "it's certainly not putrid, either."

"I've taken great pains to keep it clean."

"So you're not dying?"

"Of course not, though I certainly *felt* like I was a day or two ago. I've been sick as a dog." He reached for the handkerchief he'd tucked under his pillow. He blew his nose, balled up the fabric and stuffed it back beneath the pillow. "Got it from Colin's youngest. Worst illness I've had in the last twenty years. Couldn't sleep, fever and chills, so Mother gave me one of her blasted Irish remedies. Thought I was past common childhood colds, but I guess not."

"All you have is a *cold*?"

"Well, maybe more than a cold, but certainly not blood poisoning. Whoever told you that?"

"You're not dying then?"

"You don't have to look so accusing, you know."

"I'm sorry," she said, pushing back a bit. "Your parents sent us a letter... they told us you had a fever, that you had blood poisoning and to expect the worst."

"That's ridiculous. If I had blood poisoning I'd be dead. My mother obviously connected the wound with my fever and assumed the worst, though I can assure you that its origin was none other than little Aaron. In any case, I'm sorry. You must feel as if you've wasted your time, coming all the way down here from Norfolk."

"I felt guilty. And the letter said you were calling for me."

"I don't remember calling for anyone."

"Well you must have been, because the letter cited my name and begged me to come. So I did. And now that I'm here, I can let you know in no uncertain terms, Captain Lord, that I was very hurt by your sudden departure. Why did you do that?"

"As I explained in my note, I was running out of time and wanted to visit my parents before leaving England."

Her eyes were accusing. "You still could've said goodbye. Properly."

"Why? Because that's what *friends* do?"

"You are being churlish. It doesn't suit you."

"I'm sick and cranky and miserable and confused. Not to mention, drugged. D'you want to know the real truth? I left because I wasn't needed anymore, and staying there watching you fawn over that... that *peacock* was more than I could stomach."

"So you're jealous."

"I'm human. A living, breathing man who can only stand so much."

"So you were serious with what you said in the barn? When you told me to leave Captain Ponsonby and marry you instead?"

"Does it matter?"

She was relentless. "*Were* you?"

"Of course I was. But that doesn't matter now, does it? You two are now courting. You won your man, Lady Grace. It was foolish of you to journey all the way down here to see to the welfare of another one. Ponsonby has his pride. He won't think highly of that. You may even lose him because of it."

Movement caught the corner of his eye and there was his mother, just pushing open the door of the room. She carried a tray, and smiled when she saw Grace sitting next to the bed.

"I hope I'm not disturbin' ye both," she said, using her heel to shut the door behind her. "I brought some chicken soup." She set the tray down on the night table and leaning over him, plumped up his pillows and then added another from the nearby chair. "Ye'll make sure he eats, won't ye, Lady Grace?"

"Oh, I'll make sure."

"I'll leave ye be, then. And get some sleep, Del."

"I've *been* sleeping, Mother."

She just smiled, cast an appraising look over them both, and left.

Awkwardness. Unspoken hurts, raw accusations, the air still throbbing between them. Del sat up and reached for the tray. But her hand was there, fingers against his chest. He looked up.

Their gazes met.

"I'm sorry, Captain Lord."

"Aye. I am, too."

"I don't want you to be angry with me."

"I'm not angry with you. I'm angry with myself. Usually happens whenever I breach my own standards of self-discipline." He sighed, the fight going out of him. "But still, you should not have come."

"But I did come, and I'm here, now. So at least let me help get some food into you."

He said nothing, allowing the remains of his anger to fade beneath the dulling embrace of Mother's dram and Lady Grace's ministrations. He succumbed to the gentle pressure of her hand and relaxed back against the pillows, watching as she shook out a napkin and laid it just under his chin. She tucked it around his shoulders. Her fingers brushed his ear, the corner of his jaw. Against his wishes, he felt a part of himself responding to her as men do when in the presence of a beautiful woman and he was grateful, very grateful, for the thick and rumpled rolls of the sheet and blanket that covered him.

She picked up one of the two bowls.

"I suppose you intend to spoon-feed me like a baby, as well?" he asked, trying to further lighten the mood.

"That is my intent, Captain."

"I'm not used to anyone coddling me, except my mother."

"Well, you're sick. Everyone needs coddling when they don't feel well." She picked up a spoon and stirred the soup in its chipped green bowl— a bowl that was familiar because it was part of his childhood, a bowl that had carried soup and porridge and fish stew to him and his siblings so many times, so many years ago. And now *she* had it in her hands, leaving her own imprint on the ongoing history of his family, on the memories it carried for him— memories that would now, always, include her.

She dug deep into the bowl, brought out the liquid, frowned when she saw the steam curling up from the spoon.

"Go ahead," he said.

"And do what?"

"Blow on it. You wouldn't want your patient to burn himself now, would you?"

She laughed, the tension further dissipating, and brought the spoon to her mouth. He watched the shape her lips made as she blew softly across it. Her lashes lifted and her gaze met his, a little sly, a little shy, and Del felt the tray shift on his lap and it had nothing to do with the blankets slipping or a movement of his leg.

Damnation.

She brought the spoon toward his mouth. Her hand was trembling, and a drop of the soup escaped the spoon and plopped onto the napkin.

"Oh! I'm so clumsy... I'm sorry, Captain Lord."

He grinned. "There's plenty more where that came from."

He opened his mouth and then the spoon was safely within, the soup, delicious and just the right temperature, sliding over his tongue, slipping down his throat, hot and salty and good.

"So tell me what's going on back in Norfolk," he said, between spoonfuls. That was surely a safe subject, one that wouldn't plunge them back beneath the surface of this veneer that covered the confusing mess that roiled underneath.

She did. About how Sir Graham had quietly gone off to the rectory where Lord Nelson had been born and raised and spent the afternoon there in the church, all by himself. How Polly was mooning about after Jimmy Thorpe had also left. About the magnificent Norfolk Thoroughbreds and how they'd all oohed and aaahed when Lady Ariadne had brought out the famous Shareb-er-rehh, put a saddle on him, and demonstrated his blazing speed with a gallop across the pasture that had had the Falconer girls screeching in delight. And when she'd returned, the great horse lathered and sucking in air through massive distended nostrils, she'd assigned the "cooling off" task to Ned, who was allowed to put his twin sisters up on the famous steed's back while he walked him around and around.

"And Sir Graham allowed that?"

"He had no choice. The twins were, um... rather vocal about their wishes."

Del laughed, envisioning his beleaguered admiral.

"After they had a ride on the horse, he let Ned have one as well. And that horse took care of those children as if he knew exactly how precious his burdens were. Walked ever so slowly, placing his feet with what was almost cringing care. Lady Ariadne was laughing... she thought it was quite funny, especially as Shareb supposedly lets nobody on his back save for his mistress."

"I'm sorry to have missed it," Del said, opening his mouth for another spoonful.

Quiet again. The heavy silence was unable to contain unspoken hurts, continue the charade that all was well, any longer. The thing between them, whatever that thing was, demanded recognition, acknowledgement, and appeasement. It had not been quiet from the moment they'd met, and it refused to be quiet, now.

She paused with the spoon just inches from his mouth, and it was then that her gaze fastened on his and shifted, no longer falsely cheerful, no longer laughing, but dark and serious.

"So where do we go from here, Captain Lord?"

There. It was said. The words were out and hanging in the air between them, and they demanded the truth.

"I don't know," he answered quietly. "That is up to you."

"Ned told me why you *really* left." She looked down and stirred the soup, watching the chunks of chicken and carrots and rice revolve within the old green bowl. "But I needed to hear you say it, yourself."

"Ned is all of eight years old. He has no idea why I left."

She said nothing, only the spoon making a little scraping noise around the inside of the bowl.

"Ned is also a deeply intuitive child," he added. "But that intuition isn't always correct."

"He said you left because I broke your heart."

That very organ seemed to stop for a moment in his chest and sitting up straighter, Del took the tray, set it on the table, and lifted her chin with his finger. She stared miserably up at him.

"Lady Grace," he said softly.

Her eyes filled with tears, and she swayed toward him for one heartbeat of a moment. And then she caught herself and looked away, her eyes tragic.

"Sheldon Ponsonby proposed to me."

Del felt everything inside of him go still. Felt his heart actually quit beating. The blood went still in his veins. Nausea flared in his belly and he was suddenly cold all over.

He almost didn't dare to say it. To ask it.

But he did.

"And...?"

Pound, pound, pound, went the stricken thing in his chest. He felt his headache returning with force, and a dizziness he thought he'd overcome with the departure of the fever.

She looked away, biting her lip, the tears in her eyes welling up to make them look huge and glassy and blue.

"Did you accept?"

Her gaze swung back to him. Her lower lip was

caught beneath her teeth, and he saw one of the tears beginning to spill over, to make a sudden run for her cheek, and he longed to reach up and wipe it away.

Longed for it in this last second of ignorance, of not-knowing, of freedom to feel whatever it was that he felt for her, and Del knew with every shred of his being that what he felt for her was love.

And in that moment he knew what she was going to say before the words actually left her mouth.

"I did," she whispered.

Del felt the soup sitting heavily in his stomach, and he wondered if he was going to lose it.

"Well, then," he said, putting on a brave smile. She'd wanted this all along. He had helped her to obtain it. It wasn't her fault he'd been stupid enough to have lost his heart to her along the way. No, it wasn't her fault at all.

His fault.

His alone.

"Well then," he said again, because he could not think of anything else to say.

"I'm sorry," she whispered, dabbing at her eyes.

"Don't be silly," he said a little too loudly, a little too cavalierly. "He's what you wanted, Lady Grace. Your childhood hero. Why, now I can sail back to Barbados knowing I accomplished some good here in England, helped make a beautiful young lady's dream come true."

She was wiping at the other eye now, her face tightening as she tried to hold back her emotion.

"You are too good for me to have as a friend, Captain Lord. Someday, some lucky girl is going to call you Husband... and she will be the most blessed woman on earth."

Del's stomach roiled some more, and he feared that he was actually going to be sick.

"Last chance, then, Grace," he said cheerfully. "Last chance to have me, instead. Because nobody is going to love you harder or longer or more than I already do."

He had slipped. Called her by her Christian name without her title. A breach in formality, one that he was too desperate to catch and she was too upset to notice.

Or maybe, she did.

She burst into tears. "I gave him my word... Mama expects me to wed him... it's been something I've wanted for a long time... how do I throw that all away when we worked so hard? How do I know that what you and I feel for each other is even *real*? I've loved him for years, and I've only known *you* for less than a month. How can I can I take such a wild gamble? I'm confused! I need time, time to think about this, time to know my own heart."

"Time."

"Yes, time!"

"Well, I cannot give you that, Lady Grace. I'm taking your uncle back to Barbados, probably within days. I don't have time." He pulled the napkin from his neck, his appetite gone, and crumpled it within his fist. "Do you not love me in return?"

"Of course I love you! You're my *friend*!"

Her friend.

That damnable, wretched, gut-twisting, heart-breaking word, that king of obscenities that refused to leave him alone.

Friend.

He put the napkin on the tray. "I think you should probably go."

"You *want* me to leave?"

"Yes. Go back to Norfolk, Grace."

"Now?"

"Yes, now. I am exhausted. I need to sleep. It's improper for you to be in my bedroom."

"But I—"

"And it's not right for you to even *be* here in Hampshire. It is not fair to Captain Ponsonby. People will talk. He will be the subject of scorn and you, the target of vicious gossip. That's no way to start your marriage."

She stared at him, stricken.

He gazed steadily back, his emotions, his demeanor, his very words belying the rising anguish in his heart that threatened to overwhelm him.

"And now, Lady Grace, if you will go find my mother, I find myself in need of her medicine. A hefty dose of it, if you please. Please tell her to bring some."

He shut his eyes so he could not see her tragic face.

So that she could not see how perilously close he was to falling apart.

The dram was wretched and foul. Miserable, even. But it had nothing on the pain of a broken heart, and Del wanted only to escape back into the oblivion that it offered.

37

For a long moment, Grace could not move.

And then she got slowly to her feet, her knees shaking, one hand on the table for support.

He had just rocked her world on its axis. Dismissed her with absolutely no hint of emotion. The tears she had only just quelled threatened to return, to become one rising wail of anguish in her own throat. How could he be so stoic? So steady and unaffected?

She looked at him lying there, his eyes shut tightly, his jaw clenched. At his dark hair curling against the clean white pillowcases. At his suntanned neck, the proud rise of his shoulders. This would probably be the last time she would ever see him, and most certainly, the last time she would see him in such an intimate setting. Once she left here, that would be it. He would have come and gone like a meteor across the sky of her life, his purpose served, the damage he'd unwittingly done to her own heart, her own ability to understand its strange movings, a scar from which she might never recover. Any interaction the two of them might have from now until the end of time would be no more than a few formally-spoken words at a naval function, a sea officer's ball, someone's wedding— and probably not even that.

And yet she couldn't end their last moments together like this. Couldn't just leave. Sick as a dog he was, and yet she ached to crawl into bed with him, to nestle up against him and rest her head in the perfectly-sized cup of his shoulder, to listen to his heart beat against her ear and weep her tears within his embrace and feel his hand stroking her hair, telling her that everything would be okay.

She didn't want their last moments together be so very, very awful.

She wanted to remember him by the memories they had made, the laughter they had shared, the friendship that could be no more.

"Grace?"

She came back to herself, pulled her attention from his shoulders and up to his face. To the steady gray eyes that had opened, colder now, resolute and giving nothing away as they regarded her with a flat detachment. She couldn't hold his gaze, and her own dropped to the broad, muscular hand that rested atop the counterpane.

"I'm sorry," she whispered. "You're right. It was unwise for me to come here, and I regret it." She swallowed hard. "But I'd have regretted it far more if I hadn't come, and you'd been as ill as was originally thought... and died."

He said nothing for a long moment. At long last, he raised his hand, brushed away the heavy dark curls falling over his brow, and reached for a glass of water near the bed. He drank. She watched his Adams apple move up and down and ached for him in a way that already made her disloyal to Captain Ponsonby.

As if she hadn't been already, in thought and deed, if not word?

He finished the glass, put it down, settled back and looked at her. "You should go," he said again.

She nodded, and when her voice came out, it was little more than a whisper. "Yes."

"I daresay that we shall not see each other again." And when she didn't respond, "Nor should we."

"No... it would be best if we do not."

"I will not be writing to you."

"Nor I, you..."

"Goodbye."

She stood there, unmoving. The situation merited that she leave, and the sooner the better. Propriety demanded it. Respect for his feelings demanded it. The offer she'd accepted from Sheldon Ponsonby demanded it. And yet, she could not move.

"I need to get some sleep, Grace."

She took a deep and steadying breath. Hugged her arms to her chest, sucked her lips between her teeth, told herself not to look at him or go anywhere near him, but to simply nod and walk away.

Instead, she stood there gazing down at him. "Thank you, Captain Lord," she whispered, and her own voice sounded tremulous to her ears. "I will never forget all that you have done for me."

He turned his head on the pillow to stare at the darkened fireplace.

She began to bend down toward him. Just to drop a kiss on his brow. Nothing more.

"Go," he said, stopping her, and this time his voice was harsh. No more gentleness, just raw pain that he could no longer hold in, let alone hide.

Grace froze, stepped back, and nodded stiffly. Then, her eyes filling with fresh tears, her head high, she turned and walked from the room. It was only once she had shut the door behind her and stood all by herself in the great corridor that she pulled out her handkerchief, pressed it to her eyes, and, pushing a fist against her mouth to hold in the sobs, made her way quietly to her own room.

Tomorrow she would return to Norfolk and whatever her future with Ponsonby held.

Tomorrow could not come quickly enough.

SHE DID NOT COME TO VISIT HIM THE FOLLOWING morning. No goodbyes, no last glimpses of her face, nothing by which to remember her save for a long dark strand of her hair that Del, staring morosely at the chair in which she had sat the night before, found on the carpet just beneath it.

He was not Ponsonby. The hair brought him no disgust. He bent down upon spying it, picked it up, pressed it to his cheek and shut his eyes. He stood there for a long moment. And then he went to the desk, found a sheet of vellum, and carefully folded it up within the paper.

He tucked the paper beneath his pillow.

Colin did come in to say farewell, avoiding the subject of Lady Grace Fairchild and telling Del he must come and spend more time with him and his family the next time he was back in England. They embraced, wished each other well, and his brother left the room. Del heard his hitching gait moving down the hall, then down the great staircase. Heard goodbyes being said somewhere downstairs, and then voices out on the lawn beneath his window.

He got out of bed. Parted the drapes and looked out to the drive below.

She was there, standing with Polly and his brother as they waited for the coach to be brought round. There was something small and fragile about her in the way she stood. Something vulnerable, but fiercely resolved as well. Del could not see her face. He stood carefully well back from the window, peering out from behind the safety of one heavy drape that he was now crushing in his hand.

There, the coach. A footman letting down the stairs. His mother and father embracing Colin, speaking a few words to Lady Grace. His mother handing Colin a basket, presumably of enough Irish bread and carefully wrapped cheeses to see them safely to the next coaching inn, if not Norfolk itself.

Go to her. Stop her. End this madness and fight for her!

Del shut his eyes, trying to ignore the voice in his head. It was not his own. It was hers, Gráinne's, fearsome, urgent and strong.

Go, my son! You will lose her!

He shook his head, watching her embrace his mother down there on the drive. "She was never mine to lose," he said quietly.

The girl he loved took his brother's hand and lifted her foot to the lowered step. Del stilled, watching her, his heart aching. But in that last moment she paused and turned her face up, searching the house, the windows, one of which he stood behind with a fistful of the drape balled in his fingers like a lifeline.

He did not move.

She could not see him.

And then she turned and continued her climb into the coach. Her maid and Colin followed her, and a moment later the driver was clambering up onto the box and the vehicle was starting to move off.

Del never saw it.

He had already turned away, the drape falling shut behind him.

❦ 38 ❦

L ater that week in Norfolk, Lieutenant James Akers
called for a side party to pipe his captain back
aboard.

The boat had put off from the dock at King's Lynn,
slicing through The Wash with unerring purpose. Now,
Sheldon Ponsonby came up through the entry port,
bright hair gleaming in the slanting light of the afternoon, nose straight and strong, jaw hard with what
looked like irritation.

And why not?

Everyone on the frigate knew he'd offered for that
silly bit of fluff, and no sooner had she accepted than
she'd fled to Hampshire to see to the welfare of the
dying Captain Lord.

Dying, Akers thought to himself, *because of me.*

He felt the ever-present cloud of guilt where that
whole affair was concerned, something that had been
eating at the pit of his stomach ever since he'd rushed
to the mark, desperate to get there before his opponent, and fired his pistol in panic. He'd tried drinking
away his remorse. Tried to ignore the whispers about
his cowardice. He didn't know what was worse; the guilt
his own mind threw at him, or the silent snickers from
his peers. He hadn't really wanted to hurt, let alone kill

the other man— that enmity was reserved for Lady Grace Fairchild, not her lovesick defender who deserved far better than that fickle bitch— but it rather seemed that he had. Now, the look on Sheldon Ponsonby's face as he doffed his hat to the quarterdeck and snapped an order to make the ship ready for the admiral's imminent return, made him wonder why the captain's visage looked so dark.

"Sir Graham and his family will be back aboard shortly, Mr. Akers, and we shall sail on the evening tide."

"Our destination, sir?"

"Portsmouth. The admiral is keen to rejoin his flagship and get the hell out of England." A muscle in his jaw twitched with irritation. "And I can't say as if I bloody blame him."

Akers cleared his throat. "Sir?"

His captain rounded on him. "I offered for the girl. Damned fine dowry, she has. But I don't hold with her flying down to Hampshire to see to the welfare of another man. I don't hold with it at all! Damned humiliating, if you ask me."

"He is just a friend to her, sir."

"Of course he is. Man's as dull as a dry stick, nothing about him to attract a girl like Lady Grace, that's for sure. No, Mr. Akers, it's what it looks like to others. Tongues are already wagging. I've caught the glances, heard the whispers that I'm already being cuckolded. I won't stand for it, I tell you. I won't!"

"Well, word has it she's back now. She didn't stay long." Akers swallowed hard. "And Captain Lord?"

"Not on his deathbed as everyone thought. Just a nasty cold."

"So all is well, then."

"It's bloody well not! Last night I supped with two frigate captains, a lieutenant from the '74, *Dolphin*, and some relation of Lord Nelson's, all of whom were making *comments* about my missing fiancée and her headlong flight to Hampshire to comfort a man who fought a duel over her. Such flagrant disobedience won't be tolerated, I tell you. I like a spirited woman as much as any, but there's a limit and she'll need to be reined in. What, does that horrify you? Yes, I'm angry! You would be too if it you were the one being mocked by your peers. Delmore Lord shouldn't have fought a duel over her and you, Akers, shouldn't have let yourself get dragged into such a damned mess. Makes me look bad, you know. Quite bad. Damn it all!"

"Do you love her?"

Ponsonby came up short, as if he'd run headlong into the mainmast.

"What?"

"I asked, sir, do you love her?"

"Love? What the devil does that have to do with anything? She's of good family, closely related to a vice-admiral, and heavily dowered. No need for love. That's for fools, not sensible men who know exactly where they want their career paths to go and are in the business of mapping out a plan on how to get there. Besides, the girl is all agog over me, so there's at least some affection there. It'll have to do for us both, I daresay."

"Perhaps you will come to... to love her in time, sir."

"Damned if I care one way or another about such nonsense. I like 'em blonde, anyhow. But it'll be an advantageous match and that's all that matters." Ponsonby started to stalk away, grabbing a glass from the rack as he did. "See to the launch would you? I believe that's Sir Graham's coach making its way to the waterfront now. Just what I need. The admiral and his out-of-control, squalling brats. I tell you, if I ever have children they'll be seen and not heard!"

Ponsonby moved off, taking his foul mood with him. Akers stood for a moment watching him, feeling an odd but useless relief about what his captain had just confessed. So, if Sheldon wasn't in love with the woman he was destined to marry and had all but proclaimed he never would be, then that meant that he, James, had a chance—

You fool. Fool!

Of course he had no chance. He was destined to be as lovesick as Lady Grace Fairchild.

His own mood deteriorating, Akers headed forward to get the launch ready to collect the admiral.

⚓

GRACE'S MOOD WASN'T MUCH BETTER THAN THAT OF her betrothed's.

She, Polly and Colin Lord had returned to Norfolk very late the previous night, and she had immediately fallen into bed, travel-weary, exhausted, and weighed down by a pressing grief she didn't understand.

Sleep had not come easily to her and when it had, she had dreamed.

Not of the man to whom she had pledged her life. But the man she had left back in Hampshire.

She had awoke with a start, her heart raw with an unidentifiable ache, her body warm and restless and moist in her secret places.

Captain Lord.

She had lain awake in the darkness, thinking of him so far away down in Hampshire. Of the miles of empty night that separated them. Her soul echoed with emptiness. Longing. Loneliness. Had it rained since they had strode together out there on the lawn just a few days ago, washing away his footsteps, his presence? Had the maids changed his bed and swept his floor after he'd so hastily left? And what of Ned? Had he forgiven her?

Grace rolled over, staring out the open window into the night. She could see the dim outline of a sycamore, hear the breeze moving through its leaves, smell the sea. A cloud moved over the waning moon, backlit by its light.

I shouldn't have let him drive me off. I should have told him how I really feel.

How *did* she really feel?

Time had passed. Her lids had grown heavy and her eyeballs ached with fatigue, but her mind would not rest. Would not stop replaying that last awful scene with Captain Lord. Would not let her forget the searing pain she'd felt when he had not come down to say good-bye. She threw back the coverlet and went to the window, clutching her chemise to herself. Out in the darkness she could see the neatly fenced pastures, silvered in the light of the moon and stars. She stood there for a long moment.

Turned and walked with resolution toward the door.

It opened quietly on well-oiled hinges, swung out into the hall. The corridor was dark, a single sconce at the far end glowing in the night. Grace shut the door behind her, crossed the hall, and went to the door of what had been Captain Lord's room during his all-too-short stay here.

She reached up, placed her palm against the smooth wood, and shut her eyes.

They flooded and burned with sudden tears.

"I'm sorry," she whispered, and her heart swelled in her chest, squeezing it, constricting the pain into an unbearable knot until she couldn't breathe. She leaned her forehead against the door. The tears spilled from her eyes, rolled down her cheeks and plopped onto her bare toes. Had the maid changed his bed? Was there any trace of him left on the other side of this barrier? Oh, what had she *done*? Anguish overwhelmed her, and she pushed open the door.

His door.

The room was silent and still. The bed was made,

tack-sharp, standing silently in the darkness and backlit by the night outside. Empty. As if he had never even been here.

My friend.

And here, right here... was where they had kissed.

More than my friend.

Grace had stood there for a long moment. Eventually she had moved to the bed, climbed up on it, hugged the pillow that had cradled his head to her chest and then and only then, had she fallen into a restless and broken sleep.

Polly had found her in the morning, cocked an unconvinced brow at Grace's excuses for being in the room, and announced that Sir Graham was eager to be done with England. They would be sailing later tonight.

And now "tonight" had come, and they would all go aboard Captain Ponsonby's frigate and make the short run back down to Portsmouth. Grace wondered if she would be seasick again and if so, who would be there to care for her as tenderly as Captain Lord had done.

Captain Lord, Captain Lord!

She was still thinking of him, unable to stop thinking of him, as she was rowed out to the frigate, settled into the bosun's chair, and hauled up the side of the black-and-yellow-painted warship.

"My dear Lady Grace." It was Captain Ponsonby, smiling and handsome in his uniform as she stepped onto his gleaming decks. "I trust you had an uneventful ride back from Hampshire?"

"Unremarkable," she said. "And Captain Lord is going to be fine. His brother said so himself."

Was it her imagination that Sheldon Ponsonby's mouth tightened ever so slightly, and what looked to be annoyance suddenly shadowed his eyes? "That is good to know," he said briskly. "Too many naval officers dying in duels these days if you ask me, Navy can't spare 'em, either. Some refreshment for you before we get underway, perhaps? You'll want to retire to your cabin, I should think. Wind's picking up, 'twill be a wet run down to Portsmouth, I daresay."

"I would feel better up here on deck, I think. Captain Lord says the fresh air is better for a person with seasickness."

"Did he, now?" Again that flash of irritation, unmistakable now. "Well, you do as you wish, my dear, but I'd worry less about you if you went below. You are rather, shall I say, accident-prone, and you're much safer in your cabin than up here where you could be hit by a block or ogled by my men or be swept overboard." His smile was tight. Insincere. A clamp-down on some inner vexation. "Besides, you'll be in the way up here, especially if you're sick. I won't have time to see to you."

She felt her own irritation beginning to rise in response. "Is that the captain of this vessel speaking, or the man who has asked me to marry him?"

"Both." He leaned close and touched her cheek, grinning, and she felt a sudden and inexplicable revulsion. "Now be a good girl and go below. I'll see you and your uncle's family at dinner."

Ned joined her as she was about to angrily shove open the door to her tiny cabin.

"I don't know why you put up with that," the boy said. "He's insufferable. He doesn't love you, you know. I'm not sure he even likes you. What do you see in him anyhow? He's nothing but a peacock who's constantly preening his feathers."

Grace reached up, put the pads of her fingers against her eyes, and pressed. "Ned, please."

"It's true and you know it."

"Leave me alone."

"You should marry Captain Lord. *He* loves you."

"Go away."

"You're making a bad choice. Captain Ponsonby is ambitious and proud, and the only reason he wants to marry you is because it will advance his career. You're worth more than that, Grace. You deserve someone who will love you. Who will cherish and adore and want to be with you. You think you'll have that with Ponsonby? Why, you'll be nothing more than an ornament to him. Captain Lord, on the other hand—"

"Stop it, Ned! Just stop it!"

"I'm not going stop it because you know it's true!"

"I can't think with you tormenting me so!"

"You'd better start thinking or you're going to spend the rest of your life knowing you made the wrong choice and picked the lesser man!"

"It's expected at this point! It was expected all along! Now go, and *leave me alone*!"

Ned, mercifully, turned and left her then, and Grace threw herself on the small bunk and punched the blanket in rage and frustration. Beneath her she felt a sudden lurch, a dizzying sway, and knew the anchors had left the sea floor and that the ship was now back in its element, free of the land. She thought of Captain Ponsonby somewhere up on the deck above her, handsome and proud in his uniform, overseeing the safe departure of his vessel and felt nothing but cold anger— not toward him, but toward herself for being girlishly seduced by the man she wanted him to be, and not the one he actually was.

I want my friend.

Her stomach swam with the motion of the ship, and she reached for her reticule and fished out the little jar of ginger root that Captain Lord had given her.

I want my friend *with me. Now. Always. I want Captain Lord.*

The ginger root was quick to do its job, but there was no cure for the hurt in her heart, no cure for the agonizing torment of her thoughts. She sat up and heard voices somewhere above her head. Lady Falconer's. The Falconer children.

Why were they up on deck but she was forced to all but hide down here?

Indignation began to swell within her.

Captain Ponsonby may be my betrothed, but he is not my husband. Not yet. And he may be captain of this stupid vessel but I'm no seaman and his authority does not extend to me. I'm not staying down here. I am not!

She got to her feet and swaying drunkenly as the ship began to heel in the breeze, headed topside.

The wind hit her immediately, the sunshine bouncing like a thousand little balls off the crests of the racing waves, the great sails above blotting out the late afternoon sun. She shaded her eyes against it. Nearby, a group of seamen hauled on a line that led to a sail high above, their efforts directed by a young lieutenant who was unable to focus on his duties once he caught sight of Grace. She smiled. He flushed, turned back to his task, and Grace moved to the rail.

The ship was gathering speed now as the sail above was finally trimmed. Grace had no idea what that sail was called, and her awareness of her own ignorance brought her to the even more painful awareness that she still knew next to nothing about sailing, and she was about to marry an up-and-coming naval officer.

From what direction is the wind coming, Lady Grace?

Lessons on a pond, lessons on a deck, with a man who was far, far away from her now.

The frigate plunged, and hissing spray lashed her face. As it slid down her cheek in a trickle of salty foam, she reached up to finger it away, unsure whether the saltiness she tasted on her fingers was from the sea itself...

Or her own tears.

D el was young and strong, determined and dutiful.
He recovered quickly from his nephew's gift
of childhood illness, caught the stage down to
Portsmouth, and with nothing but a lingering cough
that was easily quelled by the jar of homemade sweets
with which his mother had sent him off, returned to
HMS *Orion* to await his admiral.

He knew Sir Graham well. The admiral would be
restless, eager to end this English holiday, and Del
would not be caught languishing in Hampshire when Sir
Graham would expect him to have the flagship provisioned and waiting for him in Portsmouth.

Truthfully, Del couldn't wait to leave, either.

England had dealt his heart a mortal blow. He was
keen to see the last of it for a while.

The stage stopped at a coaching inn somewhere in
the chalky downs, where Jimmy Thorne retrieved Del's
uniform from his traveling trunk. It had been brushed
and pressed, none the worse for wear despite being
stored for the last fortnight. Del shrugged into it, the
gold epaulets of his rank standing proudly atop his
shoulders. Having the uniform back on restored him
somewhat. He was Captain Lord again, a man with an
identity. Authority. Purpose. The return to familiarity

and routine, to a certain anonymity of service was just what he needed to try and put the past two weeks behind him. By the time he stepped out of the stage and onto Portsmouth's damp, cobbled streets, he was the taciturn flag captain once more, master and commander of the most formidable ship in the harbor— and eager to get back to work.

He mustered a grin as his ship sent a boat, the tars rowing in perfect unison, all spit and polish, not a thread out of place in their clothing, each stroke of the oars precise and true.

Routine.

Familiarity.

Order, with no surprises, nothing to trip him up.

He scaled the tumblehome and boarded through the entry port, where bosun's calls shrilled and a well-turned-out side party awaited him, a captain returning to his ship and receiving the fanfare that was his due.

His officers as well as his clerk, Cooper, were there, wizened hazel eyes smiling behind his spectacles. "Glad to have you back, sir. Word has it you nearly died in a duel. May I say it's a relief to see you looking hale and hearty?"

"I nearly died from a cold given me by my young nephew, Mr. Cooper." He grinned. "Or rather, it felt that way. Childhood illnesses are best reserved for the young, as they are far better equipped to handle them than we adults."

Cooper inclined his head.

"Any news from Sir Graham?" Del asked, heading for the quarterdeck.

"Aye, sir. He sent word... expects to arrive tomorrow, God willing."

"In that case, I got here not a moment too soon then, eh?"

"Well, we both knew he'd be itching to get back at sea."

"As am I."

His first lieutenant fell into step beside him.

"Ship provisioned and ready to go, Mr. Armstrong?"

"Been taking on water all day, just expecting another two dozen barrels of salt pork and several bushels of peas and we'll be ready for sea."

"And a good store of spirits in for the admiral?"

"All set, sir."

"Well done, Mr. Armstrong." He shot a last glance at Portsmouth's distant chimneypots. "Sir Graham isn't the only one eager to get underway. Carry on. I'll be below if needed."

Del headed for the great cabin that was his seafaring home, office, and retreat, desperate for a further push into the familiarity of routine and the only place on the ship that was truly his own. A Royal Marine greeted him and opened his cabin door. Del returned the greeting, passed his cot hanging suspended above the black-and-white-checkered deck, passed the big guns, passed the polished mahogany table where he took his meals, mapped out his courses, entertained his admiral and officers, and finally arrived at the great gallery of windows at the very aftermost point of the ship. There he finally sat, taking off his hat and running a hand through his helplessly wild and unruly curls. No sense trying to tame them; nobody here to impress with tidiness, nobody here but himself.

Outside, a gull winged past, its shadow chasing it across the harbor as the sun began to sink into the western sea.

Del watched it until he could see it no longer.

Familiarity. Routine. Duty.

He leaned his cheek against the glass, slid a hand beneath his lapel, and into the inside pocket of his waistcoat where the little paper packet lay close to his heart.

His fingers closed around it. It was tightly folded on each end to ensure the safety of its precious contents.

A hair.

A single long, dark hair... from the woman he loved.

HE DID NOT KNOW HOW LONG HE'D SLEPT.

It might have been ten minutes, it might have been an hour. Maybe even two. But a hand against his shoulder jerked him awake with a start and blinking, Del straightened up, automatically tucking the talisman deep into his pocket as he did.

"What is it, Mr. Jellicoe?"

"The frigate *Mars* has been sighted standing in for the harbor," said his manservant. "She's flying Sir Graham's flag. The admiral has returned, sir."

A more benevolent God, Del decided, would have sent the admiral back to him in a coach, in a private yacht, hell, even in a damned wheelbarrow. But no. His superior had returned earlier than expected and in Ponsonby's ship besides, and where Ponsonby was, remained also the reminder of Grace.

Del raked a hand over his face, trying to wipe away the fatigue and despair and feeling the slight scratchiness of emerging bristle.

"I expect Sir Graham will be aboard by nightfall," he said wearily. "I need a shave. My best undress uniform, as well."

"I will see to both, sir."

Efficient as always, the steward bustled about the cabin, laying out the razor, fetching hot water, soap and a towel. Shedding his coat, Del took a seat and put the towel around his neck. From where he sat, he had a commanding view of the harbor, Portsmouth, and the mud flats.

And Ponsonby's frigate, heeling smartly in a brisk

westerly, already dousing its topsails as it skillfully threaded its way between vessels of all shapes and sizes. Del bit back an uncharacteristic and savage wish that the thing would hit something, but his wishes went unheard. By the time Jellicoe had finished his shave and wiped the lather from his jaw, the frigate's anchor was splashing down and he could see the side party already mustered, could hear Lieutenant Armstrong calling for *Orion*'s own men to welcome their admiral back aboard the flagship.

At least he wouldn't have to face seeing Lady Grace Fairchild. There was no reason for *her* to be aboard Ponsonby's warship, no reason for her not to have been sent back to her mother's home to await her nuptials.

But as Del shrugged into the freshly-brushed uniform that Jellicoe laid out for him, picked up his hat and headed topside with it tucked smartly under his arm, his senses began to prickle.

For there just across the water, a group of people were already in the boat to be rowed across to HMS *Orion*.

The admiral and his family. Captain Sheldon Ponsonby and Lieutenant Akers.

And oh, God help him, Lady Grace Fairchild.

⚓

GRACE WANTED TO DIE.

She had also wanted to be sent immediately to Sussex to wait out her engagement at her mother's home where, she hoped, she would find the fortitude to end it. She did not want to accompany Ponsonby here in Portsmouth, to go aboard Sir Graham's flagship with him as he insisted she did— an act surely meant to rub his conquest in the nose of the man who commanded it, Captain Lord. She did not want to subject Captain Lord to further pain.

But fate had other ideas. As did Sir Graham, who'd hoped that she might linger in Portsmouth for a day or two so as to help manage the children. Their nanny was down with the same debilitating cold that had moved through Colin's children, and now little Anne was hot with fever as well.

"I'd really prefer to go back Sussex, Uncle Gray. It's only a short trip by coach..."

"And so you shall, but if you wouldn't mind helping out a bit until I can get us all safely settled aboard *Orion*, I'd be in your debt, Grace."

She had complied. Not because she'd wanted to, but because she'd been asked. Or maybe she really *had* wanted to— if only to see Captain Lord one last time.

Traversing the side of a massive hundred-gun ship of the line in a bosun's chair made for a far longer, higher, and more frightening trip than it did in Ponsonby's frigate, and as the rope sling swung dizzily on its ascent, Grace shut her eyes and told herself that the butterflies in her stomach had nothing to do with the anxiety of seeing Captain Lord again, and everything to do with the staggering height of the chair itself.

Absolutely nothing.

Such a falsehood was cruelly exposed for the lie it was, however, as the chair deposited her on the deck and she stepped onto the gleaming deck and saw him.

Him.

Her throat went dry. Her lungs quit working. She tried to swallow. Couldn't.

"Lady Grace," he said with stiff formality, and took her hand over a bow.

There was nothing in his cold gray eyes. No shared intimacy. No sorrow. No pain, no flicker of interest, nothing but a chilly remoteness that pierced her heart more than she would have thought possible.

The pain caught there and spread. Grace began to tremble. And looking at him for the first time in his uniform, she wondered how on earth she could ever have thought Sheldon Ponsonby the finer of the two men. How she could ever have set her cap for a man who seemed shallow and superficial by comparison to this one. How she could ever have thought this man, garbed in his fine blue coat and cocked hat, a sword at his hip and the fine gold epaulets at his shoulder catching the sun, could have been a mere seaman, a mere *man*, with the authority he wore as naturally as he did the very uniform that proclaimed it.

How he could have been anyone but the man standing right here before her.

Ponsonby paled in comparison. For if Delmore Lord was dashing and handsome in everyday civilian clothes, the figure he cut in his blue and white and gold-laced uniform that showed off the proud span of his shoulders, his long legs and powerful physique, was enough to take Grace's breath away and stingily refuse to give it back.

"C-captain Lord," she replied faintly, the back of her hand tingling, even through the glove, where his lips had so briefly touched it.

"I must say, I was not expecting to see you again... so soon," he murmured, his voice still empty and cold, almost accusatory, every emotion she had ever known him to have now carefully contained and withdrawn.

And why not? He had found refuge here on his ship, in his world, and she had invaded both.

"I was not expecting it, either."

"And where is your... betrothed?"

His face was tight. Hard. Stony.

"He is on his way. With Sir Graham."

A muscle twitched in that hard face. "I see."

"Captain Lord... I... I'm sorry. I don't want to be here anymore than you want me to be here. I only came because Uncle Gray asked me to help him out... the twins are sick with the same thing you had and so is their nanny, and Lady Falconer also isn't feeling well."

"Noted."

"I'll stay out of—"

"Captain, sir! Launch approaching from starboard. It's the admiral."

"Muster the side party, Mr. Tremain. And prepare the ensign to be run up."

"Aye, sir."

Grace felt an urge to wring her hands. "As I was about to say, I will try to—"

"Captain?"

"Yes, Mr. Edwards?"

"Purser says five of the casks of beef we just brought aboard have a smell of rot about them and wants to know if we should send them back. It will delay our departure as we'll need to find a different supplier."

"Send them back."

The junior officer moved off.

Grace took a deep breath. "I guess now probably isn't a good time to... to talk."

"Indeed, it is not," snapped Captain Lord and with a short bow, turned on his heel and stalked off, just as the side party assembled at the entry port began to form and moments later, the shrill of pipes pierced the air.

The ship had its admiral back.

And the moment for talking to its flag captain was lost.

❧ 40 ❧

As Vice-Admiral Sir Graham Falconer stepped back aboard his flagship, his sigh of relief was enough to fill the sails and speed the ship out of England.

Or so it felt to him.

The sea was his element and the last fortnight had felt like a prison sentence. Social mores and silly sisters. Adulation from country-folk. The sorrow he'd felt, the pain of reflection as he sat all alone in the still, quiet church where his late great friend, the beloved Nelson, had been baptized and spent the earliest years of his life. Maeve, a fish out of water. Ned, surly and remote. The children, any fascination they had for England quickly replaced by pleas to go back home to Barbados.

And this crisis with Del.

He had purposely sent Grace ahead in hopes that she'd come to her senses once she saw his flag captain again. That she'd find a few minutes to speak with him and try for a last chance at resolution. Or whatever was needed to stop this insane marriage planned between her and Sheldon Ponsonby.

Maeve, a lady second and a mariner first, scorned the bosun's chair as Polly made her way into it, and came through the entry port as nimbly as any seasoned tar. Which, Sir Graham mused, was exactly what she was.

"Good to see you smiling again, my love," she said, leaning in and playfully letting her lips touch his ear. "What are you going to do about them?"

He followed her gaze, though both of them knew what she meant by *them*. There was Grace standing alone at the rail looking lost and diminutive as she gazed down at the gray waters below. Wind ruffled her bonnet, played with the hem of her skirts. Forty feet away stood Del, back rigid, his normal buttoned-up façade back in place, deep in conversation with one of his lieutenants. Everything about him indicated displeasure. Tension.

Maybe even fury.

"I'm open to suggestions," Gray said.

"I propose that you host a meal in your cabin tonight," his wife said. "Invite them all. Ponsonby and his first lieutenant. Del and his lieutenants. Grace, of course. You can call it a farewell-to-England dinner, or a good-riddance-to-England dinner, hell, call it whatever you like, but the finality of it all, the realization this is the last chance they'll have to set things right, might be just what's needed to bring this whole stubborn nonsense to an end."

"Do or die, eh?"

She grinned. "Do or die."

Ned had scuttled up behind her, his color high from the climb up the ship's massive tumblehome.

"Ned," his father said, "Why don't you go report to the sailing master, tell him you're available to resume your lessons in navigation, and we'll see you at dinner tonight in my cabin."

"Yes, Papa."

"That's yes, *sir*."

Ned, who'd looked too preoccupied of late for either of his parents' liking, managed a smile and disappeared but not before casting a quick glance at Grace, still staring wistfully down into the harbor.

Ned wasn't the only one stealing a look at her.

Del, try as he might to hide it, was also standing such that he only had to cut his gaze to one side to see her, and as Sir Graham quietly observed him, he saw his flag captain do just that.

"Going to be a long evening, I think," said his wife.

"Not if I can help it."

"This is our last chance to get them together. There's no reason for her to stay on this ship once we sail. They'll likely never see each other again."

"I know."

"This is it, Gray."

"I know."

"Will you direct Ponsonby to come with us? That frigate of his would be handy as a scout."

"I will indeed."

She nodded, her eyes thoughtful, and made to move off.

Sir Graham caught her wrist. Her hand. A hand that had once saved his own life from a vicious pirate. "Aren't you afraid there'll be fireworks at the dinner table tonight, my dear?"

Her mysterious tiger-eyes gleamed. "I would be bloody disappointed," she said softly, "if there were not."

⚓

"A DINNER?!" DEL STARED AT HIS ADMIRAL, FEELING like he'd been punched in the stomach. "For what reason, sir?"

"To celebrate our getting the hell out of England, of course."

"And—" Del took a deep breath, for it would not do to question his admiral's order, challenge it, or complain about it, and he quietly put his fists behind his back where he could clench them without their being noticed. "Who is to be invited?"

"Oh, we'll have a merry band, to be sure. What do you prefer? Chicken or lamb?"

"What?"

"For the main course."

"Sir, I do believe that you—"

"Chicken or lamb, Captain Lord?"

Del ground his knuckles into his palm in the effort to preserve his facade of unruffled aplomb. "Chicken."

"Chicken it will be, then. Rather what I fancy, myself. And will you have us ready to get underway tomorrow?"

"Just need to bring aboard a few more casks of beef, sir."

"So be it."

Del nodded crisply and watched his admiral move off. Something was gnawing at his gut and he wasn't sure what it was. Unease, certainly. Suspicion, possibly. But over what, he couldn't know.

He just knew he didn't like it.

He heard the bell chime in the forecastle belfry, saw the purser coming to report on the beef. Or so he hoped. Now that Sir Graham was happy and relaxed again at the prospect of leaving for home, it would not do to keep the admiral waiting to get underway. Damn the rotted beef and the merchant who'd supplied them. If it caused a delay, Sir Graham's good mood would quickly dissipate.

No, it was best to keep an admiral happy.

Always best to keep an admiral happy.

He caught movement out of the corner of his eye and saw Lady Grace with Ned. He quickly averted his gaze and moved away, keeping his back to her, feeling her stare upon his shoulder blades. He was a disciplined man, extremely so, and the fact that he could not put her out of his mind, could not direct his thoughts to seek and remain upon other matters angered him.

And there was Ponsonby setting off from his frigate, his men rowing him toward the flagship for this blasted dinner with which Sir Graham seemed intent on torturing him.

Del's line of sight to the other man happened to be straight out along the breech of a twelve-pounder some distance forward.

I'd like to aim that gun right at your smirking face and fire it. I'd like to see a sea monster rise up from the deep and devour you. I'd like to see you find a hundred hairs in your damned soup and I'd like to see you sail off to the end of the bloody world.

Fuming, Del glanced at Grace to gauge her reaction to her betrothed's impending arrival and in her place, saw Gráinne.

She stood with arms crossed over her chest, her hair — as black, wild and curly as his own— blowing around her strong face.

"Ponsonby hates lamb," she said offhandedly, and then grinned.

Del blinked and his great-something-grandmother was gone and Lady Grace stood once again in her place. She was looking at him in confusion and wistfulness and a hundred other emotions he could not identify.

Looking at *him* and not Ponsonby, whose boat was steadily approaching.

He flushed and turned away and saw the side party mustering to welcome the enemy captain— because how else could he think of the man?— and headed aft, sparing a word for poor Jellicoe as he ducked into his cabin.

"Sir Graham is hosting a dinner in his cabin tonight," he said sharply. "As the menu choice has been left up to me, we'll do fresh produce as it's the last we'll see of it for a while, and get out that fine wine from

Portugal that's in my cupboard, if you will. Spare nothing."

"And the main course, sir?"

Del felt an involuntary twitch at the side of his mouth. A tic that thrummed along with his angry, pounding heartbeat.

Ponsonby hates lamb.

He gave a perfectly benign smile.

"Lamb."

---

THE SUN HAD SET AN HOUR EARLIER, AND ITS GLOW still softened the western sky as though inviting HMS *Orion* to follow its descent into the sea. The stars were coming out, the 600-man crew was fed, and on the forecastle, a sailor with a fiddle was playing a jig to the raucous revelry of the hands.

The captain was popular tonight. He was not only back aboard, but had relaxed his normally tight discipline and allowed several boatloads of women to be rowed out to the ship to provide entertainment to the crew on their last night in England. Feminine laughter added to the atmosphere, and the deck thumped to the dancing of many feet.

Aft was the domain of the ship's officers and there, things were much quieter. Three great stern-galleries climbed above the rudder post, stacked one upon another beneath the vice-admiral's flag that rolled from the mizzen masthead in what was left of the day's breeze. One of those cabins glowed with candlelight from within, reflecting upon water that winked it back into the night.

Spirits flowed. Rum and wine for the men (and Lady Falconer), fruit punch for Lady Grace. A hearty spiced carrot soup had started the meal and now the main course was being served.

It was, per order of Captain Delmore Lord himself, lamb.

Sheldon Ponsonby looked down at the still-bloody slab of meat that was placed in front of him and nausea flared in his belly.

Across from him and seated at the right hand of the admiral, Captain Lord raised a brow and picked up his glass. "Not to your liking, Ponsonby?"

"It will do," Sheldon bit out.

He glanced at James Akers, already further into his cups than Ponsonby wanted to see and hopefully not careering toward another disaster, given present company. On his other side was the admiral, one elbow leaning on his polished table as he turned to address his cabin servant. Several lieutenants were also present, and Lady Falconer sat at the foot of the table. She was a calculating woman, Sheldon Ponsonby had long since concluded, and a dangerous one. In his opinion, her presence at the table tonight was quite unnecessary.

Shouldn't she be with her children?

And speaking of which, why was Ned Falconer in their midst, a boy who hadn't even seen his ninth year?

Lady Grace sat across from him, mouse-quiet, eyes downcast.

"My dear," he said loudly, pointedly, and was gratified to see Delmore Lord all but flinch. "Are you feeling quite well?"

"I am fine," she said, glancing up for the briefest of moments before picking up her fork and toying with her food.

"I hope the hour is not too late for you. You've had a trying time of it, unnecessarily trekking the length of England these past few days."

Again, her blue, blue eyes raised to him, this time with a hint of defiance. "I would hardly call it *unnecessary*," she said, meeting his gaze before returning her attention to her food.

Ponsonby felt something move uneasily in his gut, a feeling that was amplified by the fact that the tension in Sir Graham's resplendent dining cabins was suddenly drum-tight.

"Of course," he said tightly.

Akers, listening keenly, chose that moment to comment.

"Goes without saying, sir," he muttered, holding out his glass for a refill, "that she wouldn't have been trekking the length of England—" a smile in Ponsonby's direction that made the captain feel pointedly uncomfortable—"if she were not chasing after certain"—the smile grew, became a sneer, "*pursuits*."

"That is enough," Ponsonby said under his breath.

"Actually," said Delmore Lord with flat calm, "It is not."

"I beg your pardon?"

"Stop it, all of you," snapped the admiral. "I'll not have our last night in England marred by tension and bad feelings."

"Whyever not?" asked Akers. "It's been marred by tension and bad feelings for days now, thanks to your niece's failure to honor the commitment she made to my captain in favor of checking on the health of her... *friend*."

Delmore Lord's palm came down hard upon his admiral's polished table. "I'll not tolerate such insults aboard my ship, Akers, or in this company. Apologize, by God, or I'll make you regret it."

"Like you regretted the day you challenged me to a duel, Captain?"

Silence.

"Oh, my," said Maeve Falconer, and her eyes began to gleam with delight. "You really aren't going to let him get away with that now, are you, Del?"

Del was putting down his napkin and getting to his feet. Grace saw the look on his face and paled, and Sir

Graham put a restraining hand on his flag captain's wrist.

"Enough," he said quietly.

"Will you apologize, Akers?"

"I think not."

"And will you, Ponsonby, not defend the honor of the woman you plan to marry?"

"What? I—"

"Right. You what?"

"This is getting out of hand. Sir Graham is correct. Akers here, he's in his cups, we've all had some... tension, there's no need for violence."

"So you won't defend her honor."

Sir Graham was no longer smiling. "Del. *Belay*. And that is an order."

Akers pretended to study his wine. "With all due respect, Captain Lord, the defense of her honor is not any of *your* concern—" a tight smile—"but Captain Ponsonby's."

Grace, watching this escalating tension in alarm, reached a shaking hand for her own glass. And if ever things were destined to go wrong, fate chose that moment for it to happen. She reached for her punch. The heel of her hand caught the rim of the crystal vessel and upended it. A flood of red liquid rushed across the table, roared past Captain Ponsonby's plate, and ended up in his lap. He shot to his feet, aghast, his formerly white breeches now stained crimson, and before he even had the chance to respond Lieutenant Akers turned his full fury on Grace.

"You irresponsible, clumsy chit! Look what you've done to my captain!"

"*Akers!*" roared Ponsonby, but it was too late; Del's rigid control let go like a stay parting in a gale, and he went at Akers so quickly that the man's chair went over and both fell to the deck, fists flying, even as the door to the outside burst open and two marines came charging in, muskets drawn.

"Sir, we heard the yelling!"

"Are you harmed, sir?"

Sir Graham just raised a hand, staying them, and shook his head as the fight raged on.

Akers was getting the worst of it.

"I never knew our Del was such a brawler," Maeve Falconer said lightly, and reached for her rum.

"Father, he has a knife!"

Sir Graham grabbed his son just as Ned tried to launch himself into the fray to save Captain Lord. But the flag captain needed no saving. As the two men gained their feet, he grabbed Akers by his neckcloth, slammed him up against the bulkhead, and caught the man's hand before he could bring the blade into play, pinning it helplessly against the hard wooden paneling behind him.

"You will get your sorry carcass *off my ship* right now, and God help you if I ever see your sniveling face again!"

Up went Akers chin in blazing defiance, and a sparkling hatred shone in his eyes.

"I will *go* where my captain commands me."

With a snarl of fury, Del ripped the other man away from the bulkhead and in that moment, which would be caught forever in Grace's memory, Akers struck like a cobra.

He caught his balance, whirled, and slammed the knife straight toward Captain Lord's torso.

MY SAVING GRACE

❧ 41 ❧

T he blade plunged into his uniform coat.

And would have killed him if Lady Falconer's own pistol hadn't appeared as if by magic, the shot ringing out like a thunderclap in the close confines of the cabin. The ball caught Akers in the arm. The knife bit into the fine blue cloth of Captain Lord's uniform coat, through his shirt, through his skin, but before it could find the space between his ribs and slide into his lung, Akers had already dropped the knife and fallen to her knees, clutching his bleeding wrist.

"Leave it to you, my dear, to save the day," said Sir Graham, as his wife tucked the pistol back into the half-boot from which she'd produced it and reached for her rum.

"*What is the meaning of this?*" Ponsonby roared, going red in the face. "By God I'll have an explanation from you, James!"

"I had to stop it! She'll make you miserable and she doesn't deserve you! She doesn't love you!" Akers slashed angrily at tears that were now spilling down his cheeks and turned his fury on Grace. "And you don't deserve him! He only wants you for your dowry, your connections, the fact that Sir Graham here is your uncle! He's too good for you!"

316

"Cease your prattle," snapped one of the marines, and hauled Akers to his feet. "Sir Graham? How should we handle this?"

"That's a matter for the ship's captain, not me." He reached for more run. "Captain Lord?"

"Take him to the surgeon and then confine him below with a guard outside the door. I will deal with this matter after I've had my damned supper."

"Aye, sir!"

Akers, eyes blazing, was led out. In the silence, Ponsonby looked as if someone had struck him across the face and obliterated his senses. He stood there blinking.

"I don't know what to say," he murmured. "I long suspected he had an odd loyalty to me, but I never thought his feelings were quite so... strong. I am shocked. Horrified, actually."

"Never could stand the fellow," Captain Lord snapped, and as he straightened his torn coat, Grace let out a little cry and went to him.

"You're bleeding!"

"I am fine, Lady Grace."

Ponsonby shook his head. Clarity was returning to his sea-green eyes, and something that looked like anguish.

Realization.

Resolution.

He saw it all, then, when he had refused to see it before. When he had refused to believe. It was there in the way his fiancée had cried out when she'd spotted the dark stain where Akers' knife had gone in. It was there in the tender hand she laid against the gold lace of the flag captain's sleeve, the way she caught her lips between her teeth and her eyes flooded with tears.

It was there in the way the flag captain had become so protective the moment he'd sensed a threat to her— both now and, Ponsonby thought ruefully, in the moments that had brought about the duel back in Norfolk.

It was there in the way the other man had defended both her life and her honor, starting with a plunge into a muddy pond and ending with an attempt on his very life.

And Lieutenant Akers would probably swing for it.

He wiped a hand down his face, his entire world coming apart.

And Sheldon Ponsonby, for the first time in his life, felt the bitter taste of defeat when it came to the fairer sex.

He glanced at the admiral.

Sir Graham just looked at him calmly and gave a barely imperceptible nod.

You know what you have to do, Captain.

Ponsonby cleared his throat.

"Lady Grace," he said with as much composure as he could muster. "May I have a word with you in private?"

She pulled back from the flag captain, her eyes suddenly coming into focus as she realized what she had just done. Delmore Lord raised his head and looked straight out into the distance, as though he could see through the painting of Barbados that hung on the paneled bulkhead and right back to Bridgetown itself. He took a step back, rigid, controlled, and disciplined once more.

"Of course," Grace said hesitantly, and looking at her uncle for permission, received a nod.

She followed Ponsonby toward the door. He opened it and gestured for her to precede him. Her chin came up and he saw her look toward Captain Lord for the briefest of moments as though for approval, even forgiveness, before he stepped into her sightline, closing the door behind him. But Captain Lord was not looking at her. He was not looking at anyone.

Ponsonby offered his elbow and together, they walked through the darkness to the rail.

Far forward, he heard drunken laughter and the strains of a fiddle, and the pounding of feet against the deck as the ship's company danced and sang and celebrated. A splash as something was thrown overboard, more laughter.

There would be no celebration for him tonight.

"Lady Grace," he began, on a deep breath. "I have called you out here to tell you that—"

"No," she said, shaking her head. "No. Let me speak."

"What I have to say is of the utmost importance. It cannot wait."

"And if you're a true gentleman, Captain Ponsonby, you will let the lady speak first."

He inclined his head. Waiting for her apology, for her excuses, for her justifications, even as he knew in his heart what was coming.

She reached out and laid a hand on his arm. Quickly drew it back. Her eyes were both tragic and resolved.

"I cannot marry you," she said firmly, raising her gaze to his. "It is not your fault, and there was a time not so long ago when I wanted nothing more than to be your wife. Indeed, it was even expected. But I cannot go through with this, Captain Ponsonby." She withdrew her hand. "I hope you understand."

His smile was pained. "You have loved him all along, haven't you?"

Her features softened. "I have. But it wasn't until tonight that I realized just how much."

"More than a friend, then."

"Far more than a friend."

They stood there awkwardly for a moment more.

"And what was it you wished to tell me, Captain Ponsonby?"

He shook his head and tried to smile. He had failed her miserably, really. Failed to defend her honor, failed to give her his heart, failed to do for her what he would have demanded for his own sister had she not already been happily married. He would not make matters worse by taking what was left of her pride.

"Captain Ponsonby?"

"Honestly, my dear—" he inclined his head and his pained smile spread. "I have quite forgotten."

"I'm sorry, Captain."

"I am, too." He bowed. "I wish you well, Lady Grace."

"And I, the same for you."

Nothing more was said. He escorted her back to the cabin and calling for his launch, exited the great flagship and returned to his frigate.

⚓

DEL'S APPETITE WAS GONE.

He had watched Lady Grace and Captain Ponsonby leave together. She would likely be placating her betrothed, trying her best to undo the damage. Soothing him for the embarrassment of being misled by Akers, reassuring him of her affections, pledging her love for him. He had no desire to sit here with Sir Graham and the other officers, knowing they pitied him. He wanted nothing more than to be alone, though it would be rude to leave the admiral's dinner.

He felt eyes upon him and looked up to see Sir Graham himself regarding him.

"Go see to that wound, Captain."

The admiral understood. He also understood that this wasn't about the wound, but about the bitter anguish of loss. Del excused himself and stalked out of the cabin. He did not go to the surgeon. Instead, he went to his own quarters, seeking solitude.

Peace.

Refuge.

A marine stood guard outside. He jerked to attention at the flag captain's appearance.

"Evening, sir."

Del nodded curtly. The marine opened the door and Del entered his domain.

He wasn't normally one to imbibe. Tonight, though, might warrant an exception.

⚓

GRACE HEARD THE SIDE PARTY PIPING PONSONBY OFF the ship and realized she'd probably never see him again.

She did not care.

A marine opened the door to her uncle's cabin for her and she stepped inside, her eyes trying to adjust to the lantern light that seemed so bright after the darkness outside. She was escorted aft through her uncle's expansive quarters and to the great day cabin, where those who still remained had tried to resume an air of normalcy as they continued with the meal.

Captain Lord himself was nowhere to be seen.

She felt no sorrow about releasing Sheldon Ponsonby from his vow. She felt nothing but a strange and weightless relief.

Her uncle looked up at her.

"Where did he go?" she asked.

Sir Graham, who was reaching for a roll, pulled it apart and slathered it with butter. "By he, I'm assuming you mean my flag captain."

"Of course I am."

"Did you break it off with Ponsonby?"

"Really, Uncle Gray, that is my business, is it not?"

"Everything on my ship is my business."

"Last I knew, this isn't your ship, it's Captain Lord's."

"And when did you become so well- and ill-versed in naval matters, Grace?"

"Just tell me where he went."

Sir Graham laid down his butter knife. "I suspect he went to question Akers. He'll likely return to his own cabin, after that. Though I did ask him to go see the surgeon. Doubt he did, though."

"Why do you doubt that? You give an order, your captains carry them out."

"Under normal circumstances," the admiral said, and bit into the roll.

Maeve Falconer smiled. "You should go to him, Grace."

"That would be highly improper and we all know it."

At that moment, Maeve's face seemed to shift and then to contort, and as Grace stared at her in confusion, the one-time pirate queen of the Caribbean began to laugh with a gusto that was quite at odds with the cultured elegance her station demanded.

"The only one around here who was ever concerned about propriety was Del," she said, "and at the moment, I highly doubt whether or not that's uppermost in his mind since he thinks you went out to console Ponsonby and is likely staring quite miserably at the paneling of his dining cabin."

"Yes, you should go to him," said Sir Graham.

"What? But—"

"Come, my dear," said Maeve, pushing aside her plate and getting to her feet. Gone was the savage and competent warrior she'd been just moments before when she'd so effectively disarmed Akers and she was once again the lady, the admiral's wife, the vibrant red-haired beauty with the mysterious tiger-eyes. "The ship is grand. Easy to get lost. I'll take you to him."

"I would like that," Grace said.

H er aunt had not overestimated the size of the ship. Though Captain Lord's quarters were on the deck just above Sir Graham's, finding them required going up a deck and gaining entrance via the red-coated marine stationed just outside the door. This, Maeve did with a murmured word.

"Of course, Lady Falconer."

The marine stamped his musket against the deck and the door opened. A wizened old man appeared, standing on a bowed leg and a peg. He had thinning gray hair combed back into an old-fashioned pigtail and he eyed Grace with some suspicion through a smudged pair of spectacles.

"Hello, Cooper. Is your captain in or has he gone to speak to the prisoner?"

"He is in, Lady Falconer. But I'm not sure if he'll—"

"I quite understand your desire to shield and protect your captain, as that's what good people do and you are amongst the best, Coop. But Lady Grace here is concerned about him and wishes to assure herself that he's suffered no grievous injury."

It was not a suggestion. It was an order from the admiral's wife, and Cooper did not question or refute it.

"Of course," he said, bowing his head. "Come with me, Lady Grace."

Maeve laid a hand on Grace's shoulder, gave her a look that told her to make good on her chance to right things, and melted back off into the darkness.

And Grace was left with the old sailor.

He turned, not waiting for her to follow, and stomped his way across the black-and-white checkered floor canvas, heading aft. Grace, her heart pounding, followed him. A cavernous space, Captain Lord had. To her left, a sleeping cot suspended from a pole, with tented curtains for privacy. Paneled, painted doors, massive guns pulled up to open ports, the great span of deck beams arcing gracefully overhead. Closets where she suspected the steward and clerk and other servants conducted the affairs relevant to serving their captain. Through a screened bulkhead and into another great space that stretched from one side of the ship to the other, the same black-and-white canvas, the paneling painted a milky robin's egg blue that was pleasant and warm in the glow of the lantern light. A long table for dining, gleaming in that same light. Through yet another barrier and into a third and final chamber, the grand, expansive aftermost portion of the ship with its panoramic gallery of windows stretching from one side to the other. Beyond them was the harbor, a silvered expanse of water upon which the lights of other ships rode, their great masts poking at the stars above.

Her eyes adjusted and she saw that just beneath those windows were velvet cushions and on one of them sat a man, silhouetted by the starlight. He was looking out into the night.

"Captain, sir. Lady Grace Fairchild to see you."

He turned his head and got to his feet with a weariness of purpose.

"Thank you, Mr. Cooper. That will be all."

"Sir?"

"Go join the festivities aft. It'll be some time before you all have the chance to make merry again."

"But sir, I—"

"That will be all, Cooper."

The wizened sailor nodded, cast a last suspicious glance at Grace, and clumped his way to the door. It opened on well-oiled hinges, and shut behind him.

Click.

Thump.. thump... thump.

And he was gone.

For a long moment, Grace stood there in the gloom, rooted to the spot, her hands clenched loosely in front of her. She could feel her heartbeat banging in her ears. Her palms were damp. She wiped them discreetly on her skirts.

"Are you all right?" she asked, eyeing the bloody spot on his coat.

"I'm still breathing."

"May I see?"

A muscle twitched in his jaw. He opened his coat, unbuttoned his vest, yanked his shirt from his breeches and lifted it, showing her the torn bit of flesh so she could see that it was superficial. He quickly covered it again and looked away.

"Hard to see in the darkness," she murmured. "I guess I'll have to take your word for it."

"It is most unseemly, Lady Grace, for you to be here in my cabin. In the dark. Alone." His voice sounded rough in the darkness. "Your husband-to-be will not approve."

Grace stood unmoving. "I have released Captain Ponsonby from his commitment to me."

The words hung flatly in the silence. The heartbeat in Grace's ears grew louder and she waited for a reaction, a word, anything from this man who stood a few feet away.

"And why," he asked quietly, "would you do such a thing?"

She took a deep breath and looked at him in silhouette, wishing she could see his face in the gloom, his eyes.

"Because I do not love him."

He turned once more to look out over the harbor, his hands clasped behind his back in the eternal pose of a mariner, and said nothing.

"I don't love him, Captain Lord. I can't love him. And maybe I was fascinated by him at one point in time, but I never loved him. There's only *one* man on this earth that I love, and that man is you."

He remained unmoving for a long time and when he spoke, his voice was as quiet and flat as the sea spread out beyond the great windows behind him.

"Do you know what my cousin Connor used to call me?" he asked, still not turning around. "Deadly Dullmore. And he was right, y'know. I am dull. Boring. Not exactly the stuff from which a fair maiden's dreams are made."

"You are not dull. You are solid. Dependable. Honorable and kind."

"Regimented. By-the-book. Unadventurous."

"West," she said.

He turned slightly, so that she could see the strong blade of his nose backlit by the night outside. "What?"

"The wind. It's out of the west. What there is of it, anyhow."

He turned further around, the starlight momentarily glinting off the epaulet on one shoulder. "And how would you know that, Lady Grace?"

"I had a good teacher. But it is out of the west, and I know that because when Lady Falconer brought me here, I happened to look up and there was a flag, and it was flickering out in that direction," she said confidently, pointing to her right. "Which makes the wind out of the west."

"Hmm." She sensed, rather than saw, his reluctant smile. "And you are certain of that, are you?"

"I am certain."

She stepped closer to him.

He did not move.

"And how do you know that that direction is the west, Lady Grace?"

She took another step toward him. "I would like to say that I looked up at the stars, found Polaris, and deduced it that way. I would like to say that I looked at the lay of the land that is Portsmouth and figured it out from there. But the truth is, Captain Lord, I did neither of those things." Another step closer and in the gloom, her hand stretched out, her fingers reaching, finding, his. "The truth is, I made it easy on myself... and asked my Aunt Maeve."

Yes, he was definitely smiling, now. She was close enough that she could see the whiteness of his teeth, and close enough that she could stand on tiptoe now, anchoring her hand against his, stand on tiptoe and tilt her head back and—

The ferocity with which he pulled her forward and up and against him surprised her. In that simple gesture were weeks' worth of need and pent-up want, of unspoken desires left to simmer for too long, of release. His head lowered and his mouth was suddenly hard against hers, his hand coming up to thread through her hair, to cup the back of her head and draw her close. He tasted of something sweet, maybe wine, but before she could wonder at it his lips were moving against hers, his breath against her cheek, his tongue licking the seam of her lips until they opened, hesitantly at first and then, as passion lit her blood and flared through her body, with a fierce and desperate need.

Aside from him, she had never kissed a man before.

Had never *been* kissed by a man before. Not even Ponsonby, really. Her every sense was assailed. The faint roughness of his jaw against her cheek and chin. The taste on his tongue, on his lips. The sound of his breathing, the whisper of his clothing as he moved. The aroma of his soap, or maybe it was cologne, something faintly exotic, heady, masculine. The powerful arm that wrapped around her lower back like a vise, holding her close. The feeling of breathlessness until he pulled back, put his hands on the outside of her shoulders, and with reclaimed tenderness, set her back and away from him.

"Captain Lord?"

"You came here tonight, Lady Grace, for a reason known only to yourself."

"I don't want you to call me Lady Grace. I am Grace. That is my name. I'd be happy if you would use it."

"You came here tonight for what reason?"

"I told you. To tell you that I love you."

"And what do you want of me?"

The words stung and she suddenly felt foolish. Uncertain. Unsure.

"I want nothing from you," she murmured.

He stood holding her, hands still against her shoulders. "Tomorrow," he said, "I will take this ship and your uncle and his family back to Barbados. It is quite likely, Grace, that you and I will never see each other again."

He had not said he loved her.

He was going away.

He did not say he loved me. Is my heart wrong? Was Ned wrong? Have we all been wrong?

"Captain Lord," she said quietly, "I came here tonight to tell you that I was in error. That God never put Captain Ponsonby in my life in order to get me to marry him, but to get me to marry— Oh." She reddened. "Oh, that doesn't sound quite right."

"Were you about to say, in order to get you to marry me?"

"Well, yes, but, that would require your asking me to marry you and of course, that is presumptuous. I mean, you may not wish to marry me. You may think me too impetuous, too flighty, too unsuitable, too seasick. You may not love me. You may think of *me* as nothing more than a friend. And if that is all you think of me, then... then I will settle for that, because I'd rather have you as a friend than nothing at all, and—"

Again his mouth claimed hers, silencing her. Her hand came up, a small thing against the broad expanse of his chest with its fine blue cloth and fancy gold buttons, and she pressed her palm against it, felt his heart beating so strong and true beneath.

He broke the kiss, and she felt him leaning his lips against the top of her head.

"I am Deadly Dullmore," he murmured, in the darkness.

"I am clumsy and impetuous."

"I am about to sail away from here, and only God and your uncle know when I'll be back."

"Then I guess we don't have much time." She pulled back and looked up at his dear, dear face gazing down at hers, at the hesitant smile on his lips, now spreading into one of confidence, triumph, and stunned realization. Of disbelief. Of joy. "You have been a hero to me, Delmore Lord."

"And I cannot believe that I finally... finally... got the very best prize of all. You." He shook his head, grinning, the years dropping away from his taciturn face and turning it boyish with delight. "Imagine that. Imagine!" And then he sobered, got down on one knee and tenderly took her hand, bringing it to his lips. "I love you, Grace."

"I love *you*, Delmore."

"Del. Please. Not Delmore. It's too stuffy. Always hated it, to be honest."

"Del, then."

"Grace."

"Kiss me again?"

"Will you marry me?"

"I thought you'd never ask."

⚓

THE FOLLOWING MORNING DAWNED BRIGHT AND clear, with a few high cirrus clouds burning off before the sun could even gain momentum on its ascent from the eastern horizon, and the roar that issued from Sir Graham's cabin at yet another delay preventing his return to his beloved Barbados might've been heard all the way to Cornwall.

"Honest to bloody hell, Del! You should've offered for the girl two weeks ago, never let Ponsonby get his anchor flukes into her, now we'll have to be stuck in this godforsaken country another three weeks while banns are read and a wedding put together and guests invited and oh, I suppose that means going all the way back to my sister's house and putting up with more frippery from that quarter! What are you trying to do to me, eh?"

Del, standing there before him with his hat in his hands, shrugged. "Nothing saying we have to stay here in England for three more weeks, sir. We could get a common license. Or marry in Barbados. Or even have the ship's chaplain conduct the ceremony whilst at sea."

But then he saw that Sir Graham's azure eyes were crinkled at the corners with high amusement, and the thunder in his words was nothing more than good natured rumbling. The admiral grinned and got up to congratulate his flag captain and give him a hearty clap on the back.

"Damn your eyes, Del, we'll do it right and proper. Here. In England. Your family and hers. All of us. Barbados can wait."

And so, Captain Delmore John Lord and Lady Grace Emily Fairchild found themselves back where it had all started—at a summer wedding (their own, this time) at the same country estate in Sussex where they'd first met, with the same pond and the same high fluffy white cotton-clouds on a similar morning filled with sunshine and a light wind out of the southwest (Grace got it right with no prompting), and guests from all over. Sir Graham's sisters, including Grace's four-times-wed mother and her portly and still-besotted new husband. Hannah and Polly. A contingent of naval officers from HMS *Orion* as well as Portsmouth and even the Admiralty in London, all looking quite dashing in their best uniforms with their gold lace catching the sun. Peers of the realm and Members of Parliament and neighboring gentry, their wives and daughters in summer pastels. Colin and Ariadne Lord were there, with their two boys. Admiral Christian Lord and his Irish wife Deirdre, and their blonde and sunny daughters with their own children.

The chapel in the village was full to bursting, the rector beaming, and when the ceremony was over and the register signed, Grace found herself walking arm-in-arm out of the church with her new husband, resplendent in his uniform, clutching his sleeve in case she tripped over her hem or slipped in the handfuls of rice being flung at them both and went skidding on her nose.

But if there was an accident waiting to happen, it would not be today.

There was dancing on the lawn, the music provided by a group of tars whose smart neckties and coats and naval slops could not conceal the fact that these were tough and salty mariners, all of them hand-selected by Jimmy Thorne, all of them on their best efforts to tone down their language and rough manners. A few tittering young women stepped out on the cordoned-off lawn to dance with some of the young naval officers, and as the wine and rum and beer and not-so-benign punch began to flow, more and more revelers joined them. Inhibitions were dropped, Jimmy Thorne proposed loudly to Polly (she accepted), the rough-language began to reappear and really, nobody cared.

Nor did anyone care when the newlyweds, eager to begin their lives as man and wife, decided they'd had enough of the revelry.

Grace's new stepfather lent them his coach and to the cheers of the guests, and with Grace waving out the window, they wheeled their way out of the long drive. By the time the team reached the road, the horses were trotting smartly.

And it was beginning to rain.

Hard.

The sky outside the window went a dark gray, then charcoal, and a sudden gust of wind hit the coach and rocked it on its axles. A moment later the deluge started, first as a few streaks against the glass, then as a sheeting downpour.

"Oh, this will be ending things soon enough back at the wedding festivities," Grace murmured.

Del rapped on the roof and rapped again, harder, to be heard over the downpour. The coach slowed. "Turn back," he yelled. "No sense you getting soaked and besides, this is too dangerous. We'll stay the night back at Ruscombe Hall." He turned back to Grace with a sheepish smile. "I'm sorry. So much for making our escape!"

He had to yell to be heard over the sound of rain hitting the roof. Lightning cracked down from the heavens and the very ground seemed to rumble beneath them.

The driver turned the team around and minutes later, they were racing back toward the manor house. Outside the window, Grace could see the day growing blacker still. The galloping team drew them up the drive. People were scurrying to and fro on the lawn, racing to escape the deluge, servants grabbing china and place settings, the ladies shrieking.

The coach lurched to a stop and Del had the door open before the driver could even get down from his box. "I'll take Mrs. Lord inside," he yelled up. "You, man, go seek shelter! We'll stay here for the night!"

"Thank you, sir!"

He dutifully waited, bent to the rain as Del reached in and helped Grace down from the coach. Hand-in-hand and laughing, they ran toward the house. She slipped in the wet grass and he caught her, and by the time they reached the front doors Grace was soaked through and her hem and satin pumps splattered with mud.

They slammed into the entrance foyer and stood there, laughing.

Sir Graham came in, raising his brows. "Back already, are you? I thought you'd left for Portsmouth."

"Got caught in the deluge."

"Well, get out of here, you two. You've got a wedding night to celebrate."

Grace caught the humor in his voice, and even her husband grinned at the admiral. And then he caught her hand once more and together, they both ran lightly up the stairs and to the second floor, where Grace headed down the hall until she came to what was to have been her own apartments.

She pushed open the door, yanked Del inside.

He shut it behind her.

She leaned back against it, breathing hard. Water

streamed down her cheeks, and the silk bandeau she'd worn had come partially loose, leaving hanks of damp hair clinging to her cheek.

Her new husband stilled, looking down at her.

Grace caught her breath and raised her gaze to his.

Outside, lightning flashed down, turning the room purple for the briefest of moments before the answering crack of thunder rumbled through the house, shaking the floor beneath their feet.

His hand came up, tenderly clearing the hair from her cheek, his fingers warm against the little indent under her cheekbone. She closed her eyes and leaned into his touch and a moment later, his lips were against hers, seeking, urgent, and delicious.

She sighed, and a little groan escaped her throat. This... this was what she had pined for, waited for, prayed for... love. Love, with this man. *This man*. And as he deepened the kiss, his mouth urgent against hers now, his fingers sliding back and into her damp hair, she pushed herself up against him, her hands catching the lapels of his coat, trying to find relief for the sudden hungry ache that started in her belly and fanned up into her nipples, down into that secret space between her legs.

Again the lightning flickered and a moment later, the answering crash of thunder.

"I imagine," she breathed, resting her forehead against his waistcoat, "that is what it must sound like when the guns go off on that insanely huge ship of yours."

"Oh, much, much louder."

"Del?"

"Grace?"

She looked up at him, seeing his face in the flickering violet light that heralded another shaking peal of thunder. "Make me your wife."

He picked her up in his arms then, doing so with a

deft move that saw her feet on the floor one moment and her legs dangling over his arm the next. The sensation of weightlessness, the delight of being overpowered, overwhelmed by such masculine strength made her shiver a little, and she hooked her arms around his neck, pressing her breasts against his waistcoat as he carried her to the bed.

He set her down with infinite care. Outside, the rain hammered in a thousand pinging drums, streaming down the windows and blurring the gray skies beyond.

"I love thunder," she said, running her finger along the line of his jaw.

"And I," he returned, "love you."

She grinned and caught at his necktie with eager fingers, loosening it.

"Do you believe in love at first sight?"

"Yes."

"Destiny?"

"Most certainly."

"Do you think I'll make an admirable sea-officer's wife?"

"That," he murmured, leaning forward to kiss the hollow of her throat, "will depend on whether you learn east from west, larboard from starboard, and how to tie a bowline."

"Will you teach me?"

His lips were against the beating pulse in her throat, the sweet clean scent of his hair in her nose, the harsh, wiry curls tickling her cheek. She sighed in bliss and then he pulled back, gazing deeply into her eyes. She reached out and touched his face. His jawline. Felt the emerging bristle there, rough against the pads of her exploring fingertips. Felt his breath against her wrist, saw the desire darkening his steady gray eyes. He caught her fingers then and brushed them along the seam of his lips, holding her gaze with his own. The gesture was wildly erotic, causing sensation to thrum in her belly and between her legs.

Lightning lit up the room once more, a flickering flash that went on and on before it abruptly stopped and in that expectant silence before the thunder came, he kissed her.

Hard.

Her hands were already clawing at his coat when the thunder came, shaking the very walls and the floor beneath them. Any attempts at drawing out the act, of a long lead-up to a climax they both craved were abandoned, the fierce weather outside only adding to their frenzy. Downstairs, drunken revelry echoed through the great ballroom, but neither heard it; she, already beginning to breathe hard, had peeled the coat from her husband's broad shoulders while he shrugged out of the damp garment entirely, letting it fall to the floor, his waistcoat following. Her hands went to his drop front, fumbling with the buttons, feeling the hard masculine flesh just beneath. His arm banded her, drawing her close, right up against his shirt and the heart she could feel beating hard and fast just beneath.

"Grace," he said hoarsely. "We shouldn't rush this."

But she wanted to rush it. Wanted to race headlong into this flight of coming joy, a newly-fledged bird charging toward a cliff, flinging herself off it, spreading her great and newly-formed wings to see if they would carry her, allow her to soar, to fly. She raised her arms, allowed him to pull her gown off over her head, to unlace her stays as she herself kicked off her muddied shoes and his hard, rough fingers found the garters that held up her stockings and peeled the wet silk down over long shapely calves.

Outside the rain beat harder, and the lightning flashed and thunder rolled over the noble Sussex downs.

And Grace felt her body melting, going up in steam,

puddling in a spreading warmth of desire, as if every cell in her body was screaming its need for him, and him alone. Him. *My husband.* He loomed over her, the sound of his own breathing lost beneath the fury outside and the deafening tattoo of the rain against the windows, his big body leaning into hers, forcing her down and backward to the bed, his lips buried in the hollow between neck and shoulder, his bristled jaw catching in her damp hair that was already soaking the pillow, warm and wet and all but suffocating him in its cloying warmth.

He moved over her. She felt small and insignificant and overpowered and delicious, and the fire that had already flared in her body spread until she could not catch her breath.

He leaned down, cradling her face between his hands, his eyes dark in the gloom, his hair framing his face.

"I wanted to make this last," he said roughly. "Wanted to take my time... go slowly... cherish and worship you but God help me, I cannot."

"Del—"

"I cannot," he repeated, and he lowered his head to her collarbone, pressing, seeking, kissing, his breath hot against her damp skin, kissing her through the thin fabric of her chemise, his great body, so hard, so muscular, so strong and virile, pressing down on her, pressing down against her, pressing her, all of her, down, down, *down* into the deep feathery embrace of the mattress. She felt the iron brace of his arms, felt the length of his legs heavy along her own, felt his lips, *ohhh*, his lips, now wandering lower, kissing her on-fire flesh through the thin barrier of her chemise. His hand, cupping her breast. Pushing the soft globe up to his mouth until his lips closed hungrily over the nipple and he sucked it, hard.

Grace moaned deep in her throat, squirming restlessly as she sought release from the building fire. The long, hard-muscled length of his leg pinned her restless movements, pushing her down into the bed, and then his knee was there, driving her legs apart, his mouth still sucking at her breast through the chemise and his hand now seeking her inner thighs, stroking the silken flesh.

Behind closed eyelids, she saw flickers of purple, heard the earth trembling in the mighty pulse of thunder that followed, felt it in her body, felt it in his hand as its broad width swept the soft skin of her thighs, found the moist junction between her legs and began to stroke, the thumb finding a hidden part of her that made her gasp and arch and cry out in delight. Oh. Oh, dear Lord, what anguish, what pleasure, what delicious *joy*! She felt a flood of moisture between herself and his hand, his fingers, as she writhed in helpless abandon, and then he moved over her, his mouth smothering her cries as he parted her, filling her with an unbearable hardness, pushing her wider and wider apart until the searing pain was met with that indescribable building anguish once more. He kissed her. He devoured her mouth, her very senses. His movements came hard and fast now, filling her, their damp shirts grinding against each other, their heartbeats melding, until he gave a hoarse cry and she was flung once more out over that same cliff, her wings already spreading to take her on a silent, floating ride as the world unfolded in all its magnificence beneath her.

She lay there. Tears of joy fell silently from her eyes to wet the pillow beneath her head. Her husband lay atop her, his weight crushing and delicious, his breathing harsh, one leg still thrown possessively over her own. Her arms came up, encircled his broad and muscled back.

"I love you, Captain Lord."

"I love you, Mrs. Lord."

Outside, the lightning was coming more slowly, the thunder beginning to move off. Her new husband raised himself on his elbows and slid his arms beneath her own shoulders, and holding her close, rolled over onto his back.

Together they lay there, listening to the rain beginning to recede. A thin ray of sunshine pierced the fast-moving clouds outside and the room began to brighten.

"I think," Grace said, laying her cheek against the broad expanse of his chest and thinking how perfectly her head fit there in the cup between his arm and shoulder, "that I'm going to enjoy being a married woman."

"And I think that I should get up and close the drapes."

"Don't."

"Aye... I must confess, I'm not inclined to move right now."

She moved her lips, seeking the warm wedge of skin at his throat, inhaling his scent, tasting the salt from their exertions. She found the hem of his rucked-up shirt, slid her hand beneath it, brought it up to rest beside her head, only the thin fabric of the shirt itself between it and her cheek.

"So don't."

He locked his arms around her back, holding her close to him, heart to heart. She felt his manhood stirring once more against the hot, moist part of her that marked their coupling, felt her own flesh responding in kind.

"Going to be a long night," he said, with a little laugh.

"Not long enough." she replied, and kissed him.

❦ 43 ❦

Barbados appeared as a brilliant green jewel riding atop the aqua expanse of the Caribbean.

Standing at the rail of the poop deck, the massive expanse of the warship's length spread out before her, Grace threw back her head, let the warm breezes play with the frilly brim of her bonnet, and smiled. Above her head, acres of sail, one stacked above the other on what she now knew was the mizzenmast, bellied hard to the fore, braced to take advantage of the wind that had pushed them across the Atlantic these past several weeks. Their shadows spilled across the quarterdeck, the waist of the ship, the foredeck, each a place where lieutenants commanded contingents of men and organized them into work parties devoted to each sail, each task, each command.

She shaded her eyes with her hand, turned, and looked down at the quarterdeck before her. It was the heart of the ship, the place where all orders originated and the massive double-spoked wheel, manned by two helmsmen and overseen by the sailing master, reigned. It was the place reserved for the admiral and his captain and those immediately responsible for the ship's command.

And there he was. Her husband.

He stood near the great wheel, hands caught behind his back, shoulders proud beneath their gold-laced epaulets and the wind playing with the long tails of his blue uniform coat as he took a spyglass, trained it on that distant rim of emerald, grinned, and said something to her uncle. He was not immune to the feel of eyes upon him and feeling hers, he turned, caught her watching him, and taking off his hat, swept it before him in a playful, gallant bow, his smile bright.

She waved back.

In the weeks that had transpired during the crossing, she had seen the man at work, the man at worry, the man responsible for running a ship of six hundred souls who all depended on him, the man who must placate and serve an admiral on one hand, the Royal Navy's demands on the other, and the welfare and good spirits of those who served both. She had lain with him while he'd stared up into the darkness, worried about whether a shift in wind might add another week to their schedule and if that would mean they'd have to ration stores in order to make what they had, last. She'd seen him maintain his patience when a young midshipman had bumbled his relaying of an order, later having a quiet word with the lieutenant who had come down a little too hard on the boy. She'd seen him working late into the night at his desk, seen him playing cards with his clerk, seen every scar on his body, every imperfection of his skin, even the little birthmark that rode his left hipbone and seemed to bear the shape of a boat.

She had remarked on it.

"Funny-looking thing, isn't it?" he'd said, as they'd lain cozied up together on the window cushions, a panoramic view of the sea just outside. "My mother told me that it crops up every so often in her family line. Her grandfather had it." He'd smiled as she'd traced the odd shape with a finger. "It's always the same. A faint discoloration that looks remarkably like an old galley."

"A galley?"

"A sort of ship, dearest, common some two hundred years ago."

She'd put her lips to it then, kissing it.

"What does it mean, Del?"

"Well, it may be nothing more than a random coming together of pigment. But family lore claims it's the mark of a long-ago ancestress on my mother's side, an Irishwoman who was a chieftain in her own right and who sailed the seas as a pirate. She was bold and fierce and feared nothing and no one, and even sailed all the way from the west coast of Ireland to England and up the Thames to London, where she managed to secure an audience with Queen Elizabeth herself."

"That is fascinating! What was her name?"

"*Gráinne Ní Mháille.*"

The strange Irish language fell from his lips as though born to them, and Grace raised her brows.

"Yes, I speak my mother's native tongue," he said, grinning.

"And yet you could not appear more English."

"Half-English," he murmured, pulling her close and running his fingers through her hair.

She tried to pronounce the strange name, but it came out sounding like she had something caught in her throat.

He laughed. "The English had a name for her. A name that you'll find much easier to pronounce, because you share it."

"What?"

"Grace," he murmured, looking into her eyes. "Grace O'Malley."

"Oh..."

"The birthmark," he said, "is only part of it. Those who receive it are said to have a special connection with Gráinne."

"And do you believe that?"

He looked away, his gaze going out over the sea, his eyes becoming reflective and far away. "I do," he said. "The part of me that is Irish believes it entirely."

"You don't seem the sort to be fanciful, Del. But we have the rest of our lives to discover each other's secrets, do we not?"

"Aye, dear heart. We do."

And now, the fresh tropical wind and sparkling sunshine all around them, she gazed lovingly down at him there on the quarterdeck, while Ned Falconer climbed the steps to where she sat and thrust a finger toward the approaching island. "There is it, Grace. Barbados! Oh, you'll love it here, it's warm and beautiful and we even have a statue of Lord Nelson. I can't wait to show you around."

"I will enjoy that, Ned."

He sobered and looked very serious and grown up all of a sudden. "I'm glad you came to your senses, you know. There was never anyone else for you but Captain Lord."

"I know that," she said, thinking about the odd disclosure about his ancestor with whom she shared a name. About how she had loved him from the beginning, but had been too hardheaded, too afraid to take the risk, to see it.

Grace leaned her elbows on the rail and looked down at the quarterdeck below, Ned beside her.

"If that island is as beautiful up close as it appears to be from this far out, I can see why your father couldn't wait to get back to it," she said, already feeling excitement about her new home.

"It is, Grace. Oh, trust me, it is! And any moment now, Captain Lord, if he is cautious, is going to call for all sail to be struck save for the barest minimum to maintain headway."

"And if he is not cautious?"

"He'll charge into the Carlisle Bay with every sail set

and flying, turn her neatly into the wind, fire a salute and have the sails struck and the boats out before the smoke even clears. Very impressive display, that, flashy and even a bit reckless and Papa would be impressed, as it's a very easy thing to mess up and any number of things can go awry." He grinned. 'But damn, it looks good when done right."

"Ned, such language!"

He laughed.

"But Captain Lord'll take the cautious approach," he predicted. "He always does."

And he did. Perhaps it was because of the strength of the wind, perhaps it was because it was a safer bet, or maybe it was simply because while the flag captain had a smart and well-drilled crew who could sail his ship through the eye of a needle if he commanded it, Captain Delmore Lord was solid and dependable and liked things done in ways that were predictably safe rather than stylishly flamboyant— even if the latter would have impressed his admiral. They glided around the southernmost coast of the island, pushed along hard by the trades with a strong following sea, turned north, and with HMS *Orion*'s massive jibboom pointed squarely on the small forest of masts dotting Carlisle Bay, Del did exactly as Ned predicted he would do.

Grace heard him give the command.

"Strike all sail save for jibs and topsails, Mr. Armstrong. And the spanker too. Smartly, now, and prepare to come about."

"Look lively lads!"

"Anchor party, at the ready!"

The massive warship, the wind coming in now over her starboard beam, began to lose way, the pitch of water creaming past her hull lessening in pitch, her decks beginning to heel a bit to leeward.

"Ready about," the captain called.

"Ready about!"

Immediately the helmsman was turning the great wheel, the man-of-war was sliding into the harbor and quickly losing way as she met the wind head-on.

"Let go!"

The rattle of chain, a splash as the massive bow anchor was let go, sinking down, down, through the crystalline depths and biting into a sea bottom it hadn't tasted since last resting in Portsmouth's cold gray harbor several thousand miles away.

And then all the warships in the harbor were firing thunderous salutes as the admiral was welcomed home, and Del was vaulting lightly up the steps and hooking an arm around her waist and kissing her, right there in front of all to see.

The crew, all six hundred of them, sent up a thunderous cheer and threw their hats into the air.

"It may be a long time before we return to England, my dear Grace. In the meantime, welcome home," he said, grinning. "Welcome home."

EPILOGUE

Hambledon, Hampshire, England, 1820

T he ancient Celtic cross still hung around her neck.
Its hammered gold and raw emeralds gleamed as
richly as they ever had, and its mysteries continued to
beckon. As it had been for Del and his siblings, it was
now a source of fascination and mystery for their
children.

The little ones gathered around their grandmother
in a reverent circle on the floor. The boys in the group,
perhaps even some of the girls, all fancied a career at
sea just like their fathers and grandfathers before them.
Colin's four boys, Kit, Cameron, Jonathan and Aaron.
His sole daughter, Tabitha. And their cousins, newly-
arrived from Barbados, where their father had served as
Admiral Sir Graham Falconer's flag captain until his
own promotion to Rear-Admiral of the Blue.

Colin and Ariadne's brood studied their newfound
cousins, wondering if they were to be friend or enemy,
partner in crime or bitter rivals. The ritual of Grandma
Deirdre passing around the ancient cross that had belonged to the venerable *Gráinne Ní Mháille* was theirs,
and they were not all that keen on sharing it.

Or her.

Let alone, the cross itself.

As Grace, her belly already swelling with their third child, sat down on the floor beside her sister-in-law Ariadne, with little two-year-old Fiona balanced on one knee and son Justin trying to muscle his way closer to his grandmother, Del sidestepped closer to his brother, Colin.

"Which story do you think she'll tell them today? The one about Queen Maeve of Connacht, since Sir Graham's wife shares her name?"

"Oh, I'd lay money on it being one about Granuaile."

"Hmm." Del rubbed at his jaw. "Aye, so would I."

Deirdre O'Devir Lord glanced up at her husband, leaning against the door jamb and admiring his grand-children. She reached to her neck, dragged out the ancient relic on its heavy chain and let the children get a good, wide-eyed look at it. The old admiral caught Del's gaze and winked.

"*Grace O'Malley*," he mouthed, agreeing with his two sons.

"...And far, far away, in the magical place that is Ireland, there lived a strong, proud woman with wildly curling hair and a ferocity in battle that had enemies far an' wide terrified of her. She commanded her own fleet o' ships, and she was Ireland's very own pirate queen..."

"Told you," Colin said, leaning in close to Del.

Del shook his head. "Told *you*," he replied.

Their mother was warming to the tale. "Her base was on the wild western coast in a county called Mayo, where she had a castle all her own, called Rockfleet. From there, she ruled th' seas and commanded a great galley—"

"As big as Papa's ship, *Orion*?"

"Ohhh, much bigger than that," Deirdre said in her musical Irish lilt.

Del and Colin exchanged glances. Colin looked

away to stifle his laughter and Del wiped helplessly at the smirk that he was helpless to prevent. Their mother's powers of exaggeration seemed to expand with each telling of the story.

And so the tale went on. How much of it was true, neither of Deirdre's two adult sons actually knew. They stood together, listening to the timeless story with as much attention as they had in their childhood, young once more, enraptured once more, two brothers who could not be more different, their families bound across time and space to this woman that none of them had ever met, though Del, had he been asked, might beg to differ on that.

"And she went *alllll* the way up th' mighty River Thames," their mother was saying, holding her arms wide to indicate how grand that mighty river actually was, "to meet the Queen of England herself…"

Colin had his arms folded across his chest, his eyes distant and fond.

"All the way to London, Grandma?"

"All the way t' London and to Queen Elizabeth's glittering palace, where she was granted an audience with none other than Her Majesty herself! She did Ireland proud that day, our Gráinne!"

Del caught a movement out of the corner of his eye, and turning his head, saw Gráinne Ní Mháille standing there in the moonlight slanting in from the window.

She smiled and winked at him.

"It's true," she said. "Every word of it."

The others never heard her, of course. Not even Colin. But within the circle, little Fiona, who had crawled from her mother's lap and gone up to sit next to her older brother, suddenly looked toward the window. Little Fiona, who had curling black ringlets and flashing eyes and the shape of a ship high on her left shoulder.

The child's eyes widened and she turned around, seeking her father's gaze.

"Papa?"

Del knew what his daughter had seen. Knew that she would be guided and guarded throughout her life by their formidable grandmother as he himself had been.

"All true," he said cryptically, echoing their ancestor. "Every word of it."

The child nodded and returned her attention to her grandmother. The story continued.

Del looked back toward the window, but Grace O'-Malley, pirate queen of the Irish seas, was gone.

— the end —

AUTHOR'S NOTE

Dear Reader,

I hope you've enjoyed this story; Del had been waiting for some time to find love, and I don't think he could have found a better or more suitable soulmate than Lady Grace. I enjoyed telling their tale, and it was great fun for me to revisit old and established characters who have become quite dear to me and hopefully, also, to you: Sir Graham and Maeve Falconer... Connor Merrick... Kieran Merrick... Christian and Deirdre Lord... Colin and Ariadne... Tristan and Letitia. All of them have stories of their own in the Heroes Of the Sea series, more of which can be found in the end pages of this book. (In fact, if you keep reading, you can get a sneak peek of *Master Of My Dreams*— the story of Del's and Colin's parents!)

In the meantime, being a novelist can be a lonely job, and it's always validating to know that readers are enjoying our work. If you liked this story, please consider posting a review on either Amazon, Goodreads, or whatever other forums you think are appropriate. Only a few lines are needed. Reviews help authors enormously, and are always very gratefully appreciated.

Thank you, and God bless!

— Danelle

MASTER OF MY DREAMS

BY DANELLE HARMON

BY DANELLE HARMON

PROLOGUE
IRELAND, 1762

The press gang was in.

One could tell by the way a thick pall had come over the land, like mist snuffing out the noonday sun. One could tell by the way the little village that clung to the sea's edge grew quiet and seemed to huddle within itself, the people slamming shut the doors of their whitewashed cottages and watching the roads from behind slitted curtains. One could tell by the way the taverns emptied and the young lads fled into the hills that climbed toward the majestic purple ridge of the twelve mountains, where they would hide until the threat had passed.

And one could tell by the big, three-masted man-of-war that filled the harbor.

England was still at war with France—and not everyone wanted to fight.

It was an infrequent threat, the Royal Navy seeking its unwilling recruits from this bleak, storm-tossed area of western Ireland that even God seemed to have forgotten. No able-bodied young man was safe from the press gang. And so it was that little Deirdre O'Devir, holding tightly to her mama's hand and clutching with pale white fingers the ancient Celtic cross that hung from around her neck, solemnly bade her older brother good-bye. Roddy had blown her a careless, laughing kiss; then the door had banged shut behind him as he ran to join the steady stream of young lads who cheerfully whistled and sang as they headed into hiding at the ruins of the old, haunted castle, far up in the hills where even the dreaded English would dare not go.

Then she and Mama had bolted the door and, huddling together beside the snapping, smoking peat fire, waited.

Roddy had said they had nothing to fear, for the press gang didn't take lassies. But as Deirdre stood at the window and looked off toward the sea, where she could see the towering masts of the man-of-war silhouetted against the brooding clouds, curiosity got the best of her. She had to see for herself just what was so terrible about the English and its Navy, which everyone so feared and hated.

After all, her dear cousin Brendan, who'd been raised right here in Connemara, was a midshipman in the Royal Navy, and despite having a British admiral for a daddy, was as much an Irishman as she or Roddy. Surely, if Brendan was in the Navy, it couldn't be as evil as everyone said it was ... could it?

Raising her chin, Deirdre made up her mind. Mama would never know if she sneaked out for just a bit. She was a wee mite, even for a seven-year-old; it was a simple thing to crawl out her window after she had made an excuse to steal off to her room. Once outside, she vaulted over the stone fence and rode away on Thunder, her own, well-loved pony.

She waited until she was well away from the cottage before she urged the pony into a gallop and raced him headlong toward the sea. The pungent scent of peat fires hung heavily on the air, mingling with the fresh, heady tang of the ocean. Cold drifting mist, the kind that penetrated a person's bones, moved stealthily down from the mountains.

Night was coming on, and with it would come a storm.

Deirdre urged Thunder faster. Already the wind was picking up; now huge black clouds were filing in from the ocean, casting shifting shadows and colors over the rocky pastures, dragging patterns of light and dark over the sea. Recklessly, she pressed her heels to the pony's flanks, not pulling him up until they crested the last rocky hill.

There she sat, a pale little thing with thick, spiral-curling black hair whipping around a face dominated by the innocently wide eyes of a child. The wind gusted, promising rain. Far below, where the sea swapped kisses with the base of the hill, waves thundered and boomed and kicked up great sheets of spray that dewed her cheeks and tasted like salt.

A flock of rooks, shrieking, winged suddenly away, and in the distance she heard the mournful bleating of sheep. Behind her, a stone, loosened by the pony's hooves, skittered down the hill, the sound cleaving the tense stillness. Deirdre gave a start and spun around, her skin crawling with the uncanny feeling that she was being watched.

But there was no one there.

Wind blew thick tangles of hair across her face. She clawed them out of her eyes and looked anxiously toward the darkening sea.

There, a half mile out in the bay, the British warship lay, majestic in all its dread, frightening in all its beauty, the sky growing blacker by the moment behind its towering masts.

Deirdre's eyes grew huge. She reached up to touch the cross of hammered gold and inlaid emeralds that hung from around her neck, but the ancient heirloom was no comfort.

Beneath her, the pony tossed his head and pricked his ears forward, his attention caught by something out in the rising surf. Deirdre stared between his ears. A boat had been lowered from the ship and was headed toward shore, plunging through the rolling breakers and neatly avoiding the rocks, around which the surf boiled and foamed white in the gathering gloom.

Panic began to prickle up her spine.

Run, Deirdre, run! But she could do nothing except stare at the boat, forgetting the oncoming storm, forgetting the menace of the press gang, forgetting the fact that it would soon be dark and the banshees would come out.

Forgetting the awful feeling that she was being watched.

The boat was nearing shore now, its crew having a rough time of it in the rising seas as they steered it through the dark, deadly rocks that reared out of the crashing surf. But even the rocks, which had guarded this ancient coast since time began, were helpless against invading Englishmen. Oars rose and fell in perfect rhythm, and every so often the boat's bow would nose up as it plowed a wave, drenching the men and the officer in the stern with spray. Deirdre felt sorry for them. But the oarsmen's smooth strokes never wavered, the boat wasn't dashed against the rocks, and steadily it drew closer.

A cold drop of rain hit her cheek. Another splashed upon her hand. Deirdre urged the pony to the very edge of the hill—and it was then that she noticed the officer in the boat had a telescope to his eye and was training it on *her*.

With a cry of fright, she wheeled Thunder around — and ran straight into a group of the most evil-looking men she'd ever seen in her life.

"And wot 'ave we 'ere, Jenkins? A wee Oirish lassie wi' purple eyes an' the fairest 'air ye ever did see!"

Deirdre's heart stopped, and bounced sickeningly down to her toes. Wildly, she looked behind her — but there was only the sea at her back, and nowhere to go.

She bit her lip and her eyes filled with tears.

"'Ere now, wot's this, tears on ol' Taggert 'ere?" One of them grabbed the pony's bridle, causing the animal to yank its head back and roll its eyes in fright. "Would ye lookee 'ere, Jenkins. Ye must've spooked her with that ugly face of yours."

Jenkins grinned, showing prominent teeth that only frightened her all the more. An oily braid hung down his back, tied at the end with a piece of leather, and tattoos competed for space on his thick, strapping arms.

"Let me go," she said, struggling to pull away.

But they simply laughed, fearsome and ugly men with hard eyes and menacing faces. Fumes of rum clung to their breath and some of them carried clubs; others had cudgels and one or two held cutlasses.

"Hold on to that nag's bridle, Taggert! With yer luck ye'll not be seein' another lass for some time to come!"

"Aye, she's the best ye're gonna do!"

Bursts of hearty guffaws followed their remarks, and their harsh English voices were foreign and frightening.

"Might as well take advantage of 'er before the lieutenant gets here!"

"Let me *go*!" Deirdre cried, kicking out at Jenkins's thigh with her foot.

He merely laughed, plucked her from the pony's back, and set her on the ground. His hand clamped around her wrist, holding her cruelly when she tried to fight and pull away. "Now, wot're ye doin' out here by yer lonesome when it's startin' to grow dark, eh? Ain't ye got a mother to watch over ye?"

Above, the clouds massed, stalled, and began to spit more rain. One drop. Another.

"'Sdeath, Jenkins, it's startin' to pour. We've work to

do, and the lieutenant ain't gonna be too happy if he catches ye messing with a mere child."

"Indeed," said a cold, hard voice, "I damn well won't be."

Suddenly, the men behind Jenkins went still and stared with something like terror toward the hill's edge. Talk stopped abruptly. Faces paled. Eyes widened; gazes were cast down.

Far off in the distance, thunder rumbled.

There, a British sea officer stood silhouetted against the sky, leaning on his sword and watching them with eyes as cold and gray as the storm clouds that gathered behind him. His blue coat was soaked with spray, his lips were set in a severe line, and his features were as hard and uncompromising as stone.

"We've come here to press seamen, Jenkins, not frighten little girls. Unhand her this moment before you feel the bite of my anger — *and* my sword."

Jenkins released her so quickly she nearly fell. Recognizing the newcomer as the officer who'd watched her from the boat, Deirdre felt her knees begin to shake. She huddled closer to the pony's shoulder, her eyes huge with fright at the sight of the boat's crew gathering behind him, huffing and puffing as they came up the hill. They began to laugh as they caught sight of her, and several exchanged smirks. But the officer did not seem amused at all. One sharp glance from him was all that was needed to instantly quell their grins. They looked down at the ground, obviously respectful of his authority and unwilling to displease him.

Even Jenkins backed away from the pony, his hands raised as though in truce. "Sorry, sir."

Pointing with his sword, the lieutenant snapped, "Get your carcass down that hill, drag the boats free of the surf, and mind that they're well hidden. We've King's business to conduct and no time to be dallying with diversions, damn you."

"Aye, sir," Jenkins sputtered, and fled.

The officer sheathed his sword, the scrape of the blade against the scabbard sending shivers up Deirdre's spine. She stared at him, taking in the smart naval uniform and thinking that if he weren't so frightening he might actually look handsome in it, even if he *was* an Englishman. Not a speck of lint flecked the dark blue coat; not a smudge of dirt marred the whiteness of breeches and waistcoat—

But then he came forward, and Deirdre remembered her fear. The fearsome, rough-looking men parted, wordlessly letting the officer through their ranks. Cold sweat broke out along the length of Deirdre's spine and she trembled violently. A strange buzzing noise started in her ears, drowning out the crash of surf, the rising moan of the wind. Her fingers went numb and the feeling began to fade from her toes, her feet, her legs....

The lieutenant caught her when she would've fallen, his touch jerking her back to reality and stark, choking terror. She screamed in fright and struggled madly.

"Let me go!" she shrieked, kicking out at him. "Let me go-o-ooo!"

Holding her easily, he let her struggle, her childish strength no match for his. Finally, she wore herself out and stood before him, frozen with fear and sobbing pathetically

"Poor little wren," he said, his voice deep and rich and soothing. He knelt down to her level, his thumbs coming up to brush away the tears that streaked her damp cheeks. She flinched, squeezing her eyes shut and trembling violently. "I daresay we've frightened you."

Deirdre opened her eyes. She stared at him, taking his measure from close range. His cocked hat covered bright, gilded hair that was caught at the nape with a black ribbon. He had long golden eyelashes, eyes the color of fog, and a sharp, clean profile that reminded her of a hawk.

Smiling, he took off his hat and tucked it beneath his elbow. His fair hair, contrasting sharply with the deep tan of his handsome face, was bleached and silvery at the ends, as though he spent a lot of time in the sun. His body was lean, his posture straighter than any she'd ever seen, and he had a firmness about his mouth that made her think he was well used to command. But then he smiled at her once more, and little crinkles appeared at the corners of his eyes, the sides of his mouth, and suddenly he didn't look quite so stern and frightening anymore.

She smiled back, hesitantly, childishly.

"Is this your pony?" he asked, still kneeling before her and inclining his head toward Thunder.

Her gaze still locked with his, she nodded, too afraid to speak.

"And what is his name?" He seemed heedless of the way his men were once more elbowing each other and grinning.

"Th-Thunder," she managed, her voice high with fright.

His brows drew together in bemusement as he caught sight of the Celtic cross hanging from around her neck. He reached out and hefted it in his hand, studying it while she went rigid with terror. "Thunder," he murmured absently, rubbing his thumb over the ornate design. Then, replacing the cross, he sat back on his heels and cast an admiring eye over the pony. "D'you know, I used to have a pony once, just like yours, except I called him Booley. He was a naughty fellow though, full of mischief and pranks. Why, once he refused to take a fence and tossed me right off his back and broke my arm. Hurt like the devil, it did!" He smiled again, shot a glance toward the gathering storm clouds, and then his gaze grew serious once more. "So we have Thunder, here. And might I ask *your* name, young lady?"

Her gaze darted to the grinning seamen, then back at the handsome lieutenant, who didn't seem to care that the skies were about to open up. "Deirdre."

"Deirdre," he repeated, the name sounding strange on his foreign tongue. "That's a pretty name for a pretty lass." He was smiling at her, and for a moment she could almost imagine him as a knight from a fairy tale, so handsome was his face, so reassuring and kind were his gray eyes. Childishly wiping the back of her hand across her running nose, Deirdre gathered her courage and took a deep breath.

"And what's *yer* name?" she asked.

"Christian." He grinned. "Christian Lord."

"That's a funny name," she said, trying not to laugh.

"Indeed it is. My pious mother's idea of a joke, I suspect. Would that I were a John. Or a Richard. Or even an Elliott, like my brother."

"Are ye in the Royal Navy?" she blurted innocently.

"Aye, that I am, little wren."

"My mother says only pirates, thieves, and tyrants are in the Royal Navy." Frowning, she peered closely at him, searching the depths of his face for some proof of her mama's words. "But I think my mother might be wrong."

"Do you, now?" The corners of his mouth were twitching, as though he was trying awfully hard not to laugh. "And why d'you say that, foundling?"

"Because my cousin Brendan is in the Royal Navy, and he's the kindest, handsomest man in the whole wide world." His sudden laughter bolstered her courage, and she puffed out her chest importantly. "And he's not a thief, nor a pirate! His daddy was an admiral, and my mother says that someday Brendan will be, too."

"An admiral, you say?"

"Uh, Lieutenant?"

Beyond her new friend's broad shoulder, Deirdre could see another man leaning against his club and grinning crookedly. Without turning around, the lieutenant snapped, "For God's sake, Hendricks, don't just stand there. Go find O'Callahan so we can be about this devilish business."

"No need to, sir. I think I hear him coming now."

"As does the whole blasted village," muttered Jenkins.

Rising abruptly to his feet, the lieutenant donned his hat and turned toward the road. Deirdre stared at him in awe, but he seemed oblivious to her perusal. He cast a wistful glance toward the man o' war, as though he regretted being here and wanted nothing more than to be back aboard his ship. He looked once more toward the road. His mouth went hard, and when he looked down at her again, his mood had changed and his gray eyes had become determined and resolved.

"Time for you to run along, little wren."

"But don't ye want to hear about my cousin Brendan?"

"Next time, foundling." He reached down, put his hands around her waist, and lifted her up to the pony's back. The motion was quick and sure; the manner in which it was done brusque and businesslike. Numbly, she allowed him to stuff the wet reins into her hands, noticing that he was no longer smiling, and that his mouth looked tight and strained. He gave her hair, damp now with mist and rain, one last tousle before turning away. "Now, off with you, before it gets any darker."

"You can't let her go, Lieutenant, she'll spread the alarm!"

"A pox on you, Hendricks!" he barked with sudden anger. "'Tis too late for any alarm, they saw us coming long before we'd already lost the element of surprise. Hail O'Callahan's party and let's be done with this. By God, 'tis miserable enough business as it is, without having to spend the entire night in this godforsaken hellhole, damn you!"

Deirdre shrank back, the lieutenant's swift change of mood confusing and frightening her. The rain was falling steadily now, gathering momentum, growing colder by the minute and pulling little curls of steam from the pony's neck. She looked at the lieutenant, standing there in the rain, and waited for him to come back and talk to her again — but he did not. Why was he suddenly so angry?

Deirdre was just about to turn Thunder away when she heard men coming up the road. She couldn't see much through the rainy gloom, but the sounds that came to her were sharp and clear: the stamp of boots and rattle of muskets; dragging feet and angry shouts; the click of a flintlock, the dull thud of a club against flesh, and a man's howl of rage and pain. English laughter ... an Irishman's swift curses.

Another blue-and-white-clad officer was in the lead.

"Lieutenant!" he called, saluting. "I've got some for you, prime lads who'll do the ship proud!"

The fair-haired lieutenant cast a cold eye over the approaching group. "By God, that was quick."

"Aye, well, being born an' raised in this part o' the world sure has its advantages." The man's voice was Irish, familiar and dear among the strange tongue of the Englishmen. As the British seamen approached, Deirdre saw they had a smaller cluster of men with them, herding them like frightened sheep and threatening them with swords and clubs to keep them in line.

She frowned and craned her neck, her hands tightening on the wet reins. The rain was coming down hard now, pitter-pattering against the nearby rocks and heightening the scent of earth, grass and the pony's hide.

Somewhere out to sea, she heard the low rumble of thunder.

"And where were they hiding, O'Callahan?" The English officer strode toward the new arrivals, his long blue coattails dark against the back of his white-clad thighs.

"Just where I thought they'd be. Out in th' hills, and drinking themselves senseless in the ruins of an old castle."

"Splendid work, O'Callahan," the lieutenant said, yet there was an odd tonelessness in his words. "I shall make note of it to the captain."

But Deirdre's horrified gaze was not on the lieutenant, not on O'Callahan, not on the group of English seamen. She stared at the frightened, angry men whom the English tars surrounded. Their clothes were dirty and torn, their faces sullen, and some of them were cut and bleeding. Yet there was no mistaking who they were. Seamus Kelly ... Patrick O'Malley ... the brothers Kevin and Kenny Meeghan....

And Roddy.

It took a moment for the truth to hit. Before she knew it she was off the pony and racing across the wet grass. She slipped on a rock and went down hard, scraping her chin and knocking the breath from her lungs. "Roddy!" she cried. *"Roddy!"*

Her brother's head jerked up, and she saw horror in his eyes at the sight of her — horror that changed quickly to rage. Without a second's hesitation, he slammed his fist into the jaw of the nearest seaman and sent another sprawling with the deadly hook that had earned him many a free ale at the village tavern.

Chaos erupted.

Deirdre scrambled to get up. In a daze, she heard the shouts of the Englishmen, the barked commands of

366

the lieutenant, the wild yells of her neighbors. Fists slammed against flesh; guttural groans and curses were all around. Managing to get to her feet, she resumed her flight toward her brother, only to be neatly snared by Hendricks. Sobbing wildly, she saw Roddy struggling between three burly seamen, spouting curses and kicking savagely out at their legs, their groins. A sharp cuff across the face stunned him; then, someone kicked him in the belly, and a cudgel's blow brought him to his knees.

With Roddy retching and coughing, the rest of the Irishmen quieted. They looked hatefully at O'Callahan, then at the fine English lieutenant. Their eyes were sullen, their backs rigid with pride.

"Take them to the boats and let's be off," the lieutenant snapped coldly. "We're done here."

Deirdre felt Hendricks release her, and she stood frozen as the seamen hauled Roddy and his friends down the hill, slipping on wet rocks and cursing the Irish rain, the Irish cold, the Irish seas that awaited them. She stared dazedly at the proud profile of the English naval officer, suddenly realizing just what he had done.

No fair and handsome knight was he.

"My brother!" she wailed, throwing herself at him and beating her hands against his back. "Please, don't take my brother!"

He turned and caught her flailing fists. "I said go home, foundling."

"But ye can't take Roddy! Ye just *can't*! He's my brother!" She struggled madly against his iron grip. "Roddy!" she screamed as the last seaman disappeared over the far side of the hill. "*Roddy!*"

Her struggles quieted, and hanging from his grip, she collapsed in great, convulsing sobs of terror and grief. She heard the wind moaning across the dark pasture, and the voices of the seamen fading to a few barks of laughter, a curse, then nothing as they reached the beach far below. Her cheeks streaming tears and rain, her wet hair hanging in straggly spirals around her face, Deirdre raised desperate eyes to the lieutenant. He stared down at her, an anguished look on his handsome face, and for a moment she thought he was going to recall the men and release her brother. Then his jaw turned hard and unyielding, the set of his mouth resolute. "We are at war with France," he said harshly. "And while I despise the methods our Navy must employ to obtain its seamen, as an officer my loyalty and duty lie with my country, not with my own inclinations." His eyes softened. "I'm sorry, little wren."

He abruptly released her and turned on his heel, striding down the hill without a backward glance. She watched him melt into the darkness, heard his footsteps fade, until she was all alone with nothing but the sad patter of falling rain and the mournful crash of waves against the beach far below.

Moments later, she saw lights bobbing out on the sea, fuzzy and dim in the mist, as the boat headed back toward the man-of-war and carried her brother away forever.

Deirdre stood there for a long time, the wind blowing her hair in wild, wet tangles around her shoulders as she watched the lights fade to tiny pinpricks in the foggy darkness and then to nothing. At seven years of age, she had just learned there were more frightening evils in this world than the banshees whose low moans could even now be heard through the darkness of the gathering night. Choking on a last sob, she wiped her eyes, gripped in both shaking hands the ancient cross that had once belonged to her formidable ancestress, and raised her chin, her gaze fixed out to sea.

Someday, she'd be old enough to go to England by herself, seek her cousin Brendan, and obtain his help in getting her brother back.

Someday, she would find that English lieutenant and make him pay for what he'd done.

Someday, she vowed — she would see that English lieutenant *dead*....

⚓

Buy *Master of My Dreams*

Scandal at Christmas

Pirate in My Arms

ABOUT THE AUTHOR

New York Times and USA Today bestselling author Danelle Harmon has written twenty critically acclaimed and award-winning books, with many being published all over the world and translated into numerous languages. She and her family make their home in New England with numerous animals including  several dogs, an Egyptian Arabian horse, and a flock of pet chickens. Danelle enjoys reading, photography, spending time with family, friends and her pets, and sailing her 19th century reproduction Melonseed skiff, Kestrel II. She welcomes email from her readers and can be reached at Danelle@danelleharmon.com or through any of the means listed below:

CONNECT WITH ME ONLINE!
Danelle Harmon's Website
Danelle Harmon's Blog

Want to know when the next new title from Danelle is released? Click here!

Even more ways to connect:

ABOUT THE AUTHOR

New York Times and USA Today bestselling author Danielle Darvon has written twenty-one full-length, award-winning books, with many being published all over the world and translated into numerous languages. She and her family make their home in New England with numerous animals, including several dogs, an Egyptian Mau, a horse, and a flock of pet chickens. Danielle enjoys reading, photography, spending time with family, friends, and her pets, and selling her 19th-century reproduction Model-era dolls.

Want to keep in the know? Sign up for her newsletter at [website].

Connect with the author:
Danielle Darvon's Website
Danielle Darvon's Blog

Want to know when the next title is available? Follow Danielle at:
Website Channel

Even more ways to connect:

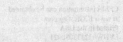

CPSIA information can be obtained
at www.ICGtesting.com
Printed in the USA
LVHW032333080921
697407LV00025B/961

9 781648 390180